PENGUIN BOOKS

THE STRANGLER VINE

'A stylish, enjoyable adventure . . . Convincing, sympathetic, beguiling, steeped in atmosphere. *The Strangler Vine* is a considerable achievement, which left me waiting impatiently for a promised sequel' *The Times*

'Intelligent, extensively researched and packed with period detail, *The Strangler Vine* evokes both the attitudes of the British colonials and the India of the period . . . with its ingredients including murder, gambling, opium wars and crime, it's an imaginative read' *Metro*

'The best elements of an old-fashioned ripping yarn unite with a plot that makes clever use of recent historical ideas about the British in India . . . Carter's twisting devious narrative is enhanced by her vigorous prose and her convincing delineation of her characters, whose further adventures, already announced, can be keenly anticipated' *Sunday Times*

'A tonic: an intelligent book that unashamedly celebrates acts of courage and daring . . . full of hairsbreadth escapes from tigers, nasty natives and even nastier white men. There are mysteries aplenty to solve, and new light shed on the period. Armchair adventure lovers should enjoy this' *Sunday Express*

'A vivid, historical page-turner, a rattling good yarn, an exciting fictional debut. A well-informed and enlightened modern book . . . I do not remember when I enjoyed a novel more than this. Finishing it would have been unbearable had it not been for the reassuring promise at the end that Blake and Avery will return for more adventures.' A. N. Wilson, *Financial Times*

'Fresh and original with many surprises in store . . . Avery is the guileless Watson of the partnership, and Blake the opaque Sherlock . . . it is a relief to know that the two will be reunited in a sequel. A cracking good plot' *Evening Standard*

'A great new double act for a super new series of adventures' *Sunday Sport*

'*The Strangler Vine* is a splendid novel with an enthralling story, a wonderfully drawn atmosphere, and an exotic mystery that captivated me' Bernard Cornwell

'M. J. Carter has cooked up a ... dish ... *...nstone*, a dash of Sherlock and a soup... ...endid romp and just t... ...iam Dalrymple

'This is a gripping story of conspiracy and betrayal set in an early Victorian India that is rendered with complete conviction. And as a historian, the author offers a thought-provoking re-interpretation of the Thuggee story' Charles Palliser

'Tigers, a murderous sect and all manner of deadly double-dealing . . . compelling' *Mail on Sunday*

'A ripping yarn . . . meticulously researched historical novel with a subversive and startling sting in its tail' *Spectator*

ABOUT THE AUTHOR

M. J. Carter is a former journalist and the author of two acclaimed works of non-fiction: *Anthony Blunt: His Lives* and *The Three Emperors: Three Cousins, Three Empires and the Road to World War One*. M. J. Carter is married with two sons and lives in London.

The Strangler Vine

M. J. CARTER

PENGUIN BOOKS

PENGUIN BOOKS

Published by the Penguin Group
Penguin Books Ltd, 80 Strand, London WC2R 0RL, England
Penguin Group (USA) Inc., 375 Hudson Street, New York, New York 10014, USA
Penguin Group (Canada), 90 Eglinton Avenue East, Suite 700, Toronto, Ontario, Canada M4P 2Y3
(a division of Pearson Penguin Canada Inc.)
Penguin Ireland, 25 St Stephen's Green, Dublin 2, Ireland
(a division of Penguin Books Ltd)
Penguin Group (Australia), 707 Collins Street, Melbourne, Victoria 3008, Australia
(a division of Pearson Australia Group Pty Ltd)
Penguin Books India Pvt Ltd, 11 Community Centre,
Panchsheel Park, New Delhi – 110 017, India
Penguin Group (NZ), 67 Apollo Drive, Rosedale, Auckland 0632, New Zealand
(a division of Pearson New Zealand Ltd)
Penguin Books (South Africa) (Pty) Ltd, Block D, Rosebank Office Park, 181 Jan Smuts Avenue,
Parktown North, Gauteng 2193, South Africa

Penguin Books Ltd, Registered Offices: 80 Strand, London WC2R 0RL, England

www.penguin.com

First published by Figtree 2014
Published in Penguin Books 2014

ISBN: 978-0-241-96655-6

www.greenpenguin.co.uk

MIX
Paper from
responsible sources
FSC® C018179

Penguin Books is committed to a sustainable
future for our business, our readers and our planet.
This book is made from Forest Stewardship
Council™ certified paper.

For my boys

Historical Note

The East India Company was launched in 1600 by a group of British merchants with ambitions to trade with the East. Over the next two centuries it built up its own private army and gradually gave up its trading interests in favour of taking over and ruling large parts of India, making money out of taxation and out of its monopoly in the opium trade with China. It became a peculiar mixture of private company and instrument of the British state, and was arguably the world's first multinational.

By 1837 the Company dominated the subcontinent, controlling much of what is now India, Bangladesh and Nepal, with Calcutta as its capital. Within these borders there still existed many independent princely states, however, which struggled to find ways of existing alongside their powerful and hungry neighbour.

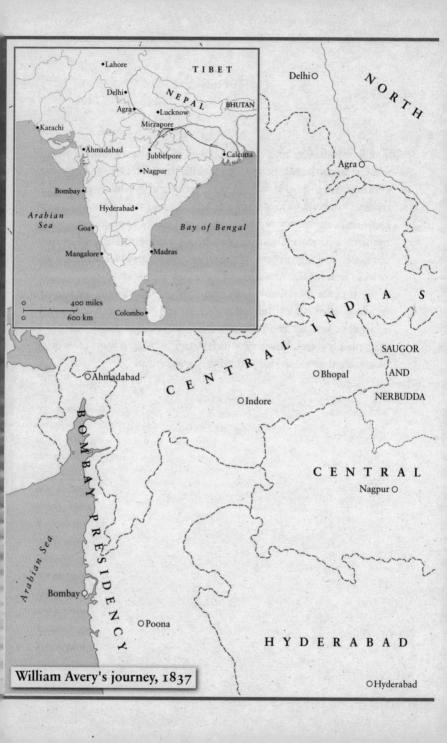

William Avery's journey, 1837

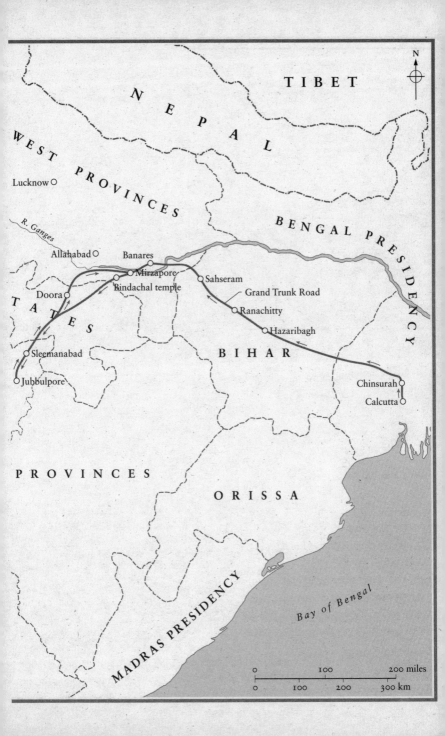

TIBET

N

NEPAL

WEST PROVINCES

Lucknow

BENGAL PRESIDENCY

R. Ganges

Allahabad   Banares
         Mirzapore
Doora   Bindachal temple   Sahseram
                                    Grand Trunk Road
TATES   Ranachitty
                               Hazaribagh

Sleemanabad   BIHAR

Jubbulpore   Chinsurah
                                        Calcutta

PROVINCES

ORISSA

Bay of Bengal

MADRAS PRESIDENCY

0   100   200 miles
0   100   200   300 km

Prologue

Central India, June 1837

He stumbles out from the mango grove and at that moment the thick monsoon clouds, which colour the night a dull charcoal grey, shift. A sliver of moonlight shines through and he sees their bright, curved knives. Had the clouds not parted he would have blundered, laughing, straight through the gates, straight on to their blades.

As it is, he is in a befuddled haze, and pretty far gone. He has been alternately laughing disgustedly at himself, and seething at their crimes, their banality, their complacency. He has been imagining how he will pay them back.

Before he even understands what he has seen, an old instinct causes him to throw himself on to the sodden ground and scramble into the shadow of the tall, mud-spattered outer walls. The effort winds him and makes his chest hurt and his knees jar, and he wheezes. The sober part of him tries to quieten his breathing, noting now the soft patter of dripping water and understanding that the sounds of the monsoon have covered his approach. *I have had too much*, he thinks, *and my bones are too old for such things.*

He knows they are there for him. He can see two of them standing silent and still, behind the gates – gates that have always seemed too imposing for such a modest building. They are barefoot, their dhotis and turbans dyed or muddied so they blend into the dark, but the moon lights up their swords and the dark sheen of their young bodies. Another step and he would now be so much skewered meat. He winces at the coarseness of the phrase, and then suppresses the urge to giggle.

Awkwardly, he twists his neck to face the wall. Days of heavy rain have penetrated the mortar and worked on cracks and holes. His hand shaking a little, he pulls away a little sand and gravel around one hole until it is large enough for him to see through into the compound.

Two lanterns on the grass give out a dim ambient light. Two men – he recognizes neither – armed with knives, speak in an intimate tone, too quiet for him to make sense of the words. Another comes on to the verandah, which means they have searched the house. One man's knife is already dark and shiny with blood. The other lifts up something small and human-like, and dangles it by its long hairy arms. The watcher starts. A shiver runs through the creature's limp body. He thinks he hears it whimper. The man tosses it up and catches it by its arms. Then, in a swift, practised, efficient movement, he places his hands round its neck and wrings it – a short, brutal twist – and the other man drives his knife into its chest. The watcher feels an unaccustomed pang of distress. He cannot remember the moment when the monkey parted company with him. It may have been hours ago. The assassin tosses the creature on to the ground, and with his comrade strolls over to the gates.

The one with the bloody knife speaks to the young guards. It is a Marathee dialect the watcher knows. He tells them to walk the walls once more. 'He may be cowering in the shadows.' The watcher knows he will never make it to the trees. The sober part of him feels, not precisely fear, but rather a sense of failure. They will kill me, and even if they do not find the papers, the truth will be lost. I will die and my grave will be unmarked and no one will know, and I will be forgotten. That thought is almost the worst.

As if in a dream, he watches the gate guard pad towards him, a knife at the ready in one hand, a long scarf in the other. The scarf. How appropriate, he thinks. Some fifteen yards from him, the guard crouches down and feels the ground where he cast himself on to the mud. He beckons the second guard. The watcher shrinks into the shadow of the wall, his mouth as dry as he can remember.

Step by step they draw closer to him, like some absurd parlour game. As they cover the last few yards he finds that, without realizing it, he has raised his arms in supplication, and is mildly disgusted by the intense desire he suddenly feels to live.

PART ONE

Chapter One

Calcutta, September 1837

The palanquin lurched again to the left and I felt a fresh wave of nausea. I pushed the curtains aside in the vain hope of a current of cool air, and waited for the moment to pass. The perspiration started anew from my neck and my back, then soaked into the chafing serge of my second-best dress uniform. The dull, sour odour filled me with dejection. Our uniforms were not washed quite as often as I would have liked as it caused the fabric to disintegrate even more swiftly than it would otherwise have done.

'*Khabadur you soor!*' Take care, you swine! I shouted at the bearers, more to relieve my feelings than anything else.

'William,' said Frank Macpherson, 'it will make no difference.' Nor did it. There was no response, nor had I expected one.

Calcutta was hot. Not the infernal, burning heat of May, but rather the sticky, enervating sultriness of September. We were the only thing in the empty afternoon streets of Whitetown – it was too hot as yet for afternoon calls. It had been a relief when the monsoon had arrived in June, but the rain had persisted and persisted and now, after three months, the depredations of damp and standing water had become almost as tiresome as the raging heat before it. The city existed in a permanent state of soupy dampness. Books and possessions rotted. Diseases lurked in its miasma. Most of my acquaintances were down with fever or boils. At the Company barracks, where the walls gushed dirty brown water when it rained, there was said to be an outbreak of cholera.

Even in Tank Square, the grand heart of the city, one could smell mould in the air. As our palanquin left the square to make for the Hooghly River ghats, it semed that even the adjutant birds perching one-legged on the parapets of Government House drooped in the heat.

'I reckon the temperature is about ninety-five degrees,' said Frank, who knew about such things.

We were on our way to Blacktown. I had been ordered – by the Governor General's office, no less – to deliver a letter to a civilian called Jeremiah Blake. Frank had decided to come too, for he was curious and we had neither of us ever been into Blacktown proper: it was not the place for an English gentleman. Even on its outskirts, the sides of the roads were piled with filth and refuse and gave on to open ditches carrying all imaginable kinds of effluent. It was not unusual to find animal corpses rotting in the street and rats scuttling over one's feet.

I was ambivalent about the commission. On the one hand, any recognition from the senior ranks of the Company was gratifying, and any relief from the tedium of barrack life to be welcomed. On the other, carrying a message to some civilian gone native felt like yet another demeaning, irksome, pointless task. Besides which, I had dipped deep into my cups the night before and was suffering greatly from the consequences.

'Damn me, it is too much,' I said, for the millionth time, pulling again at my collar to absolutely no effect. We shifted ourselves about a little. There was not quite room enough for two in the palanquin.

'My, my, we are ill-tempered and sore-headed this morning,' Frank said. 'Must have been the fish. Certainly nothing to do with the gallon of claret, nor the ten pounds you lost.'

For nine months I had been kicking my heels in Calcutta, waiting to be summoned by a cavalry regiment in north Bengal which had shown no inclination to avail itself of my services, and I was not far off hating the city. One might have supposed that being an officer in the army of the Honourable East India Company would have its compensations. But after nine months they seemed dispiritingly few, while its deficiencies were unignorable: the monstrous

6

climate, the casual barbarities of the native population and the stiff unfriendliness of the European society. Calcutta was a city in thrall to form, status and wealth, and Frank and I were at the bottom of the pile. Keeping up appearances, whatever the expense, appeared to be the most pressing duty. We drilled in the mornings before it got too hot, and studied for the Hindoostanee diploma – which no one took very seriously. Most of the officers got by with soldier bat, a few words of Hindoostanee, and in Calcutta it was not really the thing to be seen speaking the local lingo too well. The only man I knew who had actually learnt any was sitting next to me, and Frank Macpherson had no desire to fight or command troops. He had just effected a transfer to the Political Department and his ambition was to become a magistrate or some such, running a station somewhere up country. He had already passed his diploma in Hindoostanee and was now studying Persian. He had been managing his company's accounts and administering to his sepoys' welfare since shortly after he had arrived. Now I envied his activity. Idleness left me enervated, lethargic and irritable.

'I hate these damned litters, they make me ill,' I grumbled.

'Whereas I love them. I shall say it once more, now I am in the Political Department I shall travel India in a sedan chair and never sit on a horse again.' Frank looked me over. 'Oh, William, for heaven's sake, would you rather be going to Blacktown on an errand for Government House that at the very least will keep you occupied for an afternoon? Or would you rather be dead?'

'You know, Frank,' I said, rubbing my temples hard to dispel the ache, 'there are times when I think I would rather be dead.'

'You should be ashamed to say anything so stupid,' he said, severely. 'You should be careful of what you wish for.'

'I am sorry, Frank, forgive me,' I said, instantly remorseful. 'I am good for nothing in this state.'

I set my jaw against the throb in my temples, and smiled as much as I could manage. The truth was death came with alarming and casual ease in Calcutta. We had seen our fellow cadets taken overnight by the cholera, or a sudden fever, or some horrible unforeseen accident. One had died when a bullock cart loaded with sharpened wooden staves had collided with his horse. September was a bad month for fevers and diseases in Calcutta. The chaplain of Frank's regiment said that though the month was but half over, he had already seen thirty burials.

'Why they are sending me to deliver this thing I do not know.'

Frank raised an eyebrow. 'You said you were bored.'

'You!'

'I simply mentioned that my able and presentable friend was at a loose end.'

He thrust a water bottle into my hands. I made a face, but drank. I had assumed I had been chosen to go to Blacktown because I was the least occupied, least sickly junior officer to hand. It had never occurred to me that Frank might have had a hand in it.

'Besides, I wanted to have a look at Blacktown,' he went on, 'and I could not very well volunteer myself. And are you not curious to know who this Jeremiah Blake is?'

'Some tragic, leprous, broken-down old creature gone native, too opium-addled to collect his own pension,' I said heavily.

'Mebbe,' said Frank. 'Ah! The scent of the ghats is pungent today.'

The palanquin drew up to the Hooghly River ghats. These are the large steps that descend to the water and pass as quays in India. The river was like Calcutta itself. From a distance, it seemed picturesque, the gilt-covered barges of the rich natives and the bumboats selling fruit and fish, and the glimpses of the graceful mansions of Garden Reach on the other side. But close to, it was a different story. The ghats were always chaotic, crowded and dirty, and the stink of stale fish lay over them like a fog. Beggars in tiny boats waved their stumps for coins, and the native food-sellers were aggressively accosting or sullenly inscrutable. Worst of all were the half-burnt corpses that floated through the murky water. The Hindoos brought their dead down to the ghats to burn them, but they rarely spent enough on fuel to do more than burn the skin off before tipping them into the water. Once the funeral rituals were performed, no further attention was paid to these hideous objects, as if they no longer existed. Native men and women washed themselves and even filled pigskin water bottles – the creatures returning to their former animal forms as the water re-inflated them.

'You know,' I said, 'I often think that if one wished to commit a murder in Calcutta, a perfect way of disposing of the body would be to partially burn it and tip it into the Hooghly. Everyone would ignore it.'

'What a ghoulish thought, though it would make a splendid story,' said Frank.

Frank was my personal compensation for Calcutta. I thanked God for him every day. We had arrived in Calcutta at the same time and moved out of the grim cadets' quarters at Fort William as soon as possible to mess together. The rowdier among our messmates regarded him as the most tremendous spoon: he drank barely a drop; he did not shoot or gamble or ride, all of which I did excessively. Nor did he visit nautches or keep a *bibi* – a native mistress. He cared nothing for what anyone thought and he was always good-humoured, a quality I had thought I possessed until I had arrived in India. While Calcutta conspicuously exposed my own weaknesses, it brought out the best in Frank. His conscientiousness was a daily reproof to my impatience, my sore head, my occasional indulgences in the fleshpots of Calcutta, and my nightly gambling losses. (I was, like most ensigns, horribly in debt.) Despite this, I liked him enormously.

We turned into an unfamiliar street of small open cupboards that passed for shops, selling clay figures painted into the gaudy like-nesses of the Hindoo gods: Shiva, Durga and the hideous Kalee, patron goddess of Calcutta, her red tongue lolling out of her gro-tesque black face, a necklace of heads round her neck.

'The potters' neighbourhood,' Frank said, happily.

Truth be told, I had arrived in Calcutta expecting to be as seduced by its ancient traditions and exotic scenes as Frank still was. At first the lush vegetation, the sight of a camel or elephant, had been an excitement. But as time passed the notions I had harboured about the beauty of the place, and my hopes of distinguishing myself, had been replaced by an intense and bitter homesickness for England

and the realization that it was more than likely I would never see it again. The odds – well understood but never spoken aloud – were that most of us would die before ever we returned.

The one enduring romance I still found in India was in the glorious prose of Xavier Mountstuart. I had discovered Mountstuart as a boy in Devon, where I had attended a small school for the sons of the local gentry kept by the local vicar. One of his assistants had lent me a copy of *Knight Rupert*. I had been thrilled by it. My family were not readers, but Xavier Mountstuart's writings had inspired and transported me. I had devoured *The Courage of the Bruce* and *The Black Prince*, then graduated to the Indian writings: *The Lion of the Punjab*, of course, and the tales of bandits and rebels in the *Foothills of Nepal*. I had read of white forts and marble palaces and maharajas' emeralds; of zenanas and nautch girls in the Deccan; of the sieges and jangals. I had even read a short tract about Hindooism, vegetarianism and republicanism, which had left me a little confused. Mountstuart seemed to me the very acme of Byronic manhood. It was not simply that he was a poet and writer of genius, but that he had lived his writings. He was the reason I had come to India – something I had not, of course, confided to my father. He had approved of my going to India because, having bought a commission in His Majesty's army for my oldest brother and set up another (now dead) in the professions, there was no money left to do anything for me. In the East India Company's armies, positions were not sold but contacts counted for something, and since the family had a few Company connections, I had been sent off, cradling my precious volumes of Mountstuart's works.

Recently I had scraped together the wherewithal to purchase a brand-new copy of the first volume of *Leda and Rama*. This was causing a most tremendous furore in Calcutta for, under the guise of being a stirring, even immodest, romance about forbidden love and warfare between rival Indian kingdoms, it was a thinly veiled account of adulterous entanglements and corruption among some of Calcutta's most elevated worthies. People talked of nothing else. Mountstuart was no longer *persona grata* in the city's drawing-rooms, but Society – from the most respectable elderly matrons to the most junior clerks – all wanted to read his book. Nothing so exciting had happened in an age.

The bearers took a series of turns down muddy lanes barely wide enough for the palanquin until we arrived on a wide thoroughfare next to a noisy chaotic bazaar. A large cow stood moodily in the middle of the road like a rock in a fast-flowing stream forcing the waters to part around it. Around us a column of natives carried whole dead animals on long bamboo poles. Even inside the litter I could feel the crush and smell of bodies.

'William! See the fakir!' Frank cried, delighted. The creature was sitting by the roadside, smeared in ash, wearing only a long white stringy beard that dangled past his stomach. But it was his hands that drew the eye. They were hideous: the fingernails had grown through the flesh of the hands and emerged through the knuckles, long and horribly twisted. Where I felt repulsion, however, Frank experienced only cheerful curiosity and an enjoyable shudder of wonder. Though I was a better messmate, a better shot, and blessed with stupid good health, I was gradually coming to accept that Frank – short, pale and prone to chills – might be better suited to India than I.

The palanquin came to an abrupt stop and began to shake alarmingly as if the bearers were trying to roll us out. We had come to stop at the corner, or what passed for a corner, of an even narrower lane.

'*Bas you budzats!*' Enough, you blackguards, I shouted.

Awkwardly we climbed out, one after the other. A wave of hot smells assailed me: sweat, over-ripe fruit, heavy and sweet, and beneath, other ranker scents I did not care to identify. The road was soft and oozing, mud already specked my white breeches, native bodies surged and shoved, entirely too close. We were the only white faces. The *harkara* who had been running alongside the palanquin bowed and pointed down the narrow muddy lane. I spoke loudly and slowly: 'Up here?' Then, even louder, 'English-wallah live here?'

He nodded unconvincingly. Frank looked at me.

'If they are going to work for the Company, they should damn well learn our language. Up here?' I said again to the *harkara*, before Frank could start yabbering in Hindoostanee. He nodded and advanced up the lane at a loping trot.

'Will you come?' I said.

'No,' said Frank. He was already striding among the stalls, his breeches edged in mud, oblivious to the native press about him. He gazed about him; he was happy. 'I shall be looking at the caged animals and the druggist's stall. I think I saw a pangolin somewhere along here.'

I followed after the *harkara*, my boots sinking into the ooze. The dwellings started out as tumbledown mud-and-thatch hovels, then became more substantial, flat-fronted and flat-roofed, with cracked green shutters. The *harkara* stopped before one and pointed. I mopped the drops from my forehead, wiped the inside of my collar, straightened my jacket, pressed down my hair, checked my pocket watch – I was not supposed to wear it with my uniform, but it looked rather well around my cross belt – walked up to the dirty green door and knocked.

It seemed an age before I heard anything. Then came a number of wrenchingly slow footsteps, an elaborate coughing and throat-clearing, a series of locks drawn back at what seemed like five-minute intervals, then, finally, a sleepy-looking elderly *darwan* pushed his nose between the doors and gazed at me. I stood to attention.

'I have a message for Blake Sahib,' I said. 'He lives here?' I ventured, a little louder. The man contemplated me quizzically but did not move and would not open the door any further.

'I must enter,' I said slowly and clearly. 'I have a letter from the Governor General's office.' I could not help thinking that the task would have been better done by a native clerk. The *darwan* and I regarded each other for a moment, and I was about simply to push past him when, with an air of utmost reluctance, he opened the door, inch by inch, to admit me. I stepped into darkness, my eyes taking a moment to adjust.

It was a cool anteroom with broken matting on the floor, and a number of dusty bows and arrows mounted on a wall. Beneath these was a long console table of native inlaid design on which there were a number of curiosities, also dusty, **which** I could not make out. Through a doorway was a courtyard in the Indian style. The darwan looked expectantly at my feet. It took me a moment to understand that he wished me to remove my boots. His expectation seemed so utterly demeaning, so intensely insulting, it was as if all the indignities and disappointments of India were suddenly met in this one gesture. A surge of irritation leapt in me.

'No!' I said. 'No.' I shook my head violently.

The *darwan* regarded me speculatively for a moment, as if deciding how far he should press me. I stared furiously back. 'I must see your master!' I said, loudly.

Slowly, he walked through to the courtyard and I followed. He gestured to show with his hands that I should remain, then disappeared through a dark doorway on the far side and I was left quite alone. It was not the reception I had expected. I drummed my boots against the paving and fiddled with my sabre. The place had seen better days. The courtyard was shaded and well proportioned, its floor paved in mosaic that must have been handsome when new, but was cracked now, and there was an air of disintegration. Broken pieces of furniture gathered dust in the corners. Two bolsters had clearly sat through the monsoon and showed signs of rot. The small fountain was silent and clogged with weed.

'*Qui hy?*' Is there anybody there? I called out at last, which brought me, more or less, to the limit of my serviceable Hindoostanee. There was a mumble of voices from the rooms at the far end of the courtyard. Then nothing.

'I must see Blake sahib,' I called out. 'Now! *Jaldi jao!*' Quickly!

I waited, hovering between anger and embarrassment. Then, finally, another native appeared. Whereas the *darwan* had been at least neatly presented, this one was dirty. Wrapped in a large cotton blanket, he shuffled into the courtyard, apparently oblivious of my existence. He was a poor thing, grizzled, puffy-eyed, wearing a mangy beard, and barefoot. Beneath his blanket I could see an unkempt muslin shirt and a pair of dirty white pyjamas. Then, when he was but a few feet from me, he turned to one side and from his mouth issued the most enormous wad of wet scarlet pan,

13

which he spat on to the ground inches from my feet. I stumbled backwards, almost losing my footing, but the red droplets were already making a fine pattern on my muddied boots and breeches. I looked at him, aghast. I expected an immediate apology in the voluble manner of the Bengalee. Instead, he looked at me mulishly.

'You clumsy oaf!' I shouted, losing my calm entirely.

'Fuck off, lobster,' the man said.

I record these words – the insult to my uniform made obscene by the filthy words that accompanied it – only to convey the outrage and disgust I felt upon hearing them. At the same time I was completely astonished that the apparition before me was an Englishman. But there was no doubt he was. As I stared at him I could see that he was not quite as dark-skinned as I had thought, his beard and moustache the product of unkemptness rather than native custom. He was a head shorter than me, his shoulders slouched, and his hair hung greasily to his neck. His face had the unhealthy, yellowish tinge of a European to whom an annual bout of fever is no stranger. His skin was blotchy, his lips cracked, and his deep-set eyes were sinisterly ringed with grey. He was old too, at least forty.

'Is there anything in the words "fuck off" that you do not understand?' he said, in an accent in which I was sure I recognized the smell of the Thames, and he continued to fix me with an unfriendly gaze which I found extremely discomfiting.

'I am Ensign William Avery,' I said, as coldly as I could, resisting the instinct to flinch, 'and I am to deliver a letter personally to Jeremiah Blake. It comes direct from the Governor General's office. I am required to bring back an answer.'

He snorted and grimaced. 'Well, you'd better hand it over then.' He held out his hand, the blanket falling from his shoulders and on to the damp tiles. He appeared to be wearing some sort of baggy native garb made out of old sacking.

I regarded him sullenly, an unpleasant realization coming over me.

'I am Blake. Now hand it over,' he said.

As slowly as I could I retrieved the letter, and as I passed it to him

I looked deliberately through him. 'I am required to bring back an answer,' I repeated. He looked over the envelope for a moment.

'Perhaps you would like me to open it for you?' I said with exaggerated courtesy.

He ignored me, tore off the top, pulled out the contents, and scrutinized them.

'The answer is no.'

At first I could not quite believe what I had heard. When the Governor General's office issued a request, one did not say no.

'What?'

'You heard me.' He shuffled round, dropping the letter on the ground as he went. I scrambled to pick it up and though under normal circumstances I should never have done so, I read it. It was a summons to Government House the following evening to discuss 'a confidential matter, which touches closely upon your own affairs'. It was signed with a name I did not recognize, 'on behalf of the Governor General and the Secret and Political Department'. Irritation and anger were swiftly overtaken by mild panic. I could not deliver this answer to Government House. I cursed the ill luck that had sent me on such an errand, though I found it hard to imagine how such a broken-down creature could be of any interest to anyone in Government House.

'Sir, I really think you must comply.'

Jeremiah Blake kept on walking.

'Sir,' I said more urgently, 'I cannot deliver a refusal to the Governor General's office, you must know this. It is simply not done. You must attend. At the very least you must be sensible of the honour you are being paid.'

He looked round, his face quite expressionless, and said, 'I have no interest in the Company's affairs.'

I took a deep breath. 'I beg you, sir.'

'No.' His refusal met something angry in my own breast and though I should not have spoken, I did.

'Mr Blake, I have travelled all the way through Blacktown, a place which seems to me to demonstrate only too vividly the degradation and miserable depths to which this godforsaken country has fallen, to deliver your letter, and I wish to let you know' – I could hear my own excitability, but I could not stop – 'that I regard my reception at your house as having been notably lacking in courtesy. I have been treated by your servant and yourself with incredible rudeness. I can only attribute this state of affairs to your marination in the lowest native ways. Whatever my own qualities or lack thereof, I am a representative of the Company and should have been treated with respect.' I looked pointedly at where the pan was splattered in a large red bloom on the ground near my feet. 'Your language was disgraceful and your *darwan* was offensive. He virtually refused to allow me in and he tried with the greatest insolence to force me to remove my boots.'

Jeremiah Blake, who had thus far continued to show me his retreating back, paused and turned.

'Listen, Ensign,' he said. 'I'm no longer a member of the Company's army. I live in Blacktown so I can live as I wish and not be troubled by the fastidiousness of ignorant lobsters and swoddies who find my habits too oriental. As for respect for the Company – it can whistle for it, as far as I'm concerned.'

As he limped away an old native woman appeared in the opposite doorway. Ignoring me, she came and picked the blanket up from where it had fallen, and wrapped it carefully about him, speaking quietly in Hindoostanee as they left the courtyard.

The house was very silent. 'Goodbye, Mr Blake,' I called. 'Good riddance!'

I returned to the anteroom and heaved open the front door. It began to rain with heavy beating monsoon drops, and I was in an instant entirely soaked. I walked out into the alley and down towards Frank and the palanquin. He would be drenched and up to his knees in mud by now.

At least, I told myself, I would never have to see Mr Jeremiah Blake again.

Chapter Two

Music from the feast drifted over the palace's lakes through the open window of the Maharanee's rooms. Had the events of the evening been possible? Had she imagined the fire in the Sheikh's eyes, the brief sensation of burning when his hand touched hers? Did she imagine still these mysterious sensations, so shameful and yet so enticing, that she felt even now?

'She turned to the window and almost cried out. As bold as the day, as mysterious as the night, unmoving, unsmiling, there stood the Sheikh. The light silk curtains swayed about him as if they were clouds, as if they were wings. Yet his eyes were black as pitch. He had exchanged his flowing native robes for European attire. Was he angel or devil? thought the Maharanee. How could I know? I am only a woman. A woman alone in a room with a man with whom I should not be left alone. She felt her heart fluttering, bird-like. The Sheikh took a step towards her.

'"You do not know what to think," he said, his voice low, hypnotic. His eyes glinted, and for the first time she felt a surge of fear in her bosom. It could not be. He took another step.

'"Is that because you are a woman, and I am a man?"

'The Sheikh took another long stride.

'He whispered, "Is it because you are fair, and I am dark?"

'He strode forward again. They were no more than a yard apart. The Maharanee could hear wild drumming in the distance. With dread she understood that it was her own treacherous heart.

'"Or is it because you know that you should say no . . ."

With a final stride, he reached her, and as breakers throw the prow of a ship on to the rocks, as an earthquake causes a city to quiver and fall, so she was consumed by a terrible compulsion to submit. Yet she knew she must resist, though he whispered in her ear, ". . . but every fibre of your being longs to say 'Yes!'"

'"No – yes – I cannot," cried the swooning Maharanee, as he drew her to him—'

'You are making that up!' I protested, outraged.

'I deny it!' said Frank, snapping my copy of *Leda and Rama* closed. 'Well, perhaps just the last part. But you must admit, it is a little much—'

'It is not! It is a *roman-á-clef*, and quite in keeping with its exotic setting.'

'William, it is appalling old nonsense, but you are so enslaved to Mountstuart you cannot tell the difference!'

'You talk rot!'

Frank and I shared a small cache of novels. Our tastes, however, did not always agree. Mine ran more towards the heroic, Frank to the more satirical and comic – though he had converted me to his latest passion, *Pickwick Papers* by Mr Boz, whose monthly instalments he had begun to receive off the boat from his sisters in Edinburgh. It was one of the few things in Calcutta that made me laugh.

Before we could argue more, the *khansaman* – our steward – came in, bringing with him two invitations to the levee at Government House that very evening. Both of us were rather wary of him, as we were of all our servants. It was one of the peculiarities of European life in India that everyone employed vast numbers of them. Even we ensigns were obliged to employ at least seven each – it was both the custom and necessary, because each caste would do only their small allotted task. I had a *bhisti* to carry water, a *dhobi-wallah* to do the laundry, a *punkah-wallah* to work the ceiling fans, a *syce* to care for my horses, a valet, a *khitmatgur* to make my morning coffee and wait at table, and a grass cutter for the horses. Macpherson and I shared the *khansaman*, the cook, the *napi* who shaved us, a low-caste *mehtar* who swept and cleaned, and the occasional use of a *dirzi* to make clothes. Their salaries – *tuncaw* – ate horribly into our pay, and they all seemed entirely beyond our control. Most spoke barely a word of English. The *syce* was often drunk. I had once found the *khitmatgur* straining my punch through my stockings. Moreover, my possessions were disappearing week by week, but I could not be sure who was taking them. All the while, the *khansaman* insisted he would 'arrange it all', and never did.

We gazed at our invitations. We were last-minute invitees, added to swell the numbers.

'They are truly scratching down to the chaff,' said Frank. 'There really must be a great many sick officers.'

'After my achievements yesterday,' I said, wincing, 'I would have thought that even if the entire officer corps was dead they would not have asked me.'

It was mid-afternoon on the day following my ghastly encounter in Blacktown, and in hindsight the whole Blake incident seemed quite baffling. On my return to Government House I had prepared myself for the inevitable dressing down, having confessed to Frank that my ill temper and impatience had made everything a thousand times worse. Yet when I made my report to Captain Turpington, the aide who had sent me, he had seemed not at all surprised.

'I really do not know what to say, sir. I am very sorry to report – I did all I could, sir – that Mr Blake says no.'

Captain Turpington looked up from his desk. 'Say that again, Ensign.'

'Mr Blake, he declined to come to the interview. Tomorrow.'

'Did he say why?'

'I am sorry to say . . . well, sir, he said' – I swallowed – 'he said he had no interest in the Company's affairs. I did my best to reason with him, sir, I truly did' – *While in the grip of fury*, I thought to myself. 'But not with any success.'

I thought I saw the edge of Captain Turpington's mouth twitch, but the rest of his face remained entirely unsmiling. 'I see. And how did he take that?'

'He was somewhat abusive, sir . . . in fact extremely abusive.'

'Indeed.' Captain Turpington put his elbows on his desk, folded his hands under his chin and leant upon them. I fidgeted, waiting for the inevitable reprimand. Instead, he said at last, 'Well, that would appear to be that. You are dismissed, Ensign.'

Perhaps I was not as deep in disgrace as I had thought.

'I think we should definitely make an appearance,' said Frank, who never wasted an opportunity to mix with the senior ranks. 'The temptation of three new issues of *Pickwick Papers* straight off the boat does hold great attraction, but I am all for going – see if I can't find out what's happened about my posting. And you must fly there on winged feet, because the Fairest She is bound to attend.'

I was divided about such occasions: it was an honour to be asked, but Calcutta society, more than anywhere else, was all about rank and precedence, and one might just as easily find oneself slighted and patronized as favoured. But it did seem more than likely that She – Helen Larkbridge, the loveliest, most adorable girl in Calcutta – would be there, and that would make up for the rest.

The *dhobi-wallah* had for once done a good job on my best dress uniform. I donned red shell jacket, white muslin shirt, white breeches, and we set off for the Governor General's levee.

'If I were the Governor General I would have had Mountstuart deported by now.'

'Yes, but no one knows where he is.'

'I heard he had gone up country to research Thuggee for some poem.'

'With any luck the Thugs will get him.'

'But have you actually read it? Who are Sheikh Habeebee and the Maharanee of Oleepore? I mean, I've heard various theories.'

'It does not matter a jot who the characters are. The book is an attack on the reputation and respectability of Calcutta. It portrays the place as a hotbed of untrammelled lust and greed. It could do untold damage. The native news sheets are already dangerously critical of Company policy. And it could damage our reputation in England too.'

'You exaggerate. It is nothing more than a superior "blood and thunder" – and an entertaining one at that.'

We had arrived at Government House some five minutes before. Frank had marched into the melee immediately, as he always did, while I hovered at the edge for a moment, a semi-detached member of a deferential audience listening to four senior Company civilians fuming over Mountstuart's book.

I sipped my champagne and let my attention stray. The Marble Hall was the biggest room that I had ever entered. The vastly high ceiling was supported by two avenues of white columns which dwarfed everything else, and it was lit by three of the biggest chandeliers I had ever seen. There was little in the way of furniture – a series of plinths holding marble busts of the twelve Caesars (most of whom, I vaguely recalled, had come to bad ends), and a somewhat dilapidated gilded seat that was said to have belonged to the infamous native warlord Tipoo Sultan. Even now, the hall filled with a crowd of Calcutta's great and good, voices still echoed, though it was also blissfully cool.

There were familiar faces, but in Calcutta one was never quite sure if someone senior to oneself might cut one dead. The men, as ever, vastly outnumbered the ladies. The civilians sweated in black broadcloths, though here and there one glimpsed a blue silk necktie or striped waistcoat. The military men ran the gamut from red-faced brigadiers through sallow middle-aged majors finally in sufficient funds to find a wife, to younger officers, most more senior than I. An army of white-clad natives carried trays of champagne and iced claret. As for the ladies, the plethora of gems caused the company to twinkle almost as brightly as the chandeliers. Emeralds and pearls glittered off every ear lobe and rested on every satiny bosom. In Calcutta everyone with a little money had precious stones, and this was where they wore them. An ungallant observer might have observed that the Indian climate was not always kind to the ladies, as it was not at all to the men. It swiftly and ruthlessly killed the rosy bloom on a skin accustomed to English cloud and climate.

My attention was drawn to the centre of the party where, surrounded by every marriageable man in Calcutta, the unattached young ladies recently off the boat from England were to be found – along, naturally, with their chaperones. Wits called them the fishing fleet because they had come out to catch a husband. Peering into the midst of them, I began to search for signs of She.

I launched myself into the crowd, smiling and nodding as I went, scraps of conversation assailing me – Mountstuart's book,

Mountstuart's whereabouts, the Governor General's tour to the Upper Provinces, the opium harvest, the good-for-nothing natives.

'Ensign Avery!' a large woman called out to me, and tapped my wrist with her fan. Mrs Merchantly was a Calcutta matron who prided herself on taking care of new arrivals. There was no option but to stop. 'We haven't seen you in such a long while! You are looking as handsome as ever.'

At that moment a fracture opened in the crowd and I glimpsed Miss Helen Larkbridge, lovely, fresh, golden – and quite unaware of my presence. I winced inwardly as I saw that her attentions were simultaneously being claimed by a tall lieutenant, a red-faced major and a civilian who was just now expansively and confidently waving his hands about.

I turned to Mrs Merchantly and bowed. 'You are too kind, and it is my pleasure, as always.' I wondered how quickly I could extricate myself.

'My goodness, what a delightful party!' Mrs Merchantly grinned, and her dimples wobbled. 'Now, have you read Mr Mountstuart's book, Mr Avery? Everyone seems to be talking of it.'

'As a matter of fact I am in the midst of the first volume,' I said.

'The man ought to be ashamed of himself,' said Mrs Merchantly's friend, Mrs Kincaid, who stood beside her. With her high clipped Scottish tones, she reminded me of a small fierce bird. 'It is a book not suitable for maidenly eyes, and I am not sure it is not too profane for any woman.'

'But is it true,' said Mrs Merchantly, 'that the Sheikh is a portrait of – well, you would know, Mrs Kincaid, you know everyone in Calcutta.'

Mrs Kincaid nodded beadily. She could never resist an audience. 'There are two candidates for that *honour*,' she said, lowering her voice so we bent towards her, 'and although perhaps I should not speculate, many people are of the opinion that it is Willoughby Greening.' She looked at us triumphantly, having named one of the two richest men in Calcutta, a man I had thought beyond reproach.

'Do you still have that good-for-nothing *khansaman* I told you to get rid of, Mr Avery?' Mrs Merchantly interrupted. 'Is he still stealing from you? What he needs is a good *refreshing*.' I was lost for a moment, then remembered that she meant a beating. 'You are too kind for your own good.'

Mrs Kincaid said, 'The natives are kindly creatures, most of them, but they are simply by nature dishonest. Their ungodly heathen religion enslaves and has degraded them. They do not understand the difference between good and evil. They are addicted to lying.'

'Yes indeed,' said Mrs Merchantly enthusiastically, 'you know that they say, "What horns are to the buffalo, deceit is to the Bengalee."'

'The Rajas and their courts are the worst,' said Mrs Kincaid. 'So corrupt. No sense of duty to their people. Constantly murdering each other. It would be better for everyone if the Company simply took over the native states.'

At that moment my saviour appeared, weaving his way expertly through the clustered guests.

'Mrs Kincaid, Mrs Merchantly!' said Frank, grinning widely. 'What an unexpected, unanticipated and unsought pleasure!'

'Mr Macpherson,' said Mrs Kincaid, 'you've not been by in an age!'

'I know, Mrs Kincaid, I have been most remiss, and I will address it, but I fear I must drag William from you. There is someone he absolutely must speak to immediately. A very particular errand.' He gestured into the crowd.

'I wonder if it concerns one of those charming young ladies over there. The lovely Miss Larkbridge, perhaps?' Mrs Kincaid said sharply, while Mrs Merchantly's dimples vanished. 'All the young gentlemen seem to like her excessively.'

I bowed and Frank followed, bowing so deeply that even the two ladies could not have failed to spot he was making fun of them. I turned to nudge him hard, and he grinned broadly and muttered, 'Rescued from the harpies in the nick of time.'

'That's most ungenerous of you, but I am eternally in your debt,' I whispered back.

He pointed into the throng where I could see Miss Larkbridge and the party about her, and pushed me through, trotting after. There was the old red-faced major from up country whose name I could never remember, on the lookout for a wife. There was Moore, the plump, well-connected Company writer – a glorified clerk and accountant – who was given to wearing absurdly coloured neckties and waistcoats; tonight he was in turquoise-striped silk. And there was Keay, a lieutenant in one of the British army regiments, Her Majesty's 31st foot, down from Banares. I envied Keay. He was infernally sure of himself, seemed to walk in a glow of promise, and was handsome in what I considered a rather predictable way – sleek and well kept like an expensive horse. He had even seen active service.

'So how did the two ensigns manage to catch themselves an invitation?' said Moore, the Company writer, disagreeably.

'We were invited fair and square, Moore,' I said mildly. Miss Helen Larkbridge looked over. She smiled at me. I stared at her, trying to hold her gaze – her eyes were two shades of blue, the paler contained by a ring of the darker – but she shifted her gaze.

'Mr Avery, Mr Macpherson,' she said. She had removed her glove and, as if forgetting this, held her bare hand out to me, allowing me briefly to touch the tips of her rosy fingers. I swear, my heart turned in my chest.

'Mr Keay's senior officer has told him he must do better with his study of the native languages,' she said, looking slightly bored. 'But since he is an officer in a British regiment, with British soldiers, I cannot see why.'

Frank made some elaborate and quite inexplicable gesture with his fingers, muttered to me, 'Do not get too comfortable,' and withdrew back into the crowd. He had no time for the rivalrous circle round Miss Larkbridge.

'There is no point in studying Hindoostanee,' Keay said. 'I get by perfectly well with soldier bat, my servants understand me well enough. If blackie wants to get on, he should hurry up and learn English.'

The red-faced major frowned when Keay said 'blackie' and looked over anxiously at Helen. 'In my own opinion, Miss Larkbridge, Mr Keay's captain is correct,' he said. 'One cannot get on up country without some knowledge of the languages, though it is

24

true that these days there is less mixing between ourselves and the natives now than when first I arrived in India.'

'In the dark ages,' Keay muttered at me, rolling his eyes.

'Up country!' Miss Larkbridge said. Her hair was the most intense burnished gold. There were small silk roses entwined in it. 'I dread the thought – more insects, more natives, the enforced eating of curry!' The Major and Keay, who knew they would never keep a permanent posting in Calcutta, laughed politely but looked slightly crushed. Moore cheered up.

'I must say, I agree with Lieutenant Keay,' she went on. 'I have no desire to get to know Hindoostanee or the Hindoos any better than I do now.'

'Ah, you are as always a most obliging little divinity, Miss Larkbridge,' Keay said, laughing, and seized her hand. Helen let him hold it a moment, then snatched it back, giggling. I grimaced. The truth was, I was jealous of all of them, even the old major, for they all enjoyed better prospects than me, and Keay was actually quite likeable. Moore cleared his voice and attempted to recapture the initiative.

'Let us then, Miss Larkbridge, return to Calcutta matters. I am told Mr Mountstuart's book is so scandalous it should not be seen by female eyes.'

'I have a copy,' I said. 'Apparently Sheikh Habeebee is a cipher for Willoughby Greening.'

'Is he really, Avery?' She looked at me, her eyes wide. 'How very clever of you.' Moore gave me a cross look. I had evidently stolen his fire.

'Well,' he said quickly, 'that is only one of several theories, but the truth is the book has tremendously riled my superiors on all fronts – it makes all kinds of salacious accusations not just about financial improprieties, but improprieties of other kinds.'

'Goodness!' said Helen, shifting her gaze to him. 'What improprieties?'

Moore looked sheepish. 'I am sorry, these are matters I should not have mentioned before a lady.'

'I think he's the most tremendous blackguard,' Keay said, and now Helen had turned to look at him. 'I'm told he's disappeared, gone into hiding and no one knows where he is.'

'I heard he has gone deep into the Mofussil to write a poem about the Thugs.' I felt a little thrill as Helen looked again at me.

'Have you seen the article about the Thugs in the *Edinburgh Review*, Avery?' said Moore. '"The Thugs or the Secret Murderers of India"? It has caused a tremendous stir in England.'

The Thugs were a particularly monstrous species of bandit gang – notorious for strangling unwary travellers using a special scarf called a *rumal* as a sacred ritual to the goddess Kali – whose existence had only relatively recently been exposed. They were an ancient and secret fraternity with their own customs and language and a reach across the whole of India, and they had been responsible for thousands of deaths – one Thug had confessed to over 900 murders. They were undeniably fascinating and macabre, but I thought them hardly a subject for a party, and I was sure I had heard everything that could possibly be said about them.

'As I understand it,' said the Major, keen not to appear provincial, 'the article concerns the evils of Hindooism. Of Kali worship in particular: a religion that is pure, unmixed evil, and professedly devoted to the destruction of the human race. Hindooism enslaves and degrades its adherents, even encouraging them to kill their fellow man. The sooner we convert the natives to Christian ways and English morals, the sooner we can raise this country up.'

Keay yawned.

'Are you an admirer of Mountstuart, Avery?' Helen said.

'I adore him.'

'I too. What I would give to meet him! He is so dashing: *'There is a curious rapture among the lonely peaks—'*

'Where the inchoate darkling twilight to my lonely, tired soul speaks,' I finished. We smiled at each other.

I was happy. Helen shared my admiration. I could have quoted line after line. Then before I could make good my advantage, someone tapped me on the shoulder. There was Macpherson and behind him Captain Turpington looking as impatient as I had ever seen him.

'Mr Avery. I have been searching high and low for you. I am only grateful Mr Macpherson was able to find you.'

'Looking for me?'

'Yes. Your presence is required at a meeting downstairs. Immediately. No time to waste. Come along.'

I stood, stupid. 'For me?'

'Yes, Mr Avery. Now.' Macpherson grinned. Hesistant, I murmured, 'Sir, are you sure there has not been a mistake? It is really me you require?'

The Captain gave Macpherson an irritated look. 'I am quite sure, Ensign Avery. I hope you are not questioning my ability to execute my duty?'

'Never, sir, never. Might I perhaps just take leave of . . . ?'

He looked over and took in Miss Larkbridge. 'Quickly, Mr Avery.'

I turned back. Keay and Moore had leapt into the breach and were deep in conversation with Miss Larkbridge.

'Gentlemen, Miss Larkbridge,' I called. They all looked up, and Helen turned her golden smile upon me – but only for a moment.

The sound of the reception retreated as I followed the Captain down a flight of stairs and through several gloomy storerooms, stepping carefully over what appeared to be large bales of linen but were in fact the servants of guests upstairs, wrapped in muslin and sleeping as their masters made small talk above. Finally, we came to a pair of dark wood doors. Turpington knocked and stood aside for me to enter. I hesitated.

'Mr Avery?' he said, rather as a stern schoolteacher berates a faltering charge. I walked in and the door closed behind me.

I found myself in a cool room dimly lit with candles and lined with old leather-bound volumes, some very dilapidated. One man sat behind a long wooden desk; another sat before it. He turned and I saw it was Jeremiah Blake. He looked ghastly; if anything, even worse than he had at our last meeting. His face resembled sweaty putty, blotched with patches of red, peeling skin. His eyes glistened unhealthily, and he was dressed in a dreadful mongrel hybrid somewhere between uniform and mufti: a tired-looking moth-eaten blue shell jacket, a damp-looking cravat, and white military breeches, striped at the sides, that had seen better days.

He stood up. 'No,' he said.

'You will sit down, sir,' said the man behind the desk. 'Ensign . . . er' – he looked down at a sheaf of papers – 'Avery. Good evening. I think you have met Mr Blake?'

I nodded, more bemused than before and now somewhat anxious, but the man immediately turned back to Blake. He shook his head and sat back down, while I, seeing there was nowhere to sit, pushed myself back into a bookcase in a vain attempt to make myself inconspicuous.

I recognized the man who had spoken as the Chief Military Secretary, Colonel Patrick Buchanan, who handed out promotions and positions for the Commander-in-Chief. He was a handsome fellow in early middle age, with a full head of chestnut hair that showed no sign of grey, and a carefully tended moustache. He smiled pleasantly and raised his eyebrows as Blake pulled out a crumpled handkerchief from a baggy pocket and wiped his neck.

'As I said before, it has been a long time, Blake,' Colonel Buchanan said cheerfully. He had what I had come to recognize as one of those Irish accents that sounds almost Scottish.

Blake shrugged. Buchanan looked amused.

'We have a very particular task for you.'

Without stirring at all, Blake said very quietly, but clearly, 'I didn't ask for this. I don't want it, and I won't do it.'

'How interesting,' said Buchanan. 'You have regressed to the accents of your childhood. But I know you, Blake. You are our man. A spell away from Calcutta will do you very well. It is time you returned to duty. You have obligations to the Company. And it is the kind of work you favour: independent, in the field, no one to answer to.' The cheeriness took on a mocking tone. 'In a few days we both know you will be quite recovered from the fever and perfectly able to travel.'

Blake seemed hardly to be listening. There was a long pause. Eventually he said, 'I'm surprised you're still here, Patrick. What do

28

you need with the Political Department now you're getting rich on all those promotions?'

'You cannot insult your way out of this, Blake, and you may call me Colonel Buchanan.'

'No Collinson? Where is he, hiding in some corner?'

'Sir Theophilus has moved on. I have oversight of the Secret and Political Department now.' He paused dramatically.

'The task is to find Xavier Mountstuart.'

Involuntarily, my head jerked up. Blake did not respond at all.

'Mountstuart returned to Calcutta at the end of last year and brought the Governor General's office the manuscript of his novel. Naturally, the Company was not especially happy with it, but it seemed harmless enough. He had done a great deal for us over the years and his literary standing is – or was – high. It was decided not to do anything to hinder its publication – a foolish decision,' Buchanan said, leaning back in his chair. He seemed to be enjoying himself. 'Which the Company now bitterly regrets. Mountstuart smuggled a deal more scabrous detail in afterwards, and the exceedingly rich Willoughby Greening is threatening to take all and sundry to court for libel, and has made a formal complaint about the Censor's office to the Governor General. At the time the Company agreed not to hinder the book's publication, as long as Mountstuart agreed that he would return to England before it came out and undertake never to return to India again – a promise he freely made.'

Blake looked up. 'He agreed to leave for good?'

'The climate no longer agrees with him. His health is not what it was. It is not so surprising. But that is not the issue. The fact is Mountstuart has not left India. And no one knows where he is. In March he set off on a trip into the Mofussil to research his next book – a long poem about Thuggee. The Company gave him permission so long as he guaranteed that he would be back in Calcutta before the monsoon.'

It had not occurred to me that the rumours I had heard bandied about in Calcutta's drawing-rooms might actually be true.

'He has vanished,' Buchanan went on. 'He was last seen in

Jubbulpore in Saugor and Nerbudda territory where he was visiting Major Sleeman's Thuggee Department. He has not been seen since. It is the most tremendous mess and we need his whereabouts or his fate established and the whole matter tidied away as swiftly as possible. In a few weeks the Governor General Lord Auckland begins his tour up. The Company has a mass of important policies and there's enough trouble in the country as it is. We need this resolved with little fuss and, most of all, as cheaply as possible. Naturally,' Buchanan grinned, 'I thought of you.'

'I've heard nothing from Mountstuart for years,' Mr Blake said. 'And Jubbulpore is seven hundred miles away.' Looking at him, it was hard to imagine he would manage seven miles let alone seven hundred.

'Do not argue with me, Jeremiah,' Buchanan said. 'You have no choice in the matter and do not pretend you are not entirely curious to know what has become of him. We believe he left Jubbulpore in June or July. He may have gone to the kingdom of Doora. The place is ruled by a troublesome Rao who is said to harbour Thugs, but our man in Doora has seen nothing. Who knows' – he grinned mischievously – 'he might even have been taken by the Thugs themselves. Or he may simply have chosen to disappear or go native for a spell. He can be, as you may recall, unreliable.

'I will give you a week to prepare. You will take the overland route on the Grand Trunk Road. If you change horses every three to four days I reckon you could make Jubbulpore in three weeks.'

I suppressed a cough of surprise. No one travelled at those speeds on land except camel messengers; they might do fifty miles in one day, but not day after day. The average regiment would take two months to cover such a distance.

'I will give you a couple of natives, like the old days. I have in mind a man we've used many times.'

'I'm not taking the boy,' said Blake. 'You're clearly planning to foist him upon me.'

'You will do as you are told,' said Buchanan.

It took me a moment to understand that Blake meant me. 'I beg your pardon, sir?' I said.

Blake said, 'He won't do. He's never left Calcutta, and he has no languages.'

Naturally I had wondered why I was in the room, and was discomfited by my presence there. It did not, however, seem possible that they might consider someone as inexperienced as I was for such an expedition. As I realized this was indeed the case, all that I could think – despite my admiration for Mountstuart – was that there was nothing in the world I wanted less to do.

'Sir, I am sensible of the honour you do me,' I burst out, 'but really I cannot accompany Mr Blake. I am very soon to join my regiment. I can think of at least six other men who would suit far better than me in the circumstances.'

I would have protested further had not Buchanan waved me down.

'Quiet, Ensign! This is a great opportunity for you and we will hear no more cavils.' He turned abruptly back to Blake and began to talk about me as if I had not been in the room.

'He was not our first choice, I grant you. But we intend to send a Company officer with you. Someone presentable, who can take the pace and will not be too much missed. The truth is, just now there is no one else. The more experienced subalterns have already left for the north in advance of the Governor General's entourage. A quite extraordinary number are down with fever. The boy has a strong constitution. His senior officer says he's well liked – even if he has not found favour with you. Let us be practical, you need an Englishman who can hold a gun, he sits a horse well and he's said to be a good shot.'

So I was, it transpired, in the strictest sense, the Company's last choice.

'By the by, Blake,' said Buchanan, 'You may have your old captaincy back if you want it.'

Blake shook his head. 'I'm done with all that, Buchanan.'

'Well then, we must come up with a title for you which confers a little Company authority without too much compromising your precious independence. Special Envoy, perhaps?'

He mused for a moment. Blake snorted.

'Yes, a little papist, perhaps. Special Investigator? Too inquisitorial. Now, they have a name for men like you in England. What is it? Oh yes, "Special Inquiry Agent". Is that agreeable?'

Blake shrugged.

'Then you may go,' said the Colonel. 'The Quartermaster General's office is at your disposal. And Collinson sends his regards.'

Barely acknowledging these words, Blake rose heavily and began to walk – or rather hobble – towards the door. Then he turned.

'You should know that in my opinion Xavier Mountstuart is either dead or does not wish to be found. In either case, I'd say I am as likely to find him as I am the philosopher's stone.' He shuffled out.

I hung back a little, dreading the thought of having to accompany him as we navigated our way back through the building, but he limped along so slowly I could not see how it could be avoided. Colonel Buchanan, however, resolved the problem by calling me back.

'A word, Mr Avery.' He stood up and walked around the table.

'Sir?'

'Shut the door behind you. Come here. That's right. A remarkable day for you.'

'Yes, sir.' The words tumbled out on a great exhalation. I felt quite dizzy.

'Sit down. Take a moment to gather yourself. This must have come as a great surprise.'

'Yes, sir.' I was grateful for the chair. I sank into it and tried to tame my thoughts. *This is a great chance*, I told myself, but another voice in my head was saying, *But I do not want it. Let me go back to the levee, I just want my posting.*

Colonel Buchanan placed his hand for a moment on my shoulder and looked down at me. I could see a drop of moisture between his nose and his moustache. 'You know who I am?'

'Yes, sir.'

'Then you know, Mr Avery, that I have the power to make and break careers in India. Now I can see that you are not best pleased with this arrangement. I am right, am I not?'

'It is a rare opportunity,' I said. 'I can see that.'

'Let me ask you something. Where would you like to be in one year's time? Think carefully. Give me an honest answer.' There was something unvarnished and direct about the Colonel's gaze. It seemed to invite the truth.

'At home. Back in England.'

The truth was, I longed to see Devon again, with a constant painful ache: summer heat that was never excessive, cold slow rain, snow on the moors, the soft grass of the hay meadows, red earth. I longed to see my sister and sit again in the nook of the fire sharing a cup of broth, our legs knotted around each other for warmth. I knew this was impossible. My memories were of a childhood long past and it would be years before I would be able to afford the passage back.

'I see.' He raised his eyebrows again. 'India has not been quite to your taste then.'

I wished at once that I had not been so honest. 'I would not exactly say that, sir,' I faltered.

'Mr Avery, let me be candid with you. This is not a great matter but it needs to be accomplished, it must be accomplished, and, to be blunt, your future rides on how you perform upon it. If you do well, I can make sure that in a year's time you will be back wherever it is that you come from, regaling an audience of admiring females of your adventures, with a tidy pension in your pocket. If, however, Mountstuart is not found, I will see that you are sent to the most remote malarial hole in Bengal where, if you are not dead of cholera within two years, you will be half-mad with loneliness and boredom in ten and still neck-high in debt. You understand?'

The dizziness returned. 'Yes, sir. Indeed, sir.' But I thought, *Why are you saying this? Why am I here? I would rather be anywhere but here.*

'Now, the enterprise may seem impossible to you, but believe me it is not. Mr Blake is a strange cove, but he gets results. And whatever he might say, we believe he can find Mr Mountstuart, and we expect you to do your utmost to aid him.'

'Yes, sir.' And I thought, *I would rather do anything but aid him.*

'But I require you to take on another task in order to ensure that the goal is achieved, one which we expect you to discharge with discretion. As I said, Mr Blake is – how shall I say? – an unusual man. He is not quite what they call here, pukka. Not quite a gentleman. He is excellent on the trail, a veritable bloodhound, and he knows Mr Mountstuart's habits. He served many years in the Company, but he is now to all intents and purposes a civilian. He went native, took a native mistress. She died. He went astray. Insubordination. Radical views, all that. There are rumours that he is an atheist, even that he has converted to Hindooism.'

'I see, sir,' I said. And I thought, *Better and better*.

Buchanan walked back round the table. 'To be entirely, entirely honest with you, we have a very small concern that Mr Blake may veer from his duty in searching for Mr Mountstuart, and that if he finds him, his first instinct may not be to bring him back. Not that we really doubt him, but we must confess to small misgivings.'

'Really, sir.' Now I was both alarmed and confused.

'Ensign, your special task is to keep a weather eye on Mr Blake. Make sure he is doing his duty. Watch for any untoward behaviour.'

'Yes, sir. I should say, sir, that – might I observe, sir – that Mr Blake appears to have taken against me. I may not be the best person to—'

'Oh, do not concern yourself with that,' Buchanan said dismissively. 'That will all be resolved in time. I assure you.'

'Yes, sir. And how should I respond to "untoward behaviour"?'

'If you do believe Mr Blake is not performing his duties, do not do anything precipitate, but observe and remember, so you can make a full report later if necessary. You might also consider taking any problems to a senior officer such as Major Sleeman when you meet him. Of course, Mr Blake is heading this expedition and you must follow his orders, I simply wish to make you aware of some small reservations we have. And to let you know there will always be someone in authority you can talk to. You are a Company man. Remember where your loyalties lie.

'Now, as a little fillip and taster of what could be in store if you are successful, may I congratulate you on your promotion.'

I blinked. 'I beg your pardon, sir?' I said.

'You are being promoted to Lieutenant, Mr Avery.' Buchanan

smiled again. 'The expedition needs a little more Company ballast. It will naturally be a temporary commission, and there will be for the moment no additional money, but if you do well, we can change that. Once the cholera has finished with the barracks no doubt there will be more than one permanent opening.'

'Thank you, sir,' I said, taken aback by his levity.

'And by the way, you may tell no one of the reason for this expedition – not even your little Scottish friend. We will come up with some story about you joining a regiment.' With an elaborate flick of his wrist, he indicated that I was to leave.

By the time I reached the marble hall again, I had sufficiently gathered my thoughts to hope that I might still find either Frank or Miss Larkbridge there. The reception, however, was all but over: the last guests were quitting the building for suppers around town, and a mob of servants were carrying away trays and tables, moving plants and extinguishing candles. I could just see Mr Blake at the other end of the hall, hobbling slowly out into the night.

Chapter Three

Five days later Frank was murdered.

On the day after the meeting with Buchanan a message arrived informing me that I could bring only a few packs of baggage. On Frank's advice I gloomily set about selling my possessions to pay off my most pressing debts. I realized he had some notion of what I was leaving Calcutta for. It was he, after all, who had brought me to the attention of the Political Department and I wanted to put a good face on it. But in truth I felt an almost instinctive revulsion at the whole idea and a lingering anxiety that some mistake had been made.

Still, paying off some of my debts brought some relief: they had been another source of inescapable anxiety. Over-excited by my first few months' income, I had spent more than I should have on what had seemed like necessities: a pair of good horses, a share in a buggy, camp equipment for the field, some fine furniture, punch ladles and a silver muffineer. Then there were the gambling debts – of which I could not bear to think – and the servants' salaries. The two horses went, along with the pair of silver-inlaid duelling pistols, the furniture, the silver – all for much less than I had bought them. At least, I told myself, I would no longer be paying the servants' salaries.

On the second day after the meeting I confessed to Frank – to my shame – both the details of the expedition and my grievances about it. I moaned that Colonel Buchanan had contrived things so as to place me entirely at the mercy of the hateful Mr Blake, who did not care if it were to end in failure; and that if we did not succeed I would find myself not merely demoted back to Ensign, but quite possibly without regiment or position at all. I railed against Miss Larkbridge's chaperone, who had flatly refused me permission to see her – suspecting that I planned some intemperate declaration, which of course I did. I spoke of my unease at the secrecy that shrouded our endeavour. My senior officers were informed that I was being sent to an irregular cavalry regiment in the north. Nor was I comfortable with the notion that I might have to spy on Mr Blake, however unpleasant he was. Perversely, though, it was the thought of leaving the loathed Calcutta – because it meant moving ever further from any hope of home – that made me most despondent.

'You're a fool, Avery!' Frank said. 'Can you not see this as the chance for adventure that you have always wished for? At the very least it gets you out of Calcutta, even if you do have to travel with the dreaded Blake. And at the end you may even meet the man you so admire.' He sounded like a patient uncle.

For the next two days I arranged my affairs and Frank was much preoccupied with his new duties. But he seemed low, and I feared he had taken my complaints to heart and was worried he had done the wrong thing. On the fifth day, I returned to our lodgings to find him sitting in a chair, with a glass of claret, a plate of bread and butter, and a book – my copy of Scott's *Ivanhoe*. He seemed tired and distracted, even melancholic. He said he was not in the mood for a night at the mess. I was sure my ingratitude was responsible for his unusual mood. I apologized for my boorishness, and told him I intended to embrace my chance.

He sighed heavily and said, 'Oh, William, who am I to force you into things you never wished for?'

It was most unlike him. I gave him a pat on the back and said, 'Chin up, Macpherson! Get yourself to bed with a hot toddy. You must be well enough to celebrate my departure.' He smiled, looking more like his usual self, and I set off for the mess.

Three hours later I was summoned home. An officer, a captain I did not know, was waiting for me. Frank had been found lying in an alley near the bazaar, a knife wound in his chest, a cord pulled tight around his neck. His purse, coat and shoes had gone.

They had brought his body back and laid it upon his bed. I went and looked at my friend, stupidly unable to make sense of what I was seeing. The body was dirty and crumpled. Over his chest and stomach his once white shirt was wetly red. Around his neck there was a biting red line. The *khansaman* said he had not realized Frank had gone out. No one knew what he had been doing. The officer told me there was little doubt that Frank had been murdered by a native, perhaps two. Such things happened very rarely – 'Usually when a European becomes mired in some low business concerning money or native women or boys.' He looked at me questioningly.

Frank had not been like that. He had had no vices. The officer said the city watchmen and the military police were scouring the bazaar to find out the cause, but I could tell he thought it unlikely we would discover the truth. It seemed a perfect illustration of all that I had come to hate about Calcutta.

I dismissed the servants from the house. For several hours I sat by Frank's body amid the city's night sounds – occasional fat drops of water hitting the roof, a pipe guttering, the howl of a pariah dog. Then I went to my cot. I lay awake until a lone muezzin began to call Mahommedans to prayer, *'Allah ho Akbar,'* then sank briefly into uneasy, spinning darkness. When I woke, my sheets were tangled about me like a shroud.

We buried Frank the next day in the Park Street graveyard. It is the most orderly place in Calcutta: a perfect little city of well-swept paths and small palaces and temples to those gone. The day was overcast and damp. The grass was a vivid green, and one could hear the cries of the peacocks and crows that made their homes between the elaborate tombs and monuments. Frank's former regiment had agreed to pay for a marble plaque and I arranged the inscription:

In Memory of Francis Stewart Macpherson, Ensign, 1816–1837.
Beloved and Honoured Brother and Friend,
His Light Shone but too Briefly.

We were not many mourners, a few officers from Frank's regiment and members of our mess and Lieutenant Keay, my rival from the levee. He came to the wake as well, taking me aside to present his condolences and to congratulate me – he said he hoped it was not inappropriate – on my promotion.

'Listen, Avery, it is a dreadful damned thing to lose a friend like this. Perhaps leaving Calcutta now will not be the worst thing. I heard you are going north – should you hit Benares, my old billet, look up my regiment. They are capital fellows, they run a good mess and will give you a good dinner. I have a particular friend, Jiggins. Just mention my name. Of course, you depart the field leaving Miss Larkbridge under siege by the rest of us. We shall keep a piece of the wedding cake for you – although I cannot swear at this moment that it will not be that milksop Moore who will end up the bridegroom.' I got very drunk.

I do not recall much of the next two days. I walked about Calcutta, feeling very little, performing my final obligations, my eyes open but taking almost nothing in. I had intended to write home, but I could not bring myself to pen the missive my father would expect, nor the letter my sister deserved. I wrote briefly to Frank's sisters. I gave the servants their notice. That was when the rumours began. I was told by a man from our mess that there was story abroad that Frank had gone to Blacktown because he had been in debt to a native moneylender, a man of the basest morals, engaged in some of the city's most loathsome vices. I dismissed the story entirely, furious that such lies could be bruited. Frank had been the acme of moderation and virtue. I had never seen him gamble.

Helen Larkbridge sent a note with her condolences – naturally, she could not have been expected to attend the funeral. I tried to write back, but all that I had previously intended to set down now seemed hopelessly trivial and unsayable. It was as if the fuel which gave life to feelings and passion in my breast had been entirely extinguished. In the end I told her that I was leaving the city, could not tell her where I was going, but hoped to return before too many months to find her still as blooming as I would remember her. I signed the letter 'Lieutenant Avery', mildly ashamed as I did so. But I did not cross it out as I knew that, feeble as it was, my promotion was my only currency as a suitor. She sent no reply.

On my last day in Calcutta the captain who had come on the night of Frank's death returned to the house. He said that they had failed to discover anything certain about the murder, but that Frank had been disastrously in debt to a native moneylender who now had a promissory note against all Frank's possessions. He did not look me in the eye. He said that the Political Department was concerned that Frank might have had papers in his possession that he should not have. Would I mind if he looked through Frank's things before they were removed? I protested that none of this made sense, that this was not the man I had known. Where had he lost all this money? Not in my company. I demanded an explanation. He apologized with great embarrassment and said he could not give me one. I said I hoped the unproven accusations about Frank's propriety would not be made public. Discomfited, he said he did not know. Later, two burly natives arrived with a cart and took everything of Frank's away.

In the early evening I sat alone on the last chair in the drawing-room with my second glass of brandy pawnee. The room was empty save for a rat that washed itself in the middle of the floor. Since the rains a vast array of creatures – snakes, frogs, various rodents – had taken up residence inside the bungalow. I could not now summon the will to chase them out. My mind was assailed with thoughts of Frank. I did not know whether to be angry or bitterly sorry. Some part of me could not believe it. I could not recognize the man I had known – the kindest friend, the best man – in the captain's descriptions. I knew that the vastness of his debts together with the insinuations about his honesty would destroy his reputation. I remembered how I had blundered on ungratefully about myself while he had never confided in me. I wondered if he had arranged for me to leave Calcutta so I would not be present for a disgrace he must have anticipated. I thought of all his promise and how he would never do any of the things he had planned and striven for. I remembered him with the hole in his chest and the mark around his neck, and I thought of the Thugs and how they strangled their victims.

I determined I would go to the mess and play a last few hands of cards. In the past, Frank had scolded me for playing. Now those exchanges had taken on a certain painful irony. I had lost a lot at cards, principally to a certain Lieutenant O'Keefe – but not, it now

40

appeared, as much as Frank. I woke every morning resolved not to play again, just as I resolved I would not get drunk, but by the evening I would come to feel that only the card table could restore my fortunes, and that only claret and brandy could provide true solace.

I rode to the mess. There were twenty of us at table, each waited on by his own servant. The dining-room had the obligatory long table of dark polished mahogany, a trio of threadbare battle flags, and a number of scenes of regimental triumphs, of blasting cannons and hilltops taken. We ate the usual succession of hefty courses: mulligatawny soup, potted beef, mutton chops, roast turkey, fried fish, then the pastries and sweetmeats. The mood was subdued to begin with. No one mentioned Frank's name. After several glasses of loll shrub I began to unstiffen. I drank a few more. We toasted the regiment, then the King. There was a toast to my departure. Gradually we lapsed into the usual chivvying, teasing and cat-calling. A few chops and pastries were thrown. My nemesis O'Keefe was sitting at the other end of the table with a number of his cronies. He was not especially well liked – outside the mess he was a rather undistinguished officer – but he had some pull within it by virtue of his skill at the card table, and his energetic ragging of cadets, which we all took well enough.

I moved to the verandah for brandy and cheroots. A few men left for an evening ride and a visit to a nautch or to go and see their girls, and pressed me to come too. A few more retired inside for billiards. O'Keefe called for cards and a table.

'Well, who is in tonight?' He turned to me, his expression mocking. 'Do you have anything left to lose, Avery, my dear young cub? Not carrying your friend's debts too?'

'I have enough for a couple of singles,' I said.

The servants brought table and chairs. There were five of us. We played loo. I started well, winning the first hand as the dealer when everyone else passed, and the next trick too when I exchanged my cards for the Miss and the rest passed again. After that, there were a few mixed hands and I played cautiously, lost a couple of stakes, won a third of the pool a few times, then began to bleed, just a little each time, hand by hand. Before long, I was worse off than I had been before I had come to the table. Eventually O'Keefe said, as he so often did, 'Losing again, Avery. How about a hand of unlimited? I'll give you a chance to win it all back from me, but you will have to put up a serious stake.'

I was drunk. 'I am somewhat short of funds.'

'That handsome silver pocket watch will do very well.'

I did not hesitate. I unhooked the chain from the front of my jacket and placed it on the table.

'I will take an IOU,' said O'Keefe, 'but naturally with Avery leaving our midst for the Mofussil I must ask myself if I shall ever see my money.'

I bridled. 'I am good for it.' I pushed the pocket watch into the middle of the table.

I cannot describe the hand. I forgot it the moment I lost it. As I lost the next, in which I staked my father's signet ring, the last thing of value I possessed. I forfeited also an IOU that left me deeper in debt than I had been before. I struggled up and clapped my hands for the *khitmatgur*. O'Keefe made me an exaggerated little bow as I passed.

'Goodbye, Avery. I look forward to seeing you settle your debts. Unlike your friend.'

I woke bilious and sick, my temples pounding, my mouth dry, with a horrible sense of having made a terrible mistake. I was being shaken vigorously.

'Mr Avery, sar, Mr Avery! You must come. Blake Sahib awaits. You are being one hour late as we speak.'

I had been told to meet Jeremiah Blake at 4 a.m. by the Royal Botanical Gardens in Howrah on the other side of the Hooghly River, where the road led out of Calcutta. I was sure that I had told the *khitmatgur* to wake me.

A broad native swathed in enormous wrappings, whom I had never seen before, was standing over me. He had a fine luxuriant black beard, and skin like polished mahogany. 'A fine good morning to you. I am Mir Aziz, sahib. I have been for many years in the service of Bahadur Company – that is to say the Honourable East India Company. And I am come to conduct you to Mr Blake.'

I sat up slowly, and the blood thundered into my ears. I stood, trying to stave off the dizzying nausea that overwhelmed me. I stumbled, and the native caught my elbow, holding it just long enough to prevent me from falling over, and letting it go as soon as I was steady. I called for my *khitmatgur*, but there was no sign of him. It appeared he had absconded in the night along with some coins and the last of my silver cutlery. My guide affected not to see my embarrassment and withdrew as I dressed and attempted to make my toilet. I gathered the remainder of my possessions, namely my weapons – a matchlock rifle, sabre and light pistol – several packs of clothing, a small air-tight drum containing two dress uniforms and a small trunk. Outside on a bullock cart was my tent, charpai, folding chair, and a beautiful copper shaving basin with a cedarwood folding tripod base for which I had paid a small fortune. I was relieved to see the *syce* was still there, though scarcely in a better state than I.

'Sar,' said the native who called himself Mir Aziz, looking over my belongings. 'I beg your pardon most humbly, but it will not be possible to bring these things. It is only pack-horse that we are bringing. Tent and charpai and' – he pointed at my basin and my trunk – 'too heavy, too big.'

I stood for a moment, gathering myself. 'Sar,' he said more softly. 'Tent is requiring three men just to carry, three men to put up every night. We are five in number. Too few. Blake Sahib has small tents. Perhaps you have not been informed of this.'

I was feeling too ill to argue and eventually I simply waved my assent. The basin, the tent and the bed were deposited by the bungalow steps. The trunk and the chair, however, I would not leave.

It was still dark and raining lightly as we made our way through the city. By the time we reached the large tangled banyan tree outside the Botanical Gardens, the sun's rays were streaking the sky. Six lanterns, each in a thick penumbra of circling insects, lit three waiting figures wrapped in blankets. Mir Aziz rode up to them and murmured something. I hung back, embarrassed. I was two hours late. The middle figure pushed his blanket from his head, and I saw it was Mr Blake. I could hardly tell him from the other two natives.

I saw we would be five, a small party indeed. Beyond them I could see perhaps five further pack-horses.

I dismounted clumsily, turned to one side and vomited. I gave the reins of my horse to my *syce*, who was to deliver him to the new owner. Mr Blake glanced in my direction, muttered something in Hindoostanee to Mir Aziz, and strode off abruptly to mount his horse. I had intended to apologize. I decided not to.

Mir Aziz said, 'Your horse.' He pointed at a small, dumpy, bay-coloured pony. It was clear that given my height I would look absurd on it. I wondered if it would even carry me. I looked wistfully at my own handsome skittish gelding, who would never manage ninety miles in three days. Then he said, 'Many apologies, sahib, but there is no place for box or chair.'

One of the other natives climbed on to the cart and threw my trunk on to the ground, where it crashed heavily and made an alarming cracking sound. I gave an incoherent shout and ran to it. On to the ground had spilled several boxes of Windsor soap, my eau de cologne – now broken – the last of my silver cutlery, some clothing and all the books I had saved and borrowed and scavenged over the years.

'I will not leave them.'

'Better to leave precious things in Calcutta, sahib.'

I knew it too well. But there was no one in Calcutta to whom I could bear to entrust them.

Mir Aziz took pity on me. 'Chair we must leave, but it is being possible to make pack for precious things, sahib.' He said something to one of the other natives. Two pieces of sailcloth were brought from the pack-horses, and Mir Aziz laid them on the cart and gestured for me to open the box. It was clear I could not bring everything. In desperation I grabbed Mountstuart's writings, a few volumes of Sir Walter Scott, Bulwer-Lytton's *The Last Days of Pompeii*, *Pericles and Aspasia* by Walter Savage Landor, and Macpherson's *Pickwicks*.

'We can be purchasing more sailcoth in Barampore or Chinsu-rah, to cover more durably,' said Mir Aziz quietly as he wrapped my books and tied them firmly. I paid off the *syce* with the last of my coins, watching him lead away my horse. As I stood there, one of

Blake's two natives shouted something to the other, and they both laughed. I looked up, certain I had recognized a couple of the words.

'What does he say, Mir Aziz?

He nodded and looked away. 'He is saying we will make good progress today, sahib.'

Blake rode past, not giving me a look.

'I do not believe that is what he said, Mir Aziz. Tell me, please.'

He gazed at me for a moment, clearly considering whether or not to conceal the truth. 'He is saying you are a *pai-makh balaak* – a milk-faced boy – and you will not be able to keep up.'

I looked at the remains of my possessions strewn in the dirt about the broken trunk: my chair, a silver-plated carving knife, a couple of forks, a broken china plate, a pair of boots, some brightly coloured neckties, and several volumes splayed out where they had dropped. It seemed a fitting end to my time in Calcutta.

PART TWO

Chapter Four

It took all the effort I could muster simply to stay upon my horse and to restrain myself from vomiting – though I had to stop by the roadside a few times to void my guts. I was somewhat distracted by the rain. It rained so relentlessly, so intensely, that I began to imagine that we must melt back into the earth from which we had come. Then I thought of Frank – earth to earth . . . dust to dust – and was filled with such a terrible emptiness that my eyes ran and I choked.

The Grand Trunk Road stood proud of the landscape around it. Through the thick, grey, incessant drops I could just make out a bare, swampy delta of birdless mangrove and marsh, twisted bushes and occasional thickets of bamboo. The road was flooded in some places and in others the rains had filled potholes with mud, and the horses – ponies rather, stout little Pegus from Burmah – stumbled into them and lost their footing. Mr Blake rode always out in front, his stiff back shrouded like a native in a cotton blanket, a constant reproof to me. He would not allow any falling back, and we made our thirty-odd miles, but not without a struggle. By the time we were done I was an empty vessel and shook with fatigue, a situation I could blame only upon myself. Then it became clear that we would not be staying in a dak bungalow such as Europeans usually stayed in, as there were none to be seen, but in small native tents which Mr Blake expected me to help to erect. Of course, with only a few natives, I realized that I would have to abandon any notion of Calcutta levels of service and that if I did not help we would all become even wetter and hungrier than we already were. And so I laboured, tired, sick, resentful and drenched. Yet it also reminded me of how at home my brothers and I had built our shelters in the woods and caught coneys and never a servant in sight, and it was just Calcutta's customs that had given me such notions about servants. But then my anger at that hateful man resurged and that true thought fought with a burst of irritation that as a white man in this land I should be forced to labour thus, until I was quite dizzy with frustration. Once the tents were up they provided shelter of a kind, but since they were already wet the rain cascaded through them. I sat alone in mine, dining off cold rotis because it was not possible to light a fire, not daring to open my book packages lest they were already pulp. Then I lay down, shivering, the dense rain a windy chorus, my thoughts all of Frank and the poor fist we had both made of things.

The next two days were much the same as the first, save that the mangrove gave way to thickly sprouting paddy fields and to our left the great grey Ganges began its lugubrious meander north. My uniform quickly became dirty and chafed against my skin. My helmet left sores on my neck. I was as tired as I have ever been. I had little idea where we were going, knowing only that we were to travel north-west up the Grand Trunk Road as far as Benares, then west on the road to Poona and Nagpore as far as Jubbulpore, the head-quarters of the Thuggee Department and the last place Xavier Mountstuart had been sighted. The distance was a mere 700 miles. The monotony was alleviated by two things. One was a stop at the market in Chinsurah, where Sameer, the youngest of the natives, went to exchange a pony that had gone lame, and where with Mir Aziz's aid I raised a loan and bought more oiled sailcloth, binding it round my two packs in a little cupboard-like stall in the bazaar.

The second was – though I was loath to admit it – Mr Jeremiah Blake. The truth was, he was quite unrecognizable from the shivering, peeling, hobbling invalid of the week before. The trans-formation seemed to me extraordinary. He was firstly not as old as I had supposed – not young of course, but not the doddering, used-up creature he had seemed. The puffy, rashy red skin was almost gone, he was clean-shaven and his face was sunburnt. I suppose some might have called him handsome – in a coarse and common way. It was not a gentleman's face, there was something pinched about it, and it bore the marks of hard living: a broken nose, an old white puckered scar through an eyebrow. His formerly greasily straggling hair had been cut, shorter and plainer than was the fashion, and one could now see that his right ear was ragged, not like a pugilist's ear, but a tom cat's, as if something had torn bits from the top of it. Occasionally he would run a finger over these indentations. He retained an almost imperceptible limp. His eyes were deep-set and hooded. I found his gaze most unnerving, and others did too. I could not make out what colour his eyes were, some mud shade I suppose. He carried about him an air of what, for lack of a better word, I called insolence, but which I felt as the days passed was more a sceptical irritation with the world. He was very guarded. To my dismay he lived as much as he could as a native – wore native dress, a kurta and dhotis or white cotton pyjamas, with slippers, and carried a curved native sword, the tulwar, which some older Company officers preferred. A part of me envied him the looseness and coolness of his clothes, but I would not have dreamt of giving up my uniform. He ate like a native too – with his fingers, tearing the roti with his one hand, then using it to scoop up the meat and rice prepared by Nungoo, the large and slow-moving fifth member and cook of our party. And he sat cross-legged upon the ground as the natives did. Having lost my folding chair, I too now had to sit upon the ground with the natives, and I could not but view it as one more of the petty humiliations that Mr Blake had forced upon me. For what was quite unchanged was that he was just as silent and rude to me as he had been before. Not once in these days did he address a word to me; indeed he spoke little at all, and invariably in Hindoostanee.

'Was Mr Blake very angry at my late arrival and conduct?' I asked Mir Aziz on the third day.

'Chote Sahib, Mr Blake is showing no anger, nor is he speaking of it.'

On the fourth day, the rain stopped. The air was still thick and humid, but it was a relief to wake to near silence. By the light of a lantern I unpacked my books and found that apart from some dampness and a little foxing on the page edges, they had survived. As the sun rose there were patches of blue and the landscape seemed washed clean. I felt my mood lighten. I looked about me. It was, I reflected, a relief to be out of Calcutta. The landscape was now dense flat scrub clothed in its fresh post-monsoon growth, with occasional thickets of jangal. Pale brown monkeys chattered in the trees. Flocks of goats and sheep and moth-eaten pariah dogs wove on and off the highway. In the distance one could see the beginnings of low brown hills. The road itself was lined with trees, and every few miles there would be a small, tumble-down, thatched Hindoo temple or an old tomb with a small tank for water next to it and sometimes a holy man or sadoo in attendance. At regular intervals we came upon old stone monuments, thirty feet high, like fat stone fingers pointing heavenward. Mir Aziz told me that they were kos minars, giant milestones placed there by the Moghul emperors who had also planted the trees to provide shade and shelter for travellers. Now and again there would be a line of stalls selling food and tobacco to travellers camping nearby, and a dak post where groups of bearers sat waiting to carry messages or post up the road. A little way from the road one could see small villages of bamboo and mud, huts green with moss and mould after the rains. The tentative thought came to me that all might not be lost; being in the Mofussil might not be so unbearable and we might after all find Mountstuart.

Mr Blake's oddities might form part of my entertainment, but he was at the same time the great shadow over my reviving spirits. I had intended to apologize to him for my conduct on the first day, but the way in which he ignored me, and the deliberateness of his use of Hindoostanee to isolate me, soon suffocated that resolve. His whole manner, moreover, seemed designed to repel interlocutors. He never rushed but he was always engaged in some activity, and even when he was eating or sitting by the fire at night, he seemed entirely preoccupied. On that fourth day, I forced myself to approach him, but I had to interpose myself between him and his horse in order to gain his attention.

'Mr Blake, I know you did not wish me to accompany you on this journey. But at the very least you might do me the courtesy of letting me know your plans.'

He had his saddle upon his shoulder, carrying it from one pony to the next. He paused, scratched the top of his ear, and said, 'Lieutenant Avery, your job is to keep up, not to hinder me, and to keep your bone-box shut. If you do that I shall be perfectly satisfied. And you never know, you may even learn something.'

I muttered something unrepeatable under my breath.

'You feel you've been ill-used? You were lucky to leave Calcutta when you did.'

'And how do you figure that, sir?'

'You're no city type, and where you were you had few prospects. The cholera epidemic will only get worse. You're badly in debt and your servants were stealing from you.'

'You know nothing, sir. My servants were perfectly honest and my finances quite secure, thank you!' This was not at all how I had expected the exchange to go.

'All griffins are in debt,' he said, which was true. 'But the last five buttons on your jacket are patkong, a cheap alloy, not silver. Your laundryman or tailor replaced them. There's a market for silver buttons in Calcutta.'

Looking closely at my buttons I saw that the last five were almost but not precisely identical to the others. I could not believe I had not seen this before. I walked back to my fresh pony, humiliated, my heart overflowing with the purest dislike of him. *He is an oaf, a coarse oaf! And I hate him*, I thought. When I looked up, Mir Aziz was watching me.

'If you are being kind enough to permit me, Chote Sahib,' he said, 'I may tell you that we are indeed on course in our travels, and I would be most pleased to show you the maps of our route.' It was half in my mind to rebuff him, but there was something in his manner that forestalled me. The words were not offered in pity or two-faced flattery, but rather with a grave courtesy. I checked myself.

'I would be most grateful if you would,' I replied.

Thus, by design or by accident, Mir Aziz became my guide. He imparted information to me and helped me accustom myself to the road. It was a state of affairs that would have caused disapproval in Calcutta, but I was grateful for it. Within a few hours he had pointed out a dozen small things to make the journey less discomfiting. He showed me how to pitch my tent to avoid the worst of the insects and how best to arrange my nets for sleeping. When I mutinously refused Nungoo's curries and native dishes – in Calcutta such dishes were often disgusting and not often found on European tables – he told me to eat and maintain my strength, and I did, dreaming of bread and butter all the while. When he saw the rashes from my uniform, he suggested I take to looser civilian attire.

'I thank you, but as we are on Company business, I believe I should wear its livery,' I said, loud enough to ensure that Blake could hear.

Mir Aziz was not tall, but he was broad and strongly set and square-shouldered. His skin was like polished wood and his thick bushy eyebrows were held in a permanent half-frown of concentration which gave him a wise and considered aspect. His eyes had that dark liquid quality so characteristic of the natives; he had a strong, sharp nose and a splendid black beard with a few silvers hairs in it. When the wind got up, he would part it carefully, pushing one half up on to one side of his head, and the other on to the other side, and tie the two sides against his yellow pugree with a scarf. His speech might sometimes be florid, but he never spoke with the gushing flattery and insincerity that I had encountered in Calcutta. What his precise role was on our journey, however, was not by any means clear and on the subject he was most enigmatic.

'I am, as goes the saying of the Romans of old, general factotum,' was all he would say. 'I am doing and making everything.' One day he offered to shave me and did so with great facility and skill. After he dressed my face with various unguents, taken from a small wooden box, he gave me a powder and a small vial, 'Multanni mitti and rose-water, Chote Sahib. It is being treatment for painful skin.' Blake, I noted, consulted Mir Aziz frequently – though he did not take advantage of Mir Aziz's barbering.

What surprised me most about Mir Aziz was how susceptible he – a Mahommedan and also so evidently sensible – was to Hindoo superstitions. He spoke often of good and bad omens, of tigers roaring and ravens cawing, of demons and evil spirits. The two other natives, Sameer and Nungoo, were just as impression-able. When we saw an elephant there were great expressions of rejoicing. I said to Mir Aziz that I had thought elephants were sacred only to the Hindoos, because of their paunchy little elephant god.

'But it is bringing us good fortune too, Chote Sahib, to Mus-selman, Sikh, Jain – and Christian too.'

Another night, after eating, Sameer produced a noise unheard in polite company – and evidently unacceptable in Mir Aziz's. The older man insisted that he leave the camp, taking a piece of burning ember with him, douse it, then hit himself with a slipper five times. Looking much abashed, Sameer did precisely as he was told; indeed he and Nungoo took instruction from him without question.

These two spoke almost no English and behaved to me with just enough courtesy so as not to appear actually insubordinate. I had never been in such constant close quarters with natives and was sure they took pleasure in serving up insults I did not understand in their own tongues, but I did not wish to be forever asking Mir Aziz for translations and so I ignored them. Sameer was little more than a boy – slight, quick-moving with a mouth full of white teeth, con-stantly bordering on insolent and skilled with the horses. It was he who had called me a milk-faced boy that first morning, a quip I dis-missed when I saw the difficulty he was having in growing a pair of wispy moustaches. When the weather improved he took to gallop-ing ahead of us, shouting something that sounded like 'Chullo bai! Chullo bai!' and scattering travellers on foot.

Nungoo was older, quiet, with a broad flat face, long moustaches and skin dark as treacle. His arms seemed to emerge from the front of his shoulders, which made his back look almost hunched, but he was extremely strong and very methodical. He reprimanded Sameer now and again, I noted, but also took a certain care in him. Both men, like Mir Aziz, were Mahommedans and so not constrained by the caste rules that bound Hindoos to certain tasks. Like him, their roles were not precisely stated: they were neither quite servants nor sepoys – though they had both served in the Company's army – but rather something in between. They rode extremely well, and carried swords and muskets. Nungoo cooked for us. Sameer saw to the horses and for a few coins washed my clothes.

That fourth night we finally spent under a roof. Not in a dak bungalow – his lordship would not have that – but a native caravanserai, a kind of circular walled cloister entered through a large gate, where each section of cloistered wall was a small room with a wooden door. Mr Blake greeted one or two natives, then went to speak to the woman who ran the cook-shop at the gate. He seized her hand and she cried out and laughed a deep guttural laugh when she saw him. I was surprised, since very few Europeans ever elected to stay in such places, but within minutes our wet clothes were being dried round the hearth, and bowls of curry, rice and small fried cakes were produced. In the yard in the middle of the caravanserai business was contracted, and natives tended camels, loaded bales and took on new grooms. At the edges, high-caste Hindoos cooked their suppers over open fires, and merchants and horse dealers moved from one shadowed cloistered room to the next, muttering and arguing. I sat at the entrance of our straw-filled room with my copy of Mountstuart's *The Courage of the Bruce*, while Blake played knuckle-bones with the merchants, several of whom he clearly knew, occasionally issuing a loud belch. I knew I was unmistakeable in my uniform, and I fancied the natives went more slowly and watchfully about their business. I was sure my appearance annoyed Mr Blake, and I was glad that it did. The presence of a lumpy charpai gave me reason to rejoice and, despite the constant burble and the savaging of insects, I lapsed into unconsciousness for a few hours.

For the next week we woke at four while it was still cool, riding five or six hours to cover the required distance of thirty to forty miles, changing our ponies every few days, resting when we could in the afternoons. Though we passed empty white dak bungalows, Blake never allowed us to stay in one. Instead nights were passed in the now noxious-smelling tents. The heat was still thick and exhausting, but the rain was dwindling and the mud was less onerous and the travelling less hard. And despite the exasperations, I found that after months of lethargy the change of air and the activity elevated my spirits. I did not cease to mourn poor Macpherson, but the longing for home came less painfully, and other thoughts began to supplant it. I determined that I would do all that was asked of me, and everything in my power to try to make our journey a success. I would show no fatigue, I would not complain – though occasionally I would gripe to myself that I was obliged to undertake chores that no European would normally perform, in conditions that no European would normally have to undergo, that my sores were starting to fester, that I could not abide the food and that the insects kept me from sleeping. I would observe Jeremiah Blake and note my observations, and whatever happened I would do my duty. I found these thoughts comforting.

The road was not yet as busy as it would become once the rains stopped for good, but it was already a full day's entertainment in itself. There were frenzied ash-smeared fakirs who gambolled grotesquely and stuck their palms out for money; women wrapped in layers of cottons – saffron, pink, blue – with babes on their hips and dull brass bracelets tinkling; small insolent boys chewing sugar cane. There were jugglers with families of monkeys in their turbans; wealthy Sikhs in yellow silk waistcoats with enormous beards and huge dastars, leading columns of camels and carts; wedding parties in red and silver, with painted elephants, encircled by the scent of jasmine; and carts of dull-eyed, ragged indentured servants.

As for us, it is impossible to overstate what an odd, un-European picture we made: a small, lamentably unkempt party, travelling faster than anything but the camel sowars delivering messages up the road. Occasionally we would pass an English civilian or officer followed by the usual eight carts of possessions and twenty or thirty servants, covering their eight miles a day, with perhaps a wife and children carried in two palanquins, all complaining bitterly. I began to dream of travelling with a tent so large and luxurious that it required its own bullock cart, my tripod basin, eau de cologne and Windsor soap, and a full complement of servants including my own cook, laundryman and barber.

By night, we'd take turns to watch for thieves and dacoits, but not Thugs. Mir Aziz said one rarely heard of them now. Even in earlier times, they had never plied the busy routes but haunted the more remote places where there was jangal into which to vanish, and they had never attacked Europeans. We were all armed – Mir Aziz always wore an ammunition belt across one shoulder, and a tulwar, which he sheathed in a beautiful and very distinctive black leather scabbard stitched with silver.

What did not change was that Mr Blake remained an utter enigma. He kept his own council, never imparted his thoughts and showed, as far as I could tell, absolutely no interest in Xavier Mountstuart. By day, he was always out in front, his straight back an unmistakeable marker of a former soldier. At night, by our fire, he might take out a small, thick leather-bound book and read from it; or he would bring out a small huqqa and suck impassively, staring into the fire. Though he sometimes looked near-feverish with fatigue, he never acknowledged it as far as I could tell. Despite his commonness he did have a quality that commanded our natives' respect. In other circumstances I might have tried again with him or even forced my conversation upon him out of sheer mischief. But there was something powerfully self-contained about him that repelled inquiry. I considered asking Mir Aziz what he knew about him, but I was reluctant to expose both my ignorance and my curiosity. I tried to imagine his life in Calcutta with his *bibi*, the native woman who had died. I could not picture him surrounded by friends or a family, or that dreary broken-down house in better days. I could see no sign of the 'bloodhound' described by Colonel Buchanan. I did not hear him inquire of a single European we encountered if they had seen Mountstuart – not an unreasonable question about the most famous man in India. Instead, at each town or station he and Mir Aziz would disappear for an hour or two. Whether he knew of my own admiration for Mountstuart I had no idea. I found the thought that he had known the poet abhorrent. As a result I took to searching out a British officer in each place to inquire whether they had seen Mountstuart. None had. There seemed to be no trace of him.

In those hours when we rode and there was little to see, or when I tried to rest and sleep would not come, I deliberately turned my thoughts from Frank to Mountstuart and the Thugs. What I knew about their practices – 'Thuggee' – had come both from the drawing-rooms of Calcutta, and Major William Sleeman's history of the Thugs and their customs, which I had read after I had arrived in Calcutta. 'Thuggee' Sleeman was the Company officer who had done most to capture and destroy the Thug gangs. The headquarters of his campaign, Jubbulpore, was our destination. It was in the Thug heartland, the old anarchic Maratha states, taken over by the Company in 1819. Since the late 1820s William Sleeman, in a campaign of extraordinary brilliance and relentlessness, had pursued and all but stamped out the Thugs, making the roads of India safe for native travellers.

Through the dry season the Thugs walked those roads, posing as innocent travellers, befriending other wayfarers. They would begin in small bands of ten or twelve, up to thirty, but might combine until they numbered over a hundred, for they were too cowardly ever to attack unless they well outnumbered their victims. They would cover hundreds of miles, choosing their quarry, then employing disguises to ensnare them, depending on their caste or religion. They might play poor pilgrims or a group of sepoys on leave or a raja's policeman with his servants, or a caravan of merchants. It was the task of the Thug inveigler or deceiver – the incarnation of fair face and foul intention – to charm the victims. Often he would be the jemadar, the chief of the band. He might sing, tell tales or recite poetry. The best inveiglers made women fall in love with them and convinced the most intransigent merchant, high-caste Brahmin or proud Sikh to sit at their fire. Often the inveiglers would suggest it would be safer to travel in a group for fear of dacoits or Thugs.

The band might spend a day or weeks charming their victims until they were entirely trusted. Then, one night as they all sat together, at a pre-ordained moment, the Thug leader would make a sign. Behind each innocent a strangler, a *bhurtote*, would be standing ready to throw his *rumal* – the long knotted orange scarf with which he choked out life – around the victim's neck. Next to each there would be two hand-holders whose job it was to prevent the victim from pulling off the scarf. The murders were, according to Sleeman, executed with great skill and precision – the Thugs prided themselves on how quickly and silently they worked. Men, women and children were murdered without compunction for no one could be left alive to tell their secret, though occasionally they would save a small child and bring it up as their own, training it in Thuggee later. There were Thugs whose parents had been victims of their own methods, and it was said these men accepted this with the calm fatalism that is one of the most perplexing qualities of Hindooism.

The most horrible aspect of Thuggee, however, was that the Thugs justified their murders as acts of devotion to Kali. She was the reason they plied their monstrous trade. They said she ordered them to. Their victims were offerings to the goddess, who delighted in blood. I had read that each gang carried a pickaxe sacred to her, with which they dug their victims' graves, and that each Thug underwent an initiation of eating fresh sugar cane called *goor*. The Thugs said the *goor* changed their natures for ever. It gave them the blood lust which made it possible for them to perform their murders, and each time they planned to kill, they would consume it again. They claimed not to be accountable for their actions, as they were merely the goddess's instruments. The fruit of their murders, the victims' possessions, were their reward for doing the goddess's bidding.

And yet one could tell that Sleeman had some sympathy for the Thugs he had captured. He had interviewed them and studied them at length, and his book described their customs, habits and their thoughts of what drove them. One Thug in particular, Feringhea, had particularly captured his imagination. Sleeman had persuaded him to become an informer, an Approver, and he had told the Major his life story. Though he had killed hundreds without compunction, he was in his way a remarkable character: he was passionately fond of his family, a fine neighbour, brilliant at executing his ruses, true to his monstrous beliefs, and yet trapped in his belief that he was slave to the *goor*, undone by the loss of his moral compass. I could, when I considered it, see how Xavier Mountstuart would think the Thugs might make a fine subject for a great poem.

*

The further we left Calcutta behind, the **wilder** and hillier and more forested the landscape became. On the road tall trees gave shade, and on several afternoons we heard growls from the forest. Mir Aziz said they were tigers, calling from the right side of the road, and that this was a good omen. On certain afternoons when time permitted, I would walk into the forest to shoot partridge and pigeons which Nungoo cooked for me – he would not eat them himself on account of them not being killed in the correct manner for a Musselman. We passed Hazaribagh, the 'city of a thousand tigers', where the land began to rise. Outside Ranachitty, where the views from atop the hills down at the thickly forested valleys reminded me of England, we saw a tiger asleep on the road. When I lifted my musket to take a shot, Mir Aziz pushed it away and Mr Blake barked in Hindoostanee.

'Tiger in the road is being very good luck,' said Mir Aziz. 'Bad luck to kill.' He glanced at Blake. 'Blake Sahib is saying most tiger is not dangerous, no, not at all.' I put my gun away, grumpily, wondering if I would ever have another chance. The commotion, meanwhile, had roused the creature, which in one fluid movement rose, stared at us insolently and strolled languidly into the undergrowth where it was immediately swallowed by the shadows.

After nine days we came to the city of Sahseram, a place of old, decaying, pink-stone buildings. It had been, Mir Aziz said, the capital of the Emperor Sher Shah Suri, who had built the great road north and was buried here. By the side of the road there were many low round mounds, suttee graves, in which were buried Hindoo widows who had immolated themselves on the funeral pyres of their husbands. Mr Blake had business, Mir Aziz told me, and I was free for the afternoon. I found myself alone with the Company civilian who had authorized our change of mounts – a short, somewhat nervous fellow who reminded me of nothing so much as a mild but anxious vicar, but who kindly invited me to pass the night at his home. The prospect of a night in the flea-filled straw of a caravanserai was not appealing, and I immediately accepted.

'Did you hear at all whether Xavier Mountstuart passed this way a few months ago?' I asked him.

'Xavier Mountstuart? Good heavens, is he supposed to have done?' The thought made him frown. '*From what turbid waters, from what darkling caverns comest thou, great giving mother Ganges?* Goodness me! What on earth could he want with Sahseram? No. No. I think it very unlikely that I should not have heard of it.' It was the same answer I had encountered all the way up the road.

The afternoon was less humid than it had been and at the civilian's suggestion I took a palanquin into the town, following the huge red dome of Sher Shah Suri's tomb. I was brought to a large, still square tank, or artificial lake. In its midst, connected to the land by a narrow brick causeway, was a palace of a tomb. It was in some disrepair but still handsome, and made – one saw when one approached – of many thousands of small pink bricks. Its large main dome was intricately encircled by many smaller domed shelters and handsome terraces, punctuated by dark-shadowed arches. Though the water was not very clean and the building somewhat dilapidated, I realized I felt at peace and almost happy. I dismissed the bearers and, having strolled about the tank, wandered back through the bazaar. I examined a stall which sold inlaid boxes, and another which to my surprise displayed tiny dolls' furniture. Further into the bazaar were the more prosaic stalls selling vegetables, firewood, oil and fresh-cooked foods. Without thinking I purchased a snack of fried gram served on a sal leaf, which I had seen Sameer eat – something I would never have done in Calcutta. It was crisp and hot and delicious.

There was little of the importuning by natives that one encountered in Calcutta and so I continued to meander past a white-domed temple and a small square tank rimmed by tiny child-sized steps. A crowd was gathered around a pan stall. I could see the potions and dried herbs. I stopped at a distance, attempting to work out what was happening. The crowd parted for a moment, and I saw Mir Aziz – I was sure it was he – bending over a native sitting in a chair. He was brandishing what looked like a long pointed sharp needle and seemed about to do the man in the chair some terrible injury while some of the crowd watched and others talked animatedly among themselves. Then some looked up, and for the first time I had the feeling that I was where I should not be. I turned on my heel, then looked back, but the crowd had re-formed and I could see nothing. I walked back to the European part of town, extremely troubled by what I had seen.

Over dinner I did my best to look enthralled by my host's talk of the Governor General Lord Auckland's upcoming visit on his way north. My thoughts, however, kept returning to the needle and the bazaar.

'Though of course the Governor General and his sisters will be travelling by boat up the Ganges,' my host said, 'the soldiers will mostly be coming up the road. It is naturally a great honour, of which I am very sensible, to put up the army, but we are only a small station, you know. Feeding and watering a 10,000-strong force here, well, we have had to scour the neighbourhood. I can tell you, the natives do not like it, not one bit. It is all a little worrying. There are whispers,' he went on, 'of famine further north. It all puts pressure on us, the civilians. We do not have a regular station of soldiers here, so if anything were to happen . . . It is of some concern to me,' and he patted a handkerchief anxiously against his forehead. 'More soup?'

I declined. 'Might I, however, describe something I saw today in the bazaar to ask if you are familiar with it?'

I described the strange sight I had witnessed: one native apparently about to do violence to another seated before him, surrounded by a considerable audience. My host began to wring his hands, pulling his fingers back towards his knuckles in an anxious manner.

'Goodness, what can it be? I have never heard of such a thing. It all sounds very alarming. I suppose I shall have to investigate. Dear, dear, more uncivilized native conduct. Very much not what we need just now, when there is enough muttering in the bazaar.'

He seemed a nice enough man and I was sorry I had worried him, but the prospect of a comfortable bed displaced all cares and I soon retired joyfully to its embrace. There in turn I began to worry. Whatever he had been doing, Mir Aziz's proximity to the pan stall was especially concerning. My senior officers had warned me that pan stalls were havens of sedition, and native druggists were charlatans peddling dangerous remedies. I felt a sneaking suspicion that his performance was connected to Blake. Perhaps, I thought, they had no intention of finding our quarry. Eventually, fatigue overcame me and I dropped off. At some point I was woken again by a thin clammy hand snaking unpleasantly around my waist. Holding as tight as I could to the shreds of sleep, I gave the body attached to it as hard a dig as possible with my elbow and then kicked backward to push it from the bed. There was a pained yelp.

'I believe, sir,' I said sleepily, 'I accepted an invitation for dinner and a bed, not for company in it.'

'I just thought . . .' my host said plaintively.

'You were mistaken then,' I said. 'I am extremely fatigued, sir. Kindly leave me to sleep.'

In the morning when I rejoined our party, I was constrained and awkward with Mir Aziz. He volunteered nothing about the previous day's activities, and I could not bring myself to ask. I felt the former easiness and understanding between us disperse, and I regretted it. There were three days of riding until we would reach Benares. I bestirred myself to think only of that. But after ten days of hard travel we were all dog-tired. Even Mr Blake flagged. I caught him swaying in the saddle and I could see when he dismounted that he ached just as I did, though he never complained of it. Sameer was sulky; Nungoo clattered about with his cooking pot. I struggled to stay awake for my watch, cursed my sores and became morose and ill-tempered, especially with Mir Aziz. The landscape offered little respite. It became flat again, punctuated by the occasional tank, a small mosque or Hindoo temple and the obligatory skinny, half-naked sadoo, and a few poor huts. We began to pass large fields where small, curly-leafed plants were pushing up through the earth. Eventually we came upon the longest, ugliest grey building I had ever seen – a vast, vast rectangular thing that stretched on and on like a series of long barns. Despite my resolution not to depend on Mir Aziz, I could not resist asking what it was.

'Manufactury for afeem. Opium poppy,' he said. 'It is new cultivation, maybe three, four year ago. Once this land was planted with indigo and lentil.'

I heard, or thought I heard, a note of disapproval in his voice and I pursued it coldly. 'But this is not a bad thing, Mir Aziz?' I said.

'I do not know, sahib,' he said.

'Opium has made India rich,' I announced. 'It has repaired the fortunes of the Company, which has brought peace, order, roads, trade to all. Now it will be able to do more. Is that not a good thing?' Ahead of me, I was sure I heard Blake snort, though it was quiet enough for me to wonder if I had imagined it.

'Of course, sahib.' I could tell he did not agree, but I had wanted to force him to bow to my opinion, and he had and I felt shabby for it. We did not speak for the rest of the day.

We came to Benares in the morning. From a distance it was like a tale from the *Arabian Nights*, a glitter of pale walls. Then as we came closer one could see the wide pewter-dark mirror of the Ganges with its yachts, pinnaces, steamboats and rafts, running past the city walls, with deep ghat steps leading down to it. From them, stretching up to an immense height, there were elegant old minarets, palaces with elaborately carved stone balconies, and Hindoo temples. The stone seemed to me at that moment to be all the colours of the dawn, from near white to pale pink to golden orange to red. On the ghats there were huge pale stone statues of Hindoo gods, sitting or reclining, and near them, tiny by comparison, hundreds of natives stood waist-deep in the water, washing or spreading their arms in prayer, or pouring liquid from brass bowls that glinted in the sun, their foreheads daubed with white smears. Other ghats were piled with hemp sacks of grain, cotton and opium ready to be loaded on to steamboats for transport down to Calcutta. From yet more twirled a constant plume of smoke, almost picturesque until one remembered it came from the burning bodies of the dead before they were tipped into the river. Closer to, Benares reminded me of Calcutta: it heaved with bodies and livestock. We made the river crossing in a shallow red boat, then pushed our way through the city gates and a labyrinth of narrow alleys to a stables where we exchanged our ponies and stowed our baggage.

Mir Aziz told me that Mr Blake had business in the city. I was free to spend the day as I preferred and might take Sameer if I wished. I declined the offer. For a few hours I wanted nothing more than to be free of Blake's arrangements, and I wished to pursue my own plans. I said I intended to seek out Lieutenant Keay's regiment and his friend Jiggins, and that if I could get European accommodation for the night I should accept it. I hired a palanquin which took me some way beyond the walls, past the wide gravelled avenues of the European cantonment to the headquarters of Keay's regiment, His Majesty's 31st. In a small hot room off the parade ground I found a large, sandy-haired adjutant poring unenthusiastically over a pile of papers. When he saw me, he leapt from the table and vigorously pumped my hand.

'A new phiz! Capital! And a new uniform. Where have you sprung from?' He was a big, sturdy fellow, with a fair bit of flesh round him, and there were the beginnings of red whiskers on his chin. When he grinned he showed a row of large, even teeth. 'Are you advance notice from Calcutta? We're not expecting the Governor General for six weeks.'

'I am up from Calcutta, but I'm travelling with a Company civilian to Jubbulpore. Do you know where I might find a Lieutenant Jiggins?'

'I am the very man! Who sent you? Jubbulpore, eh? To see Thuggee Sleeman, I suppose?' Seeing my expression of surprise he said, 'Why else would you be going to Jubbulpore?'

'Of course. Lieutenant Keay said I should—'

'Cut-above Keay, the Prince of the Mofussil? He sent you? Prime!'

I laughed, and he said, '"Cut-above Keay" – it is good, isn't it? From Calcutta, hey? Has he managed to catch himself a wife? Can't imagine it would be too hard.'

'We have been rivals, I'm afraid. I fear he'll get the best of it. But he suggested I come find —'

'Yes, of course! Do you have lodgings? I am sure I can set you up. How long are you here for? Are you a large party?'

I explained how few we were, how fast we had been travelling, and how at that moment the summit of my ambitions was to find something apart from the ground on which to sleep. His keenness was both appealing and a little overwhelming.

'Fire and fury! Never heard anything like it! No servants? You must be quite done up. Can't have that. There is at least one empty bungalow and there are rooms at the chummery. I insist you dine at the mess tonight. We always want news from Calcutta.'

He began to summon natives from nowhere and issued a stream of orders. In just a few minutes he had found me a fleet of servants, directed me to my rooms, arranged for my luggage to be collected, ordered a bath and suggested we meet again at dusk. I drew a cold bath – a luxury so delightful at that moment it surpassed all others – and dozed. I woke after an hour determined to return to the ghats. Leaving my palanquin at the gates, I pushed my way into the alleys alone on foot. I could not say quite why I felt the need to return – Benares was impressively ancient and it had a decrepit beauty, but I did not warm to its crowded chaos. I roamed about the temples and shrines, and then to the bazaar, wandering between stalls selling sky blue and pink silks, heavy-smelling perfumes, piles of musty carpets, daggers, knives and elderly blunderbusses, and ventured as deep as I could into the native parts. There were more stalls selling inlaid ivory work, and jade and ivory bangles and hairpins. From a fearsome old woman who bit my coins, I chose a box of iridescent beetles' wings for my sister in England, to sew on to a dress. Since we had left Calcutta I had put thoughts of her from me. Now I resolved to write to her. But I saw no sign of Mir Aziz.

Jiggins's mess turned out to be a jolly place, smaller and friendlier than mine, and he was its master of revelries. I was stood a fine dinner and plied with Champagne – 'Simkin, simkin, Avery, please,' said Jiggins, 'got to learn the local lingo' – which, after two weeks of warm water from a skin bottle, was very nectar of the gods. The officers were a convivial bunch, loudly complaining about whiling away their days in Benares, while up in the north there were still battles to be fought and skirmishes to be had. They could not wait to follow the Governor General to Simla, and thence, they hoped, to the border. I envied them.

'Have you seen a regiment march yet, Avery?' said Jiggins. 'It is something all right. The Governor General's procession will be all that and more. It starts with his entourage and their servants. Then after it comes at least two divisions, and for every fighting man at least five non-combatants – with large families even more. That's a column of at least 20,000 people, and tens of thousands of camels, horses, mules, bullocks and elephants, grain, salt, silks, shoes, black-smiths, saddlers, sweetmeat makers: a whole moving city, all trundling along. The front reaches its destination before the back has even started.'

'But tell us, Avery,' he went on, clapping an arm around my shoulders, and speaking for the benefit of the whole table, 'how do you come to be pounding the miles to Jubbulpore with a mysterious civilian, in double-quick time and in disgraceful discomfort, without a bearer to your name?'

There was laughter.

'We are going to Jubbulpore to see Major Sleeman. I can say no more.' I am a poor liar and when Jiggins gave me a sidelong look, I blushed a little.

'Sleeman is a remarkable fellow,' another man said. 'A politico, not a real soldier, of course.' Politicos were officers who had trans-ferred to the Political Department, taking civilian jobs running stations, as Macpherson had hoped to. 'But they don't find corpses lying in the road like they used to. Major Lawrence used to oversee the Thug-taking round here, and he's done very well for himself. But they have all done well, Sleeman's men.'

'A bit of an old stick, Sleeman. Always going on about his sugar cane and his trees and his peasants.'

'Still, they say the sugar cane got him that pretty French wife!'

'She must have had a sweet tooth!' said Jiggins, and there was general laughter and hooting. 'But if you do not mind my asking, why travel so fast? What is wrong with a little comfort? Must be said, when I saw you this morning you looked as if you had been dragged through the Mofussil by a herd of careering water buffalo.'

'My civilian, Jeremiah Blake, is a little eccentric. He wishes to make good time.'

'Sounds a bit cracked if you ask me. No servants, no proper food, no proper drink, not even a camp cot to sleep on. Never heard the like. Why be in this country if you are going to deny yourself the few lowly comforts?'

'Jeremiah Blake?' said an older captain, slightly in his cups. 'I remember a Jeremiah Blake. This one was a captain up near Sind when we were with the 11th Bengal infantry. Some kind of poor-house prodigy. Spoke everything: Maratha, Pashtun, Urdu, Persian. Promoted from the ranks. I can't remember why. They gave him a native company. Sepoys would do anything for him. Never gave anything away, very quiet. Unless he was drunk – then he could swear like a fifty-year-old Irish trooper.'

While I salted this intelligence away, for a reason I could not quite divine I said, 'I do not think it can be him.'

I was asked for news of Keay and gave as good an account as I could, admitting to our romantic rivalry to the guffaws of the company, and then recited as much Calcutta gossip as I could muster. The party had heard rumours of Xavier Mountstuart's novel. They topped up my glass and roared at the details.

'Ah, Mountstuart,' someone said. '*The love of power, and rapid gain of gold/ The hardness by long habitude produced/ The dangerous life in which he had grown old.*'

'*The mercy he had granted, oft pushed aside,*' I continued, '*The sights he was accustomed to behold/ The wild hills, and wild men with whom he'd ride/ Had cost his enemies a long repentence/ And made him a good friend, but bad acquaintance.* It is a marvellous poem, *The Lion of the Punjab*. I am a great admirer of his. I have been reading him since I was a boy. We are searching for him – among other things.' I had a sudden lurch of discomfort. I had said too much. The whole table looked expectantly at me. I wondered what Blake would have thought.

'Aha! Lost him, have you?' said Jiggins, and there was more laughter. 'So that's it! Never fear. Secret's safe with us.'

I blushed again. 'I should not really speak of it, but as a matter of fact, yes. He was supposed to be going to Jubbulpore but no one has seen him since.'

'So it would be something to find him then,' mused Jiggins. 'Are there clues in his verse to his whereabouts, do you think? Is that why they sent you?' I smiled a little nervously. 'Never read any of it myself. Always considered him a bit of a hero, though one hears things.'

'How do you mean?' I said.

'I don't know.' Jiggins swung his arm vaguely. 'Said to be a tricky cove. Irritable. Quick to take offence. Rather too keen on the natives. But that's just talk.'

'We've been told he went to Jubbulpore to meet with the captured Thugs. He is writing a poem about a Thug chief. But he went off and no one has seen him.'

'How curious. We never saw him here,' said Jiggins. 'I suppose the Thugs might make a poem. Sleeman says they have their code and all that, not like your dacoit, who will do anything. Hope you are taking care on the roads, they can be dangerous round here. Of course, he might have gone to see old Vishwanath.'

'Who is old Vishwanath?'

'Rao of Dhoora. The one who keeps the white tigers. Princely state on the Poona road? You must have heard of him. Difficult old humbug he is too. Ignores every last request we make. Will not allow our soldiers within his boundaries for anything. Ignores summonses. Lords it up a storm. Likes his gemstones: dripping with rubies and sapphires. Mountstuart is famously his friend – or that's what is said round here. Probably enjoying the Rao's hospitality and lining his pockets with a few sapphires as we speak.'

It was a sore point that we Company men were no longer allowed – as we once had been – to accept gifts from native princes. We had to turn any such reward over to the Company treasury on pain of instant dismissal and possible court martial.

We toasted the King, smoked a little and toasted him again, and I was glad the subject had moved on. Eventually Jiggins said, 'We're planning a visit to a nautch. Will you come? Town's full of *chaklas* too, probably go to one after. Some very pretty little creatures too, very obliging. Either way, a huqqa and a nautch is a fine way to end the evening. I'm sure we can find you something . . .'

By now I was in the grip of a great surge of gratitude and affection for Jiggins, and for Keay back in Calcutta too, and for all the world, and so we all set out in palanquins towards the city. We tumbled out in a part I did not recognize from my earlier explorations. It was dark but the night sky was bright and the endless small temples glowed with light – in Benares someone seemed to be praying to some god at every minute of the day. The streets were still busy, the natives laughing and chatting among themselves. There was a sense of palpable anticipation in the air. Like me, Jiggins was a little drunk. He clapped his arm across my shoulder and pointed at a painted doorway. 'Here it is. Marvellous place. Stay as long as you like, leave whenever you want. Bearers'll take you back.' At that moment sounds of clapping and whistling and shouting launched into the still night from a few hundred yards away. 'Native gathering,' said Jiggins. 'They come to hear some local doxy sing old songs from a roof. Benares tradition. All whining and yowling to me.'

The thought of a courtesan singing from a rooftop caught my curiosity. 'Might I go for a moment and take a look?'

'Whatever you desire, Avery, my dear chap. Not much to see, I'd say. Should warn you they like to tease a white man if they can, and you will stand out like a fire in an icehouse. The Resident doesn't approve of it, the singing, but doesn't do anything about it. Harmless really. Perhaps you wouldn't mind if I—?' He pointed at the door. 'The bearer can bring you back.'

'Not at all, I will be but a moment.'

A bearer at my side, I followed the sounds of shouts and whistles across several streets until the way widened and I came to a small crowd that had gathered before an old house on a corner, three storeys high, with cracked open shutters. From the roof came a long, unnerving, almost whining note. The crowd was looking upward. A woman was singing in the native style, her coarse, full-throated voice keening and swooping, weaving in and out of minor keys in no sort of pattern I could make out. She leant over a parapet; her face was uncovered, but it was too dark to see her clearly. She wore pale wraps, and her arms, encased in bangles and exposed to the elbow, were large and heavy and moved in wide, graceful, circular motions. The song appeared to start as a lament with long, solemn notes, but swiftly her voice took on an arch and pointed quality. The audience – men of all ages, some bare-headed, others heavily turbanned or hooded, with a few children running about between their feet – was quiet at first. But then they began to chuckle and clap appreciatively. I listened for a while until I felt I had gleaned what I could from the proceedings and turned to go. Immediately, the woman's voice changed again. There was a gust of laughter and shouts. I turned round. It seemed that I was the target of the laughter. Her arms were pointed at me and the mocking note in her voice was unmistakeable. The crowd cheered. I took to my heels, marching as quickly and purposefully as I could, only half-attentive of where I was going. Something had caught my eye. Through the forest of heads I was sure I had seen Blake staring up at her, listening intently.

After some minutes I realized that I had not only lost all sense of where I was, but I had also misplaced my bearer. I returned the way I had come, but I must have missed a turn for I found myself in a small dirty square that I was sure I had not visited before. About the edges bodies lay under carts, and a few dark faces looked up at me. Again I tried to retrace my steps, listening for the whistles and shouts. But the streets had begun to empty and I was in a lane I did not recognize at all. I stood, trying to set myself a landmark to make for, but the street was illuminated only by slits of light emerging from cracked and louvred shutters, and the towers and minarets looked shadowily alike. I was soon entirely lost. There were occasional bursts of noise – the murmur of voices from a rooftop, the rattle of a window being closed, and from somewhere more distant a roar of voices – but I could not deduce their direction. I wandered for a while, and as I did so a creeping conviction came upon me that I was being followed. Shadows hovered behind me, yet when I turned there was no one. The streets were still peopled, men slept in doorways and under the lee of a temple, but now the festive mood had vanished, replaced by what I perceived as one almost of apprehension. The natives I accosted to inquire for directions back to the ghats glanced uncomfortably at my uniform then stared at the ground, or darted me furtive glances, refusing to understand even my bat phrases. They muttered anxiously and gestured vaguely until I let them go.

Increasingly sober, I walked into an empty market square, where a number of ink-skinned men were talking intently in groups. There was something strained, almost a smell of uneasiness, in the air, which my presence did nothing to alleviate. Nor could I put away the notion that someone was watching me. At a corner between two large, high-walled buildings, I withdrew into the shadow to take my bearings before I set out again. It began to rain. Something fell across my head and about my neck, and a hand reached around my shoulders.

Chapter Five

It is not good time to be abroad, Chote Sahib,' said Mir Aziz quietly. 'Let us return to the ghats and find you a palanquin.'

He had thrown a large cotton blanket over my shoulders. Without a second thought, I bundled it around me against the rain and followed him. We walked briskly for about five minutes until we reached the part of the city that was full of temples washing light into the streets.

'Mir Aziz?' I said at last. 'Why is it that I should not be on the streets?'

'Let us continue,' he said, with barely a backward glance.

'No. No. Please, Mir Aziz, tell me this at least. I was with some officers in the city. I heard a woman singing from a rooftop. There was a crowd gathered below, laughing and cheering. When I left I became lost. The streets were suddenly quieter and there was something . . . What did I see? Do you say it is dangerous? Is there sedition in Benares?'

He pulled me to the side of the street. He paused and looked me directly in the eye. He said, 'Not sedition, Chote Sahib. Just fear.'

'Fear?'

'There are tales of famine north of Allahabad, Chote Sahib.'

'Yes,' I said, 'I have heard of this. But the Company, the government, will make sure that the people are fed.'

'Of course, sahib. But the Hindoo is frightened. He fears the coming of the Governor General and his army of many *lakh* of men. How to feed all? And then, after they have gone, will there be food left?'

'I am sure the Company will find a way.' I thought of the chaos of Calcutta and I was not sure at all.

'I know this, but the Hindoo fears.'

He made to walk on, but I touched his shoulder lightly. 'Thank you, Mir Aziz. Might I ask, is there more? Is this what the woman sings about?' The thought came to me that I had never spoken so openly with a native.

'No.' He laughed. 'The woman, she is one of the *tawaifs*, a courtesan, of Benares. They sing ghazals – the sad love songs – but also they are changing the words of the old songs to speak of gossip and scandal. She might sing of dishonest moneychanger, or of Company magistrate who makes taxes too high, or magistrate who likes too much Hindoo women.'

'Is that what she spoke of tonight?'

'I do not know, Chote Sahib, I was not there.'

I wanted very much to ask about the scene in the bazaar at Sahseram, but I hesitated. I said – more plaintively than I would have wished – 'Mir Aziz, I see no sign that Blake is searching for Xavier Mountstuart, and I find no trace of him anywhere. Are we truly looking for him? Can you tell me at least something?'

I was sure that Mir Aziz was smiling. 'Have faith, Chote Sahib, we search, we shall find.'

'Mir Aziz, in Sahseram . . .' But I could not bring myself to ask. 'How is it that you are so well acquainted with the gossip of the bazaar?'

'I tell you before, I am general factotum, I do everything. Now let us escape rain.'

We left Benares before the sun rose. It was eight days to Jubbulpore. I had a note from Jiggins asking me to look him up on my return, and a bad headache, but I had the sense to let no one know it. From time to time that day I would glance up to find Blake watching me. It was more attention than he usually paid me, and I found that look of his unsettling. As if he knew things about one. Perhaps, I thought, he has discovered my blunder about Mountstuart. Perhaps he knows that I saw him among the natives.

In the early afternoon outside Mirzapore we turned off the Grand Trunk Road for the road south-west. Mir Aziz told me we were to make a stop at Bindachal. The name was familiar, but I could not recall why.

'It is old, old temple where Thugs come to worship goddess Kali,' said Mir Aziz.

I remembered it then. It was the temple the Thugs made

pilgrimages to in order to bring tribute to their patron Kali, goddess of destruction, the demon devourer – she of the six arms full of weapons, and the necklace of severed heads. It was said the priests of the temple had once encouraged them in their murderous endeavours.

The landscape had become lush. The roadside was all soft green grasses, and every once in a while the trees would part and a small waterfall would tumble from rocky crags. The sound of water was everywhere. The day, however, was cloudy and heavy, and the going was muddy. Perspiration gathered in my brows and seeped into my eyelashes. The well-trodden path took us uphill a little and became stony. Along the way there were a few broken-down buildings: rude, moss-covered, thatched dwellings, an old tower, a small temple with garish painted columns all suggestive of more prosperous times. We passed several barefoot natives carrying a bowl or a wreath of flowers. Then, coming towards us, I saw a man covered in blood. It was smeared all over his face and arms and dribbled down his clothes. I looked away, appalled. At first I thought he must have been attacked, then I realized he must be a devotee of the goddess, as he was not failing and had a dogged, not pained, look about him, and he was accompanied by three grinning supporters. The day darkened and the hum of insects began almost to hurt my ears. In the trees one could see the fleeting forms of large black monkeys. At last we came to a flight of steps, worn down through many centuries of use, before which a few carts and livestock were tethered. Nungoo and Sameer remained with the horses. The trees thickened about us. Mir Aziz had been muttering with Blake. He now came to walk beside me.

'Chote Sahib, is very sacred place. The Hindoos say this is where the left breast of Kali is falling after being sliced off by god Shiva.' Through the trees we came to the place. The temple seemed to be a cave in the hill, but around it was a low wall enclosing an old stone courtyard, and across the entrance to the cave there was a carved and painted stone facade with steps up to it. There were three pilgrims in the courtyard: a wizened old man wrestling with a white goat; a farmer carrying a pail of oil and muttering in an unsettling, unending monotone; and a younger native wearing nothing but a dhoti and leaning on a staff. Another old man, a priest I guessed, sat unsmiling at the top of the steps in a white dhoti, soliciting payment. There was an old well and a large, perfectly smooth and symmetrical upright stone covered in wreaths.

I asked Mir Aziz what it was. He smiled uncertainly.

'It is Shiva lingam, sahib,' he said.

It was obvious I was none the wiser, and the temptation to humiliate me was too much for Mr Blake, for as he passed me on his way to the temple he addressed me for the first time in two weeks.

'It is a giant phallus, Mr Avery. They are revered by worshippers of the god Shiva.'

I turned away quickly. The old revulsion for India and its customs surged in me. What monstrous religion could place such a thing in public and demand its worship, or encourage its adherents to pray to the goddess of death and destruction?

Mr Blake mounted the steps and at the temple entrance stooped to give the sour-looking priest a coin and muttered something to him. He nodded and inclined his head. Mr Blake entered, then re-emerged a few moments later. He knelt down and raised his hands as if in obeissance to the old charlatan, then bowed. They began to talk. The sight of him pandering to the old priest, a creature devoted to the worship of Kali, annoyed me, but I kept my temper, reluctantly removed my boots and went in.

The place was dark and low-ceilinged and lit only by a few small flickering oil lamps, their effect diminished by wispy curls of smoke from incense burners. It smelt of damp, sweat, smoke, blood and age. It was not hard to imagine the veneration of a cult of murderers in that ancient hole. I had half expected a statue of Kali like those that I had seen illustrated in books: a grinning black she-devil with six arms, a ghastly poking red tongue, and a necklace of human heads. Instead, out of the smoky air loomed a squat black stone mounted on a plinth, with a flat face, oval silver sockets for eyes and a red smear for a mouth, like something from a child's drawing. It was draped in orange flowers and beads. And yet for all that, it emanated an old malignancy, as if it had soaked up centuries of blood and cruelty. Next to it, almost as unmoving, sat another old priest. He turned cold eyes upon me. On the ground before it there were small brass pans. One contained oil, another milk, yet another something which I eventually guessed must be hair. At the sides were a few old knives and coins. The chanting Hindoo pilgrim entered, carrying his vessel of oil. I stepped to the side. He poured it out before the idol, then fell to the ground, prostrating himself before it. As he rose the priest marked his forehead with a red painted finger and he struck a small bell three times. Then the younger native came in. Standing before the idol, he brought out a small bowl and a knife. Setting the former on the ground, he knelt and to my horror cut the palm of his hand, letting the blood drip into the small bowl. I felt my gorge rise and I pushed out into the light thinking I must leave or suffocate, and as I did so I remembered suddenly what William Sleeman had written about this place – that any honest Christian would want to pull it down and hang its priests.

Mr Blake was still muttering to the old priest. I pulled my boots on as quickly as I could and rose to go. With no warning, the old man with the goat dragged it forward, trying vainly to pull its struggling forelegs into its body, took out a knife and made a sudden downward slash into the beast's throat in a ghastly act of sacrifice. Jets of bloody red spume shot forth from the creature's neck and spattered on to the ground. The creature's head was still attached to its body; its tongue pushed out and then withdrew a few times while its back legs collapsed and it twitched repeatedly. The old man waited for the spasms to end, then dipped his fingers in the blood on his blade and dabbed it upon his forehead.

'Are you quite well, Chote Sahib?' Mir Aziz was watching me anxiously.

'I am quite well, Mir Aziz,' I said. I felt sick. The place seemed to me heavy with evil, degradation and corruption, and I could not bear another moment in it. 'I do not like this place. Do you not feel it? There is violence and destruction and ignorance, and I do not understand why we have come here!'

I marched down the hill, took my horse and rode until I felt better. They did not catch up with me for several hours. I guessed Mr Blake was displeased with me as his face was screwed into a frown all the afternoon. I did not expect him to speak to me again, but when we were removing our packs to make camp that evening he said, 'Mr Avery, do not ride off alone in the future.'

'I am sorry, Mr Blake, but the place revolted me. It is mired in evil, and I could not stay another moment. I find it hard to see why you were so enamoured of it.'

'Everyone calls barbarity what he is not accustomed to,' said Blake.

'What?' I said.

'Nevertheless, you're to stay with the party in the future. You do not know the roads.'

'I am amazed that you noticed I was not present, Mr Blake.'

'You think you have something to complain of?' He spoke in a quiet, level tone with a hint of a threat. We had stopped in a clearing by the roadside; one could hear a stream nearby. The natives, I noticed, had all vanished, presumably to the waterside.

'Nothing I would expect you to acknowledge. But since you ask, yes, I do. Why would I not be exasperated by forever following after, being ignored and kept in ignorance of even the most modest of your plans? Moreover, I fail to see any sign that you are actually in pursuit of the object of our journey. I thought that we were to seek out Xavier Mountstuart, but I have yet to see you do anything to further our endeavour. I, at least, have inquired after him of everyone I have encountered on our route. Then we find ourselves in that horrible, evil place – and for what reason? Perhaps, Mr Blake, you have no interest in the matter and are following some other quite different project of your own? I do not – mark you – complain about the, how shall I say, eccentric manner in which we travel, nor of the casual insolence of your natives.'

'I think, Mr Avery, you just did.'

'I do not complain of it, I note it. I wish to add,' I said hastily, wishing to be just, 'that Mir Aziz has been nothing but courtesy itself.'

'So you have been asking about Mountstuart. Have you found any trace of him?'

'Not one,' I said, deflated. He fixed me with a look. I think I have already said I found his gaze discomfiting. It was as if he could see one's weaknesses. But I stared back.

'You write me off entirely, Mr Blake. You are wrong to, you know nothing of me.'

'I know as much as I need to know.' Now his usually level voice was exasperated. 'You're a young buck with the usual Calcutta opinions and manners. You nurse a sore head most mornings, you speak no local languages, you know nothing about this place or its customs – you understand nothing of what you have just seen at that temple. You're inclined to believe what you're told, though in that you're no different from most griffins. And everything you think or feel is instantly etched upon your features. Let me ask you, what use can you be to me? And let's see, you're West Country from your accent. A youngest son. Your father's the squire, so you see yourself a gentleman, but there's little money or you wouldn't be here. There's a Company connection or you wouldn't be in India at all, but it's a modest one or you'd have had a commission sooner. Your mother made a pet of you, your father's a tartar, so beneath all the bluster you want sympathy and you're fretful. You fancy yourself in love with that girl from the levee.'

I was deeply taken aback; I hardly knew how to respond. 'I can only assume you must have spied upon me.' I wished to sound calm, but to my own ears my voice sounded hollow. 'Do you have anything more to add?'

'You can ride. You might be smartish but I can't tell.'

I stood for a moment, staring at the ground. When I looked up, he was still gazing at me, but I saw in his face something more galling than dislike: the look I'd seen on my older brothers when they thought they'd hit me too hard. He rubbed the rough edge of his ear.

I turned away from him, suddenly tired, and trudged to my pack. 'We stopped at Bindachal,' he called out to my retreating back, 'because I thought Xavier Mountstuart would have chosen to visit it. The temple priest told me he came in March.'

The road from the Ganges down towards Poona, Nagpore and the western coast – a road that runs over 700 miles – was little more than a rutted dirt path worn by centuries of bullock carts, camels and feet. Occasionally it would end before a fallen tree, whereupon we would retrace our steps and look for a newer, fainter track to take us onward. There could have been no greater contrast with the Grand Trunk Road, so constantly full of bustling travellers. There were far fewer journeyers and for miles at a time we passed no one. Two more days brought us out of Bengal and into the Company territory of Saugor and Nerbudda River.

'They say that the Nerbudda is so pure and clean,' Mir Aziz said, 'Mother Ganga herself is coming to wash in its waters.'

By daylight the landscape was verdant and leafy. There were moments, indeed, when I had a strange intimation of almost being in England. The earth turned dark red, like the Devon soil, and as we rode, splashing through the half-dried mud, clouds of small yellow butterflies floated along before us and on either side tiny yellow flowers sprang from the banks. The jangal – the thickest I had so far seen – alternated with flat green scrub, and far off there were soft hills covered in clusters of delicate leafy trees. Mir Aziz told me their names: the common sal with which the villagers built their huts; banyans with their thick muscular trunks and long wooded tendrils hanging down under the spread of leaves; peepul trees, tall with dark green shiny leaves which the villagers used as medicine for headaches and pains; sissos and mahua; teak with its huge heart-shaped leaves and fluffy white seed-heads.

But for all the odd moments of familiarity, for all the lushness, there were other times, especially at night, when the landscape seemed strange and sinister, an old forest harbouring an old and secret evil. This was Thugs' heartland, they had buried their victims in mango groves, and in turn Major Sleeman had hanged them from the trees. Jiggins had told me to watch for dacoits and robbers, for whom the thick monsoon growth provided perfect cover. Mir Aziz said the forests were occupied by Bhils and Gonds, tribes who had once ruled these parts and who wore bones in their ears and noses, painted themselves and preyed on human flesh. For myself, I noticed strange growths in the trees, where one grey trunk, about a fist-width, wound itself round and round another, entrapping and surrounding it even as a python squeezes life out of its prey. Sometimes there would be copses in which tree upon tree was in the course of being thus encircled.

Major Sleeman's presence and influence resonated down the road, as if combating this old evil. Twice a day we would come to a well-tended mango grove, small oases of sanctuary planted to provide shelter for travellers to pitch their tents. Most, according to the villagers, had been planted on Sleeman's orders. One village was even named Sleemanabad in gratitude for the hundred acres he had purchased for it after the local guroo had prophesied that he would have a son. At another they pointed proudly to a large sal tree on which the Major had hung the leaders of a particularly fiendish gang of Thugs.

The villages were usually little more than a cluster of huts plastered in pale blue, with a few plantain trees and fields of lentils studded with covered platforms where farmers watched over their crops. It was in these – rather than the occasional plantations we came upon – where Blake made inquiries. He would seek out the headman or guroo, while gangs of small children covered in nothing but dust surged to meet us, thrusting their fingers up to touch us, grabbing for my shiny coat buttons. The mothers, their faces covered, watched us silently from their huts. Blake would talk in the local lingo, then he and Mir Aziz would be invited into a hut, and when they emerged all would be smiling. Blake would gesture for Nungoo to bring out a map, on which he would note our position. Whether anything was vouchsafed about Mountstuart's whereabouts I did not know: I had not spoken with Blake since our exchange after Bindachal, and I was too proud to ask.

On the night before we came to Jubbulpore, we camped in a mango grove with a small, well-kept tank. Nungoo produced a pipe and trilled strange, uncouth sounds, and Sameer sang quietly along with him. Mir Aziz brought out the huqqa he had smoked in the evenings since Benares, and offered to tell me the names of the stars and some new plants I had seen. I acquiesced gratefully, glad of a little talk and aware that tomorrow in Jubbulpore such familiarities would be less appropriate.

I retired but sleep eluded me. I lay in the dark thinking about Jubbulpore, listening to the hum of the grasshoppers and the cry of a jackal. I dozed for a while. I came half to my senses and I was back in my room at home in England. It was a summer night. The window was open. I could feel the breeze and for a moment I felt perfectly at ease. Then I remembered that the gentle airs of the West Country were a long way away. I was in a tent in the Mofussil and the movement of the air around me was unnatural; something had happened. In the moment I understood this, I sensed that I was not alone. There was someone in my tent. He moved as quietly as anything could, but I was sure he was at the foot of my bedroll. I knew he must be watching me for any sign of consciousness and so I kept my eyes shut.

If he was an assassin I would already be dead. If not an assassin, therefore, a thief. It was almost tempting to lie still and let him make off with my paltry possessions so he might see just how poor a travelling sahib could be. I made a small stretching, shifting movement, as if in sleep, to free the sheet where it was tightly pinned against my chest. Then abruptly I rolled forward and dived towards him and my few small packs.

There was enough moonlight to see that the thief was entirely naked, and he glistened as if he were covered in water or oil. As soon as I moved towards him he jerked backward and as quickly as I had seized his arm, it slipped from my grasp. I saw that one side of the tent flap had been cut away; it was this that had brought on my dream of home. I lunged forward again, this time gripping his leg about the middle of the calf. He stumbled, but the oil made him so difficult to hold that almost at once he was straight away back upon his feet. He swung round at me as I advanced again, and I felt a sting all through my arm. Then he was away, half stumbling

83

and half running across the clearing to where our horses were tethered.

I took the pistol from under my bedroll where I had been keeping it, and followed after him.

'Hai! Hai! Thief!' I shouted. The grove was mostly in shadow, but the moon illuminated enough for me to take in the scene. My attacker was already halfway across the clearing. The horses were loose and excitable, and near them a group of figures were moving in a way which at first sight looked oddly like a rough country dance. Then I understood that it was Nungoo, who had been on watch, fighting off two men. Another naked thief stood by the trees. I was filled with rage.

'Get away,' I roared, running towards Nungoo and his attackers. It did not occur to me that they might misunderstand my meaning, and they did not. The second thief vanished into the trees. My thief, only a little behind, followed him at speed. Both were screaming what I imagined were angry and fearful oaths. One of Nungoo's attackers detached himself and flew towards me, brandishing a knife. I waited until he was four paces from me, then I shot him and he fell, a bullet in his throat. The second attacker, seeing the fate of his comrade, made a last thrust at Nungoo's chest, then turned to run away. Nungoo fell to the ground.

I hesitated as he ran. The pistol was a Collier repeater. There was nothing else like it. It could shoot six bullets in succession, but its wondrous qualities were somewhat offset by its tendency to blow off one's hand with the second shot if it was not cleaned. In a moment Nungoo's attacker would be all but lost in the shadows. I turned the barrel, cocked the hammer and gazed into the dark, fancying I had caught a flash of movement. I pulled the trigger.

It was a lucky shot. I heard him fall.

This whole episode took barely a minute. I was standing at the far end of the clearing when the others emerged from their tents.

'Don't follow them,' Blake shouted. 'You'll never catch them now.' He called something to Sameer, who ran to secure the horses, and something else to Mir Aziz, who with Blake went to the fallen figure of Nungoo. I followed after.

It was evident that Nungoo was beyond help. He lay on his side, his arms awkwardly splayed out like a doll's, his head twisted back, his eyes open, as if he had been thrown down from a great height. From his neck there streamed dark rivulets of blood. The moon was brokenly reflected in its viscous surface. We stood quiet for a moment. Blake leant and touched Nungoo's neck, then pushed him over so his chest was upward. There were many more dark wounds in his chest and stomach.

'Why did he not call out?' I said, more angrily than I meant.

'They crept up on him. One of them managed a cut at his throat but it didn't kill him, though I suspect he couldn't make a noise. Then he fought hard until they did for him.'

Without a word, Mir Aziz brought a lantern and lit it with the tinderbox. First he set about rearranging the body so that it lay straight. Then he began to search our baggage. The brigands had not had time to take much, but our packs were strewn upon the ground, rice and flour trampled all about. My small tent had been cut all the way up one side before I had woken. The last few pieces of my silver cutlery and a few coins had gone. One set of books lay scattered about; the others spilled out of the package my attacker had hit me with. Mir Aziz stepped carefully through the debris until he found what he wanted: a pack of cotton sheets. A few feet from him one of the thieves lay still, his long skewering knife still in his hand.

'This one is dead,' said Blake. Then he walked over to the other fallen figure in the shadows and bent down. 'This one,' he added, and there came a whimper and a splutter, 'is still just alive.'

Mir Aziz was wiping the blood from Nungoo's body. From where I stood I could see that both thieves were naked, and their oiled skin gave off an uncanny sheen in the moonlight. I had heard stories of robbers who covered themselves in grease to steal into tents and to slip through the fingers of a would-be captor. So skilful were they, it was said, they could tickle their sleeping victims with a feather, making them turn and wriggle, until they had stolen the rings from their fingers and the clothes from their backs.

Mir Aziz spread a cotton blanket over Nungoo. Sameer sliced

another into rags and they began to wash the body under its cover. I would have liked to have offered my help, but it was such a private scene it did not seem proper to interrupt it, and I noted that Blake did not. The wounded thief stirred and cried out. I was not keen to take a closer look at my handiwork – I had shot many things before but never a man – but I knew I must.

The bullet had entered the lower part of his back, under his ribs, passed through his guts and come out on the other side. I could see blood streaming from both back and stomach. He had tried to turn himself and was leaning on his side, breathing shallowly. 'What should we do with him?' I whispered.

'The bullet came out, but it will likely have ruptured his innards and he's bleeding very fast. I can't do much for him, and I doubt Mir Aziz could either, even if he wished to,' Blake said. 'It will be a slow death. You could save him pain by putting him out of his misery now.'

'I cannot,' I said. We looked at the man. He seemed barely aware of us, but the pain must have been monstrous. At last Blake said, 'I can bind the wound to slow the bleeding.'

He pulled Nungoo's bedroll from his collapsed tent and folded it, then gently moved the thief so he was lying upon it. From the little pouch about his own neck, Blake took a ball of something soft and brown, pulled a little off and pushed it into the thief's mouth, forcing a little water between his lips.

'That is opium?'

'Yes.'

'He killed Nungoo.'

'And now he too dies. A poor exchange for both of them. The opium's the best I can do for him.' He took two great swabs of rag and folded them. 'Come and help me.' We put one swab under his back, and Blake put the other over the stomach wound and pressed down upon it. The thief gasped and muttered something. I stood up. Blake looked up.

'Avery, you're bleeding.'

I saw he was right. I was still holding the pistol in my right hand. I had quite forgotten it. There was a thick gash along my arm from below the elbow into my hand. It was slick and wet and, now that I saw it, it hurt acutely.

'It is nothing,' I said, but I dropped the gun and my hand began to shake.

Leaning across the thief's body, Blake took hold of my arm and turned it over. 'At least it missed the vein, Mr Avery. Now sit down and let me see it.' But I could not.

'I must just collect my books,' I said, and I set about clumsily gathering my scattered volumes and put them into a pile, and all the while drops of blood dripped on to the covers. Blake watched me.

When I had finished he said, 'Ever shot a man before?'

'Two,' I said. 'No.'

'Come here. Take my place. Press down on the wound with your other hand.' I did not relish the task, but I did as he asked. He fetched a pile of Sameer's rags. 'We'll wrap it for now.' He swabbed my arm and bandaged Sameer's rag tight about it. Then he pulled out the purse from round his neck and took out the ball of opium. He pinched off a small piece and held it out to me. I shook my head.

'Take it,' he said. 'Like as not I'll have to stitch your wound. Take it, it'll help.'

I took the small brown ball and placed it in my mouth, and he pushed me out of the way and resumed his pressure on the thief's stomach. The opium was easy to chew, a little like beeswax but bitter, and a dusting of cinnamon had been added to it to make it more palatable.

Mir Aziz was reciting some kind of prayer over Nungoo's body. Sameer sat next to him, his head bowed.

'Were they Thugs, Mr Blake?'

He shook his head, his hands pressing hard on to the wounded thief's stomach. 'These were roadside thieves taking their chances.'

'They looked like savages.'

'They're hungry. There have been some bad years and the monsoon was thin up here, the harvest will be poor. Some are already feeling it and have taken to the roads. A bad bet on their part. Their skill is stealth. They'd have planned to strike Nungoo unconscious and counted on you not waking.'

Another minute passed. 'Those were two good shots,' he said. 'You're handy with the pistol.'

'I almost did not try the second. I thought the Collier might have my hand.'

'They're temperamental, Colliers,' he said. 'But you know your way round a gun.'

'I've been shooting since I was a small boy.' It was strange. I could not actually see Blake's eyes, they were shadowed by his brows, but under the force of his imagined gaze I felt compelled to continue.

'I grew up in Devon, between Dartmoor and the coast. A small village called Bainton. My father was – is – a fine marksman. It is the only thing I inherited from him. I've been going out after coneys and game since I can remember. I miss the woods and the fields. You were right, Mr Blake, I am not at home in the city.'

'Sisters and brothers?'

'Three brothers, two now dead, and my sister. My oldest brother Harry will have the estate, such as it is, and has a commission in the army. Fred was in the navy, he died at sea. James died when I was small, I hardly remember him. I am the youngest.'

'And your sister?'

'Louisa, she is closest to me in age. She takes care of my father.' There was something in the way he listened that slightly unnerved me, as if he heard more than I said.

'Your mother's dead?'

'Three years since.' My eyes strayed back to Nungoo's prostrate body.

'You prize your books, Mr Avery,' he said.

'As you so eloquently observed a few days ago, Mr Blake, I have little else to prize. They are virtually my only possessions.' I felt a touch light-headed and the pain in my arm began to float away. 'May I ask you something? How did you know I was in debt – I mean, beyond the obvious?'

'Your signet ring was missing; I remembered it from the first time I saw you,' he said. 'And the pocket watch. With young officers it's usually cards. The pocket watch goes before the ring. The ring is an heirloom, the pocket watch is a gift.'

I nodded.

'I observe things. Small things, don't forget them. Put them together.' There was a pause. 'There's a lot of Mountstuart in that pile of books,' he said.

'I have read almost everything he has written. You knew him, did you not, Mr Blake?'

'A little. A long time ago.' Blake took a length of clean rag and began to tuck it deftly under the thief's body. He wound it round him several times, covering each wound. The man was silent; he seemed all but insensible. Blake tied the ends of the bandages as tight as he could.

'This one cannot feel much now. Let me see your hand.' He began to probe the wound with his fingers. It was longer than I'd thought, but not too deep.

'What's *Pickwick Papers*?' he said.

The question seemed so utterly peculiar and out of place that I stumbled over my answer.

'It concerns, er, a retired London gentleman and his friends who, er, go on perambulations around the English countryside and have adventures. It is comic.'

Again Blake's silence seemed to compel me to speak. 'It was my friend Macpherson's particular favourite.'

'Short and pale, with the freckles and sandy hair.'

'Really, Mr Blake,' I said, suddenly annoyed. 'If you have not been spying on me, you are doing an extremely bad job of persuading me otherwise.'

'He was at the levee with you. I never forget a face.'

The thought of Frank brought me up short and I took a deep breath before I could recollect myself.

'That hurts?'

'No. My friend, Macpherson. He was killed two days before we left Calcutta.'

'I'm sorry for it.' He wiped away the blood. 'What happened?'

'He was killed in Blacktown.'

'The officer murdered at the Bangbazaar? That was him?'

'You heard of it?

'It's rare that a white man finds his end in Blacktown these days – though not as rare as you might think.' He turned my arm over. 'Your man used a katar, you can see by the wound,' he said. 'It's carried on the knuckles and delivered like a punch. It could have been much worse. I'll clean it and sew it. Mir Aziz would do a better job than I, but I can't disturb him now. You understand?' I nodded. The fire was down to a few embers. Quickly, he coaxed them to life.

'How did your friend Macpherson die?'

'He was stabbed and there was a cord around his neck.'

'Some story about him, wasn't there?'

'He was in debt to a moneylender.' A pause. Again, I felt compelled to say more than I quite wished to. 'Someone in the Political Department seemed to think he might have had papers he should not have. His reputation was ruined. I still cannot believe it. He was so – so good. He never drank, or gambled. He was a generous friend. But when I think back, the days before he died, he was melancholy, low-spirited. I thought it was my fault.'

Blake placed a small sealed pot among the now glowing embers. 'This is ghee. When it melts, I'll clean the wound with it. It should stop the bleeding. It may hurt.'

'I can show it to the military doctor at Jubbulpore,' I said.

'Hah.' It was an abrupt, non-committal sound. He poured the ghee along the wound. The opium did its work well.

'You do not have much use for physicians?' I said.

'Kill more than they cure.' He poured off the pool of butter, then started again. 'Why were your friend's low spirits your fault?'

'It is he that you have to blame for my presence here. He put my name forward, I think. I was not as grateful as I should have been.'

Blake finished with the ghee, then brought forth a small leather folder from which he retrieved a needle and cotton. He threaded the needle, and pulled the sides of the wound together with one hand while pushing the needle through the skin. Although I could feel it pulling and the sensation was not pleasant, the pain was remarkably reduced.

'Have you found signs of Mountstuart along the road?' I said.

In and out went the needle. 'He travelled among the natives and avoided European company.'

'That was why there was no sign of him on the Grand Trunk Road.'

'Not among the whites. He travelled with three servants and he won a monkey in a dice game.' He looked up from his work. 'You are disappointed that Mountstuart preferred to be among the natives.'

'No.' But I was. Blake was now near the last stitch and I thought I would get little from him once the stitching was done. I said, 'Did you learn much from the headmen about Mountstuart?'

'He was seen all down the Poona road in April. Made a spectacle of himself – no surprise, it's what he's known for. In one place he paid for a village feast – they were grateful, food has been scarce. The harvest was bad. In another he recited verses of the Mahabharata.' I did not know what this was, but I did not say so. 'In another, he apparently killed a boar with such fastidiousness the villagers felt able to eat it – though I doubt the truth of that. Nonsense has always accumulated round Mountstuart. There.'

He pulled the thread tight and bit off the end with his teeth.

'I thank you, Mr Blake,' I said. 'And I wish to apologize for questioning your commitment to our endeavour.'

For a moment I thought he might laugh at me.

'Accepted, Mr Avery.'

He tied my hand into a sling and said we should pack the wound with banana leaf or some herb called *brahmi*, which would speed the healing.

Nungoo's body had by now been wrapped in a clean white sheet. Mir Aziz was entirely silent. I could think of nothing to say to him. Sameer, wet-eyed, carefully helped me into my best uniform. I had spent several days agonizing over how I should present myself at Jubbulpore: whether I should break into my second bar of Windsor soap, how I might take the creases and dust from my uniform. Now such preoccupations seemed absurd.

'*Mujhe bahut afsos hai,*' I said falteringly to Sameer. I am very sorry. 'Nungoo – good man. Fine man.' I tried to take his hand in mine, but it was too painful so I brushed it instead.

'Nungoo's body must be buried within a day,' Blake said. 'We're none of us up to digging a grave. It's only a few hours to Jubbulpore, we will make arrangements to have him buried there.'

Blake brought from his packs a black broadcloth tail-coat – a little rumpled and dusty – and a white summer shirt and white trousers, and put them on. The sun had risen and the day was by now almost warm. At Blake's bidding I went to look at the wounded thief. I saw that he was dead. He had made hardly a sound. I looked into his face; he was not much older than me.

'We'll take their bodies too. We should not leave them by the roadside,' said Blake.

We rode for several hours. But though beyond the trees the countryside was verdant and well tended, with fields of papaya, pomegranate and jackfruit trees, and though the road was wider and flatter and gritted with small stones and more like a road than anything since Mirzapore, there was no rejoicing. Apart from his prayer, Mir Aziz had said no word since Nungoo's death; Sameer wept openly. Blake lapsed into silence and looked as dour and weary as I had seen him. I had been the cause of two men's deaths. It was not how I had imagined our arrival at Jubbulpore. The heat was oppressive and we passed thicket upon thicket in which the trees had been encircled by other sinisterly twisting grey trunks.

'It is as if one tree would squeeze the life out of another, and then another, and then another,' I said aloud. 'What are they?'

'They are called strangler vines,' said Blake.

And so we came to Jubbulpore with three corpses.

Chapter Six

At the edge of Jubbulpore two sentries carrying muskets and wearing jackets the colour of dust eyed us suspiciously as Blake asked for directions to the Thuggee bureau. I had rarely felt such relief in arriving anywhere, so I ignored their stony glances and looked about as we rode into the cantonment. It was immediately evident that the place was exceptionally neat and well ordered, from the freshly gravelled road lined with coconut and toddy palms, to the small barracks and parade ground, to the humming bazaar where shopkeepers were beginning to lay out their wares and the natives about their daily chores stopped to gaze at our grisly cargo.

Our gloomy escorts led us to a sprawling collection of whitewashed cottages joined haphazardly together. A long verandah was crowded with servants and sepoys, who craned to look but did not approach. After a few minutes a short, dark-haired man, dressed in the same grey-brown material as the sepoys, hurried out of the doorway and down the steps. When he saw us he started.

'The sepoy says you were asking for the Thuggee bureau,' he said, surveying us. 'What is it that you want?'

'We were attacked on the Mirzapore road, about two hours' ride back,' Blake said. 'There were four of them. My assistant despatched two, but was wounded and is in need of care and rest.' I turned to stare at Blake and tried to hide my surprise. It would be no exaggeration to say that he was a different man. The edges had been brushed off his voice; it was filled with authority. He even sat on his horse differently. 'Another of our party was killed and requires burial. We have brought the bodies of our assailants since we assumed the Thuggee Department would wish to inspect them.'

'Well, I am afraid you cannot come into the Thuggee bureau,' the man said, looking us over with an expression of distaste. It must be admitted that we were not impressive: we were dusty, somewhat creased around the edges and possibly a little malodorous.

'What is your name, sir?' said Blake sharply.

'Captain James Pursloe, Assistant Superintendant of the Thuggee bureau,' the man said. There was something slightly petulant about his manner, though he looked to me a good ten years older than I.

'A captain, eh?' said Blake. The man squirmed uncomfortably under his gaze. 'Captain Pursloe, I have come 700 miles, all the way from Calcutta, in three weeks, to see Major Sleeman. I have letters of introduction from Government House. I have three bodies and a wounded man. I want accommodation, medical attention for my assistant, and to bury our Mahommedan companion, according to his traditional rites, within the day. I hope that is not too much for you.'

Captain Pursloe pulled himself up and squared his shoulders.

'Yes, sir.'

Now another Company officer appeared: an enormous, burly officer dressed in the same grey-brown material as the others, with a sunburnt face and a jutting jaw that gave him a belligerent air. The big officer gave Pursloe a careless nod.

'Lieutenent Mauwle,' the latter said, a little nervously I thought, 'these gentlemen have come all the way from Calcutta. They were attacked on the road to Mirzapore, not two hours since.'

'How many?' said Mauwle curtly.

'Four,' said Blake. 'Oiled and shaven. Two dead, two escaped. Here are the bodies.'

'They'll be Bhils,' said Mauwle. He had a thick Scottish brogue. He barked an order in the local lingo and the crowd about us slowly began to disperse. Then he advanced on them, and they scattered. He came alongside our horses and lifted back the head of one of our attackers, grunted and dropped it again.

'I'll take some men out, they'll not get far.'

'An attack is, I assure you, a very rare occurrence here,' Pursloe said. 'The roads around Jubbulpore are very safe these days. You are a very small party, Mr er—'

'My name is Jeremiah Blake, and I am the Company's Special Inquiry Agent.'

The sulky, persecuted look was replaced by one of alarm.

'I cannot say I have ever heard of a Special Inquiry Agent,' he said. 'May I . . . may I ask what your visit concerns?'

Lieutenant Mauwle, mounting the steps of the Thuggee Department, turned round.

'We are here in search of Xavier Mountstuart.'

Pursloe blenched. Lieutenant Mauwle laughed, a throaty, scornful sound.

'You've come a long way for nothing then,' he said. 'You won't find him here. And all mention of him is forbidden in Jubbulpore.'

The rest of the day was somewhat befogged in my memory. We were shown to an empty bungalow that smelled of dust. It was surrounded by high compound walls closed by a pair of substantial gates. Our hosts seemed keen to rectify our first impressions, for within a few hours the place had servants, food and bedding and the station's grumpy old medic arrived. He approved my stitches but tut-tuttingly removed the paste of leaves that Blake had packed around them. I took a bath. In the late afternoon a troop of sepoys escorted us to a small overgrown Mahommedan graveyard where Nungoo was to be buried. I reflected that in Calcutta one would very rarely have attended such a ceremony; and that I was glad that I had come. Blake and I stood slightly apart as Mir Aziz and Sameer and a local Mahommedan holy man said verses and cast earth over the body, which was laid in a shallow grave, wrapped in white shrouds. I found I was too tired to think, too tired to speak. At the bungalow we dined off boiled chicken and rice, and then I crawled under layers of mosquito nets to my bed. The night air was thick with swarming insects, and I was glad of the nets.

The last thing I recall noticing was that the bed legs were sitting in cups of water.

At some point the squeaking of rusty hinges and metal clanging against itself penetrated my dreams. After that I slept for nearly two days.

*

I dreamt of Devon again. The window of my bedroom open. The view of rough fields and hedgerows stretching on. The wood beyond. In the wood the leaf mould, a hound padding at my heels. A soft, wet, overcast day.

When I woke, my clothes had been laundered and folded on a small chest, my books unpacked and propped up in a glass cabinet, and an unfamiliar servant with a pot of fragrant, steaming coffee stood at the end of the bed. My head throbbed, but I was gladder than I could say to find myself among the fruits of civilization. After I had bathed I ventured on to the verandah. The gates to the compound, rusted but tall and imposing, were locked. Blake was sitting very still, whether thinking or praying I could not have said. I would have returned quietly to my room, but he called my name.

'The gates,' I said.

'Yes, they say they need to lock us in each night for our own safety. Mir Aziz and Sameer are taking a few more days of mourning. I'm calling on Major Sleeman this afternoon.'

'I should like to accompany you,' I said, rather cool.

To my surprise he said, 'All right.' Truth to tell I did not feel entirely well, but I was determined not to be left behind.

I struggled with my clothes, the bandage making everything difficult, and when I presented myself on the verandah at the appointed time, I had only been able to get on one arm of my best uniform jacket.

Blake was clean-shaven, with a high-collared white muslin shirt, a white necktie, a well-cut blue dress-coat, and pressed white nankeen trousers. I had never seen him so finely dressed, and I did not forebear to stare. He guided my arm into my sleeve and fastened my buttons one by one, then brushed me down.

'And I had thought myself the beau,' I said. 'May I comment on your transformation, Mr Blake? Even your voice is different.'

I thought he might take offence, but he said, 'Got to look the part.'

We were escorted from our lodgings by a large unit of sepoys. Major Sleeman's residence was the grandest dwelling in Jubbulpore: a two-storey stone mansion in the classical style, with Greek columns holding up an elegant portico and long windows behind them. It was surrounded by a flourishing walled garden, watered by innumerable little irrigation channels. The Major, however, was not yet at home.

We were shown into a large cool study. Finding myself less robust than I had hoped, I let myself into a chair. We sat in silence. The windows were stretched with fine muslin, and the walls lined with glass cases filled to bursting with books and stuffed animals. There was a large three-quarter-length portrait of a man in a blue regimental jacket, and in the middle of the room a long desk, polished wood with inlaid ivory, on which small rocks and minerals were displayed.

After about five minutes there came the unmistakeable sound of English voices, signalling, I assumed, the arrival of our host. We waited and I felt the beginnings of nausea. Then into the room strode a grey-haired man whose features I recognized from the portrait, though he now had considerably less hair.

'Aha! Our visitors!' he said heartily. 'Might I introduce myself? I am Major William Sleeman.' He was sturdily built, not tall, with a ruddy farmer's face, small flinty blue eyes and that yellow, worn-out look that told of decades in India. But all of this was trumped by the general amiability of his countenance and his tremendous air of energy and activity. Behind him came Captain Pursloe and a slight, pale, freckled man with a beaky nose.

Major Sleeman thrust out his hand to Blake, and would have grasped mine in its sling had I not removed it swiftly from his range, waving it slightly instead.

'Ah, yes, yes. Of course!' the Major said. 'The attack!' He shook his head emphatically. 'May I present my condolences on the loss of your man. We regard the safety of the roads about Jubbulpore as our responsibility. I am deeply sensible that we have failed you.' He seemed genuinely upset.

'Uncle – Major Sleeman,' said Pursloe, 'may I present Mr Jeremiah Blake and er . . .'

'Lieutenant William Avery,' I said.

'Of course, attacks close to Jubbulpore are usually very rare,' said Pursloe.

'I imagine they were hungry and took their chances,' said Blake, more mildly than I expected. 'We were a small party. I've been speaking to the headmen on the road – I hear there have been some bad harvests.'

Major Sleeman shook his head. 'But an ill deed is a choice, Mr Blake. And this is a reminder that I cannot relax my exertions for a moment. Your assailants were Bhils, a troublesome, nomadic race whom we had hoped we had pacified. You are most fortunate, young man. They are known to poison the tips of their knives.'

'I'd not heard that,' said Blake.

'You know the Bhils?'

'I have encountered them once or twice.'

'That is, if I may say, most unusual in a Calcutta civilian,' said Major Sleeman. 'Lieutenant Avery, I hear you managed to kill two of them. Well done, sir!'

'It is a great honour to meet the discoverer of the Thugs and the author of *Ramaseeana*, sir,' I said, slightly breathlessly. 'Everyone speaks of your work in Calcutta.'

The small blue eyes fixed upon me. 'Avery is a West Country name. Do I detect a trace of Devon?'

I nodded. He grinned. 'Cornishman myself, born and bred. Hope to see it again, one day. Now, we do not stand on ceremony here, the Company population is too small. You have met our captain, James Pursloe, I think? May I also present Mr Edward Hogwood, my deputy magistrate, who shoulders so much of the burden of running Jubbulpore. I would not know what to do without him.'

Hogwood, who had remained so quiet I had almost forgotten him, smiled, nodded and seemed to stand a little taller in the glow of the Major's approval. He was a worn, amiable-looking man, about the same height as Sleeman and Pursloe, with dark half-circles under his eyes. I felt perspiration begin to trickle down my forehead.

'Our little triumvirate does most of the work both of running Jubbulpore and the Thugee bureau, along with Lieutenant Mauwle. Of course, now that I have been appointed Commissioner of Thug-gee for all India, I do far less of the day-to-day work. But we are still a small, tight-knit community – Pursloe here is my nephew; the doctor is my cousin. My wife has supervised the growing of new strains of sugar cane in the region. Some might accuse me of nepotism, I suppose' – he grinned broadly again – 'but we feel our results speak for themselves.'

He gestured for us to sit, though he remained standing. 'Let us furnish you with some refreshment. Tea or iced sherbert?' He clapped his hands. 'Now, welcome, or as the Moghuls have it . . .' and he came out with a stream of something of which I could make no sense at all.

To Sleeman's evident surprise, Blake answered in the same lingo. I cannot even begin to reproduce the sounds he made.

'So you know Persian, Mr Blake. I own I am surprised. It is not always done to admit a taste for it in Calcutta these days and certainly not such high-flown prose. For myself, I never got on very well with Calcutta. So much time wasted, so much energy dissipated, so many temptations to peculation.'

'I would not disagree with you,' said Blake.

Sleeman produced another wave of Persian, and again Blake answered. Pursloe suppressed a yawn.

'Most impressive!' said Sleeman. 'And do you have any other languages?'

'A few.' A silence.

'And they are?'

'Hindoostanee, Urdu, Bengalee, Marathee, Pashtun, a little Sanskrit – but that was a long time ago.'

'May I ask where you acquired such fluency?'

'I had good teachers.'

Sleeman smiled. There was no disguising Blake's reluctance to speak about himself.

'James tells me you made Calcutta to Jubbulpore in three weeks. That is a very considerable feat. How did you manage it?'

'Small party, little baggage, changed our horses every few days,' said Blake. 'I have covered considerable distances the same way up in the north. The worst of the monsoon is done, and the heat was quite bearable.'

I thought ruefully of the nights of soaking tents and cold wet ground.

'How practical!' said Major Sleeman. 'More Company men should travel as efficiently. Too wedded to their comforts. So, Mr Blake, may I ask in what capacity you come to see us?'

Evidently Pursloe had not mentioned Mountstuart.

'I am the Company's Special Inquiry Agent.'

'I was not aware the Company had a "Special Inquiry Agent",' said Major Sleeman. 'It has a rather severe and ominous ring about it. May I be candid? Calcutta is a long way away from here and we have become a little wary of its interventions.'

Pursloe cleared his throat and clasped his hands together. He looked, I thought, extremely discomfited. The other man, Hogwood, raised his eyebrows slightly and smiled.

'Major Sleeman, I'm not here to interfere with your work. I've come to investigate the disappearance of Xavier Mountstuart. He was due back in Calcutta four months ago, and it now appears that Jubbulpore was the last place he was seen. Here are my letters of introduction.' He stood up and extracted an envelope from the pocket of his black coat.

It was as if all the warmth and liveliness slid from Major Slee-man's face. The blue eyes narrowed, the lips grew thinner. There was a silence. Pursloe, meanwhile, looked at his feet. He said in a low voice, 'Major Sleeman does not choose to speak of Mr Mount-stuart.'

'Does not choose to speak of him?' Blake looked broodingly at the Major.

'I cannot help you, Mr Blake,' the Major said with chilly deliber-ateness. 'I will not have the man mentioned under any circumstances.

'Surely there must be some mistake?' I said – I really was not feel-ing myself. 'Major Sleeman, you have to help us.'

'I beg your pardon, Lieutenant, there is no mistake.' His tone was icy. 'I must ask you not to pursue the matter. He was here, he left, he did not deign to tell us where he was going. You have made a wasted journey.'

'Major Sleeman, I do not wish to provoke you,' said Blake. 'I am sorry this inquiry is so unwelcome to you, but I have a task to perform.'

'Mr Blake, you are most welcome in Jubbulpore as long as you steer away from that subject. We pride ourselves on our hospitality and we will do our best to make you comfortable until you are ready to travel. I must ask, however, that you adhere to our rules.'

'You mean being locked into our compound each night and required not to go into the town on our own.'

'There is a Thug hanging next week. It makes the station unsettled. What with concerns that a bad harvest may prompt native unrest, we believe it is safer to ensure that visitors are secure.'

'I thank you for your hospitality, Major Sleeman,' said Blake abruptly. 'We will take our leave.'

I stood up dizzily, but my legs were not ready for me and though I attempted to follow Blake to the door, the next moment I found myself lying on the Turkey carpet, not at all certain how I had got there.

'Lieutenant, you are soaked with perspiration!' said Major Sleeman. 'We will arrange a palanquin. Mr Blake, your assistant is clearly not well at all' – this said accusingly. 'I will have the doctor visit you at once.'

I tried to protest, but I was steered back to a deep chair from which I thought I might never rise, and cold towels were brought. With a hint of ill temper Pursloe disappeared to arrange a palanquin. We waited; the sandy-coloured man, Hogwood, hovered. The Major sat at his desk, and Blake examined the bookcases apparently unconcerned by the increasing awkwardness of the silence.

Blake began to talk about some essays the Major had written about orchards and fruit trees. The Major seemed very taken aback that he'd seen them. Then Blake said, 'But Lieutenant Avery is the keen student of plants and trees.' And I thought dizzily, *Am I?*

'In that case, Mr Avery, perhaps I might show you around my garden before you leave Jubbulpore?'

I nodded obediently, and mopped myself with the towels. Silence returned.

Blake wandered over to the table on which various rocks were arranged. He began to talk about the rocks, identifying each one. 'And these are ammonites, if I am not mistaken. I have only ever seen them in books. I had no idea that fossils had been found in Hind.'

The Major seemed both surprised and pleased. 'I believe I am the first man to have identified fossils in India,' he said. He said he'd found other similar things a few miles outside Jubbulpore, including the bones of an enormous beast, like the skeletons of the giant reptiles they had discovered in England. Dinosauria, he said they were called. I wondered slightly if I was hallucinating.

'See, Avery,' said Blake. He opened his palm to reveal a shiny black stone on which was etched what looked like the carved relief of a very large snail. 'This is the petrified remains of an ancient sea creature, but we're thousands of miles from the sea.'

I shook my head. But I remembered seeing such things in childhood on the beach in Devon. We'd called them snake stones and devil's fingers.

'Mr Blake,' the Major was saying, 'may I ask how you come about your own knowledge? I do not know above five men in the country who take an interest in such things.'

'I came across a copy of Lyell's *Principles of Geology* in Calcutta.'

'Indeed.' The Major laughed. It was a pleasant sound. 'Where do you stand on . . .' and he said some word like 'uniformitarianism'. Blake had some answer, but I could not hold my attention upon it. Then the large double doors opened and a small, dark-haired white woman swept into the room, accompanied by a native woman holding a wriggling child, two more servants and, trailing behind, a sulky-looking Pursloe.

'Amelie!' said Sleeman. 'This is my wife, gentleman, and my daughter Louise.'

'*Eh bien, enchantée, Messieurs,*' said Mrs Sleeman. I had the impression of grace and exceptional neatness, and a brisk deliberateness similar to the Major's.

'My wife is French,' the Major said with evident pride. 'And very clever. She is, among many things, an expert on strains of sugar cane.'

'William!' she said, in a tone between exasperation and pleasure. 'Is this the sick gentleman from Calcutta?' she said, fixing upon me. 'The palanquin is prepared. Please let us know if there is anything we may do for you. My dear, I hope you have invited the gentlemen for next week. I am holding a dinner for our regional officers and planters; I do hope William has mentioned it.'

'Ah, yes, of course, we would very much like you to attend,' said Major Sleeman, as if the earlier awkwardness was all forgotten.

'We should be delighted to come,' said Blake.

Mr Hogwood came forward. 'Let me help escort the Lieutenant to the litter.'

I said that I could make my own way, but Blake insisted I leant on his arm. I could read nothing in his face.

The doctor unwound my bandages. The wound was swollen, red and seeping. He placed a hand on my forehead.

'Little to be done,' he said. 'Brandy at regular intervals to take down the fever.' He poured me a small glass. 'I have a powder somewhere about me. I see you take an interest in native remedies, Mr Blake.' Blake nodded. 'I do not,' the doctor said crisply.

'Care for a glass yourself?' said Blake.

'Oh, no,' the doctor said. 'I imbibe only sparingly. We all do in Jubbulpore. Major Sleeman demands the highest standards.'

'You're his cousin, I think?'

'I am,' he said, mildly suspicious. 'And Captain Pursloe is his nephew. We are devoted to him, and the cantonment works much the better for it, I should say.'

'Can you tell me anything about Xavier Mountstuart?'

The doctor looked down. 'Ah. Yes. Well, as you know Major Sleeman simply will not have the man mentioned.'

'But you must have met him,' Blake said, coaxingly. 'Can you not tell me what you remember? Even in the privacy of the sickroom?'

He shook his head and frowned. 'I have nothing to say.'

Blake touched his arm lightly. The doctor's features softened a little.

'Didn't like him. Very slighting of my work. I have had a number of well-received articles published in serious journals on the subject of Phrenology and the Thugs.' The doctor's mouth tightened into a disapproving moue.

'Phrenology?' I said.

'It is the scientific method by which one may deduce the character of an individual – or potentially a whole race – by means of mapping the lumps on their skull. My conclusions have been received with great interest. We had the skulls of various captured Thugs measured and then sent the dimensions to Edinburgh, where they were analysed by the experts. The results were fascinating. Firstly, they showed that the Thugs' skulls and therefore brains are smaller than ours, and secondly, the shape of their heads revealed that they are not naturally predisposed to evil, but they are, like children, easily swayed and yield to cruelty. They require guidance.'

'And Mr Mountstuart disagreed with you?'

The doctor took a breath. 'He was – is – not a man of science.' He shook his head again, as if he might have said more but had decided not to. 'I must go.' He picked up his case and bustled out. Blake followed. He returned a few minutes later carrying one bowl of ghee and another of an unattractive green paste.

'Pompous fool,' he muttered, and sat down by my bed where he began to unwrap the doctor's bandages.

'You do not believe in Phrenology?'

'I do not believe you can determine the character of a group of people by the measurements of a few men's heads. And life has taught me not to trust too much to appearances.' He swabbed the wound with the ghee, then picked up the bowl of green paste, picking out a few black insects before he pressed it upon my wound. 'The insects here are as bad as anywhere I've ever been.'

'So, what is your plan, Mr Blake?'

'Should I have a plan?

'You are the Company's Inquiry Agent. Colonel Buchanan said you were a bloodhound in pursuit of your quarry.'

'Did he.' He poured me a small brandy and tipped into it a brown powder.

I swallowed it. 'Ugh! This is vile! Do you not wonder what Mr Mountstuart can have done to so enrage the Major?'

'I can imagine almost anything. He has a talent for enraging people.'

'Oh.' I was disappointed.

He began to wrap the bandage around my arm again. 'What do you make of Jubbulpore?' he said.

'You are asking me?'

'No one else.'

I was half-minded not to answer since he had been so unforthcoming himself. But it was better to be on speaking terms with Blake than not.

'It is as well kept and comfortable as anywhere I have seen in India. The constant escort and the locking up at night is tiresome, but perhaps that is the price of order in the Mofussil. You would know better than I. The Major is impressive, but his refusal to speak about Mountstuart – well, it seems rather excessive. And I find his nephew the Captain disagreeable.'

'Your fever was a piece of luck.'

'I'm so pleased you found it useful.'

'I have something to ask you.'

'Yes?' I felt my pulse quicken.

'Don't recover any faster than you must. I need time here.'

'And what will you do?'

'I will find out what happened to Mountstuart.'

'And my contribution is to play the invalid,' I said, again disappointed. 'Surely you have a better use for me?'

'Not for now. Take heart, Lieutenant Avery,' he said, 'you already proved yourself the other night, on the road.'

Despite myself, I was gratified.

I slept fitfully. My wound ached and my mind raced horribly. I dreamt of a flowing stream and a white pitcher of clear water, but the thought of drinking the swirling water made me nauseous. I felt I would never be cool or refreshed again. When I woke my sheets were soaked and Mir Aziz was sitting by my bedside with a pot of coffee and another of the doctor's noxious infusions. I was glad to see him and told him so.

'Will you rise?' he said. 'It is nearly afternoon.'

'Where is Blake?'

'He is away.'

I pressed him.

'I am not knowing, Chote Sahib.'

'I do not believe you,' I said. He smiled. I told him about Major Sleeman's anger over Mountstuart. 'I have no idea what Mr Blake's plans are,' I said, hoping he might take the bait and share what he knew.

But instead he said, 'Let me shave you, it will be making you much refreshed.'

'Are you a soldier or a barber, Mir Aziz?'

'I have been many things, Chote Sahib,' he said, as the razor came close to my ear. 'Healer and moonshee too.'

The blade glided across my cheek. 'Am I never to get a clear answer about anything?' I said.

By the time Blake returned I was restless and bored. He, however, was in a fine mood and surprisingly well turned out, his cheeks freshly shaved, his hair oiled. He opened my bandages and pulled away the now-blackened paste. The swelling was much improved and the wound had stopped seeping.

'Where have you been, Mr Blake?' I said. He did not answer. 'Does the bloodhound have the scent?' I said, irritation larding my words with sarcasm. He poured a small glass of brandy and gave it to me.

'I think you went to the bazaar. That is, I assume, what you do. Jaw with the natives and all that.' Silence. 'I saw you that night in Benares when the woman, the *tawaif*, sang. Mir Aziz said there was discontent in Benares,' I went on, 'and that the *tawaifs* sing about such things.' I wrenched my arm away from him. 'Good God! It is like talking to oneself!'

Blake sat back. 'The Company is not popular in Benares,' he said. 'There's discontent all the way up the Grand Trunk Road. A famine has begun north of Mirzapore. The people are frightened, and their fears spread to other matters.'

'What about here?'

'Famine hasn't reached here yet. But there's some discontent about rents and fear about the poor harvest.'

'So what do they complain about in Benares?'

'They think the Company takes too much in taxes and is sending its profits back to England and they will be left with nothing. The country people complain that crop yields have gone down, so there's less food, but the Company goes on taking the same or more and forces them to plant opium instead of food. The city dwellers fear the arrival of missionaries: they think they may be forced to convert. They say the Company is disrespectful to their wives and daughters. They fear change.'

'Is that what the *tawaif* sang about?'

'No, she sang about Mountstuart. He likes to be known as *malik-al-shuara*, "the king of poets". In Benares his book was the talk of the bazaar.'

'*Leda and Rama*?' I said, utterly amazed. 'How would the natives know about that?'

'They are not stupid,' he said. 'Why should they not know about something that touches so deeply on corruption and misdemeanours among the Europeans?'

'But how do they know?'

'I imagine from the *akhbarat*.'

'And what is that?'

'It's a news sheet.'

'But why would an *akhbarat* write of it?'

'Why wouldn't it? The book is all about the wickedness of the Calcutta Company sahibs, their greed and their immodesty.'

'But the Hindoo and Musselman princes are hardly patterns of virtue!' I said. 'Good God, after the stories one hears about the princely courts.'

He shrugged again. 'Do you want to take a walk?'

'Forgive us for inconveniencing you, Major Sleeman,' said Blake.

Accompanied by our inevitable sepoy escort, we had walked through Jubbulpore to the Thuggee bureau. It was late afternoon and the palm-shaded streets thronged with natives in white and yellow and pink, carrying pots and baskets and bundles of vegetables. Blake wore a black tail-coat; I was saddled with my sling. Major Sleeman stood on the verandah of the Thuggee bureau with Mr Hogwood, the deputy magistrate.

'I am afraid we do not allow visitors in the Thug bureau,' the Major said. 'Our work is confidential. I am pleased to see Mr Avery's colour is a little better. And you, Mr Blake, I hope you are comfortable? Is there anything we might do for you?'

'I wanted to let you know that once Mr Avery is strong enough we'll be going north, probably to Doora,' said Blake. 'In the meantime we would be glad of some distraction – your sepoys are so very diligent it is hard to stray far from home and, of course, we are locked in at night.'

'The city has a gaol full of murderous men, Mr Blake, and the days before a hanging are always a trying time. Even in Jubbulpore we must be vigilant. Mr Hogwood's bungalow was broken into just the other night. One of his servants was seriously wounded by the assailants. We must ensure that everyone is safe.'

'I am sorry for that, and I don't wish to contravene your rules, but I know that in the past, in daylight hours at least, you have shown visitors something of your work.'

Major Sleeman frowned. For the first time Mr Hogwood spoke.

'I cannot pretend I have an abundance of unoccupied time,' he said, 'but I would be happy to accommodate the gentlemen. They could visit the School of Industry, perhaps? And Mauwle and I are going out to investigate an old Thug grave in a day or so. Mr Blake might accompany us?'

He waited, almost anxiously, for the Major's response. Sleeman nodded. 'It is not a very edifying sight, an exhumation, and it will be a long day – taxing for the Lieutenant, I should think, but it will give you a vivid idea of the horror of Thuggee.'

'Something to talk about in the drawing-rooms of Calcutta,' said Hogwood, with a half-smile.

'And you should see the School of Industry too. It is our new prison, constructed especially for our Approvers – our Thug informers – and their families, a more constructive demonstration of what we do. You will be among its first visitors. You will understand us better.'

'And of course, Major, there is always Feringhea,' said Hogwood.

Feringhea. The most notorious of all Thugs. It seemed very peculiar to think he should be living somewhere in Jubbulpore.

'You have heard of him, Lieutenant?' said Hogwood.

'Everyone has,' I said. 'I must confess it would be extraordinary to see him.'

'Then I shall take you up on all your invitations,' said Blake.

I was determined I would not be left behind.

In the middle of the night I woke to find my sheets drenched, my bladder full, the mosquito nets encrusted in flying creatures, their din in my head. Dizzy and half asleep I staggered outside to relieve myself. As I stood in the dark a native wrapped in a blanket emerged from the back of the compound. I would have raised the alarm, but before my eyes he transformed into Blake.

'Where have you been?' I whispered.

'Nowhere, Avery, nowhere.'

I stumbled back to bed. When I woke I thought I must have been dreaming.

Chapter Seven

'It is a charming spot, is it not?' said Mr Hogwood. It was seven and we had ridden for three hours. Blake was not pleased I had come; he thought I should have stayed in the bungalow playing the invalid, but I could not bear to. We were in a mango grove with a grassy clearing in its midst. There were signs of several recent fires.

'According to our Approvers it was a very popular *bele* – a burial ground for Thug victims – for decades. Major Sleeman once found thirty-six corpses in one grove. The Thugs bury their victims with great care and artfully disguise the earth so they cannot be found by man or dug up by beast. Without our Approvers, they would never be found.'

Further along the road about thirty ryots, men, women and children, had gathered from the nearest village.

'They are summoned to witness the excavations,' said Mr Hogwood. 'They may recognize pieces of clothing or stray possessions.' The headman, an old man with white in his beard, in a dirty white blanket, approached Mr Hogwood's stirrup and touched his forehead to the latter's hand.

We had travelled with two Approvers, who wore long white pyjamas. Underneath these their ankles were shackled. They were small men with dark skins and faces much lined, though strangely empty of expression. You would not have picked them out as hardened murderers. They had sat on one horse, one behind the other, their chains draped across the saddle and rattling all the while. Now they slid awkwardly off their mount, and a nujeeb guided them with the flat of his sword.

Lieutenant Mauwle loomed even larger in person than he had in my memory. In the early light he looked as if he were made of some hard, dull material, impervious to everything, and he had about him an air of menace. His bite, one felt, would be as bad as his bark. My one attempt to politely engage him had dismally failed.

'What is this cloth you wear?' I had asked, pointing at his odd grey jacket, for though it failed on every criterion of elegance and fashion, it did appear in its way sensible, as it was the very same colour as dust. The Lieutenant looked at me as if it was quite the most stupid question that had ever been conceived of.

'It's called *karkee*,' he said shortly.

Now Mauwle said something in their lingo, and the Approvers picked up their chains and began to shuffle about through the trees. From their saddlepacks, the nujeebs unpacked shovels and pickaxes. A bullock cart laden with boxes and cloth hove into view, and two wallahs dismounted and began to form the cloth into a large open tent, embroidered with blue thread. Carpets were laid on the ground, and a table erected on them, and from a cluster of sticks, several chairs emerged. We sat in the shade of the tent and were served breakfast. The villagers sat by the wayside and murmured quietly to each other, occasionally sharing small packets of food.

'How long have you been in Jubbulpore, Mr Hogwood?' Blake asked.

'Oh, five years now. But I was promised to India from an early age and I went to East India College. I had a few years in Calcutta then I came to Jubbulpore just after the last of the big Thug trials in '32. I am deputy magistrate and much of my work concerns the running of the cantonment, but rooting out Thuggee has become so thoroughly entwined with the Major's other work that inevitably I am more of a general aid.' He rubbed his forehead.

'You are tired, Mr Hogwood,' said Blake.

'It has cost me the last vestiges of my good looks,' Hogwood said wryly, passing his hand through his thinning hair.

The Approvers shambled about to little effect. Occasionally they alighted on a particular spot and a nujeeb dug a few shovelfuls, only to change their minds. Increasingly impatient, Lieutenant Mauwle watched them. At last he strode up to them and, bending over them, began to speak slowly and deliberately. There was no mistaking his meaning. The Approvers' faces grew more empty and distant.

Hogwood, seeing this, went over and laid a restraining hand on Mauwle, who looked mutinous but stepped back. The Approvers moved more quickly after that, but they still found nothing.

'I imagine an exhumation is a rare thing,' Blake said. 'Now that Thuggee is all but crushed in this district, and you have been acting on Thug testimonies for ten years.'

Mr Hogwood said, 'That is true. We are more likely to be beset by mountains of paperwork than Thugs. The gangs in this region have been largely caught – one still eludes us, but it is barely active now and it dares not kill near Jubbulpore.'

'It seems strange to pursue murders that took place so long ago with no notion of who the victims are,' said Blake.

'It may seem so,' said Hogwood. 'But no rumour of a murder is too petty or too distant for us. In the past the natives were unwilling to report a crime – you know how corrupt the native police are. It is only through Thug confessions that we hear about them, and then they may be years old. We are the only ones who give justice to the dead.'

'And how many natives do you think the Thugs have killed?'

It was Mauwle who answered. 'The Major believes that at their height they murdered 40,000 people a year across India. He says they may have claimed a million in all.'

'A million lives?'

Unable to restrain himself, Mauwle began to make his own passes up and down the grove, touching the trunks and shifting the leaves with the toe of his boot, while Hogwood watched. After a while he got up and followed. Mauwle had stopped under an old tree. Hogwood cleared away a circle of dead leaves.

He beckoned to us. There were the remains of a fire.

Mauwle said, 'All the signs are there. Tamped-down earth, a fire on top.' Close to, his blunt features were studded with pockmarks. He nodded at the Approvers. 'Waste of time bringing them. They've not earned their keep today. If they do not deliver, they'll hang.'

'They could not possibly have known of this,' said Hogwood placatingly, 'if it is as recent as you think.' He turned to us. 'Lieutenant Mauwle has an extraordinary nose for Thug activity.'

The nujeebs were summoned to dig. The earth was crumbly and gave easily, and before long a hard clod protruded from the shallow sod. A digger brought a wide soft-haired brush and swept away the damp earth. Five toes and a foot emerged. More soil was cleared. The grove grew quiet. Working in silence, the nujeebs uncovered the edges of a circle, perhaps six or seven feet wide. With every shovelful of earth the lineaments of a horrible scene were more clearly displayed, and we were assailed by a terrible odour which forced us to cover our faces with scarves and handkerchiefs.

Within the round pit was a muddy, bloody mass of stumps and branches that gradually resolved itself into a number of horribly contorted corpses. When I forced myself to look at them, I saw that they were naked, their skins marbled black and livid green, their tongues protruding from their mouths, and where their stomachs had been there was a ghastly red and white mess. I tasted bile and stepped back; Hogwood – as green as I – followed me back to the shelter of the tent.

'I thought they strangled their victims,' I said, my chest heaving.

'They do,' Hogwood said, drawing great breaths and leaning his hands on his knees, 'but afterwards they break the bones and cut the sinews, so they can fit all the bodies into a single hole. Then they slice open the stomach so the noxious gases may escape, so they will not explode as they decompose. Come, sit down, Lieutenant Avery, you look very ill. I shall say no more.' He mopped his face.

I began to breathe more easily. The villagers had withdrawn to the roadside as far from the grave as they could. Only Lieutenant Mauwle and Blake were left watching the diggers; Blake, sombre and still, the Lieutenant rallying and haranguing as if supervising some military exercise.

'I confess,' Hogwood said, 'I have never seen so fresh a burial and I hope I never do again. It can barely be a month old. But there is no question it is a Thug grave. A perfect circle, dug with the short pick-axe they dedicate to Kali. The trouble is, we should certainly not be finding anything so recent.' He rubbed his fingers along the bridge of his nose as trying to iron away a headache.

'Well, Mauwle,' he called, 'this is a rare cut-up.'

Mauwle looked up. 'Kitree band,' he grunted. 'Who else?'

'Who are the Kitree band?' said Blake.

Hogwood and Mauwle exchanged looks.

'I imagine it is something the Major would rather I did not speak of,' said Hogwood. Mauwle gave a dismissive grunt. Blake came to the tent.

Hogwood sighed. 'They are the Thug band of whom I spoke earlier. They keep to themselves. They winter together rather than returning to a village when the season ends, as most do. As we have pulled our net tighter, so they have retreated into the jangal and mountains – and over the border into Doora. Other Thugs are caught because we have gathered details about each one from the testimony of arrested Thugs. It is one of the cleverest parts of the Major's system – another thing of which I probably should not speak.' He smiled deprecatingly. 'We have a list of every Thug we have heard of. Each is given a number, and gradually we draw a portrait of him. His aliases, his associates, his crimes, his caste, his role, which gangs he has belonged to, and distinguishing marks – moles, or one eye and so on – and at last his family and his home. From this list of upward of 4,000 names, we have drawn up family trees, genealogies, maps, and built cases against each. There is nothing like it, nothing so scientific and systematic, anywhere in the world.

'But' – and he sighed – 'the Kitree band do not follow the pattern, and they remain elusive. We know they are led by a man with many aliases whom we know as Rada Kishin, and they hide in Doora where the Rao puts up a hullabaloo if Company soldiers set foot in his lands. They are the last true Thug gang in these parts.' He sat back, looking more weary than ever.

The grave contained seven bodies. The native clerks, with handkerchiefs across their faces, drew their positions in the pit. Then Lieutenant Mauwle and the chief jemadar climbed into it and disentangled the bodies, placing them one by one on a white sheet.

'Nothing seems to daunt or disconcert Lieutenant Mauwle,' Mr Hogwood murmured, 'he prides himself on it. Your Mr Blake is also made of stern stuff. I am afraid I am not.'

Laid out, the little party was both ghastly and dreadfully pathetic. There were four men, one woman and two children, a boy and a girl. An odd matter-of-factness overtook the men clustered about the bodies. Mauwle and his nujeebs examined them inch by inch for any small identifying detail. The clerks drew and wrote. The nujeebs searched the empty grave. The villagers, muted and unwilling, were rounded up to look at the bodies and give testimony. It seemed impossible that they could remember anything, so unrecognizable were the faces, but one man claimed he recalled a strip of cloth, and a nujeeb found two tiny gold earrings. The afternoon shadows lengthened. Hogwood spoke quietly to the headman and gave him some money so the villagers would bury the bodies, for they could not be transported in such a state.

My mind was numb – or not quite numb, for I could not help imagining the events that had led to the scene before us.

Hogwood returned from his exertions. 'I am sorry you have seen this; an old exhumation somehow puts the horror at a distance. I do not know what we shall say to the Major. That something like this should happen now . . . But there cannot be a more vivid illustration of what our work is and why it is important. Every small detail brings us closer to the murderers, and now we may at least be able to discover who these poor creatures were and then the correct prayers and burial rites may be arranged. But you may imagine how months, years even, of exhumations work themselves upon our minds.'

He called for more water and offered me a glass, which I drank noisily. I bestirred myself. Something useful must, I told myself, come out of the day's proceedings.

'Mr Hogwood,' I said in a low voice, 'forgive me for asking, but you are not a member of the Thuggee bureau, and clearly you are not entirely wedded to the Major's habit of hiding his achievements under a bushel. Would you consider telling me—'

'I know what you would ask, and I cannot speak of the man. I am sorry, but you must understand, we all admire the Major beyond measure, we all owe him our careers. If he demands that we do not speak of . . . of that man, we are bound to listen to him.'

'It is such a small thing,' I said dejectedly. 'And we have been sent here by Calcutta. And come such a long way, and at no small cost.'

He looked apologetic. 'Perhaps Mr Blake might try writing to the Major, setting out your argument on paper? That may make him reconsider. He may seem stubborn – it is easy to become wary of outsiders when you spend years in the Mofussil – but he is not deaf to sensible argument, believe me.'

'I will suggest it, but I am sure Blake will not. He is not precisely free of stubbornness either.'

Hogwood gave me a quizzical look. 'I am sorry I cannot be of more help. To be honest, I do not think you will find anyone in Jubbulpore with a good word for Mountstuart.'

'Will you at least consider?'

He shook his head. 'I cannot.'

The ride back was interminable. For mile after mile the strangler vines choked the sal trees, one grey trunk encircling another, until the whole jangal appeared like some terrible tangled knot in which it was impossible to tell murderer from victim. I felt hot and dizzy, though whether it was from the fever or the sight of the Thug grave I could not exactly say. Ahead of me, Blake and Lieutenant Mauwle rode side by side in silence. It was dark when we arrived at the Jubbulpore sentries.

'I suppose you've taken many Thugs, Mr Mauwle,' said Blake suddenly.

'Hundreds.'

'Tell me, do you release many?'

Mauwle laughed. 'None.'

'Not one?'

'Maybe eight or nine in the time I've been here,' he said dismissively. 'We know our men. Some are caught red-handed on Thugging expeditions, in the act as you might say. The others are arrested on good evidence. The system does not make mistakes.'

Blake nodded. We rode on.

'Lieutenant Mauwle, did you ever find the thieves who attacked us on the road to Jubbulpore?' Blake called out.

'Yes.'

'And what's to become of them?'

'They are to be food for the worms, Mr Blake. They resisted capture, so we shot them. I strung them from a tree as a warning.'

I felt so all in by the time we returned that I went straight to my bed. A few minutes later Blake came in with a bowl of curry and a rice cake and another of the doctor's vile powders.

'Why do you force these things on me when you have such a low opinion of the doctor?' I said irritably.

'They are not the doctor's powders, they are mine,' Blake said.

'Yours! What do you know of fevers?'

'More than any army sawbones.'

'What is it, then? Where did you come by it?' Silence. 'I will not drink it unless you tell me.'

'It works. That's all you need to know.'

I put a damp cloth over my eyes and lay back. 'Mr Blake, I swear that you would let me perish rather than reveal a single detail touching yourself. I've never known anyone so keen to ask questions and so reluctant to answer them.'

'How' – I went on after a few minutes of silence – 'how do I know that your powder does not bring on fever rather than take it away, and that you force it on me to keep me ill so you can do whatever it is you occupy yourself with here? And, by the way, I should like to know what you *are* doing here.'

Blake sighed. 'It's called *quing-hau*. I had it from a fellow up near Saharanpore by the Thibet border years ago. It's a kind of wormwood, which accounts for the bitter taste. It's the best cure for fever I've ever found. Though of course, I could be lying. It might be poison.'

I drank it up.

'What were you doing at the Thibet border?'

'Company business.'

That night my dreams were of Thugs and blood. I was glad to be woken by Mir Aziz.

'Major invites you to his garden this afternoon, if you are well enough,' he said. 'Will you say yes?'

'Is Blake in?'

'He is not, Chote Sahib.'

'I will say yes.'

In the shadow of a cluster of toddy palms, the Major surveyed his garden. He seemed quite immune to the heat, though his nose had gone scarlet and there was a constant trickle of perspiration from his forehead.

'May I say, Lieutenant, how sorry I am that you had to witness so ghastly a sight as yesterday's exhumation. At least you can now comprehend the evil we struggle against. And it is most kind of you to accept my invitation. I am afraid that anyone who shows a modicum of interest is thus importuned. Do not let me over-exert you. My wife reminds me that I have a tendency to forget others' needs. How are you today? Arm still in the sling I see.'

'Better today, thank you, sir, though still a little tired.' I had no idea where Blake was. 'And I am glad to be here, sir. A garden such as this, it reminds me of home.'

'Does it? What do you see, Lieutenant Avery?'

'Ah,' I ventured a little nervously, 'coconut palms, tamarisk, mango, young teak over there, a small neem, pomegranate . . .'

'You have a countryman's eye,' said the Major. 'I love the pomegranate's gaudy red flower. These are blooms you could never find in an English garden. And over there a jackfruit tree, another exquisite bloom. Custard apple – so much better looking than they taste, I always think, but the natives love them. Now, what are these?'

I followed his brisk stride between the beds, felt myself begin to droop in the heat, and surreptitiously loosened my cravat.

'The garden is not merely a pleasure and our orchard, Lieutenant Avery, it is also my "laboratory". I improve our yields with scientific methods which I then endeavour to pass on to the ryots, and I am teaching my gardeners to prune and irrigate. I firmly believe it is our duty as rulers to demonstrate to the people of this country that we have their best interests at heart.'

'Is that what prompted your campaign against the Thugs, sir?'

The temperature suddenly fell several degrees.

'As I said before, Lieutenant, we do not discuss Thuggee and certainly not at home,' the Major said sharply.

'I'm sorry, sir,' I said, mortified.

'No,' he said, relenting at once. 'I am sorry. Your question is reasonable. I am stuck in my habits. The Thuggee Department has crushed the Thugs by means of the strict and persistent application of a precise system. As part of this I demand absolute obedience. I forget that it is a different matter beyond Jubbulpore and that I myself have made the Thugs a subject of discussion in the wider world. Though I confess the extent of the excitement and interest they provoke seems extraordinary to me. To answer your question: for me, ridding the natives of this plague of murderers is both a duty and a demonstration of our intentions and our effectiveness.

'My duties in the Thuggee bureau are another reason I so love the garden, Mr Avery. As I think I have mentioned, I was recently made Commissioner for Thuggee and dacoity throughout India.' His pleasure in his promotion was unmistakeable. 'Living in the shadow of such darkness, delving into it as deeply as I have, is a burdensome thing. The weight of those horrors can be hard to shake off.'

He leant forward and scrutinized some long spiky leaves. 'May I ask you, Lieutenant, have you known Mr Blake long?'

'No, sir, I met him only shortly before we left Calcutta.'

'Indeed.' He took out a paring knife and began to cut an odd-looking green and yellow nubbly fruit from its base. 'Please, do not feel obliged to say anything you would rather not, but he is a most surprising man.'

'I am afraid I know very little about him. I believe he was formerly a common soldier who worked his way up to Captain. I have never come across anyone so good at asking questions and so reluctant to answer them.' Before the words were out I wished I had not said them.

'I like a man who rises by his own efforts,' said the Major mildly.

'Of course, now he works for Government House. They seemed to think he was the only man for the job.' In my embarrassment I laughed.

'Well,' said Major Sleeman, 'he is certainly something of an enigma. And he has an extraordinary grasp of Persian. You might let him know that I am aware he has been asking questions of my staff.' He stared at his paring knife. He drew himself up, his jaw locked and his hand closed over the knife. Through clenched teeth he said very slowly and emphatically, 'I must ask that he desists.'

He strode off to a new vantage point, beckoning me to follow. 'My one regret,' he said, 'is that I cannot plant peepul trees here. I like them most particularly – those delicate pale green leaves that rustle. The natives say it is the gods sitting in the branches that make them do so.' He smiled. 'But their roots ruthlessly undermine any building. It makes me think of how I conceive of my work in Jubbulpore: preserving and encouraging the best of native custom and introducing European advances, while uprooting those evils that lurk in Hindooism – Thuggee, widow-burning, infanticide – so they cannot undermine the good. Ah, here is my nephew. I have arranged for him to escort you back.'

Captain Pursloe walked into the garden, his reluctance evident in every stiff step.

'It is most kind of you, but I would not dream of distracting the Captain from his work,' I said.

'Nonsense! James can show you what we have accomplished in Jubbulpore.'

Pursloe rode ahead of me. His rigid back could not have more perfectly expressed his exasperation with his task, though why he should have so thoroughly taken against us I did not know.

Evening was not long off, and the natives were out carrying water pots or bundles of vegetables and fruit. Jubbulpore was not especially distinguished, but I was once again struck by how clean and clearly thriving it was. On every road there were small tanks shaded by tamarind trees, and new buildings seemed to be rising up everywhere. Beyond the town, the fields were in luxuriant cultivation: nature both fruitful and tamed.

'Is an escort really necessary? The town seems so orderly and so peaceful I cannot imagine there could be anything to fear.'

'There is a hanging in a few days. It is always a difficult time,' Pursloe said coolly. 'Besides, we have had a number of burglaries – even in Jubbulpore it is not always possible to keep evil at bay.'

'Nevertheless, the place is most handsomely kept.'

Pursloe's pride in his uncle overrode his dislike of me.

'Major Sleeman created Jubbulpore. It was a nothing after the Maratha wars and it is far from a plum, but he has transformed it. Soon there will be half a regiment here, and a department of engineers and munitions. Planters arrive every month. And, of course, there is the School of Industry, the new model prison for our Approvers and their families.'

'We are to see it tomorrow. I must say I am surprised that they should have a special place to live.'

'It is the Major's idea. They were promised their lives and security for their families in return for turning King's evidence. It is a way of ensuring their children are not lured into Thuggee and will allow them to be productive. Major Sleeman has in mind to set up a carpet manufactory in the prison. He wishes to have their children educated. We are waiting to hear from Calcutta if they may be taught to read and write.'

'You admire the Major very much.'

He turned sharply as if he suspected I was somehow teasing him.

'He is a great man. And he and my aunt – Mrs Sleeman – have been like a father and mother to me. I came out to Madras when I was very young; they have taken great pains with me.'

'What becomes of the prisoners who are not Approvers?'

'There is a prison on the north side of Jubbulpore for those awaiting trial or hanging, and those serving out sentences.'

'Might I see that?'

'No.'

'How big is it?'

'I cannot divulge such details.'

'And you cannot tell me about Mountstuart either.' The heat was making my head ache and my temper was suffering. 'Though you could. Your uncle is not here.'

'How dare you ask me about him!'

I rode up behind him. 'I do not pretend to know why you have so clearly taken against us, Captain Pursloe, but the sooner we find out what became of him, the sooner we can leave.'

He did not acknowledge that I had spoken, and after a few minutes I gave up hope of an answer. But as we drew up to the gates of the compound he burst out, 'He was a cad. He may be celebrated elsewhere, but we all disliked him intensely.'

'Mountstuart is a great man and a brilliant poet,' I said.

'Have you met him?' he scoffed. I did not answer. 'I did not think so. Let me tell you, we do not know where he went. He did not choose to inform us of his departure, which was typical.' He looked away. 'My uncle – Major Sleeman – allowed that man into the Thuggee Department. He went about as if he owned the place, with that infernal monkey all over him like some malevolent imp. He was disgustingly rude to my uncle. He talked a deal of nonsense about the Thugs. He made a romance of them, called them outlaws. Rot! I have seen what they do to their victims. There is nothing picturesque about them, let me assure you. I *loathed* him.' Pursloe's face contorted with rage. 'And now you and your civilian are here, raising things that are best left alone. Wasting our time, and what for? For *nothing*.'

We glared at each other.

'You should just go to Doora. Mountstuart was apparently a boon companion of the Rao – and a more corrupt and dishonest native prince you will not find.'

Chapter Eight

We met the Major at the School of Industry, a great square red and white fort, its entrance crowned with a vast triangular pediment. We had already been conducted on the tour, and seen the outside walls being painted by a troop of wretched skinny convicted Thugs, shackled to each other by leg irons, and observed by sepoys brandishing muskets. We'd seen the inside too: clean, white, as yet almost unoccupied, no prison bars or cells. At the far end of the courtyard some Approvers were building the huts they would occupy with their families, just as the sepoys did on the military lines.

'Whom do we have here?' the Major said, beaming. 'Choka – a strangler; Golab and Aviga, both jemadars of their own gangs; Gumoosh, a second-in command to a powerful jemadar; and Motee, an inveigler. Between them I think they have upward of one hundred murders upon their consciences. They speak a rather specialized dialect which you may find a little difficult to follow, Mr Avery.' The Approvers knelt and Sleeman launched into a flood of native talk, which I – too craven to admit my ignorance – pretended to follow.

It appeared to be some kind of lecture; as the Major spoke, the Approvers nodded, looking thoughtful. It was most peculiar watching the smiling, paunchy old men in their cotton coats, having witnessed a few days before victims of the horrors they had once performed. They might have been a group of village elders beneath a banyan tree. One had lost an eye, which gave him a rascally aspect. Another glowered ferociously beneath a ledge of bristling eyebrow. But the others might have been plump, benevolent grandfathers, and the Major himself looked on like a proud father. After perhaps a quarter of an hour, the Major dismissed them and we withdrew to the shelter of the portico.

'Are you not reluctant to remind them of their old lives?' said Blake, as we stood in the cool, watching them.

'I believe it never hurts to have them revisit their crimes in bright daylight. To remind them of how they lived in darkness, and to encourage them in the habit of speaking the truth. One can go too far, of course. My old assistant up in Lucknow, Captain Paton, gets his Thugs to enact their crimes, to demonstrate the use of the scarf or *rumal* for visitors. I find that distasteful.'

'They all seem to be high-ranking Thugs – chiefs and stranglers.'

'Men of high status are of most use to us. They have more to tell; they know the plans, the circumstances of the crimes and what was gained. The lower sort often move among gangs or Thug for a season here or there, and have little understanding of the old traditions and beliefs.'

'So the "lower sort" end up in the prison?'

'That is a little harsh, Mr Blake. There are men of all castes and roles in the School of Industry, and in the prison,' the Major replied. 'The men here have of course committed grave crimes, but without them we could never have crushed Thuggee, and they will never be released. Their thirst for blood cannot be appeased. The temptation to return to killing would be too great.'

'Temptation?' said Blake. 'That's a strange word.'

'The evidence shows that Thugging contaminates them, the urge to kill becomes a constant temptation.'

'Does it?'

'You have to understand, Mr Blake, that Thugging contaminates them, and that for many whose families have Thugged for generations, it has become almost an hereditary impulse. And of course, their worship of Kali commands them to such evil.'

'Forgive me, Major, but you almost sound as if you believe in the power of Kali.'

The Major's faced clouded.

'I mean no offence,' said Blake. 'So, the children will live here too?'

'As I said, Thuggee runs in families, like a contagion. Without supervision the sons would go on to become the next generation.

Wives and children must therefore be incarcerated too. But as you see, the conditions are quite unlike a normal prison. Can you imagine anything as well conceived in England?'

'But the children have committed no crime,' Blake said.

Major Sleeman cleared his throat. 'We must cut this off, Mr Blake, root and branch, root and branch. I have high hopes, however, that with education these children can be raised up, and one day they may possibly be released. Let us not disagree on this. Now, I think the Lieutenant is keen to see the famous Feringhea?'

'I am indeed, Major,' I said quickly. I realized, as the Major did not, that Blake was angry.

'I must tell you something about Feringhea before you meet him,' said Sleeman. 'As you may know, he is called the Prince of Thugs. His family are Brahmins from north-east of Gwalior, Thug leaders for generations; his uncle made a fortune by Thugging, which is very rare. From his extreme youth Feringhea was famous for his abilities as an inveigler – the Thug who deceives the prey with fair words and charming manners. He led his first band when he was but twelve. He was at the heart of the Thug conspiracy, and when we captured him – it was, I think, seven years ago now – I knew that I would break Thuggee. He perfectly illustrates the terrible seduction of Thuggee for those who have been initiated into it. He might have had another life. For a time during the Maratha wars, he left Thugging and served under Sir David Ochterlony, as chief of his messenger service. Think: he arranged the dissemination of Company intelligence in the north! But the call of Thuggee was too strong and he returned to his old ways.

'I knew we must take him, but he kept eluding us. To catch him I was forced to hang his nephew and arrest his family – though I was loath to do it. His love for his wife and child was so great that he could not bear to be too far from them. Instead of fleeing north beyond our reach, he took to sleeping a night in one of five villages so he would not be too far from them. I could not spare enough sepoys to watch all the villages at the same time, and so it took weeks, but we caught him in the end. I travelled to Saugor to escort him to Jubbulpore, and saw how valuable he would be. Though his crimes were terrible – and I would say I am more familiar with them than any man but he – I saw that his intelligence, memory and knowledge would make him an exceptional Approver.'

'And was he?' I said.

'Indeed he was. We owe the capture and prosecution of hundreds of Thugs to him, and of course he has furnished me with invaluable descriptions of Thuggee itself.'

We set off toward a small cottage that stood by itself on the other side of the yard some way away from the Approvers' huts. It had small high windows in plaster walls, and the door had three large locks.

Major Sleeman entered first. The sepoy and his nujeebs, holding their muskets in a manner which did not suggest entire easiness, came next, and finally we two. It was dark and it took a moment to adapt to the light.

There were two sepoys, a small table with a candle, two chairs, and a rug, and on this, cross-legged, his back supported by several large bolsters, sat a still, dark native. Major Sleeman spoke, and though I could not understand the words, it did not strike me as the way a gaoler commonly addressed a prisoner. The native looked into Sleeman's eyes, and his voice was soft and murmuring. He smiled slightly as he spoke, and the Major half-smiled back, as if both had forgotten that there were others in the room.

'Gentlemen,' the Major said at last. 'May I present Feringhea, our most important Approver. He is willing to answer your questions.'

He wore no shackles and was dressed in a simple white kurta and dhoti and a neatly tied orange turban. He had evidently been handsome as a young man. Now his cheeks were gaunt with age, the flesh on his arms and shoulders sagged over the muscle, and his moustache and beard were more grey than black. His face was long and aristocratic, his nose aquiline and thin. He had a large full mouth. But his eyes were unnerving: wide, unblinking, olive green speckled with black, like some appraising reptile. He was entirely composed and gave no appearance of humility. He sat as if the whole room were at his command, and there was something excessively probing in his gaze that I did not like, as if with a look he was convinced he might place us all under his spell.

Nor did I relish having to admit at this moment that I spoke no Hindoostanee. I looked hopefully again at Blake. But it was the Major who rescued me: 'Feringhea will not speak Hindoostanee. If you do not have Persian you may speak English and we will translate.'

Again I glanced at Blake.

'Ask what you like,' he said. 'When will you ever again speak to a Thug?'

I thought for a moment. I did not want to appear stupid. I did not want to seem impressed. 'I would like to ask him if there is any true difference between a Thug and any other thief.'

The Major translated. The question seemed to offend him, for he sat up haughtily, spoke in the same soft, persuasive tone; once again, the Major translated.

'Feringhea says that a thief is a contemptible being, but a Thug rides his horse, wears his dagger, shows a front! Mere thieving? Never! If a banker's treasure were before him, even entrusted to his care, even if he was hungry or dying he would spurn to steal it. But let a banker go on a journey and he would certainly murder him.'

As the Major spoke the Thug's words, a chill stole over me though the room was warm. For a moment he seemed not to be himself but only the mouthpiece of the Thug. I would have stopped there, but the Major said, 'Do you have another question?'

'Does he feel any remorse for his crimes?' I asked. Feringhea turned his cold green eyes on me as he spoke.

'He says,' the Major said – and the Thug looked back at him, and I was relieved – 'when he Thugged, it was as it is when the sahibs hunt big game. You hunt tigers and boar, he hunts men. You have only the instincts of the wild beasts to overcome, whereas he has to subdue the suspicions and fears of intelligent men and women, often heavily armed and guarded. He asks, can you not imagine the pleasure of the pursuit, of overcoming such protection during days of travel in their company, the joy of seeing suspicion change to friendship, until that wonderful moment arrives when the *rumal* completes the *shikar*? The soft *rumal*, which has ended the life of hundreds? Remorse? Never! Joy and elation, often!'

I shuddered.

'But Thuggee is being defeated. Why does he think that is?'

'He says that the goddess turned from the Thugs. They transgressed for the love of money. His band killed a number of women and others proscribed by the goddess. And now the *iqbal* – the power, the luck – of the Company is stronger than the Thugs and it has defeated them.'

'Does he still worship the goddess?'

'He says the goddess has turned her face from him.'

'Is that why he turned Approver?'

'He says, I am a Thug. My father and grandfather were Thugs, and I have Thugged with many. But before the sound of the Company's drums, sorcerers, witches and demons take flight. How can Thuggee stand? Let the government employ me and I will do its work.'

As I fumbled for another question, Blake said, '*Iqbal* is an interesting word to use. Such a Mahommedan word for such a Hindoo cult.'

But I had another question. 'I want to know, how did he choose his victims?'

The Major muttered with the Thug. 'He says, when he is on the road, from the time that the omens are favourable, he considers as victims any the deity throws into his hands. If he and his gang were not to kill them, she will never again be propitious to them.'

'Of course,' said Blake, 'if the Thugs had murdered Europeans as well as natives, the Company would have run them down years ago.' I could tell he was impatient.

The Major looked pained. Feringhea looked at him questioningly, and he translated. They murmured together. The Major straightened up, and the enchantment at last dropped away from him.

'The jemadar does not wish to offend,' he said, frowning, 'but I believe he thinks the blood of Europeans would not be acceptable to the goddess. This stems, I understand, from the Hindoo belief that the touch of an unbeliever is tainted.'

There came a knock at the door. It was Pursloe. He gave us a sullen look and told the Major he was needed back at the Thuggee bureau.

'May I ask a few more questions?' said Blake, suddenly animated. 'I will never have another opportunity. Perhaps your nephew might stay to oversee us?'

The Major havered. He was disconcerted by Blake, but also eager to be gone.

'James will stay with you,' he said, 'and return to the bureau afterwards. The hanging is tomorrow. You are welcome to attend it, but by no means obliged to. I bid you good day.' He bowed to Ferginhea and strode from the room. I could hear him calling to the sepoys as he walked away.

Pursloe looked extremely put out.

Blake began to talk to Feringhea in Persian. I understood nothing, but it seemed to me that under his questioning the Thug's air of macabre threat diminished, and with every minute he seemed just another wily rascal. At the same time, however, Pursloe became increasingly exasperated. At last he burst out, 'That is *enough*, Mr Blake.'

Blake and the Thug looked at Pursloe with surprise and something else – in Blake's face something like pity; in the Thug's, something like contempt.

The sepoys opened the door and we followed the Captain out. I turned for a last sighting of Feringhea; he had settled back on to his cushions and was watching us with an expression of great complacency; I should almost have said that Pursloe's discomposure pleased him. The Captain stalked his way through the School of Industry and out of its gates, every step a little explosion of rage.

'Sir,' he said to Blake at last, 'my uncle made it quite clear and yet you asked those questions against his express request. You realize I shall have to inform him.'

'Will you? And did you also inform him that you had spoken of Mountstuart to my assistant?'

Pursloe glowered.

'I don't think your uncle told Feringhea not to speak of Mountstuart.' Blake touched Pursloe's arm. 'We don't seek to do him any harm.'

Pursloe trembled, walked jerkily to his horse, mounted it stiffly and rode off without a backward glance.

'Confound it, Blake! What did you say to Feringhea?'

'What they deserve. Fobbing us off with Thug burials and Feringhea, thinking they can distract me from Mountstuart.'

'What did you say?'

'I asked him if Sleeman had brought Mountstuart to see him. He said yes. I asked him what he thought of him. He said Mountstuart seemed like one in the grip of a passion, careless for his own well-being. Like someone half in love with death, as if he might go in search of it. Then he told me that Mountstuart had asked him if Sleeman had tortured him.'

'And what was his answer?

'He said it had given him great pleasure to serve the Company since first Major Sleeman had asked him. Because of this, the breaking machine had not been required.'

That night, for the first time since we had arrived in Jubbulpore, I was not exhausted when I went to my bed. I lay awake, and when I judged from the creaks and footfalls he was about to leave, I crept from my room. He was wearing a kurta, pyjamas and a pugree. He carried a lantern.

'What is this?' I demanded in a hoarse whisper. I looked about for Sameer and Mir Aziz, expecting to see at least one of them, but he was alone.

Blake sighed. 'Please return to your bed, Avery.'

'I will not. Where are you going? Into the native quarter?'

He refused to answer me, but I would not be deflected. At last he said, 'I am going to the gaol. There is no good in your coming.'

'The gaol!'

'Do not argue with me, Avery. I cannot tell you what I am about.'

'But the gaol! With the Thug prisoners?'

'I cannot force you to return to your bed. But I'm asking you to.'

'God knows, I do not wish to challenge you, Blake, but what are you doing? You have got yourself caught up in some dangerous political obsession. This is not why we are here.'

'Something is wrong here. Do you not feel it?'

'No. I see light and order and civilization in the midst of darkness and ignorance.'

He shook his head. 'Why are we surrounded by sepoys wherever we go? Why are we locked in each night? Who is Sleeman to insist that no one in Jubbulpore may speak to us?'

'He is fighting the darkness,' I said. 'Not just Thugs, but everything: widow-burning, the fakirs with their mutilations, the thieves who will poison a passerby for a silver spoon, the filth.'

'Have you been to London, boy? Never seen the rookeries, I'll bet, or what a hungry man will do for a silver spoon? There's terror and evil everywhere, you just haven't seen it. Now, I am leaving. You will have to lay hands on me to stop me.'

I knew I would let him go. 'I must know where this is leading. And I am not a boy. I do you the courtesy of treating you as a gentleman; you should do the same to me.'

'Be patient.'

I returned to my bed. I lay awake thinking about what Colonel Buchanan had said about Blake's 'untoward behaviour'.

My aunt once took us – without my mother's permission – to watch a famous murderer and card-sharp take the noose in Exeter. She liked to frighten my siblings and me with descriptions of hellfire, for the sake of our souls, she said. There was a carnival air – hurdy-gurdy men, and boys selling twists of roasted nuts, and a loud, eager crowd – and something else. A sense of barely curtailed riot. As if the crowd might erupt if the right spark caught. I recall little of the event itself, save that we boys affected great bravado and jeering, while my sister was horrified. Afterwards, the man's form, bucking and struggling as the life was choked from it, and that sense of disquiet, returned to me constantly in dreams, and I felt my sister's disgust as a rebuke.

Blake had decided to go to the Thug hanging, and though I did not much wish to witness it, I wished to keep an eye on him.

The execution place was outside the prison walls in a part of the town I had not visited before, a bare piece of ground not far from the fields, which I supposed had been cleared for just such a purpose. There was a unit of sepoys, and a unit of mounted nujeebs. In their midst stood three tall thick posts. Across them stretched a long beam from which fourteen nooses hung. A temporary platform had been constructed beneath, for the condemned men to stand upon before they dropped off the side into eternity. There were a number of Europeans, several of whom I had not seen before; no ladies, of course. We stood to the left of the posts and were separated from the native crowd by more sepoys. The crowd was large and growing all the time, until the sepoys and nujeebs were making every effort to keep them from pressing in on the gibbets entirely. Major Sleeman sat on his horse, in a blue dress uniform with a thick gold embroidered collar and gold epaulettes. Behind him came Mr Hogwood. Pursloe stood with the sepoys; Mauwle stood by the gibbets, supervising the hanging.

When the Thugs emerged from two covered bullock carts, some in the crowd jeered, others shouted what seemed like cheers, and I felt that same sense of barely restrained chaos. The prisoners were shackled one to another and each was crowned with a garland of white flowers. They seemed extraordinarily calm for men going to their deaths. One young Thug was even laughing and joking. One by one they were unshackled and mounted the platform, each followed by a sepoy. They lined up behind a noose. Then, before the sepoy could manhandle them into the ropes, each took hold of their noose and placed it around their own neck. The crowd fell silent.

I looked at Blake. He said, 'So that they will not be tainted by the touch of a lower caste – or at least that's true for some of them.'

Suddenly, the young laughing man lifted up his arms, cried out, 'Kali ka jaee!' and stepped deliberately off the platform.

'What did he say?' I whispered.

'Kali is great,' muttered Blake.

The body twisted and jerked. The crowd gasped, then a great shout went up and some native women at the front began weeping and keening and pressing themselves against the sepoys as if they would push past them. There were two gun-shots. Mauwle had his arm raised and two sepoys had shot over the crowd's heads. At once the crowd quietened, but it seemed to me unhappy, mutinous and muttering. Around the edges, young men began to run, shouting angrily. Major Sleeman, imperturbable and ignoring the noise, called out to the Thugs, asking for their last words. One protested his innocence, another that some charity might be dispensed in his village, which had lost so many men. The others continued to laugh and shout at the crowd. Then the platform on which they stood was drawn sharply out from under them, and they swung. I watched. Blake looked down.

'They walked smiling into death,' I said. 'No penitence, no remorse.'

Death roused the crowd again. Those at the front began running, some at the sepoys, who used their rifle butts to fend their attackers off. At the back, women scattered, screaming, and groups jostled with each other. The Europeans, with the exception of Sleeman's men and us, swiftly left the ground. The nujeebs rode forward to line up with the sepoys and once again raised their rifles to shoot. On Mauwle's signal they fired their weapons. There were screams. Parts of the crowd began to run. Then thirty mounted nujeebs appeared from behind the prison walls. Sleeman watched, entirely calm, and Mauwle moved the soldiers around with what appeared to be almost imperceptible gestures. After that the crowd was quelled very quickly. Those who could took off. The others were rounded up by the soldiers and some were knocked to the ground, while others knelt in supplication. The entire episode had taken about five or at most ten minutes. The women and some of the men were permitted to leave in small groups until a final cluster of twenty men were hauled off by the nujeebs. Meanwhile, the sepoys had cut the dead men down and carried them into the two carts in which they had come. I must confess I had not expected anything like this to happen in Jubbulpore and found myself a little shaken. The conduct and discipline of Mauwle's men, however, had been most effective.

When the last natives had been taken from the ground, Mauwle strolled over.

'Seen enough, Mr Blake?'

Blake shrugged.

'Trouble is always close to the surface.' He grinned, a hard smile, as if to force Blake into retreat.

Blake stared back him. 'I suppose having so many criminals – thousands – imprisoned in such a small cantonment makes people anxious. That and rumours about the famine.'

'Reasons do not matter. Order does,' said Mauwle. He strode over to where a sepoy held his horse, forcing Blake to double his stride simply to keep up with him.

'There must be more Thugs in Jubbulpore than anywhere else in Hind now,' Blake said. 'They must pour in.'

Mauwle nodded. 'A Thug may be caught in Orissa, but come from Oudh, and commit murder in Bihar. Where else should he be tried? We are well set up to try them, sentence them and, if need be, hang them. You cannot trust justice in the native states: there a bribe will get you out of anything.'

'And in Bengal an Approver's testimony cannot stand in Court,' said Blake. 'They will not accept the accusations of criminals as evidence. But in the Territory you do. And your magistrates have more authority than elsewhere, too. You can pass any sentence, you need no confirmation from Calcutta.'

Mauwle took the reins from the sepoy. 'I'm no magistrate, Mr Blake, you'd have to ask the Major. But we try more natives than anywhere else,' and he gave Blake a flinty look.

'I believe you. The Territory has a great reputation for efficiency. Thug trials are held in secret, isn't that so?'

'There is no need for an audience.'

'I mean, there is no jury, there are no opposing arguments.'

'The evidence is damning and the natives lie freely. They're murderers. They cannot be played with. I'd have thought you'd understand that.'

'I do understand, Lieutenant Mauwle. It is necessary to be ruthless with ruthless men.'

'It is.'

'But sometimes the nujeebs arrest innocent natives and extract ransom payments for their release, and sometimes they arrest on the word of very unreliable local informers.'

'I do not know how you come by your information, Mr Blake, but what do you expect? It happens. But not often.' He lifted his saddle and tightened the girth.

'I have one last question.'

'You can ask what you wish. Whether I answer is another matter.'

'I've heard tell of a breaking machine.'

Mauwle laughed. 'And I thought you were going to ask about Mountstuart.' He put his foot in the stirrup and swung himself on to his horse. 'The breaking machine. The truth is, we do not need it. The Major's system is the breaking machine: the maps, the lists, the family trees. That is what has broken the Thugs. Now they fear us. Of course, they imagine we have racks in our dungeons. But we do not need them. And if the Major heard you ask about such things, he'd say you were in league with our enemies.'

'What about Mountstuart?'

He laughed again. 'Disliked him. A pestering kind of a man with a high opinion of himself.'

Chapter Nine

'Sar,' Mir Aziz said in my ear, 'the Major comes.'

It was early – the sun had barely risen. I pulled on the clothes I had to hand and rushed on to the verandah to find a dozen nujeebs wrestling to unlock our gates, and behind them Major Sleeman astride an elephant. The procession entered the compound, almost entirely filling the yard in front, and the Major, aided by a mahout, dismounted from the elephant's neck on to its bent thigh and thence to the ground. By now Blake had joined me.

'You are most splendidly dressed today, Major,' he said. Sleeman wore a blue regimental uniform with a great deal of gold braid and a feathered cocked hat. The elephant was draped in silk and covered in silver meshwork, and the nujeebs wore yellow silk turbans.

'I am making my tour of the local villages,' he said, and gestured at himself. 'Naturally I cannot appear less impressive than the land-owners. It's necessary to quell local concerns about yesterday's events. Such things happen. I am sorry you had to witness it. The crowd whips itself up about nothing. We plan to continue with our dinner. I hope we shall still see you there. I understand you leave tomorrow?'

'There is no more reason to stay.'

'Where will you go?'

'To Doora.'

'I see.'

'Perhaps you would like to direct us somewhere else, if you think us mistaken?'

'I would not presume to,' said the Major. 'But I would advise you to take care. The Rao is extremely hostile to Company emissaries. In fact, I should say he loathes the Company. His court is rife with intrigue, and he is almost certainly not to be trusted. Moreover, we

136

believe he provides protection to at least one Thug gang in return for a share of their plunder.'

Blake gazed impassively at the Major and gave a tiny nod.

'Oh, he is not the worst. Our attempts to stamp out Thuggee have often been undermined by the collusion of native princes. Among the rulers of the central states I should say there is not one truly admirable man. Robbers and murderers all, with no sense of duty towards their people. I take the Rao of Doora's resistance particularly hard. He should know better. He had the advantage of an education in Calcutta, among the best European minds.'

Major Sleeman tapped his fingers on the hilt of his sword.

'Mr Blake, it has not escaped my attention that you have been quizzing my people, though I expressly asked you not to. I imagine you have found it of very little help. But I also wish to clear up what may be a misconception.' The bright blue eyes gazed at Blake, whose expression, as usual, betrayed nothing. 'My nephew, James, Captain Pursloe, came to me. I fear he said things in anger to Lieutenant Avery regarding the man you seek that he regrets. That imply things he did not intend. He can be very excitable, but he is devoted to me and to his duty. I want you to understand that though he was very provoked by . . . by that man's behaviour, he would certainly never have done anything to harm him. He is a good boy.'

'I never thought otherwise,' said Blake.

'Good. I hope we understand each other.' The Major coughed. It was an uneasy cough. He looked to one side, as if he could not quite meet Blake's eyes. 'Your quarry. The poet. I should say that he had the look of a man who did not want to be found by anyone. I should say he was beyond hope.'

Later, Mir Aziz removed the stitches in my arm. The little red scars and scabs made the skin look as if it had been laced on to my bones. I made a fist, dismayed by how weak it felt. As each little thread was pulled from the skin, I reflected upon our journey and Nungoo's death and how little we had achieved. I told Mir Aziz about the

School of Industry, and Feringhea, the riot at the hanging and what the Major had said about Pursloe.

'I thought I would go to see Hogwood again. To ask him if he will tell me what happened when Mountstuart was here. What do you think, Mir Aziz?'

Mir Aziz considered. 'Nothing is being lost by it, Chote Sahib.'

Mr Hogwood was in the magistrate's office signing letters on a desk piled so high with boxes and documents that he was all but invisible. One by one he handed them to two dak runners who stood restlessly by.

He looked up at me. 'Just one moment, almost done. Endless reports, most of them never to be read.'

'I hope you do not mind me calling upon you, Mr Hogwood. But we depart tomorrow.'

'I thought I should be seeing you and Mr Blake tonight at dinner with the Major. May I say how sorry I am that you had to witness what happened at the hanging. Unfortunately, even in the best-run stations such things happen.' He sat back in his chair and stretched a little, and the bones in his shoulders cracked. He looked at me meaningfully and dismissed his runners.

'Mr Hogwood, I have not only come to say goodbye.'

Hogwood sighed. 'I am truly not sure that anything I could tell you would help you.'

'We have come so far. And we leave with nothing.'

'You would have to promise not to reveal the provenance of the story. The Major would feel it a great betrayal if he knew.'

I was surprised but I hid it. 'I swear I will not divulge it to anyone but Blake.'

He stood and stretched again. He shook his head and sighed. I pulled up a chair and sat down.

'Mr Mountstuart arrived in late May, or was it early June? He had no servants, only the monkey and a letter of introduction from Government House, just like your Mr Blake. He stayed for almost a month. He said he was writing a long poem about the Thugs and he wished to know as much about them as possible. The Major was happy to help him. He brought him to see the Approvers and

Feringhea. He allowed him into the Department, which he very rarely does. Mountstuart seemed a little eccentric, with his monkey and all, but we were all very impressed by him and pleased that he had come to Jubbulpore. He and the Major had a good deal in common, with their languages and their love of the country.

'But after about a week, perhaps ten days, things began to go awry. Mountstuart became cool towards the Major. I still do not understand quite why. One day everything was good, the next it was bad. He became irritable. Then he began to be volubly critical. He was deliberately contrary, even though we did our best to accommodate him. It was at this time that I accompanied him on an exhumation. He seemed to view it as some macabre entertainment. The grave was an old one; we found a number of skeletons. That cursed little monkey stole some of the bones and ran off with them, and Mr Mountstuart considered this amusing and would not call him back. The natives were . . . well, they should not have seen it. Then he asked the Approvers to demonstrate the use of the *rumal* upon each other, and gave them some coins to do so. It was very unseemly. He had an absolute mania for the Thugs, by the way. He wished to speak with them endlessly.

'It came to the point where he and the Major could not agree on anything. Even matters on which they should have shared views. They argued especially about the native princes. Then Mountstuart took to wearing native robes and wandering about the bazaar. This is not something we do in Jubbulpore. The crust of civilization is still very thin here. There are only a few Europeans, and keeping order and peace in the cantonment must be a priority. Wearing native clothes gives quite the wrong impression. Perhaps we should not have been surprised – he is a poet after all and we provincial Company men are prosaic creatures. But looking back, I do wonder if perhaps he was not quite himself – if he was entirely well. Years in the tropics can have an effect on a man.'

'You mean that he was mad?'

Hogwood shook his head. 'I could not say for sure, but he was most erratic.'

'So, what then?'

'The Major invited Mountstuart to dinner. It was an attempt to make peace. He came, but two hours late. He was argumentative and rude and sullen. I tried to pacify him – but he only grew louder and more uncontrollable. He stood up, and before everyone he said that the Company was an institution whose sole purpose was to immiserate the natives, and that Jubbulpore was the worst. He said, "You are no better than criminals, and you know why." Then he repeated it in Hindoostanee and Marathee for the benefit of the servants. And then he said it again. "You are no better than criminals."

'I have never seen the Major so angry. He ordered Mountstuart from the house. Mountstuart laughed and said he was going, and that when he had finished with us the world would shun us like Cain.'

'Good God!'

'You are upset,' said Hogwood.

'It seems foolish to admit it, but I have admired Xavier Mountstuart since I was a boy. His writings were what brought me to India.'

'Sometimes it is better not to approach one's heroes too closely,' Hogwood said, almost sadly. 'Better to meet them only on the page. Anyway, the next day he had gone.'

'What do you mean?'

'The servants at his compound, where you are staying in fact—'

'He stayed in the same place as us?' Had I been sleeping in the same bed as he had?

'Why yes, did I not say? The servants came to me saying that he had disappeared, and the monkey too. We went to see if we could discover what had happened. There was no trace of him anywhere. It was nearly July and the monsoon had started, so any tracks had long since vanished. There were rumours that he had left Jubbulpore walking north. But it was a hard time to travel, especially for a man not young, nor in the most robust health. I honestly do not know if he is alive or dead: I prefer to think that he walked to Doora – they say he knows the Rao. But there has been no news that he was there.'

I nodded. 'I have a question. About Pursloe.'

Hogwood sighed. 'He is inclined to become over-excited.'

'He told me he hated Mountstuart. He was shaking with rage.'

'He has a very strong attachment to his uncle. He feels the need to defend him from all comers, even when it is not necessary. He felt Mountstuart belittled the Major. But for what it's worth I do not think he would . . . I myself feel certain that Mountstuart left Jubbulpore.'

'Better to know this, even if we do not know where he went,' I said. I had a sudden intimation of Mountstuart dead, somewhere in the jangal. 'I thank you.'

'The truth is invariably duller than one's imaginings.'

I stood up. Then a thought came to me.

'Mr Hogwood, might I ask your advice in confidence? A delicate matter upon which I am at a loss.'

He drooped a little, but said, 'How may I help?'

'I am sorry, you have quite enough to think about.'

'No, no, believe me, so much of my work is dull administration – the projections of the mango harvest, road repairs in Sleemanabad – it is a relief to be called upon to think about something different.'

'It concerns Mr Blake.'

'Ah.'

'In Calcutta I received my orders from the Chief Military Secretary, Colonel Buchanan.'

'I know of him. Everyone does.'

'Indeed. He told me that one of my duties was to keep an eye on Blake to make sure he did not stray from the task. And if he did then I should consider reporting him to a senior officer. He mentioned Sleeman by name.'

'I see.'

'It is a charge that goes against all my training and instincts.'

'It would be a most awkward position to find oneself in.'

'This is in strictest confidence, Mr Hogwood. I have become quite anxious about Blake. I felt confident at first because, well, because he asked me to make my recovery as slow as possible, so as to give him more time here. I thought that must mean that he was investigating Mountstuart. But he seems to be entirely preoccupied by the

Thugs. He disappears at all times of the day and night, and refuses to tell me anything. And he seems determined to enrage everyone. Feringhea mentioned a breaking machine. So Blake asked Mauwle about it.'

Hogwood grimaced. 'How did Mauwle respond? It is the case that they are very sensitive about all that. Jubbulpore is not perfect. I know the Major can seem arrogant. When one is left to run things as he has been, so far from civilization, one comes to rely upon one-self and one's own judgement. Also, the fight against Thuggee has been hard, the things we have seen, the way it has insinuated itself into our lives . . . but I swear, I've seen nothing that would lead me to believe a breaking machine exists, nor anything else of which the Major should be ashamed. And he has many fine qualities – great qualities, even – as I think you would agree.'

I nodded. 'That is not all. A few days ago I discovered Blake had done something that truly alarms me. He seems to have broken into the prison.'

Hogwood looked at me in astonishment. 'He what?' He paused and rubbed his forehead. 'Broke *into* the prison? How odd. I am sure that none of the prisoners has escaped.'

'Apparently that was never his aim.'

'I had considered Mr Blake an intelligent man, even if he is not one of us – a gentleman, I mean. You know, this all reminds me of Mountstuart's visit.'

'They knew each other, a long time ago. But I do not think they were friends.'

'How can I advise you?' he said, rubbing his head again. 'I suppose you should tell the Major, but Mr Blake may end up in the lock-up, or worse. On the other hand, it does not seem that he has actually done any real harm, and your Colonel Buchanan evidently takes a rather cautious view of him. You are off tomorrow – you could say nothing. I wish the Major had spoken to you, but he was sorely provoked. If you warned him, at least he would be able to counter any wild accusations from Blake. In the meantime, I swear I shall not say anything of what you have told me.'

I thanked him, almost more confused than before.

'Watch out for yourself, Avery. If you go to Doora. It is a dangerous place.'

I had not sat down at a dinner table with ladies since I had left Calcutta, and I had missed it. Just like her husband, Mrs Sleeman had a talent for order and organization. In the soft glazed light everything in the room seemed to glow or shine: the polished mahogany of the dinner table, the porcelain and silver, the crystal candlesticks, the light reflected off the long looking-glass – a little tarnished by the elements – the ladies' pearls. Outside, the insects hurled themselves against the muslin stretched across the windows. There could not be, I thought, another room like this, such a grand but comfortable haven of familiarity and Englishness, for hundreds of miles in any direction.

There were twenty of us at the table: the Major and Mrs Sleeman, Hogwood, Pursloe, Mauwle, the doctor and various officers and engineers from the new cantonment and their wives, two district officers from south of Jubbulpore and two recently arrived planters and their wives.

No one had mentioned the hanging, and I realized, with some relief, that no one would.

'I know it is usual now to serve many European courses,' the Major was saying, 'but I find such dishes very hard on the constitution. I cannot work on a diet of pudding and roast beef in thick English sauces. The native habit of eating little meat suits me. Amelie and our regular guests are kind enough to humour me, although Lieutenant Mauwle takes a rather different view of the subject.'

'I do, sir,' said Mauwle, lifting his glass to him.

Meanwhile, the planters' ladies had primped themselves and gazed at Blake all evening, trying to gain his attention. I wished they would not, as he was in an unfriendly and uncompromising mood. He had slung himself along the back of his chair, his arms crossed, his chin pointing into his chest, and his expression did not suggest he welcomed questions.

'There is a great mystery about you, Mr Blake,' the slightly larger of the planters' wives said, simpering a little. 'Try as we might all night, we have not been able to discover what brings you to Jubbulpore.'

'I cannot say, madam,' Blake said. 'Major Sleeman has expressly forbidden discussion of the matter.'

The lady persevered. 'Oh!' she said, and mouthed the word 'Mountstuart?', arching her eyebrows questioningly. Her husband coughed and nudged her, and several awkward conversations were suddenly struck up. The *khitmatgur* filled my glass with chilled claret. The second planter's wife, sitting on my right, began to whisper loudly.

'Is it true? Is it the poet that brings you here? We so wished to meet him, but we never had the opportunity. We are told he behaved very badly. But no one is to speak of it. You must tell me what you know. Has he disappeared? Do you think he was murdered by the natives? Or did away with himself in a fit of melancholy?' She giggled. I raised my hand for another glass of claret and buried my face in it so I should not have to answer, until her husband shushed and frowned her into silence.

'Lieutenant Avery,' Mrs Sleeman broke in. She was perfectly dressed in white muslin with not a hair out of place. 'I am sure you have many stories from Calcutta society. It is an age since we heard any of the gossip. Do tell us what they are talking of.' The tone was charming but steely. I brought forth my Calcutta chatter, carefully skirting around the subject of Mountstuart's book, and kept the planters' wives entertained for some time. After several glasses of claret I could not exactly tell them apart, but they were determined to enjoy themselves and were very good-humoured, and that was a relief. Occasionally I looked over to see Pursloe, silent and mulish next to his aunt, who talked briskly across him. Eventually I exhausted my store of tales and we began to listen to the doctor, who was expatiating on the School of Industry.

'It is not really a matter for the dinner table, I admit,' he said, 'but in my opinion the regime is far too liberal. To be honest this is the case at the prison too, where the vast majority of Thugs serve their sentences. The only real discomfort is that of breathing the noxious prison air, which is, admittedly, foul. Their hard labour is not hard enough.'

'Is it not?' said Blake.

'Not in my opinion, sir. They are simply deprived of their liberty.' These last words tumbled into silence: the rest of table had become quiet.

'You are responsible for the health of the inmates, are you not, Doctor?' Blake said. I had been praying that he would speak all evening, and now I longed for him to remain silent. 'They die, I'm told, at a rate of two or three a week of dysentery and fever, and thus far not a single Thug sentenced even to the shortest seven-year stretch has lived to see release.' The doctor looked furious.

'I cannot but wonder where you came by such misinformation – and at your naivety, Mr Blake,' the Major said. 'The spread of disease is a problem for prisons everywhere, from Bombay to London, and I think you would find a gaol in a native state a great deal worse. You cannot lay the blame on our doctor. And you have seen how seriously we have addressed these things in the School of Industry.'

'To which only a very small proportion of your prisoners are sent.'

'Let us agree this is not an appropriate moment to discuss such matters,' said the Major.

'Oh, Mrs Sleeman,' cried one of the planters' wives. 'Tell your husband not to cast us all as shrinking violets. We are starved of good and lively conversation and we are all fascinated by the Thugs.'

Mrs Sleeman laid a hand on her husband's cuff.

'Well, well,' he said, reluctantly. 'What I can say is that in our new School of Industry cleanliness and sanitation will be admirably maintained. And that we plan to counter the future threat of Thuggee by educating our Approvers' sons to cultivate the virtues of benevolence and conscientiousness. We shall win them from the evils of Thuggee.'

'But they will still be natives, untrustworthy, incessant liars,' said one of the planters. There was a murmur of agreement.

'I protest,' said the Major. 'One cannot generalize in such a way. It is true that many natives do not understand "truth" in the way that we do. The Thugs do lie incessantly – it has been a great problem in the Courts. But this is not simply because they have no moral understanding. Over the years at this table we have often debated the capacity of the natives, especially the poorer sort. Some believe that they are not capable of feeling in the same way that we do. I used to think this. I have learnt they are wary of us – I wish they were not. Their own native governments have mistreated them for generations, and we do not make sufficient effort to understand them. But we can win them to the light and drive out ignorance and superstition by showing them the benefits of civilization, by demonstrating we are worthy rulers. By – for example – making the roads safe for them to travel. What native princeling has done this?'

'You are too soft-hearted, Major Sleeman,' said the other planter.

'Major Sleeman,' said Blake, 'is there not a contradiction between your conviction that the natives lie, and your reliance on the testimony of your Approvers?'

'I do not see one.'

'It is the case that the Company has done much more than any native prince to bring order and prosperity to this land,' said the first planter.

'Has it?' Blake said.

'Mr Blake,' said Major Sleeman impatiently, 'you must agree that the Company has brought great benefits to India. You who are familiar with so many of its languages, and have seen so much of it, know better than most what it has accomplished.'

The whole table turned to Blake, save me. I prayed for some blessed interruption: for the ceiling to fall down, for a large snake to enter at the window. I drank a long draught of claret.

'At one time I would have agreed with you,' said Blake quietly. 'But I am no longer so sure. I have seen corruption and chaos in the native states, just as you have. I marched with the Company into Assam and Manipore, Bahalwapore and Mysore. But after more than sixteen years I cannot say that the natives' lot is any better than it was before. Why should we be surprised? The Company came to India to profit from it. I appreciate, Major Sleeman, that your governance has brought peace to a region blighted by wars, but all around I see the natives poorer for the existence of the Company. And even here, the natives are anxious and angry.'

The table went deathly silent.

'I would dispute your conclusions, Mr Blake,' said the Major crisply. 'After twenty years of peace, the ryots of this territory are far better off.'

'Would they agree with you?'

'Of course, they complain,' the Major said. 'But that is because they have forgotten what life was like under the Marathas. They say they cannot grow enough, and they say it is because they are encouraged to perjure themselves in our courts, or because of the eating of beef, or the prevalence of adultery or the impiety of the surveys we make of the local populations. The truth is over twenty years of peace their families have grown and they do not let the earth lie fallow.'

'But I see something different: I see the Company demanding higher and higher rents,' said Blake softly. 'I see the old relations between landowner and peasant broken. The Company has turned the zamindars, the landowners, into its rent collectors. They extort money from the peasants however they can, no matter how bad the harvest has been. I see men arrive in Calcutta every day, driven off the land and starving, or indentured as all but slaves because they cannot pay their rents. They are forced to plant indigo and opium poppy when they should plant food. The Company extends its rule and the country becomes poorer.'

'When you say "men",' one of the planters' wives said, 'do you mean natives?'

Blake stared at her.

'You are a Jacobin, sir!' said her husband.

'You cannot truly believe that, Mr Blake?' said Mr Hogwood.

'Just now the Governor General's party and an army of 10,000 are travelling north up the Grand Trunk Road into the famine areas north of Allahabad. What will that 10,000-strong column do, do you think? Bring bread and honey to the starving natives? Or pass through and onward like a plague of locusts?'

The company looked at Blake as if he were mad and dangerous.

And I realized that he did not care at all. Across the table Hogwood caught my eye.

'Mr Blake, you are jaded indeed,' said the Major.

'Maybe I have seen too much.' He stood up. 'Gentleman, ladies, I bid you good night.'

I stood too. I had to follow him. 'Major Sleeman, Mrs Sleeman.'

But Blake had already taken off into the night. As I waited for my horse, I could hear the Major talking to his guests.

'Of course, some of their superstitions are very picturesque,' he was saying. 'My dear Mauvli, who advises me on Mahommedan matters, tells me that lightning is a flaming arrow that Allah throws at his foes. Our local zamindar, the little Sarimant of Deori, of whom I am most fond – he is the most polished, graceful and elegant creature, all rose-coloured silk and azure satin – insisted when we had our influenza epidemic some years ago that we must get the local guroo to choose a couple of goats and to chase them out of town into the forest. Scape goats, you see.'

The company laughed, and part of me wished I was back in the dining-room, laughing too.

Our packs lay on the bungalow's drawing-room floor – the sum of our meagre baggage. Blake sat on a chair, scribbling in a notebook. He had put off his European clothes and donned kurta and dhoti. He looked grizzled and creased, and the scar on his brow bulged a little more than usual. He looked, indeed, more like himself.

'Was that necessary?'

Blake did not answer.

'Why will you not talk to me? Have I not shown that I deserve it?' I said. 'Have I not reported everything I have seen and heard? Did I not discover what Mountstuart did here – though you show little enough interest in it?'

'You did. And I'm grateful for it.' He returned to his scribblings.

'You enrage the Major, you insult his guests, you disappear for hours and say nothing. And for God's sake, Blake, you broke into the damn prison! Just explain it to me. Just a few words and I would willingly accept it all.'

He did not even raise his head.

'Do you truly not care how these people regard you? What is it that you so dislike about Jubbulpore?'

'Everything.'

I went to bed. I rose at first light and walked out of the bungalow. Outside the gates two natives stood guard. I told them to take me to the Thuggee bureau.

PART THREE

Chapter Ten

The road to Doora followed the meanderings of the Son River. On its far side we could see verdant rice and millet fields, bounded at their lower ends with mounds of earth to hold the rainwater after the monsoons. Beyond them the rocky sides of the Kaimur hills stretched north. Tributaries splashed down the rock into small waterfalls and rushing streams. My arm was healing well enough, though hours of riding made it ache.

Blake and I barely spoke. With the native robes had returned the old coarse manners – the unshavenness and the taciturnity – and I was not inclined to press my company upon him. For myself, I was in a state of gloomy brooding, my head full of contradictions. Now we had left Jubbulpore, my recollections of it were less rosy, and I was surprised at the relief I now felt, but I feared there would be little for us in Doora. Blake's silences exasperated me, but I worried over what I had said to Major Sleeman.

Mir Aziz reckoned it would take five days to reach Doora. On the first night when we pitched camp, he brought out his huqqa, lit it and said, 'If Chote Sahib permits, I will teach him Hindoostanee. I am excellent moonshee.' In truth, it was the last thing I wished to do, but it seemed churlish to refuse and I was touched by his kindness. And so, in front of Blake and Sameer, I was forced to expose my tiny reservoir of Hindoostanee words, the knowledge that Mir Aziz meant well fighting a rising testiness as Sameer laughed loudly at my ignorance and Blake barely seemed to notice. It was the same the following night, but after Mir Aziz pronounced the lesson at an end, I asked him if he would tell me his story, and he agreed. He had been born, he said, in the kingdom of Oudh and had left his village at sixteen to travel to Bengal with his two uncles to join the Company's army. One uncle, he said, had been a jack-of-all-trades, a hakim, a healer of sorts, a writer of *akhbars*, and a sometime moonshee and teacher of languages. He had taught Mir Aziz to write and some knowledge of figures.

Before he came to Bengal, Mir Aziz said, he had never seen a white man.

'I wished to take service with the Bahadur Company, but I was most frightened. We had heard the sahibs were born from an egg and were terrible giants who stood many gaz high. The European ladies were said to be fairies or, if old and ugly, witches who would cast spells upon us.'

'Were you disappointed when you saw them?'

'A little disappointed, Chote Sahib. The first sahib I saw was very young and soft-faced, like a woman. No whiskers. A young officer with a skin the colour of milk, short of stature. He is not filling me with fear. Among us, a warrior must have a beard. But he could speak my tongue and he could write a page faster than I could mix the ink, and his house was four times bigger than that belonging to the headman of my village. His eye was sharp like a hawk. And he gave me this,' and he pointed to his tulwar with its handsome leather and silver scabbard.

'Sometimes I am fighting with the armies of His Majesty. They love to fight, and they worship Rum and Brandee. It takes their fear, and makes them fight like lions. I have seen it bring them back to life, and kill them too.'

'But you did not remain just a soldier?'

'No, Chote Sahib, after two years my officer is coming to me and saying I could be of more service elsewhere. He is telling me to go to my uncle, the hakim. I go, and my uncle is teaching me doctoring, writing, Persian. After this, I returned to the Company, and I began to perform tasks for the Company, up and down the road, from Calcutta to Lahore and beyond. Sometimes fighting, sometimes missions.'

'Has the Company treated you well?'

'It is putting clothes on the backs of my children. It is providing my wives with perfumes, sweetmeats and servants. It is giving me employment with honour.'

I looked over at Blake. I could not imagine him ever speaking so freely about anything.

On the third day, Mir Aziz and Blake's manner changed. They became watchful and uneasy. Every once in a while Blake would nod and Mir Aziz would dismount and scour the ground, or Blake would ride ahead looking from side to side, as if to peer into the impenetrable undergrowth. They constantly exchanged glances. Never had I more felt that the two were engaged in some secret dialogue from which I was excluded. Sameer and I were obliged to follow, neither of us sure what we were to look for. When I asked Blake what he was watching for, he would only tell me to be attentive to anything unexpected. They did not relax their watchfulness for a moment. I began to worry that my healing arm would render me unable to help as much as I wished.

In the late afternoon we crossed from Company territory into Doora. We stopped at the first large village we came to; Blake disappeared with the headman, and made arrangements that we should sleep there in an empty hut, rather than camp at the roadside. When I pressed him, he would only say that if we were to encounter trouble, better that it should be by daylight.

We rose before first light. Blake urged us all to prime our weapons.

'We may be safe, but the headman tells me there are a number of places up the road that are good for ambush.'

'Why should they be so keen to attack us?' I said. 'They will bring down the Company on their heads. Whoever was pursuing us would be wise to pass on to some easier prey.'

Blake shrugged. 'They would.'

Half the village, including the headman, accompanied us for almost a mile out of the village. After that, we rode on as briskly as we could. For almost half an hour we continued at a good pace, and with every moment I felt myself relax. Our pursuers would have to be mounted, and the chances of a Company party being attacked by a gang of mounted brigands, even in Doora, were remote indeed. The morning bird calls and shrieks were almost deafening. The jangal thickened and loomed and the path bent out of view. A bird screeched loudly. I would not have particularly remarked on it had not Mir Aziz turned back to look at me suddenly, taken his musket into his hands and kicked his horse to a canter. Blake wound his reins round the pommel of his saddle and brought out his musket, and Sameer plucked his up too. We followed the path round the bend and there, ahead of us, was a vast tree trunk that had fallen across the road.

We stopped, and just as we did so, two figures crashed out of the trees to my left, their arms outstretched to snatch my reins. The first and closest man was slow, and it was not hard to keep still and shoot him in the chest as he reached forward. The recoil of my musket caused pain to flare in my hand. I swivelled to aim at the other attacker, who ducked backward out of the way. Other figures were running from the other side of the road. There came a loud report of another gun, and then another, and after a moment a third. Both Blake and Mir Aziz were shooting at the brigands. The plan had clearly been to ambush us as we reached the fallen tree trunk, but we had stopped in good time, so our horses had more room to manoeuvre. This greatly disadvantaged our ambushers. I could see Mir Aziz using his musket as a bayonet with extraordinary force and skill. Blake was swinging his tulwar, and dealt one man a great slice in the face. The fight, it seemed, was going our way. My remaining assailant made a grab at my reins. He missed and I kicked out at him, but he had a long wooden stave and dealt me a stunning blow across the shoulder. I had reached for my pistol but the blow caused me to drop it, and he thrust at me with the stave, trying to unseat me. Instead of resisting, I let myself slide from the saddle and on to the ground next to the Collier. As he stepped around my bucking horse to finish me off, I had it ready in my left hand and I shot him in the face.

I stood up and looked about me. Two more of our attackers appeared to be down. Sameer had one man at his feet and was driving off another. Blake had two to contend with. I ran up and dealt the one with his back to me a blow with my sabre – reflecting as I did so that in England I had never envisaged myself doing anything so ungentlemanly. I had not used a sword on a man before, and it was not pleasant. The blade went through his ribs and he sank to the ground like a broken sack. Blake stabbed the other in the stomach. The rest, seeing the damage inflicted upon their companions, fled.

Sameer marched up, patted me on the shoulder, grinned widely and waved his bayonet in the air.

'Shaabaash,' he said. This means 'well done'. It was not clear whether he referred to me or himself.

There were five bodies on the ground and, increasingly distantly, we could hear the cries and stumblings of the rest of our attackers as they escaped through the jangal. We were winded but unharmed, there was barely a scratch on any of us. A trail of flattened grasses led us through the trees to five horses and the marks of a fire. We roped the animals together and added them to our pack-horses.

'They were using the horses to follow us, but they are finding it hard to keep up with us,' said Mir Aziz, complacently. 'They fight on foot, they are not in the way of being good cavalrymen like us, and thus we took the advantage.'

'Given that the roads around Jubbulpore are so famously safe,' I observed, 'we have certainly been exceedingly unlucky in our encounters on them.'

'There's no luck in it, or accident,' said Blake. 'They've been after us for two days.'

'Do you truly believe they were deliberately sent after us? They did a poor job of it.'

'We were prepared. Mir Aziz, Sameer and I are used to fighting, and you did well. Very well.'

'Who would want us dead?' I said.

'Someone in Jubbulpore. Someone in Doora.'

'I suppose you are going to suggest that Major Sleeman is trying to have us killed,' I said, my voice rising with irritation and incredulity. 'This is perfectly ridiculous.'

Blake grunted.

'No, Blake Sahib,' said Mir Aziz gravely. It was the first time I had ever heard him contradict Blake. 'I do not think. We are small party, we travel fast. They see one Company officer – the Chote Sahib who is in uniform. They smell: urgent. They think: money. They track us one day and one night. They attack. Nothing more.'

Blake said nothing, but I knew he was not convinced.

There was no question of taking the bodies of the fallen with us, or of burying them. We dragged them to the side of the road and rode on as fast as we could. At the first village we stopped and Blake told the headman what had happened. We pressed on and camped by the roadside that night. We did not speak much of our attack.

On the sixth day the road began to fill with other travellers. Mir Aziz discovered from a large party of revellers that Doora was celebrating the seventh birthday of the Rao's heir. As Doora was the largest state in the region, this would be a great event.

'You've not met a grand Hindoo before, I'll bet,' said Blake, who had risen in a better mood than I had seen him in days.

'I've seen those rich Calcutta baboos. A few of them.'

'Not the same animal at all. They might seem exotic to you, but the Calcutta merchants and zamindars are half-European in the eyes of the rulers of the princely states. Take care with your manners.'

I eyed him, unimpressed. 'You are giving me a lecture on manners?'

'When it comes to native etiquette, Mr Avery,' he said, 'yes. It will pay to be courteous and I expect you to be. Take care not to touch anyone of the court unless they make it plain they wish you to, and then, like as not, they'll be wearing gloves. Don't touch any water or food bowls unless they are particularly offered to you. Don't eat or drink from anything which a native guest has eaten from. Don't show any curiosity about the zenanas. Remove your shoes whenever you are asked. And finally, prepare to feel insulted, and resolve to do your utmost – your utmost, now – not to show it.'

'Why would I feel insulted?'

'You heard Major Sleeman. Our visit is unlikely to be welcome.'

I pressed him to explain, but he would only say that there was no use painting a picture of disaster before it had befallen us.

'What do your omens tell you about our visit to Doora?' I asked Mir Aziz.

'Chote Sahib, the omens are mixed,' he said, knowing I teased him. 'I am hearing the cry of a lone jackal at night. But also I am seeing the black crow on the left of the road. And that is a good sign.'

Doora appeared under a pale blue hazy sky. It lay at the far end of a wide green plain, the river swelling into a lake before its far-off walls. A mile before the gates Blake made us stop by a small tank and broken-down temple and we changed into our most official weeds – he in dark broadcloth, I in a uniform as well turned as Sameer could make it. He had Mir Aziz shave us both, but kept the beginnings of the moustache and beard he had grown. Then we passed through the city gateway, a mass of broken brick and peeling plaster. On each side stood a small contingent of native soldiers in silk waistcoats holding unsheathed tulwars. Natives carrying baskets of bamboo, custard apples and timber streamed around us.

Mr Crouch-Symington was a tired, perspiring, cross little man – that much was evident from the moment we saw him. Lines of exasperation were grooved into the Company Resident's worn, yellowing face, and his mouth was puckered into a tight little pout. The news of our attack he greeted not with horror, but with exasperation.

'Well, I must say,' he repeated, 'it really could not have come at a worse moment. The Rao's ministers are likely to see it as a provocation. And there is nothing to be done about it. The perpetrators will never be found. I have the greatest respect for Major Sleeman, but just now Thuggee officers on Doora territory would put me in a most unenviable position.'

But that was far from the worst of it. We were not at all up to muster.

'To be blunt, Mr Blake, if the Company meant to send the Rao a real mission, it could surely have done better. I would have expected a lieutenant colonel, or a major – a senior civilian at the very least – and a decent complement of servants. You should know very well that these native princelings expect a senior member of the Company with a proper entourage. It is too bad that you do not have a contingent of Company troops. And no gifts. You must know they expect gifts. And your timing is quite disastrous. We are in the midst of the heir's birthday celebrations. I am expecting a number of very distinguished Europeans who will be staying in the Residency.'

'Mr Crouch-Symington, as I said before, this is a confidential mission arranged in short order. It was of the essence that we travel speedily. Luxury and scale were neither appropriate nor possible.' Blake had put his Company manner back on, but there was something very slightly off – insolent even – in his manner towards the Resident. He stared him full in the face and the man wriggled with discomfort.

'Perhaps you might read my letter of introduction from Government House.' Blake brought out an unimpressively bent, yellowed envelope.

The Resident rubbed his eyes and looked at it as if it were giving off an unpleasant odour. He drew out a pair of pince-nez which he squashed on to his soft little nose, and set to studying it.

'Very brief,' he said. 'Very uninformative.' He looked Blake over again. 'I will see what I can do. But I cannot promise that you will have any joy of him. You must understand Vishwanath Singh is a very difficult person.' He lowered his voice at this, turning to look surreptitiously at the five or six bearers who busied themselves in various corners of the room. 'He is slippery. One never knows what is really happening at court. The Dowager-Begum has far too much influence. And he is an out-and-out heathen, with all the debauched habits that implies. I have had to have words with him about his zenana, and the number of his wives and *bibis*.'

'I had no idea that the Company was concerning itself with such matters,' Blake said, and scratched his ear. 'Been in Doora long?' I knew the tone. He considered the Resident an idiot.

The Resident glared at him. 'I regard it as my Christian duty to speak to him on the subject. I have been here nine months, since you ask. I must say, I find it hard to believe that your suit is worthy of such secrecy. Frankly, it is most important that relations with the Rao improve. My Company guests are coming with the express intention of pouring oil on the waters. I need your assurance at least that you will not cause any further decline.'

'I will certainly do my best, but I can give no guarantee as to how the Rao will take my request.'

The Resident looked most put out. 'Well, if the Company letter to the Rao is anything like this one here, I hardly think it will persuade him to receive you.'

'I had thought that was your job,' Blake said.

The Resident's face creased and folded into such a scowl that I wondered if it would ever regain its former shape.

'I should have been informed weeks ago that you were coming, sir,' he grumbled. 'It is customary for formal missions to be met at the state's boundary and escorted by the Rao's troop to the palace. But perhaps you did not know that.'

'As I said, Mr Crouch-Symington, we are not that kind of mission and we have travelled faster than a formal welcome could have been negotiated. May I assure you that I have travelled all over the north and into the Punjab in similar circumstances and never encountered any trouble in gaining audience with a native ruler.'

The Resident looked unconvinced. 'Well, I can offer you accommodation at the Residency for two nights. After that you will have to move elsewhere. We will be full for the celebrations. Now, I am exceedingly busy, and I am afraid I have no more time to give you. I will let you know the outcome of your request. The *khansaman* will show you to your rooms. Your sowars can sleep in the stables. Good day.' He turned, barked at one of the servants, gave a short, derisory wave, and walked out. I waited as long as I could bear.

'And you told me to be courteous!' I burst out. 'Why did you not tell him we are here looking for Mountstuart?'

'It wouldn't have made any difference.'

Though Blake had hardly been polite, I was surprised and down-cast that a Company Resident could prove so unwelcoming to emissaries from Government House. Blake, however, seemed quite unsurprised. Naturally he would not tell me why. But I suspected he was a little pleased. I even wondered if he was somehow responsible for the Resident's rudeness – perhaps he had deliberately held back some crucial paper. Late in the afternoon, however, we received a message summoning us for an audience the next day. I cast my sus-picions aside and gave myself over to thoughts of my first visit to an Indian prince's court.

Rao Vishwanath Singh's palace buildings were a long white fort with a line of elegant arched porticos along its second floor. It seemed to me to resemble nothing so much as a long white ship; a long white ship encrusted with a series of little white rotundas and domed buildings, a classical balustrade, several miniature Hindoo temples, and a lush garden full of exotic palms and fronds. These gave it a somewhat jumbled but energetic aspect.

The palace entrance was a vast imposing gateway of two mas-sive red sandstone pillars. Around their circumference were carved dancing nautch girls, two-humped camels and scaly ser-pents, and along the lintel two whiskered fish eyed each other. The doors themselves were huge battered slabs of oak held together by thick iron braces, coated in peeling green paint. Before them stood four of the Rao's guard in his personal livery: pink silk robes and green silk churidars, chainmail waistcoats and shining pointed helmets. They might have come straight from a poem by Mountstuart.

Mir Aziz dismounted and spoke quietly to the guards. Today he looked every inch an eastern emissary, his beard oiled and teased, his white kurta immaculate, an embroidered waistcoat, and on his feet gold embroidered slippers with curled toes. Manifesting barely a flicker of interest, the solidiers looked us over and slowly opened the gate. One of them called into the courtyard, another beckoned us in. On the other side we found ourselves in an enormous yard. At its centre stood a vast and grand old banyan tree, its runners creat-ing a curtain of brown tails down to the dirt under its crown of leaves. Hundreds of men in the Rao's various liveries wandered about. Close to, the walls of the fort had the same mildewed look as the buildings of Calcutta.

A groom had us hand our horses over to a gang of stable boys and then we were claimed by two natives, both in long white robes tied at the waist by red and gold sashes. We followed them through a smaller white gate before which two more heavily armed soldiers stood, through a small courtyard lined with carefully pruned trees, into a high-ceilinged anteroom painted green. There we were passed into the hands of a pair of rather more grandly dressed native officials, in long pink-embroidered jackets – jamas, which were fitted tight to the chest and arms and fell into a long pleated skirt. They in turn led us into a perfect cloistered garden. Four shaded arcades, supported by elaborately carved pillars on each side, enclosed a series of small square hedges, four small pools each in the shape of a tear drop, rows of orange marigold-like flowers, shrubs and small trees and fat-leafed palms in pots, and in the centre a circular pond on which deep-pink cupped lotuses floated.

Stalking the paths were four splendid peacocks. In the trees there were small green parakeets. Once again I had the sense of stepping into one of Mountstuart's poems. At the garden's far end was a high doorway and through this was another anteroom, this time dark-shadowed and dominated by tall black wooden doors beyond which one could hear the murmur of a crowd. Following Blake's example I removed my boots, whereupon a servant poured perfumed water over our hands.

'Remember,' Blake muttered. 'Do what I do. When the natives prostrate themselves, we go down on one knee and bow our heads. It's the Company's protocol. And whatever happens, don't show any irritation.'

Before I could press him for further explanation, the tall doors were opened and we walked into a large hall in which brightly dressed natives, all barefoot, were pressed around the walls. We took up position just inside the doors, with a dais and low throne opposite us. Blake and I were the only Europeans, and some of the natives stared openly at us. Most, however, took no interest. The room was like nothing I had ever seen. The lower walls were painted in bands of mustard yellow and a deep forest green. Above this was a cornice of scalloped arches picked out in gold, under which the plaster was painted with twisting stalks, tendrils and blossoms. Massive studded and embossed wooden pillars supported two sides of the hall, and from the high ceiling were hung two enormous elaborate glinting chandeliers. The throne, one of those low chairs that are called *gaddi*, which more resemble beds, was made of embossed silver, and the seat was a plump blue silk cushion. Before it on either side were a large pair of silver lions, embossed with patterns and bearing impossibly curling tails, each holding in one paw what looked like a mace. Between them was a red velvet carpet.

'Why are the lions there?' I whispered to Blake.

'The Indian princes do not prize originality. They all call themselves "Singh", which means lion.'

After some minutes a procession of sorts began. From a curved archway to one side of the throne, two natives appeared, each beating a drum. They were followed by a portly gentleman in a large orange silk turban, processing very slowly; then by a troop of bearers holding long pikes and giant feathered fans; and then by a cluster of bejewelled native gentlemen in embroidered jamas, carrying curved tulwars in ornamented scabbards. More finely dressed men emerged slowly, these carrying long staffs, followed by more servants holding fans and giant fly-swatters. And finally, in a tableau of silk-covered soldiers, servants and officials, a slender, finely made man who sparkled and wore pointed gold slippers – the only shoes in the room – padded slowly towards the throne, making no attempt to acknowledge his audience. He did not sit on the throne, however, but on the carpet before it, between the lions. The plump native in the orange turban approached the dais, with some difficulty went on to one knee and then flattened himself on the floor. The rest of the company followed. Blake knelt and bowed his head, and I did likewise, while straining to gain a glimpse of the Rao. After a pause, he stretched out his hand and, with an air almost of exasperation, gestured for the multitude to rise.

Orange Turban got awkwardly to his feet and the audience followed. He began to address the assembly in a deep, sonorous voice. It was clear that he knew the words well and that the audience had heard them before, for no one was very attentive. The speech went on for some time, and I took to studying our circumstances. Orange Turban I guessed must be the Grand Vizier or some such. He wore a heavy gold necklace over his thickly embroidered robe. He spoke with great earnestness, and made large emphatic gestures. Rao Vishwanath Singh, meanwhile, was much younger and had a small, very neat upturned moustache and a short, tightly clipped beard. He wore a wide turban of a deep burgundy silk, a gold and white embroidered robe and burgundy silk pyjamas. But the jewels were the thing: he glittered from his head to his gold slippers. On his turban was a jewel shaped like a curved flame and studded with diamonds and emeralds, with a spray of pearls dangling from it. Around his neck he wore string upon string of pearls – so many one could hardly see the tiny embroidered designs of his coat. Jewels sparkled in his ears, there were rings set with rubies on his fingers, and his robe was fastened by a belt of emeralds. The body beneath all this finery was rather thin and pale, and when I took a fleeting glance at his face he appeared to be suffering the event with ill-concealed irritation.

The Grand Vizier ceased speaking, and another, taller man, with a long face and deep-set eyes ringed with grey, came forward holding a scroll and feather quill. A tall, pulpit-like table was brought for him. He began to speak. I had assumed this would be our moment, and looked to Blake attentively for a sign. Instead a burly man accompanied by a boy of perhaps eleven or twelve came and knelt before the Rao, and began to speak in an urgent manner, pointing every so often at the boy. It was clear he was gripped by a sense of grievance and expected redress. The talk went back and forth between him and the scribe for what seemed an eternity. Eventually the Grand Vizier spoke, the Rao nodded, the man withdrew, evidently disappointed but apparently not surprised, and the scribe scribbled something on his paper. Once again I prepared myself for our summons. But now another native came forward and made his obeisances. Then another, and another. As suit followed suit, I fancied the native audience was whispering about the evident affront being done to us. I glanced at Blake. He did not move; his expression was almost serene. Mir Aziz, to one side of us, remained ramrod-straight; Sameer, behind me, was, I was sure, struggling to restrain himself. I felt myself begin to simmer.

It seemed to go on for hours. The Rao never spoke, but nodded occasionally with an air of great boredom. Finally the scribe beckoned Mir Aziz, and they conferred. The Rao stared at us coldly. Blake knelt, and I knelt. There was a silence. The Rao did not invite us to rise. Blake turned to the Grand Vizier, who looked nervously at the Rao and gestured for us to rise. Blake began to speak in a melodious, rhythmic tongue which I assumed must be Persian. The Grand Vizier nodded loftily.

From his breast pocket, Blake extracted a white envelope with dark seals and held it out. Mir Aziz took it and gave it to the scribe. After conferring with the Grand Vizier, the scribe began a great dramatic dumb show of opening the envelope with a great flourish, then plucking the letter from its envelope, unfolding and beginning to peruse it. He whispered urgently to the Grand Vizier. Blake cast his eyes down and began to speak clearly and quietly, but the Grand Vizier raised his hand to stop him and took the letter from the scribe. Blake fell silent. At that moment the Rao moved suddenly from his reclining position into a cross-legged one, and made it clear he wished to see the letter. The room was at once utterly still. Producing a silk square which had been tucked into his cummerbund, the Grand Vizier wrapped it around his hand – he had, I saw, grotesquely long thumbnails – took the letter and presented it to the Rao. The Rao looked over the letter. He scratched his nose delicately and then looked at us as if he would very much have enjoyed watching us being exquisitely tortured. The Grand Vizier's expression had shifted from diplomatic to insulted. He frowned with evident displeasure. Blake spoke again. We stood in awkward silence for what seemed like many minutes. The Rao spoke two words. The room stirred, uneasily. The Vizier smiled, but his smile did not reach his eyes, and he replied to Blake. Even I could tell the words were curt. Blake bowed again and withdrew to our former position. The Rao, meanwhile, stood up and swept out, followed by his entourage. The rest of audience left through another anteroom to the side in an orderly column of twos and threes, all studiously ignoring us.

I was both outraged and bitterly disappointed, but I had given my word and so I obediently followed Blake back through the garden. Now it seemed to me alien and chilly, the peacocks' cries shrill and strange. We came into the palace yard, where we waited while Sameer went in search of the horses.

'How could they treat us like that? Keeping us waiting as if we were nobodies! Summarily dismissing us! Publicly insulting the Company! But you knew, you expected something of this sort.'

'There was little that could be done. They were already ill-disposed towards us. Buchanan had nothing good to say of the Rao, and Jubbulpore regards him as an enemy. That witless Resident won't have helped things either. If I were Vishwanath Singh I would have taken his appointment as an affront. And we're a modest party – I have no real rank as far as Company matters go, and you're only a lieutenant, so the Rao and his officials would calculate we are easy to insult with impunity, as long as he's all honey with the Resident's grand guests. Also I suspect our letter of introduction was even more brusque than I expected it would be. All in all we were ripe for snubbing. The object of the audience was to show how angry he is, and that he will not help while relations continue as they are.'

'You did tell him we seek Mountstuart and have no interest in Thuggee?'

He gave me a look. 'I tried, but he would not have him spoken of – or at least he ignored my reference to him.'

'Why would our letter from Government House be brusque?'

'That is a good question and I have no good answer to it, except that Calcutta is often bad at bending a knee even when it would be politic to do so.'

I sighed with disappointment. 'So the Rao insults and dismisses us. We have no good reason to suppose that Mountstuart was even here – unless of course you know something which you choose not to share with me.' I paused, but he did not rise to the bait. Indeed, he looked almost too unconcerned and innocent. 'What is it that makes you so sure that Mountstuart was here?' I said, almost pleading.

'Just a feeling,' he said and, seeing how downcast I was, 'Be of good cheer, Avery.'

I would not be comforted. 'Then what the devil are we to do next?'

'We will enjoy the festivities.'

We moved out of the Residency the next day and were glad to go. There was something lowering about the place, not unassociated with Mr Crouch-Symington's dyspeptic ill humour. Mir Aziz had found us rooms in an old building not far from the palace which belonged to a native merchant. Blake claimed the few European billets had long since been taken. I took secret pleasure in the place's exoticness, its long arched windows and the old embroidered carpets and cushions draped everywhere, and the way it was permeated with oriental smells – spices, dust, incense. Nonetheless, regarding Mountstuart we were at stalemate. Blake, however, was almost cheerful. Once our few belongings were moved he prepared to go out, putting on a long robe over his native clothes and winding a pugree about his head. With his new moustache and the beginnings of a beard, he might almost have passed as a native.

'You wish me to be of assistance,' I said. 'Will you not take me with you?'

'No.'

There was an almost tangible air of anticipation about him. Most suspicious. I, meanwhile, lay back on my charpai, a picture of lassitude, examining my arm and the small scabbed holes where my stitches had been, opening and closing my fist, my books about me. The moment he left I followed swiftly behind. The narrow street was packed with crowds of bustling natives, the men in dhotis or long robes fluttering red, orange, blue, their wives in bright saris which covered their heads and sometimes their faces. Excited children capered and screamed, taking bites at some sticky sweetmeat clasped in their fists. Of course, I was lost almost immediately, but I was confident that I would find the bazaar in due course, and I did.

I found Blake at a pan stall with Mir Aziz. A crowd had gathered. I placed myself at a distance, by a seller of brass vessels, and gave the woman a few coins to let me stand in the shadow of her stall. A table had been set upon trestles with a bolster at one end, and upon it lay a native. Nearby sat two more men, and to each Blake administered a small ball of something – I was sure it was opium. The crowd about the pan stall chattered and examined little bottles and pouches.

Then, with a very precise flourish, Blake brought out a large soft purse and handed it to Mir Aziz. I could not see what was in it, but I guessed some tools of some sort. Blake pinned the man down by the shoulders, and Mir Aziz took up one of his implements, a long curved needle, placed across his nose a pair of spectacles that I had not seen before, and bent over his patient. He appeared to pull open the man's eye and brought his needle down into the eyeball itself. I held my breath and so did everyone else. The man, presumably well dosed with opium, did not flinch. From my post all I could tell was that Mir Aziz seemed to make cuts in the man's eye while his audience watched, fascinated. Then he washed it with what I guessed was melted ghee, and followed the same procedure with the other eye. Once it was complete, his patient sat up, threw up his hands and cried out with joy and amazement. Two men came forward to help him, but he pushed them away and hobbled to his feet, exclaiming. There was a great deal of chatter, the crowd surged around him and I could see nothing; when it parted, the man had been borne off. The next patient presented himself. Mir Aziz performed the procedure three more times, and each time the crowd gasped as the needle came down.

For some time afterwards neither Blake nor Mir Aziz could move from their places by the pan stall, so besieged were they by the enthusiastic crowd. But even after the people had dispersed, Blake and Mir Aziz continued to talk to the pan seller and a few others. Blake then went to the next stall, a barber's, and was shaved. And all the time he chattered away. Now I recalled all the times that he had departed from us unshaven and returned smooth-faced. Finally, he walked to a stall at which there seemed nothing to buy. It was draped in thick red cotton blankets and within it sat an old biddy with no teeth. He produced something and presented it to her with a small bow. She cackled and took it, and they began to talk. I had never seen Blake so at ease.

I departed then, and as I left the bazaar passed two or three European parties – including a lady with dark brown hair, swaddled in layers of muslin, and her entourage, who were examining a stall of silks. She made no attempt to disguise her curiosity about me, and under other circumstances I would have introduced myself, but I was eager to return to our rooms before Blake and so I made do with a polite nod. Blake returned some fifteen minutes later with two pairs of soft Bundelkand boots, and a vial of oil which he claimed was good for rheumatism. He was in an immensely good humour.

I said, 'So you were shaved in the bazaar, though Mir Aziz is himself a barber.'

He looked up.

'For who knows more of everyone's business than a barber?' I continued.

'Get a good look, did you?'

'I saw Mir Aziz performing some bizarre ritual with a needle upon the natives' eyes. It looked extraordinarily dangerous.'

'He does not cut them, he removes cataracts. He restores sight. It is an ancient and much-prized skill. It "opens doors", as they say.'

'Why would you not take me?' I said.

'You are of no use to me in the bazaar.'

'I do not see its great appeal,' I said.

'Open your eyes. Everything comes to the bazaar. All news, all truth, all lies end up there. Where do you think I first heard of the breaking machine?'

'So why could you not take me? My authority, my uniform, might encourage them to speak.'

He sighed. 'Listen, Avery. For most natives the Company barely touches their lives. Do you know how few Europeans there are here? Do you not recall that Mir Aziz did not see one of us until he was, what, sixteen? To them we are a burden to be borne and at best ignored. The sooner you understand that, the better. If you stand behind me in your redcoat, the words will dry in their mouths. In the bazaar you're of no use to me. But I speak better street Hindoostanee and Marathee – and half a dozen other tongues – than any European you'll ever meet. I used to know every barber and matchmaker between Calcutta and Lahore – the best carriers of news in all Hind. A few still remember me.' This was said wryly. 'What's more, I like being among them.'

I gritted my teeth and picked up one of my books.

'It is not your fault,' he said after a moment. 'The Company teaches its people to shrink from contact with the natives.'

'Why, thank you,' I said. Then, trying to drain the exasperation from my voice, 'So what great jewels of intelligence have you discovered today?'

'Tomorrow there's to be a public execution, before the festivities for the heir's seventh birthday begin. It's unusual – the princes generally like to show off their mercy at times of celebration. But this man's an assassin who got into the Rao's bedchamber and nearly killed him barely two weeks ago. All is not steady in the kingdom of Doora. The court is full of factions: the Rao is liked well enough – his mother the Dowager-Begum is very popular – but there are said to be several sardars who see themselves on the throne. They say the assassin belongs to one of them, but no one is sure whom. Vishwanath Singh is worried because he had no son. Everyone expects another attempt on his life before the heir is fully installed.'

'What d'you mean, he has no son? The heir's having his seventh birthday.'

'No. The Rao has an army of wives and concubines, but no son. He's adopted a cousin – it's a widespread practice among the native princes if a son can't be begotten. But the child only formally becomes his heir after the thread ceremony in a few days' time, in which he is initiated into his caste and religion. If the Rao dies before that, everyone knows what'll happen.'

I waited expectantly. 'What?'

He shifted impatiently. 'The Company will march in and take over, put in a puppet and that'll be the end of an independent Doora. Don't look surprised, the Company does it all the time, in the name of security or stability or order. And the Company particularly dislikes this Rao. In the bazaar they say that the Company has one or all of the Rao's rivals in its pocket.'

'I do not believe that!'

'It might be gossip. But it would give the Rao a good reason for hating the Company. And that, Mr Avery, is what I discovered in the bazaar.'

'And did the bazaar produce any news of the whereabouts of Mountstuart?'

'Not a word.'

Blake said we should watch the execution. I did not relish the thought, but I came with him. We were the only Europeans I could see, and our presence at first occasioned some attention but after a while the crowd turned back to the impending event. From the palace's red gateway there issued an elephant, led by its keeper, or mahout. The Rao's soldiers pushed the crowds back to clear a space for it. The elephant stood to the left of the gates. The crowd kept surging into the space, and the soldiers kept pushing it back. Then a thin column of more soldiers carrying muskets issued from the fort. To my surprise it was commanded by a European.

'Who's that?' I whispered.

'He'll be the Rao's master of artillery or some such. Native princes often have a European to train their armies. Former Company, or more likely French.'

The line of men split in half to reveal a dirty creature in shackles, escorted by two soldiers bearing bayoneted muskets. People in the crowd shouted out angrily when they saw him. The wretch was barely aware of where he was. He looked about mutely and dazedly, unaware of the huge beast before him. In Calcutta we had all heard of native rulers using elephants to execute miscreants, some-times letting them torture a man for hours, but I had not expected to see the thing in the flesh and I felt my gorge rise. The secret pleas-ure I had taken in Doora entirely evaporated.

The man was led by his two captors towards the elephant. He made no attempt to resist, and was slowly pushed into a kneeling position with his back to the crowd and his head before the ele-phant. A rope was tied between his shackles and a large ring bolted into a heavy cornerstone so he could not move. The elephant was coaxed forward. A soldier appeared with a drum. From the red gate came a deputation of men in fine dress. I recognized the Grand Vizier and some of the faces from among the Rao's sardars. They stood in a cluster outside the fort gates. They did not look pleased to be present. Blake whispered with Mir Aziz.

'Who are they?' I muttered.

'They are the leaders of the court factions. There's the diwan, the Rao's first minister' – he nodded at Orange Turban – 'and the Rao's eldest cousin, and his senior sardar, the richest man in Doora. I don't know the others.'

The elephant lifted its foot. The mahout moved it into position over the condemned man's head. I held my breath. I looked away. There was a drum beat, and an odd muffled crack. I will not describe the scene when I looked up. We all turned quickly away and made our way back to our rooms.

'Well, you have reminded me of all that disgusts me about this country, Blake.'

'I take no pleasure in watching a man die. But was that worse than the execution we saw in Jubbulpore?'

'It was the most barbarous thing I have ever witnessed. Do not try some appalling comparison.'

'Why not? The man probably felt nothing, and it was over far more quickly than for those poor creatures who swung.'

'Felt nothing! Good God, man, his brains were spread all over the town square! And he had no doubt been tortured beforehand.'

'Not so different from Jubbulpore then.' I turned away, disgusted. 'Did you not see that he had been heavily drugged?' he persisted.

'He was hardly conscious, and the beast had been trained to kill quickly.'

'Damn me, Blake, if you hate the Company so much, why do you still work for it?'

He looked at me and passed his hand through his hair.

Some hours later Mir Aziz brought a message that, along with the rest of the Resident's guests, we had been invited to the banquet given for the Rao's heir.

'It would be too great a slight to ignore us completely,' Blake had said complacently. 'And a certain well-placed bribe helped.' Mir Aziz inclined his head.

The next morning we arrived at the Residency in two hired palanquins, with Mir Aziz and Sameer as our *khitmatgurs*, and took our place at the back of the procession of Company guests on horses and in palanquins with their platoons of servants and sepoys. News of our disgrace clearly preceded us, for no one attempted to speak to us, though we received more than our share of covert stares. At the front with the Resident I could see a very senior Company officer, a major general, riding a splendid black Arab, and next to him an elaborate palanquin, no doubt his wife's. The Resident himself was attempting to clamber on to a modest-sized elephant with a green and gold howdah atop. He did not appear to enjoy the experience.

When all was ready we left the Residency yard, one by one, for the street, joining the many small, brightly arrayed processions on their way to the fort. As before, we entered through the red gate, but now we turned left towards the fort's large gardens in which a series of large tents had been pitched.

We alighted in the palace courtyard, where we were encouraged to stand to await the arrival of the Rao, who was, Mir Aziz told me, making a tour of the city with his heir before returning for the banquet. Then through the red stone gates came native soldiers, six abreast marching in step, in spiked helmets and chainmail, holding their swords in their scabbards, their faces severe. After them came scarlet-turbanned natives in white embroidered pyjamas, some bearing muskets, others carrying red and gold pennants. They were followed by horsemen, their scarlet turbans striped with gold thread, and their horses draped in red cloth embroidered with gold, each carrying a small arched silver howdah; musicians blowing long thin brass trumpets; bearers with giant fringed parasols around a cage on wheels holding two sleepy pale tigers; ten long, slim, black-spotted cheetas held on leashes by ten long, slim women in gold-edged saris. Beyond the gates the crowd cheered and whooped. There were more elephants, perhaps twenty; then at the end of the procession, two large elephants of identical size, each with a jewelled headdress and their legs wound about with gold chains, pulled a vast wooden cart painted scarlet and decorated in beaten gold filigree. About the cart, bearers strolled, carrying golden parasols, silver rods, giant fans made of peacock feathers, and huge red fly-whisks. Upon it sat the Rao, inclining his head this way and that; next to him was a small boy and behind him three retainers.

The procession slowed and some parts disappeared into the fort while others stopped. The tigers' cage was set down by the tent. The Rao and his heir, a small thin child with a shaved head and a white dhoti, a strip of gold cloth around his waist and a heavy gold necklace on his small chest, slowly climbed from their cart, and with a band of soldiers and courtiers they walked into the tent. The various parties followed behind, each passing the cage of tigers. When it was our turn, I could not forebear from staring at the creatures and saw that not only was their fur so pale it was almost a ghostly white, but their eyes were blue like sapphires.

'White tigers!' I whispered to Blake. 'I thought they were a fairy tale.'

The tent was vast and airy, and one side was entirely open. It was lined with crimson cloth, every inch of which was embroidered with gold thread in serpentine patterns. Rugs and carpets covered the vast floor. In the centre of the tent sat a small orchestra playing long, stringed native instruments, issuing the usual unearthly twangs.

On a small dais behind them sat the Rao and his heir, cross-legged on a velvet rug. Europeans were seated on low chairs to his left; on the other side of the tent, to the Rao's right, hundreds of natives sat on rugs, dressed in their brightest best and talking animatedly. Approximately one-third of the tent to the right of the Rao was screened off by a curtain stretched between bamboo poles in which there were many small holes. The Resident, the Major General and his wife and the other Europeans, proud civilians of a type I recognized from Calcutta, were closest to the Rao. We, by contrast, were as far away from him as a European could be.

A troop of servant girls, all slim and pretty, threw necklaces of fresh flowers over our necks, and others offered us a small bowl of pale white porridge.

'Almond-paste to wash your hands,' Blake muttered before I had – as I intended – gathered a spoonful and put it in my mouth.

Another fleet of serving girls brought silver bowls of water to rinse it off. Then fifty *khitmatgurs* brought dishes in silver bowls: curries and pilaus, roasted meats, rice with almonds, dressed with a gold and silver leaf. There were small cups of chilled sherbert. Blake immediately gathered up rice with his fingers. When I hesitated, a servant promptly brought a silver spoon and fork. There were so many bearers and servants Mir Aziz and Sameer were all but idle behind us. Wine arrived too. Having surveyed and helped myself to the constant stream of courses, I stole a glance at the Rao and his party. He seemed all glitter and shine. He wore a large pink silk turban with a band of gold damask around it and a turban jewel – a *sarpech*, Blake called it – of sapphires with a spray of pearls. Once again there were strings and strings of pearls about his neck, and in his lap he held a sword in a jewelled scabbard. He ate nothing, but between him and the Resident, and creating a distance between them, was a large silver huqqa with an impossibly long hose wound round and round about it. Behind him stood a cluster of servants holding giant horse-hair swatters and peacock-feather fans, and amidst them were more gaudily dressed guards carrying guns and swords. There were, I now saw, armed soldiers at every entrance of the tent. The Rao's little cousin looked rather tired and overwhelmed. He was flanked, I noted, by two large guards who effectively shielded him from the native guests. Occasionally the

Rao would bend over the child and say a quiet word. Otherwise he listened, expressionless, to the Resident and the Major General, with whom he made occasional desultory exchanges. The Resident looked enormously awkward while at the same time trying to appear courteous. Since I had little reason to like either man, I had to admit the scene was rather amusing.

Periodically natives would come to pay their respects, prostrating themselves upon the ground and actually kissing the Rao's slipper.

'Is that not a little much?' I whispered to Blake after the third instance of foot kissing.

He looked up from scooping a handful of rice into his mouth and shrugged. 'These Rajputs claim to be descended from the sun or the moon or some star. Likely they believe a kiss on the toes is all we mere mortals deserve. I've always had more of a fancy for the Maratha princes – they pride themselves on being descended from cowherds and farmers.'

I snorted.

The musicians took up their instruments, and three wrestlers, tattooed with henna and wearing jewelled vests, lifted weights, juggling clubs and climbing poles. Then came the nautch dancers, slender girls with dark-painted eyes wearing fine pleated petticoats that flew out when they turned in circles.

At some point I became aware that we were being watched. Among the second division of European guests, several chairs down from the Resident, the large lady with dark brown hair whom I had seen in the bazaar was staring straight at us. Catching my eye, she raised her eyebrows. I looked away. When I looked back she was in deep consultation with the man next to her, whom I recognized as the European who had commanded the Rao's troops at the execution. With the help of her *khitmatgur*, the European gentleman and several servant girls, she was bundled rather awkwardly to her feet, and approached the Rao on the hand of the European. She stopped a respectful ten feet from him, and made a deep curtsey. The Rao waved his hand at her and she – somewhat unsteadily – rose up. The Rao addressed her. I was most surprised to observe that he spoke with a good deal more animation than he had shown to anyone else. I had the impression that the Resident and the Major General did not like this one bit. After a short exchange, the small heir stood up, came forward and took the lady's hand, and they both made their way to the white curtain, and disappeared behind it.

'Where has she gone?' I asked, though I had already guessed.

'That is the *parda*. The Rao's mother and his wives will be behind it, watching through those small holes.' Blake was looking as cheerful as I had ever seen him.

'She was staring at us.'

'She was,' he said.

The meal ended, the servant girls reappeared, doused our hands in gram flour, rinsed them with water and wiped them with attr of roses. The Resident stood and drank to the Rao's health and his son's accession to manhood. He bowed low once to the Rao and once, awkwardly, to the curtain. With an expression that somehow managed to combine graciousness with mild disdain, the Rao got to his feet, inclined his head to his European guests, and turned to his native guests, who applauded and bent as low as they could over their dishes. Then, surrounded by his entourage, he processed slowly out of the tent, acknowledging one or two persons on his way with a regal nod. When he passed us he shot us a brief but particularly cool look.

The *khitmatgurs* returned, carrying baskets, and began to cast objects from them at the guests. On closer observations these turned out to be precious stones, embroidered shawls, bolts of cloth, and long necklaces made of tinsel silver. The Company visitors stood motionless, letting the precious gifts slide off them on to the floor. The Company ordered that the fruits of the native princes' legendary generosity could not be kept for personal gain; disobedience led to instant dismissal. Anything accepted out of courtesy must be handed immediately to the Company coffers. I watched as two red stones slid from my shoulder down to my feet. They were obviously rubies. Just one would have relieved me of a good part of my debts. I left them nestling in a fold of the rug.

Blake smiled.

*

The next morning we received an invitation to call on a Mrs Parkes. Who could it be, I thought, but the lady from the Rao's feast? I was certain Blake knew for sure, but he evinced such an air of secretive self-satisfaction that I would not ask him. I dressed in my best uniform, but when Blake presented himself he looked nothing like the Company's man. He wore the most casual of civilian outfits, with a loose muslin summer shirt, baggy pyjamas of a distinctly native cut and a wide-brimmed straw hat.

'What?' he said, when he caught me staring. 'You're sucking your teeth like some up-country matron.'

'I am a little surprised by your toggery, Mr Blake,' I said.

'I assure you it'll pass muster.'

Mrs Parkes was staying at a white bungalow of recent construction on the far side of Doora. We found her in a room without chairs or much order of any kind. There were bolsters and embroideries scattered about and a thick velvet rug. Several boxes seemed to have spilled their contents on the ground. A number of pencil sketches were propped up against a wall and servant women bustled about looking busy but not appearing to accomplish very much. Mrs Parkes sat cross-legged against a pile of worn velvet cushions, wrapped in layers of muslin and a large shawl of fine pink wool with gold thread woven through it. She was attempting to play the sitar, the long stringed instrument beloved of the natives, and she leant the hollow chamber of the thing against her left knee as she plucked a jumble of vibrating notes.

It was not at all what I had expected.

'Gentlemen,' said Mrs Parkes, looking up from her instrument, then laying it carefully to one side. She was, of course, the lady from the feast. 'I would stand, but I have reached the point in my life when I find elevating myself from a cross-legged position requires both effort and a minimum of two servants. Would you mind perhaps sitting instead?' She patted a couple of bolsters. 'I have chairs, but the move from the Residency was such an undertaking that I have not had the heart to unpack them. And, of course, one can only play the sitar cross-legged. Also I find that despite the aches in my joints, I rather enjoy reclining on cushions. And if my rheumatism comes on

I find a cube of opium helps tremendously – though it gives me a terrible headache in the morning.'

I had never been received in this manner by a lady, and for a moment was rendered quite dumb. But Blake answered immediately, assuring her that he was a firm believer in the efficacy of opium and that we would like nothing better than to recline on her bolsters. He sat down with far greater ease than I, as his pyjamas were looser than my close-cut military trews. Mrs Parkes called for tea, which was placed on a low table with a round brass top. All the while, I was aware that her eyes were alight with curiosity. She was a full-boned, rounded woman, but her voluminous wrappings made her seem larger than she was, and her thick chestnut hair, piled and pinned on her head, showed signs of grey. She had broad, rather emphatic features which had once been pretty, but her face was still rendered engaging by the liveliness of her eyes and her intelligent expression. I guessed she was some way on the far side of forty.

'Now, my dear young men, you have come from Calcutta, I suppose? You must tell me all the news. It is a woefully long time since I was there.'

'Lieutenant Avery is the man for Calcutta stories, Mrs Parkes,' Blake said, picking up a delicate tea cup which seemed far too small for his hands. Once again I trotted out my little cache of gossip, and Mrs Parkes made suitable expostulations. When my stories had been exhausted, I asked her how she came to be in Doora, and she said that her husband was often ill during the cool season, and since they had no children, it was better that she travelled. I would have inquired further had not Blake told her of our attacks by robbers and dacoits, and had me show off my wound, whereupon Mrs Parkes said she had an ointment from a Mahommedan gentlewoman in Delhi that was marvellous for healing scars and she would send it round to our lodgings. Blake asked if she had been there lately – he had not visited for years and I had seen nothing of the north. She described the red fort and the court of the old Emperor and how she had sailed down the Ganges in a pinnace. She talked extremely well. Blake said much had changed since he was there, and then he frowned and said he'd heard the Methodists had moved in, in force. I had never heard him so warmly talkative.

Mrs Parkes said, 'I am not an admirer of the fashionable new piety. I see ambitious civilians I knew years ago in Calcutta who barely went to church, praying themselves into higher salaries. And all this talk of converting the natives, and how we are tainted by proximity to them and their beliefs. It was not thus when I first came to Calcutta.'

'Nor was it for me, Mrs Parkes,' said Blake. I was a little non-plussed by the forthrightness with which she expressed such views, but I could tell that all the time she was watching and weighing us up, and I had the strangest feeling that there was some current between Blake and herself which I did not fully understand.

'When I came to India fifteen years ago,' Mrs Parkes went on, 'there was some respect and a wholesome curiosity about the customs and languages and great achievements of the natives. We visited the baboos and we learnt much from them. I learnt Hindoostanee, and a world opened to me. Ten years later Bentinck was trying to sell the Taj Mahal for marble to put a few pennies in the Company treasury. And now youngsters coming out here are encouraged to have as little as possible to do with the natives – I am sorry, Mr Avery, if I offend you, but I speak of what I see.'

'Not at all, Mrs Parkes,' I said, and with as much bite as I felt safe to venture, 'and I am sure Mr Blake entirely agrees with you.'

'Does he indeed.'

There was a pause. Mrs Parkes lifted her cup to her lips, sipped, swallowed, and said, 'And so, my dear sirs, please satisfy a matron's curiosity and tell me what two young Company men are doing in the city of Doora during the heir's coming-of-age?'

I expected Blake would fob her off, but instead he said, 'We come from Jubbulpore, Mrs Parkes, where we saw Major Sleeman.'

'Ah yes, Major Sleeman. A remarkable man. You had the full tour, I suppose?'

There was something very dry in the way she said this, and Blake caught her eye and grinned at her as if they were sharing some joke, and said, 'Indeed we did.'

He is flirting with her, I thought. And the notion was so startling that I almost choked on my tea.

'I was in Futtehpore in 1830 when they found three bodies in a well. I followed the articles about the Thugs in the *Calcutta Gazette* for several years. I even saw a Thug trial in Cawnpore. But of course, Mr Blake, you have not yet answered my question.'

'No, Mrs Parkes,' he said. He leant forward and rubbed his lower lip as if choosing his words carefully. 'We're here to see the Rao, but he's not inclined to see us. Still, I think you know that already. There are many good reasons why he would not wish to see us. To begin, we are a somewhat eccentric, even lowly, party. I have a peculiar status – they call me a "Special Inquiry Agent" – and Avery is all but a griffin.'

Rather than looking offended, Mrs Parkes seemed amused.

'As a mid-level civilian's wife who travels alone, I am quite used to such attitudes.'

'And of course the Rao might well be feeling less than warm towards the Company.'

I began to feel uneasy.

'It may interest you to know, Mr Blake, that the Rao's zenana is abuzz with talk of the two handsome Company officers and how they are not in good odour with the Rao. Usually they see only whiskery old Company officials.'

'The zenana?' I said, extremely impressed. A zenana is the Indian equivalent of the Turkish harem.

'Don't get yourself too excited, Avery,' Blake said, and I scowled. 'A zenana is the home of the women of the court. Its true importance is as a centre of gossip and intrigue, not as a den of concubines. The Rao's zenana is ruled over by his mother, who is the former regent and a person of great influence at court. Isn't that right, Mrs Parkes?'

'So I hear, Mr Blake.'

'I think you know very well, Mrs Parkes. You went behind the *parda* yesterday and were escorted by the Rao's European.'

Mrs Parkes smiled, 'Monsieur Lartigue, the Rao's master of artillery.'

'They call you "the lady of the zenanas".'

Mrs Parkes waved for some more tea. 'They do?'

'Fanny Parkes, the confidante of begums and bais. You taught the Bai of Scindia to ride side-saddle and persuaded her to go into exile in Benares on a Company pension. You are a friend of the old Begum of Oudh and, of course, of the Dowager-Begum of Doora. I heard she calls you the "great aunt of my granddaughter".'

Mrs Parkes' eyes narrowed. 'My goodness, Mr Blake, you are well informed. You will know then that I am not so much famous as infamous. These days the Company suspects those who see beauty in the lives of the natives, and I am accused of befriending native ladies for my own enrichment. But I am useful to Residents' wives and the Governor General's sisters as a translator, for they will never learn Hindoostanee themselves and they have no interest in understanding local customs and courtesies.' She spoke in a hard, matter-of-fact tone.

'Mrs Parkes,' said Blake, 'I do know you. We met in Calcutta many years ago, but I don't think you remember me.'

She stared at him now. 'I do not, and yet I felt when I saw you that there was something familiar about you.'

'I was a shrimp of a boy learning Hindoostanee from the same moonshee as you. I was a holy terror, the regiment's mascot, a drummer boy with no manners. I kicked your horse and spat at your sircar.'

'Bless me!' The expression on Mrs Parkes' face mirrored my own. She stared at him. 'A filthy-mouthed little rascal who frightened the horses and thieved from the bazaar . . . Jemmy, Jemmy Blake!'

Blake nodded.

'I would come to Writers' Building to have my lesson,' she continued, 'it gave me an excuse to walk through the bazaar, and you had the lesson afterwards. You were only a boy, but already far better than me. They had you at Sanskrit and Persian before long.'

'I was older than I looked, but yes, madam. They taught me Pashtu, Marathee and Gujuratee. I remember that you were kind to me. You gave me sweets and once a rupee.'

'Did I? I had quite forgotten and I am sure you did not deserve it,' she said. 'You knew a great many words that I had never heard before, and I hope never to again. You were thrashed for it too. You were someone's experiment. I always wondered what became of you. Bless me! And now you are the Company's . . .'

'Special Inquiry Agent. My relations with the Company are complicated. I became a captain, but it's a long story. I lost my appetite for certain things. Lost many things.'

She sighed. 'All our relations with the Company have become complicated. Are you married? Have you family?'

He hesitated. 'Had. Lost that too, madam. A wife.'

'I am so sorry.'

'And I. But if I may test your patience, I would very much like to know what else they are saying in the zenana.'

Mrs Parkes looked at him appraisingly for a moment. 'They say that your letter of introduction was brusque to the point of rudeness, and your – forgive me – lack of rank is an insult. They say your story of being attacked outside Doora is most ill-timed, deliberately ill-timed, perhaps. They say you came to harangue the Rao about his relations with the Company and to accuse him of confidentially protecting brigands and even Thugs. But I think you had guessed all that already. Some in the zenana are more charitable. They say how can two such personable young men be up to no good?'

He stared back at her. I might as well have not been in the room. 'And what do you think?'

'The Resident seems quite as exasperated by you as the Rao. As far as I am concerned that is in your favour. But then again you could simply be extremely tactless. I wonder, however, if you haven't come to ask the Rao about Xavier Mountstuart.'

'Mrs Parkes,' Blake said quietly, and his eyes glittered, 'you are a clever, clever woman.'

She gave him a frank, but slightly mocking, look. 'I am a silly, easily flattered woman.'

'Has he been here?'

'I really do not know. There was the whisper of a rumour in the zenana about the *malik-al-shuara*, but that's all. Nothing certain, but enough to pique my curiosity. He has not been seen in public, but the Rao's palaces are very large. I wonder why he would be in hiding?'

Blake shook his head. 'Perhaps you have heard rumours?'

'Not for the sake of a *roman-à-clef* about Calcutta, I'll be bound. Something about things going awry in Jubbulpore? But stories like that always followed Mr Mountstuart. The thing is, as I have been thinking about what I remember of you, Jemmy Blake, I recall that you knew Mountstuart in Calcutta. You were his experiment, weren't you?'

'In a manner of speaking.' He pushed himself back from the table, in retreat. 'I had hoped that perhaps you might help us to get back in to see the Rao.'

She laughed. 'I see. You want me to talk to the Begum. To ask her if she will persuade the Rao to reconsider your suit.'

'Just so.'

For a moment her face fell, as if disappointed, but she recovered herself quickly.

'It will be at the farthest reaches of my poor influence. And I am still not sure if I should help you. I like and respect the Begum more than I can say, I would do nothing to hurt or hinder her. And it is presumably the Company that has sent you to find Mountstuart?'

'It is. But I swear to you, Mrs Parkes, my intentions are honest.'

'Yes, well, honest intentions do not always beget honest acts. I will do what I can, though I can promise nothing. I am a fool with a bad taste for meddling. And I must leave in two days for Mirzapore to meet the Governor General's caravan to the north. The Misses Eden want a translator to conduct them through the zenanas. I hope for both our sakes you are who you say you are, and who I would like to think you are. Neither of us will come out of this well if you are just another Company agent. I will tell them that you have a particular relationship with the *malik-al-shuara*, which explains your peculiar status and why you are here.'

'May I ask, Mrs Parkes, if we had baulked at sitting on the floor, would we have passed the test?'

'No, Jemmy Blake, you would not. Do close your mouth, dear Mr Avery. You have such a nice face and it does not become you.'

*

I could not sleep for thinking over what Blake had spilled out so freely to Mrs Parkes; descriptions that prompted more questions than they had answered. I wondered about his association with Mountstuart – how close it had been and still remained – and how a drummer boy had risen to the rank of captain, only to lose it.

The next day we received a letter from Mrs Parkes – which I transcribe here – and a small package.

My dear Mr Blake,

What an extraordinary sleight of fate has brought us together after all these years! Or is it fate, I wonder? I cannot help feeling there is something of what I recall of young Jemmy – quick, never trusting to chance and too clever for most mortals – in the older Mr Blake.

I have entrusted this letter to my sardar-bearer, a man I have known for many years and whom I entirely trust. I do not know quite why, but I feel inclined to advise you to make sure this letter is seen by no one other than yourself and Mr Avery. I saw the Begum yesterday. I enclose the following description because I am afraid I cannot resist an opportunity to show off my own cleverness – you will have to forgive me – and because I fancy it will entertain the boy I knew, and will interest the young almost-griffin Mr Avery, in whom I detect a taste for the romantic and the exotic. Am I right, Mr Blake?

I found Her Highness seated on a plain wood gaddi surrounded by her attendants, ladies and several daughters. She is small and delicate, and carries herself with that light-footed grace which we European ladies so noticeably lack. She has tiny hands and feet, and a deep, melodious voice. Her hair is the colour of gunmetal and drawn simply back from her face. Because she is a widow she has set ornament and comfort aside and wears plain cotton, and no adornment but a couple of simple gold bracelets, and sleeps on the bare ground. But have no doubt, she is still a force in the land. When the Rao was a child and sent to Calcutta, she ruled the kingdom with such sense and moderation that the local Resident never interfered and rather sang her praises to Calcutta. Now she has taken off the mantle of power – with some relief,

I fancy – but it is well known that the Rao still consults her on thorny matters. Mr Avery may be interested to learn that most of the ladies of the zenana are lively looking, rather than beautiful, and most are quite old, attendants of the Begum since youth. They all dress with the utmost decorum, in long petticoats and trousers beneath, save for their pretty hinna-ed feet. But one, the Rao's newest wife, is truly ravishing. She wore a small tight shirt and a long piece of purple Benares silk with a golden border wrapped around her, and walks with tiny, graceful steps. She has velvet brown eyes, and a small mouth like a perfect piece of ripe fruit. She wore toe rings and silver ankle bracelets, and round her neck were the ubiquitous strings of pearls. The Rao's new wife is the niece of his first minister. Between her and the Begum there is said to be little love lost – I leave you to draw your own conclusions – though before me they behaved to each other with the greatest courtesy. Nevertheless, this led me to think that I would have to be careful in how I broached the matter of your suit.

I had arranged to bring a remarkably beautiful Arab which belongs to my cousin to the zenana, as the Begum is a good judge of horse-flesh, and has always been curious about the side-saddle. It gave me a chance to lead the Begum into her courtyard, away from the new wife, who takes no interest in such things. The courtyard, incidentally, is a vast space, handsomely laid out with fountains and paths, and walls high enough so that even a man standing upon an elephant could not see over them. The Begum keeps two rhinoceroses within it, and feeds them oranges and sweetmeats – though today they were locked away. She liked my horse and examined it with the help of several rather fearsome female attendants who carry tulwars. I had promised to demonstrate the side-saddle, and so wore a black riding-habit, which caused great amusement among the ladies. They said I look like a European doctor and frightfully ugly! Nevertheless, I put the Arab through his paces and showed them how English ladies ride.

The Begum was vastly amused by my exhibition and insisted I try a native saddle with great iron stirrups on either side. I was persuaded to change into Rajput costume, and mounted one of the Begum's horses, feeling a little like Queen Elizabeth giving that speech before the Armada.

The scene appeared to have pleased the Begum, and so I requested that I might speak to her on a difficult matter, making it clear that I would desist if the subject displeased her.

I reminded her of the two Company officers in bad odour with the Rao. Naturally she knew all about you, as she had seen you through the curtain at the banquet. I told her, as succinctly as possible, that I had known you as a child; that you had known Mountstuart for many years; and that I suspected that your quest was not quite what the Rao assumed it must be. I told her, knowing that it might be a mistake, that you had fallen as foul of the Resident as of the Rao – which interested her mightily. She was nevertheless hesitant. She said she would think upon the matter, and determine if she could raise it with her son. She intimated that the matter was not at all straightforward. As we spoke, the newest wife appeared in the courtyard saying that the attendants had told her that my riding had been most entertaining and she wished to see the horse. The Begum changed the subject instantly. I am sure that she believes the new wife to be the First Minister's spy, sent to report on the extent of her influence over the Rao and to limit it.

When I left, my hands were powdered with attr, I was presented with pan, and an attendant sprinkled me copiously with rose-water – as you will know, the more lavishly one is doused in rose-water the greater the compliment, so I concluded with some relief that I had intrigued rather than insulted my hostess.

This morning one of the Begum's male servants came to tell me that an audience with the Rao was not possible, but that you and Mr Avery are to be invited on the Rao's shikar, which takes place tomorrow at Vishnagarh as part of the celebrations. It will be a tiger hunt, most unusually for the season, but apparently the Major General has asked especially. I do not know if the invitation is on the part of the Begum or the Rao, but it is at least a start. An invitation under normal circumstances is regarded as an honour. If you conduct yourselves well, it is possible it may lead to something. I am sorry I cannot conjure more. Clearly there is more to this whole matter than a simple audience. But you know that better than I.

I am making my final preparations for quitting Doora, and so I shall not have the chance to tell you this myself, nor the pleasure of satisfying my curiosity as to the consequences of my endeavours, and yours. What-

ever the outcome, I hope our paths may cross again and I sign myself,
your friend,

    Mrs Fanny Parkes

P.S. I also send a pot of the ointment I told you of, for Lieutenant Avery's
arm.

'What was Mrs Parkes like when you first knew her in Calcutta?'
I said.

'She was prim, but she never shrank from the country, she liked
it. Always off to the bazaar, or to see some puja festival, even then.
I remember nothing about the husband. He was said to go mad in
the winter, and she would go travelling. Over the years she has done
a number of people I know a few discreet good turns.'

Chapter Eleven

The thought of going on a Raja's *shikar* – and a tiger hunt at that – overthrew all thoughts of Jubbulpore and even of Mountstuart. I re-read his description of stalking the beasts in *Lays of the Rajputana Hills*, and cleaned my sword and rifle again, putting from me the thought that I might not be up to firing it. Sameer was quite as excited as me. For my Hindoostanee lesson that afternoon Mir Aziz made me translate his boasts: 'We shall stalk the tiger and bring it down! We shall outdo the Rao's heavy-footed hunters!' Tigers, Mir Aziz said, were more common in Doora than anywhere else in India, and they were hunted as much as pests as royal game. But in the lush greenery after the monsoon they would be hard to catch sight of. Blake, however, had lost some of the almost-cheerfulness I had detected in him at his reintroduction to Mrs Parkes. Mir Aziz thought he might be disappointed about the *shikar*. 'You may be seeing the tigers, Avery Sahib, but more than likely, no Rao.'

We rode the six miles to the Rao's lakeside residence at Vishnagarh that night so as to be ready for the early start the next morning. The lake shone and undulated like silk. Next to it a city of embroidered tents had risen up – or rather three distinct communities of tents: one for native courtiers, one for European visitors, and the smallest for tradesmen and hangers-on. A little to the left of the tents and separated by an avenue of trees, the Rao's palace was a rambling complex of white domes and pediments and curving balustrades. Beyond it was thick jangal.

Mir Aziz repaired to speak to the chief huntsman. He reported that a part of the jangal had been separated from the rest with stakes and fences, and within it there were said to be several tigers, perhaps up to five, including a parent and cub which had been preying on local livestock. His other news confirmed what he had predicted. While the Rao and his chosen few would be hunting on elephants, we Europeans would be watching and shooting from machans – platforms constructed in the trees. The tigers would be lured to the machans by buffalo carcasses that had been left nearby the day before, and driven towards them by a line of beaters. Sameer and I were disheartened. We had imagined ourselves stalking the creatures on foot or on horseback, not trapped on some platform.

Before the sun rose, a large crowd of villagers had gathered outside the Rao's palace. Some held torches, some carried drums, and several bore elderly firearms that looked as if they had not been fired in a century. The Rao arrived on horseback with a party of sardars. On the far side of the multitude there was a large canvas screen kept aloft by long bamboo posts tied to it at intervals, behind which I guessed some of the Rao's zenana sheltered. A *shikari* led us to a spot just next to the Resident's party of himself, the Major General and four other gentlemen. There was no disguising our mutual antipathy. Mr Crouch-Symington just about stirred himself to acknowledge us, but his guests ostentatiously looked in any direction but ours. Blake ignored them, but I found their rudeness awkward, the more so when it became clear that we would all be placed either on the same machan or on two close together.

The beaters, armed with their drums and torches, were split into smaller groups and sent in single file to create a vast circle which would drive the tigers towards the Rao and the machans. The Rao's party disappeared into the jangal on several elephants, then mounted *shikaris* led us through the jangal into a great meadow at the far end of which there was a ravine and a waterhole, by which were the carcasses of two water buffalo. The machans were balanced in the trees nearby, hidden in the leaves. The Major General, two gentlemen and a fleet of bearers carrying water bottles, drinks, metal trays of refreshments, and ammunition, climbed awkwardly into one. There was nothing for the Resident to do but to bring his spare guest to join us – along with a slightly smaller, but still lavish, contingent of servants with trays of food and sherberts. Mr Crouch-Symington's tight yellow face was a picture of vexation. He nodded slightly at us then positioned himself and his friend as far from us as possible. Hidden in the trees behind us were two *shikaris* on horseback, each brandishing a long spear. Despite myself, I began to feel excited. Blake looked out across the meadow.

'What?' I said.

'I never thought there was much sport in rounding up creatures and driving them into an ambush.'

Mir Aziz had told us the beaters would start on the signal of a single gun-shot and then move forward in an orderly line without a break. But the shouts, drums and flashes suddenly came with no warning, from a ridge some way north of us. Falteringly, confusedly, the other beaters followed.

Order was lost almost at once. From our platform we could just see some sections advancing quickly in one direction to volleys of shots, and others holding back or moving in the opposite direction. There was no line. We waited.

'You are gloominess itself, Blake,' I said after a while.

'I don't like it,' he said. 'These hunts are usually organized with great care. This is not. With the line broken and all in disarray the creatures may turn back on the beaters.'

We waited for what seemed like a long while. Then from the east came a wild beating of drums and great shouting. It sounded as if something ill had occurred, but we could see nothing. We waited. The Resident and his guest helped themselves to their refreshments and murmured quietly to each other.

Then, out of the trees, a tiger came padding swiftly but calmly as you please, heading for the waterhole. I raised my gun, but as I did so, there was a cracking below us, and to my horror the machan listed and began to slide downwards. I could see the Major General's party in their machan across the ravine, standing in consternation. The machan gave a shudder and jerked off its branch on to the ground. Blake, Mir Aziz, Sameer and I – all leaning against the paling that ran about each side of the machan so as to prevent one misstepping and falling out – grasped on to it and protected ourselves from the worst of the fall, but I swear I felt its impact through every bone in my body.

The bearers – trays and broken glass about them – lay sprawled and dazed. But in a worse state were the Resident and his friend who had sat themselves away from us. They had both been flung through the air, out beyond the shelter of the tree, clear on to the ground, where they had fallen into crumpled heaps. Blake and I were stuck between a mass of broken branches and the paling of the machan, otherwise we would have run out to help them, but instead it was a mounted *shikari* who galloped out from the trees to their aid.

The collapse of the machan did not frighten the tiger one whit. It walked straight past the waterhole and the buffaloes, and on towards the Resident and his friend. Seeing this, the *shikari* swerved to distract or drive off the beast, but his horse was startled and the *shikari* was thrown down, his mount galloping terrified to the other end of the ravine. The two gentlemen had barely moved, while some of the bearers scrambled up but seemed uncertain where to run. Ahead of us the Major General's party shrieked and called and someone loosed a bullet, to no effect. Mir Aziz and Sameer had by now managed to extricate us from the branches, and, somewhat stunned, I tried to stand up. Another shot went off.

The unhorsed *shikari* began to haul the Resident's friend to his feet while shouting at the tiger and waving his sword, and the Resident slowly brought himself to his knees. The beast would not be distracted. It leapt towards the tumbled figures, grabbing the Resident by the neck. I thought I heard the man moan. The *shikari* rushed at it, thrusting with his sword, but the beast simply batted him out of its way, a claw ripping him from cheek to breast. Mir Aziz and Sameer shouted and ran past me. I could not take my eyes from the tiger. With Mr Crouch-Symington between its jaws, it turned and ran back into the forest.

The hair on my neck and arms rose, and I could hear my heart pumping in my ears. 'I am going after it!' I shouted to Blake, and I ran to where the creature had disappeared into the shadow.

'Avery, you fucking half-wit!' he shouted. 'You don't know what you're doing! Damn you, Avery, stop!' I heard him shouting in Hindoostanee at Mir Aziz and Sameer. I felt light-headed, and a bubble of laughter rose up through my chest.

'Don't worry,' I shouted, 'I'm an excellent shot! It's all I'm good for!' And I ran. It was not hard to see where the creature had gone. Its passage had left the grasses and twigs quite crushed, the victim's body left wavy patterns in the mud and there was a light but regular spotting of blood. One part of me acknowledged how foolish I was being, yet another part felt absurdly confident, as if my sight and hearing had been miraculously enhanced, and some sixth sense allowed me to apprehend the whole jangal. I was sure the creature was some way ahead, but I slowed down. After some minutes I heard someone coming up behind me – the breathing and rhythm of the steps clearly human. Blake was holding his musket. 'You bloody fool! Come back.' I shook my head and smiled, pointing down.

'You came after me,' I said, and took a drink from my water bottle.

'I left Mir Aziz to take care of the *shikari* and bearers and get them into the other machan,' he said. 'The other *shikari* rode off for help.' He caught his breath. 'I didn't trust Sameer not to go charging off with you on some idiot pursuit. Your hand isn't fit to shoot with.'

'It is perfectly fine. We cannot go back. What about that poor fellow, the Resident?'

Blake looked at me.

'Well, he's a rather awful fellow,' he said, 'but we cannot leave him to the beast.'

He took a drink from his own canteen, and looked about. 'These creatures are clever and unpredictable. This one has a taste for men and might easily be circling round behind us. It might be sitting behind that rock watching us. If there is more than one, the beaters will have riled them. Something has gone very wrong with this *shikar*. I had a bad feeling from the start. We should get back to the machan.'

194

I shook my head. 'I will not leave that man to his fate. I am going on. Leave me to it, if you fear for yourself.'

He frowned and looked about. 'You're a fool, Avery.' He thought for a moment. 'Don't point your gun at me. Make as little noise as possible. Don't speak.'

I grinned. We stepped slowly forward. Some hundred yards up the path we found a pitiful shred of clothing and more blood. The tiger had stopped to rest and had taken a bite of its prey. The tracks – the pug marks – and the blood were clear to see, but on each side the grasses grew so high and the undergrowth was so thick that there could have been a dozen tigers not inches from me and I would never have seen them. Then the trail turned back on itself the way we had come. Blake was right: the creature might be just behind us.

It became peculiarly quiet, as if the jangal were holding its breath. There was just the sound of our feet breaking dead leaves and twigs, and the receding cries of the beaters. The usual chorus of morning birds had fallen silent. We walked on. From time to time there were skitterings and hooves in the undergrowth. Once a heavy black sambar deer leapt across the path ahead of us. From higher up in the trees came the occasional chatter of monkeys and birds sounding warning cries. Among the sal trees the strangler vines were doing their work.

The trees opened out into a small clearing, and I could see the sun through the leaves. A monkey was chattering, a high-pitched nicker. I heard Blake take a breath. I spun and levelled my gun, but there was nothing. Then, behind the curtain of leaves and vines, something padded past me. Without thinking I stepped backward, almost falling over Blake. 'Look there,' he said. Beyond us, under a tree, was a small sorry pile of flesh, bone, hair and clothing that had once been Mr Crouch-Symington.

Blake knelt by the remains. 'You're a fool and I'm another,' he whispered. Then he tugged my arm and pointed at the pug marks around the body and raised two fingers. There were two distinct sets: one splayed; the other neater, as if pressing less heavily upon the ground. Two tigers. He pointed at a tree that looked easy enough to climb and pushed me firmly towards it. One after the other we balanced our muskets on our backs and pulled ourselves up into the branches as high as we could, finding places to sit where we could watch the little clearing. After some time, there came a sound like a heavy cartwheel going over a grate; like gravel poured from a barrel; like a series of tuneless piano strings plucked: a sound I had never heard before, the sound of a tiger snarling. The noise came from a nest of boulders on the right side of the clearing. The beast growled intermittently and we sat silent in our tree. Then, deciding perhaps that we were not dangerous, or of any interest, or had gone, or that it could not wait another moment to feed, the creature walked out from behind its boulder.

It looked right and left as it went. It was a long creature, not in its first youth. Its coat was shaggy – even slightly mangy – and its stripes the colour of flame and charcoal. It padded over to the body, leaving me with a fine shot along its side, and I raised my gun. But just as I meant to pull the trigger, it sensed me and looked up. My barrel rustled through the leaves and I shot. I was sure the bullet had met its target. The creature flinched sideways, but then picked itself up and crashed out of the clearing.

I turned to Blake in apology. He pulled his hand through his hair, and wiped the perspiration from his forehead.

'We must try to finish it off.'

I hung my head and slowly climbed down the tree. My arm throbbed dreadfully. I dared not look to see if the wound had re-opened, and pulled my shirtsleeve down to cover it. At the bottom Blake told me to reload my gun.

We walked on, following the trail. I lost track of the hour, but the sun seemed high. Eventually, we reached a point where overhanging leaves hid the way forward. Blake put his face up to the leaves, and I did the same. I could see a large meadow that led distantly towards the ravine where our machan had formerly sat. Far off, much further than I would have expected, I could see the other machan high in the trees. It seemed to be empty.

Before us, an elephant was staggering across the grass. Its mahout, riding on its neck holding a short metal pole, was quite unable to command it.

Out of the trees, perhaps fifteen yards from us, the tiger launched itself so fast that the line of its body seemed almost liquid. It was as if the jangal's dappled shadows had turned themselves to flesh. One moment a ripple of breeze and shade, the next a snarling beast. It flung itself on to the elephant's hind legs, as a cat climbs a curtain, and sank its great jaws into the hide to gain purchase.

The elephant wheezed and trumpeted in panic, its legs skittering and hopping, its little eyes popping. The howdah on its back lurched unsteadily, and the two occupants clung to its sides. The tiger released itself from the elephant's hide, and the huge grey creature staggered forward and then began to topple, precipitating to the ground the mahout, who rolled clear of the creature, as well as the howdah. The two men were thrown wide of the collapsing elephant, their headgear shaken from their heads, swords tangled between their legs, guns knocked from their hands. As they scrambled to their feet, the tiger sprang towards them with a mighty leap. But the mahout flung himself between the monster and its quarry, and the tiger brought him down instead. The man screamed – a horrible, high-pitched mewing, as the tiger buried his jaws in his face and the back of his neck, and placed itself on top of him chest to chest, leaving me with a sight of its whole side. I fell to the ground, found my position, aimed and shot. I knew it was good even before the tiger shivered, reared slightly and tumbled sideways. The force with which it did so seemed to make the ground shake.

The mahout continued to scream. I stood up and ran into the clearing. I was dimly aware that Blake was behind me. As I ran, I saw that one of the two men was the Rao. He was sitting on the ground looking dazed. Behind him his companion, a lavishly dressed sardar, was leaning on his gun. The elephant, half-crazed, pulled itself up and hurled itself towards the trees. Blood oozed bright from the claw marks on the animal's grey haunches. From those trees came a crashing of grasses and leaves. The elephant sheered off to the right. The sardar was so startled he almost leapt into the air. He lifted his rifle and aimed – somewhat wildly – into the trees. Nothing appeared, but the sounds beyond the trees continued.

The sardar, still unaware of us, still standing behind his Rao, his weapon still primed, straightened and took aim at a target I should never have expected. I acted without thought. I turned to Blake and he gave me his musket – I had had no time to reload my own. As the butt fitted into my shoulder my head became clear. I could tell the sight and the barrel were not perfectly matched, and made what allowance I could. Blake shouted in Hindoostanee. The Rao turned. The sardar looked up. As the Rao apprehended with horror the muzzle pointed at his head, I shot and the sardar fell into the dirt.

'Reload!' said Blake, putting a hand upon my shoulder. He ran forward and scooped up a handful of earth and pebbles and threw them at the tiger. Satisfied it was dead, he rushed over to the still-whimpering mahout and endeavoured to prise the man's head out of the dead tiger's jaws.

From the other side of the meadow came distant shouts. The Rao subsided on to the ground. I went to help him, passing the fallen sardar. From the corner of my eye I saw that the bullet had entered under his arm and gone into his chest, for he had been standing sideways to me. I retrieved the Rao's turban and the *sarpech*, which gleamed red and gold among the grasses, and made to help him up, offering my hand under his elbow. He looked up at me, grimaced, drew his elbow back and regained his feet alone. I remembered that such high-caste Hindoos abhorred the touch of a European. I thought I might laugh out loud. 'I do apologize, sir,' I said, then remembered he would not understand me.

I scrabbled for a few words.

'*Mujay maaf kijiye Maharaj*,' I said haltingly.

I held out his turban and the jewel. I made to bow, but my legs seemed to buckle and instead I found myself on one knee. It seemed, nevertheless, the correct thing to do. The Rao smiled imperially and, without actually touching my hand, took them delicately from me. *I have at last performed an almost heroic deed*, I thought. *And I have killed another man.* Behind the Rao, Blake had removed his jacket and was proceeding to tie it tight round the mahout's face. I saw him look past the Rao at me and give me a quizzical half-smile.

'Come here, Avery, and hold this man's head. There is something I must do.'

I stood up, bowed to the Rao and walked over. My movements were jerky; I did not quite have mastery over my own limbs. The mahout was alive, but he had fainted. Blood poured from his face, and I endeavoured to hold his head steady, but my hands were shaking. Blake strode towards the Rao, whose expression had regained its characteristic haughtiness. Blake bowed.

'Maharaj!' he began, and then issued a stream of quite unintelligible words in which I thought I identified the word 'gun'. The Rao, who was using his as a crutch, stared at Blake as if he were mad. 'Maharaj!' Blake ventured again. The Rao glanced behind him. His courtiers and servants were some distance away. Quickly, he lifted his gun. It was a beautiful thing, inlaid with silver filigree. He opened the barrel and looked into it. He nodded. From within it he fished out a wad of blackened cotton with his long, delicate fingers and let it fall on the ground. Quickly, Blake bent over, picked it up, put it in his pocket and took several steps back.

Within minutes the Rao was surrounded by *shikaris* and sardars. I could not really hear what they said, and I have a vision of Blake fending them off in that quiet, stubborn way that I imagined they would find infuriating. Someone came and spirited off the mahout. We stood waiting for mounts. I was extremely thirsty and my wound hurt but had not reopened. The sardar's body was thrown across a horse. Rao and his entourage were borne off on elephants. Against the dirt and tufts of thick green grass the tiger looked impossibly bright and powerful, even in death. Its head was huge. It had whiskers and a kind of moustache and several of its teeth were broken. A small rosette of red had spread across the hide where my shot had pierced its hide and rammed into its heart. The *shikaris* stretched the body out and eventually a couple of sapling trunks were brought and its legs were tied to them and it was carried away.

I wondered idly what had become of Mir Aziz and Sameer and the Resident's party. I later learnt they had long since been taken back to the safety of the tents. At last the Rao's soldiers conducted us back past the beaters. Blake rode close to me, and when we reached our tents, there was Mir Aziz on my other side. Neither spoke, but I had the feeling they believed they were protecting me. The thought mildly exasperated me. The soldiers gathered up our tents – they looked small and poor indeed next to the Rao's city of tents – and we rode up to the riverside palace, where I was given a large, airy room. Noisy native servants kept arriving with boxes and food, and demanding things I couldn't understand. My head hurt. People wished to talk to me. Blake closed the door on them. I was, I recall, extremely tired.

When I woke there seemed to be an army of barbers and bearers carrying a tub and pitchers of hot water, and *khitmatgurs* with coffee and platters full of breads, fruits and dahls. Sameer stood at the foot of the bed, unsure whether to send them away or order them in. I was starving. I took a bath and then ate until I could fit in no more. When I was done, Blake arrived, dressed in a pure white kurta and churidars. Mir Aziz and Sameer had, he said, been offered various grand dishes, but had insisted upon cooking their own meal.

'I sent back the jewels and the silks. There were some very large rubies,' he said.

'I should have liked a ruby,' I said. 'Just one. How is the mahout?'

'It seems he might live. Lost a lot of blood, and he'll never be pretty, but he might come through. The *shikari* who tried to save the Resident will not. The Major General, who has temporarily taken on the late Resident's duties, has offered us hospitality in the Residency. He is loud in his praises of your brave deeds and would be only too pleased if we join him, not least, I suspect, so he can put a first-hand description in his despatch to Calcutta. I'm told he said it was "a very palpable hit for the Company".'

'But not so good for the Resident.'

'No. I declined his offer. He's more of a . . . well, I declined his offer.'

I laughed.

'It was well done, Avery,' he said. 'And the Company will make something out of it: the Lieutenant who saved the native prince from tiger attack and assassination.'

'It was certainly strange. The machan collapsing, and the tiger and the elephant, and the sardar,' I said.

'The elephant had been cut before and the machan was supposed to come down. If the Rao had survived the attack, a machan populated by Europeans collapsing would certainly have provoked an incident with the Company. The Rao has determined enemies. The sardar must have expected to lose his life, but he tried to kill the Rao anyway. The tiger was an unforeseen addition. Still, your two shots have got us a private interview with him. When I returned the gifts, I asked for an audience. It has been agreed. I'm indebted to you.'

It occurred to me that Blake had traded my chance to pay off my debts and marry Helen for a few words with a native prince.

'You couldn't have kept them,' he said. 'But you should know that for a chance to speak to the Rao alone, I would have given them up even if you could have kept them.'

'Why should you imagine that my desire to find Mountstuart is any less than yours?' I said. I was irritated now. 'He has been my idol. I do not know what he is to you. Moreover, Colonel Buchanan made it quite clear that my future depends upon our success or failure.'

'Did he? And what else did he say to you?'

'He said that if we failed he'd send me to a hole in the Mofussil and keep me there until I went mad or died of the cholera.'

'And if we find him?'

I looked away. 'I can go home.'

'Is that what you want?'

'I no longer know. I hated Calcutta so much, all I could think of was home. But what I chiefly missed was the place and my sister, Louisa. If I were to return now, the rest of my family would regard me as a failure. Certainly my father would. We do not see eye to eye. There is little for me there.'

'What about your sister?'

'She is the best person I know.'

'Not married?'

'He will never let her marry. She is to be the crutch of his old age.'

'Well,' he said. 'I think those two shots may have placed you beyond Buchanan's reach.'

I fidgeted. 'So,' I said brightly, 'we have given up a raja's treasure for a few minutes in which to make him even more annoyed with us than he was before.'

'That's the ticket, Avery. We'll make a Special Inquiry Agent of you yet.'

The room was high and bright. Small windows, set in a painted frieze of brightly rendered birds and flowers high in the walls, ushered in the light. Below the painted frieze there were glazed bookcases stuffed with leather-bound volumes along one wall. I could not quite make out the titles, but I was sure some were in English. On a stand in one corner of the room an enormous green and red parrot delicately ate a nut, and on the floor beneath it was a gold-enamelled huqqa. In another sat a *punkah-wallah*, and in another a musician on a cushion plucked single notes from a sitar. On various intricately patterned occasional tables were a globe, a telescope, a sextant, a chess set. There were also four extremely large, bearded and heavily armed guards, whose hands never left the jewelled scabbards of their tulwars.

In the elaborate garden outside, in which the white tiger paced up and down a shaded cage, our clothes and persons had been minutely searched by more burly guards.

The Rao stood behind a long mahogany desk, poring over a pile of papers with two elderly, bearded companions. The desk was covered with a number of tiny perfect objects: small boxes inlaid with enamel, inkwells encrusted with tiny rubies, a magnifying-glass. He wore a simple pleated robe of white muslin, and over it a pink silk coat embroidered in gold, and over that he was once again garlanded with row upon row of pearls. There was another spray of precious stones attached to his turban.

We waited, barefoot of course. Eventually the Rao tilted his head and looked at us. He dismissed his companions, who shot us curious glances as they bowed low and backed out of the room. The musician departed too. The Rao looked over our heads and began to speak, a great flood of Hindoostanee poured from his lips. After a minute or two, he stopped. Blake bowed low. I did the same. Blake replied in kind. After two or three sentences the Rao waved his hand impatiently.

'Yes, yes, Mr Jeremiah Blake,' he said, 'let us dispense with the florid addresses. I expect it from my own subjects, but it sounds absurd coming from an Englishman of the Company, and besides, it bores me.'

I am ashamed to say that I goggled in a rather impolite fashion.

'Yes, Lieutenant William Avery, my English is very good, is it not?' said the Rao. He seemed rather pleased at my surprise. 'I do not choose to use it often these days, but I have not lost it. Now, let me say again, I thank you for saving my life. It was most impressive marksmanship. A difficult shot, I believe. It will be the talk of my court for a thousand years. I am indebted to you. Your Hindoostanee is quite dreadful, by the way. Now come, come.'

He beckoned me over. From a gold box he drew out a black bag tied at the top by a drawstring. From it he poured out a handful of precious stones, which clicked satisfyingly against each other in his hand. He held them out to show me.

'Sir, Your Majesty, Maharaja, you know I cannot accept them,' I stuttered.

He sniffed. 'Yes. The Company has rules about such things. I wish you to know that I am grateful, and am sensible of your courage and skill, and I wish to be magnanimous. But Mr Blake has asked for an interview. I will be honest and say I wish you had chosen something else. The letter you brought was, you must know, insulting, for all that your own words dripped with honey. Your story of an attack outside my walls I cannot but regard as a provocation. But you have saved me from beast and assassin and I am grateful. Nevertheless, I shudder to think of the uses to which the Company will put this story. Now, please to be quick.'

He stopped, but then took another breath as if he could not quite restrain himself.

'But let me say before you advance your suit, I have no interest in how the Company regards the running of my kingdom. I have adhered to all the arrangements laid out in the accord between my family and the Company. I say again, as I have said many times, that I do not give, nor ever have given, succour to Thugs and bandits, as Major Sleeman persists in insinuating. I regard them as a menace to my people. Rather, I believe that my prerogatives are daily being undermined by the Company, my word mistrusted and the Company's manner increasingly peremptory.

'Where does it say that Company troops may come riding into Doora to pick up whomsoever they like on some flimsy charge? Where was it ever agreed that a Resident's authority might include delivering lectures on Christian morals to a native prince? The late Resident – I fear I cannot altogether mourn his departure, though I would not have wished such an ending upon him for all the world – had the impudence to tell me to put away my zenana and dress more like a European. I regarded this as both rude and well beyond any remit ever given to a Resident, and mentioned nowhere in the annals of the relations between the Company and the princely states. I wish to point out that my family and I enjoyed excellent relations with the former Resident, who was a precious support to my mother in the years of her regency, while the Company was trying to make a little Christian of me in Calcutta. In our view, he was removed with summary and insulting abruptness. It is not I who have changed, but the Company. If my views are still not clear, let me say without any obfuscation that I believe there are those in the Company who look for reasons to take my lands – but because I do not poison my first ministers, or murder my cousins, the Company cannot justify sending its armies here, and thus looks for other ways of relieving me of my throne. Now, you may take that back to Calcutta.'

I gasped and would have protested, but Blake placed his hand on my shoulder.

'Maharaj, I – we – are not here to harangue you about Thuggee, nor to deliver a homily from the Company. And please, I beg you to believe me when I assure you that I am of the opinion the attack upon us had nothing to do with Doora.'

I pressed my lips together and set my jaw. I was by no means sure that this was true.

'We come only in search of Xavier Mountstuart. I know he rejoiced in calling you friend. I do not know why I was furnished with such letters from Calcutta – or rather I have an idea and I believe the reason was to damage us in your eyes so you would be unwilling to help us, though I do not entirely understand why.'

The Rao sat down on a carved wooden chair and placed his hands on the arms. Two of the guards came to stand on either side behind it. He looked slighter and more delicate than ever, but his expression was still haughty.

'I have an obligation to you. But I do not choose to talk of my friend Mountstuart Sahib to "all and sundry", as the saying goes.'

'Maharaj, may I remind you that I may have come to you with the Company's letter, but without the Company's uniform. I come because I wish to discover what has become of the *malik-al-shuara*, whom I too once called friend.'

'Then I must disappoint you, Mr Blake, for as you say, no one has seen Mountstuart Sahib in Doora this many a long year. Why are you so sure he has been here?'

'We had been told he planned to come to you after visiting Jubbulpore, which we visited only to search for him. We ask simply if there is anything you can tell us about what might have become of him.'

'But you have no evidence of his coming to Doora?'

'No, sir.'

'Well then, for my part I would say your question is answered. I am sorry you have come so far for so little. Let us at least part in good faith. Let me give you both something to thank you for my deliverance. You, Mr Blake, as well as Mr Avery, for I have not thanked you for preventing me from firing my gun. How did you guess it was blocked? An amazing piece of clairvoyance. Your Hindoostanee, by the way, is really not bad at all.'

'You are too kind, Maharaj. It was not clairvoyance, but reasoning. Your' – he chose his word carefully – 'opponents wished to leave nothing to chance.'

The Rao said, 'My opponents planned well indeed. My household is penetrated, and who can I trust? Not the Company. If I were to die before little Arjuna is anointed, the Company would sweep us into the Bengal presidency for lack of an heir. '

Now I burst out. 'Sir, that is completely untrue and an abominable impugning of our and the Company's honour! Our deeds should show our intentions! We sought only to help!'

The room seemed to become uncomfortably quiet, the guards quietest of all, as if awaiting a word from their master. Even the parrot looked up. I had perhaps overstepped the mark.

'Maharaj, you know we saved your life,' Blake said. 'I think you amuse yourself with us.'

The Rao said, '*Chote Sahib bahut accha nishaana-baaz hai – awr chahra bhi khubsurat hai – lekin mujhe lagta hai voh kuch be-waquf hai?*'

'*Larke Ko maaf kar dena Maharaj. Voh abhi jawan awr jald-baaz hai – awr sirf thora sa be waquf,*' Blake said.

The Rao raised his eyebrows. I caught the word 'boy', *larke*; and the word 'stupid', *be-waquf*.

'And so, Maharaj, since, as you say, we have incurred your thanks and obligation, let me speak one more word on that subject for which we came?'

The Rao sighed as if his patience was being sorely tried, but nodded.

'Let me tell you that Mountstuart was a good friend to me – as good as he was able to be. I owe him much, and I think I knew him well. Well enough to recognize the third ring on your right hand.'

The Rao looked bored. I looked at his hands, but he had wrapped left over right.

'It is a gold signet ring with the insignia of a white rose. It belonged to his father's family, who are from Ayr in Scotland. It was given to him by his mother, who hoped he would be a poet. I know he was here, and I do not believe he would have given it to anyone whom he did not trust. For myself, I would say that only someone he trusted would know its provenance. And though it would be presumptuous of me, Xavier Mountstuart would have told you that your first minister's and your cousin's treason are the talk of the bazaar. Though you, of course, know that already.'

The Rao lifted up his hands and admired the gold signet ring that was indeed on his right hand. He began to laugh. 'Mr Jeremiah Blake, who are you?'

'I learnt my Hindoostanee and Sanskrit from Xavier Mountstuart. I had a talent for languages. Once he had schooled me, I accompanied him on certain expeditions.'

'Where?'

'Sind, Punjab, Coorg, several visits to Burmah before the war. Many places.'

'I see. So, you were the boy.'

'I was the boy.'

'*My country! In thy days of glory past/ A beauteous halo circled round thy brow,*' said the Rao.

And Blake said, '*And worshipped as a deity thou wast/ Where is thy glory, where the reverence now?* It's not often that a Rajput king quotes an atheist firebrand, Maharaj.'

'Or that a Company civilian does either. Henry Derozio introduced me to Xavier. Calcutta was a freer place in those days. I cannot imagine such associations now.'

'Mountstuart introduced me to Henry Derozio. He gave me a copy of Thomas Paine's *Rights of Man*, and later *The Age of Reason*. Might I ask, Maharaj, how you met Derozio?'

'It is, of course, quite irregular for a commoner to interrogate a prince in such a manner,' the Rao said languidly, 'but you have stimulated my curiosity and so I will answer. At Drummond's Academy in Calcutta. The Company took me into its keeping when my father died. I was eight. My mother fought to keep the regency and to save my throne. In Calcutta they gave me two tutors, German Lutheran missionaries, who failed to instill Christian beliefs in me, I fear, but gave me the Enlightenment instead: mathematics, botany, astronomy, music and poetry. And they sent me to classes at David Drummonds' Academy. They thought that since he was a dour Scot he must be a Presbyterian, but in fact, of course, he was a notorious free-thinker!' The Rao laughed and brought his hands up to his face as if to hide his wide smile. His recollections had transported him to another time.

'What a place it was! And Henry Derozio was its most brilliant boy – several years younger than me, but already his mind was so alive! Poor Henry. Of course, his free-thinking and his republican ideas and his *Rights of Man* went too far for me. But we shared a deep sense of our country's former greatness, and desired to see it raise its head again in pride. And we found fellowship in that neither of us fitted. He was neither native nor European, and far too radical for either Hindoo or English. I was a prince, admiring European learning, but tied to my Hindoo heritage – never enough of one or the other. In Calcutta I was too Hindoo. When I returned to Doora I was too European. You know, I brought in laws against suttee and infanticide before the Company did; I had children vaccinated against smallpox. I have made Doora a centre of music such as it has not been since the days of my ancestor Rabindrath, the great friend of the Emperor Akbar. Calcutta gives me no credit for this, and accuses me of intransigence, yet my sardars mutter that I desecrate tradition. And now I find I am fighting for my throne and must seem more Hindoo than the most Hindoo in order to hold on to it.

'Henry and I were fascinated by Mountstuart, the Scotsman who wrote such beautiful verse about our homeland, who spoke such perfect Hindoostanee, who shared with us an admiration for Byron. Of course, he also shared Henry's tiresomely radical views, but I always think Mountstuart embraced them mostly because he so enjoyed shocking the fat Company moneybags, rather than because he truly believed them.'

The Rao recollected himself. He said, more coolly, 'Mr Blake, I am told Mrs Parkes describes you as "of the Company and not of the Company". Explain yourself.'

Blake thought for a moment.

'I came here at fourteen or fifteen with the Company. I have spent more of my life here than in England. Mountstuart gave me an education. I served in the Company's armies for many years, but slowly and almost without realizing it, I lost my appetite for working in its employ. I came to believe I could not continue in good conscience. I rose to become a captain in its armies. It did not suit me; I did not suit it. I lost my rank.'

'They wanted to restore him,' I interjected, 'but he refused them.'

'If I wish to stay in Hind I must remain in its employ, but I will not wear its uniform. So in the last years it has used me to find things. And men.'

'So you are on the Company's errand.' The Rao was suspicious again.

'It sent me to Jubbulpore, but I came for my own reasons. I believed Mountstuart to be in danger – that is not unusual. But certain things I was told. . . .' He looked directly at the Rao. 'And now I know he was here.'

'Well, I will tell you what I know. Even if you are the Company's man, I do not think it will take you very far. He came from Jubbulpore, seeking refuge. It was when? In the Christian calendar it would have been, I think, June or July. He had travelled up through the jangal in disguise after the rains began. Not an easy journey, but this year the monsoon was mild. He was not well, and he asked me to hide him. He said the Company had played him false.'

'This does not surprise me.'

I looked between the two. 'Blake, what do you mean?'

'We will speak of it later. May I ask how he seemed to you, Maharaj?'

The Rao paused. 'He was physically quite weak, but after some days of rest, his capricious self again. Though quite agitated.'

'You said he was not well, Maharaj?'

'I did not see him every day,' the Rao said, 'but I made sure he was comfortable. He was quite obsessed with the Thugs. He was writing, furiously, often through the night, and sleeping in the day. He became possessed by the notion that he must meet with a certain Thug gang, whom he said were still at large. I considered the idea ridiculous, but of course I could not dissuade him. He was sure that there were those at court who knew how they might be contacted. I have worked hard to root out brigands in Doora, and I did not want to believe him. But there are dark corners of the court, as you know, and in the end I allowed him to send out his message. Within a week a messenger came with a place and a time. Another sign, no doubt you will say, that I am not master of my own court.

'I told him not to go. He was stubborn, and he gave me the ring. He said if he did not return, there would be no help in searching for him, and requested that if Company men came looking for him I would not give him away.'

'Maharaj, may I inquire if he said anything more about the ring?'

'He said if he did not return within a year it should be sent to his sister. He said someone might come who recognized it, but not whom.'

'He left two months ago. We have heard nothing since. I found the messenger. He told us where he had taken Xavier. It was off the road to Mirzapore in the direction of Allahabad. I had soldiers there for three weeks. I had every path followed. We found nothing.'

'And he left no message for anyone at all, Maharaj?'

The Rao shook his head.

'I would like to go to that place. I would like to speak to the messenger.'

'That will not be possible. He is, as my Lutherans used to say, no longer with us.'

'Nevertheless, Maharaj, I must go there.'

'That is a fool's errand, Mr Blake, though I respect your persistence. I regret having helped Mountstuart. It would be improper to repay my obligation to you in such a manner. Can you not enjoy my hospitality, take a few stones, keep them for what I pray shall be a hale old age, and leave with my blessing?'

'I think you know that I cannot. *Lekin shayed aap larke ke liye kuch kar saken.*'

Again I caught the word 'boy', and I bridled. The parrot turned noisily on its perch. The two guards stood like statues. The Rao picked up one of the pages he had been studying and turned it around so we could see it. It was a large, detailed and beautiful drawing of a lotus flower.

'It is lovely, is it not?'

I nodded. Blake said nothing. I reached about for something to fill the silence.

'Maharaja, may I ask a question?'

He nodded graciously.

'Why was it – in the throne room on the day of our audience – that you did not sit upon the throne, but rather at its feet?'

The Rao smiled. 'The *gaddi* is not for the raos, Lieutenant. It is for Vishnu, our true ruler, the protector, the restorer of balance, bringer of light. We consider ourselves his servants and must sit at his feet. And might I ask, Mr Avery, since it is directly to you that I owe my life, whether you believe that my debt to you should be paid in the way Mr Blake demands?'

I took a breath. 'We came to find Mr Mountstuart, Your Highness. We must do our best, everything we can, to discover what has become of him. We need your help to do so.'

The Rao pursed his lips. He looked exasperated. 'I could discharge my debt by having my men show you where Xavier went. I could furnish you with lavish provisions and stores and pack-horses. I could arrange for a fleet of guards to accompany you. I could even plant rumours in those dark places of the court so that those you seek may perhaps hear of you. But I ask you, do not do this thing.'

Blake said, 'Maharaj, I cannot take your guards.'

The Rao looked cross. 'If you choose to go alone and do not return, I will regard my obligation to you at an end. I will not come and save you.'

'I understand.'

The Rao looked at Blake and then at me. He frowned. 'You may go. I will think on it.'

He clapped his hands, and at once the two guards by the doors opened them and two more came to escort us out through the garden. Blake made a small bow.

'I thank you, Maharaj,' he said. As ever, I followed him.

The Rao said, 'Lieutenant, please, one moment.' Blake was already past the tiger's cage in the garden. The Rao waved my guard to follow him.

'I am sorry, Maharaja, if we displease you. We must do our best.'

'That is not why I detain you. Here.' He took out the small bag of gems. 'Take it. Place it in the hands of the Company's treasurers if you must. But you must take it.'

He dropped the bag into my hand, making sure he did not touch me.

Chapter Twelve

It was not until we were back in our rooms that I felt free to speak.

'So, you would trust the Rao?' I said.

'I would.'

'He gave me these.' I held out the bag.

Blake said, 'You should keep them. They'll pay off your debts and get you back to England, at the very least.'

I gaped at him and put the bag down.

'But you said – never mind.' I rubbed my forehead in the vain hope that it would help me to think more clearly. 'If he is harbouring Thugs as Sleeman says, he could have had Mountstuart killed and taken his ring. This Thug story is very convenient. He could have sent Mountstuart off to the jangal and had him killed.'

'It's possible.'

'He did not mention Mountstuart's monkey.'

'You're quite right. I'd forgotten him. Stupid of me.'

'I did not miss that you called me a stupid boy.'

'Your Hindoostanee is improving. He called you a stupid boy; I called you a rash boy. He also said you were handsome and a fine shot.'

I looked at him stonily. 'And who is Henry Derozio?'

'Was. A teacher in Calcutta. A brilliant man. I never heard anyone speak so well – it was all rationalism and Tom Paine. Enough to make a man drunk with ideas, and for a few years I was. It did not go down too well with the Company redcoat, I can tell you, but Mountstuart was amused. Henry got a post teaching English at the Hindoo college – the school for the sons of rich baboos – when he was seventeen. He could have passed as Portuguese or even English, but he chose to call himself a native. I don't know what he was –

half-caste, I suppose.' As he spoke, it seemed to me that Blake, like the Rao, was transported back to a happier time.

'He was a few years younger than me, but he seemed older. He brought his poetry to Mountstuart; they both admired Byron. He died about seven years ago, just after he was dismissed by the college. He was twenty-two. Some said he was poisoned, but it was more likely the cholera. He made a space for himself and what he believed, which no longer exists in Calcutta now. The Hindoos feared him because he encouraged their sons to question their beliefs; the Europeans hated his talk of republicanism and the rights of natives and India's great past.'

'Oh.' I did not like to ask who Tom Paine was. 'So, now' – I hoped he was settled into a talking mood – 'will you tell me what it is you suspect happened at Jubbulpore?'

'Truly, Avery, it would be better for you to remain in ignorance. If you will carry my despatches, you will have done the best you can.'

'Carry your despatches?'

He cleared his throat. He looked evasive.

'You will go to Mirzapore and then on to Calcutta – unless there are orders to join your regiment. I have several reports and they must reach the right hands in Calcutta. I want you to deliver them. You will take Sameer. I'll make it clear that I ordered you to return. I'll say that you have undertaken all your tasks with great conscientiousness, and with the reports about the hunt and how you single-handedly repaired relations with the Rao you'll be well placed for the future. Though how much longer he will be able to hold on to his throne, I don't know.'

'You are planning to go and find those Thugs without me.'

'I have to try to find what became of Xavier Mountstuart. It's why I came – the only reason.'

'Do you think I will slip off obediently now, before our work is done, and when you refuse to explain all those dark suspicions you hint at? Because I will not!'

'You will. You take orders from me.' His calmness was infuriating.

'I will not! I will not allow it.'

'You will not allow it.' He sighed. 'We've gone beyond Company business now, Avery. You're not bound to this, but I am, for my own reasons. I must follow this to its end. And it may not turn out well – it is quite likely not to turn out well. You know that. You have gone as far as duty and your orders oblige you, as far as the Company can expect.'

'What you mean is, you are deliberately going out on your own to find the Thugs who took Mountstuart, and you reckon they are as likely to kill you as not,' I said. 'Do not condescend to me. Do you think I act purely for my own advancement? Have I not done enough to show that I do not? And what if you found Mountstuart and brought him to Mirzapore, and I was halfway to Calcutta?'

'Listen to me, I don't doubt your courage, but you are young.'

I bristled.

'That is not an insult, Avery. Make use of it. It doesn't last for ever. I have obligations and bad old habits. You do not.'

'And what of Mir Aziz?'

'I expect him to return to Mirzapore too.'

I thought of the stones in my pocket.

'I will not go to Mirzapore.' I realized I was close to tears.

The Rao housed us in luxury while we waited for his answer, but wherever we went the palace was full of soldiers. The day after our audience, he sent the tiger's skin, complete with its head, for my inspection before it was taken to the tanners for curing, and his *shikaris* took me out on a ride.

It was impossible to speak to Blake. Every time I did so it ended in argument. But it never occurred to me to suggest that he should not go into the forest and instead return to Mirzapore with us, for I knew he would not. The next day the Rao agreed to Blake's request, as I had known he would. Blake set about making his plans, and those for our departure for Mirzapore. I refused to take any part in them. I packed up my modest bags and went out to shoot game with the Rao's *shikaris*. When I returned, Mir Aziz told me the palace was abuzz with rumours that the Rao's first cousin had been imprisoned, and that Orange Turban had decided to retire to his estates and relinquish his position as diwan. That night I buried myself in Macpherson's now almost unreadably worn *Pickwicks*, and their absurd, warm-spirited Englishness.

We left the next morning, riding out of the city on the road for Mirzapore with a sizeable escort. After several miles, where the road forked left in the direction of Allahabad, Blake stopped and Mir Aziz with him. Both were dressed almost identically in native garb. I realized that Mir Aziz was going with Blake. Half the guards peeled off to accompany them. We had stopped by the side of the path, which was flattened by the pounding of hooves and feet like so many others we had traversed together. Blake made to take my hand and shake it. I refused.

He took my hand anyway. 'Goodbye, Avery. You'll realize this is the right way of it. Good luck.'

I glared at them both. I found it hard to speak. Mir Aziz said, 'We will see each other again, Chote Sahib,' and bowed.

An hour on, I said goodbye to Sameer, as we had previously agreed, and we parted, though not without argument. He wished to follow them too, but I persuaded him that one of us must deliver Blake's despatches. We had arranged that he would go on to the Company cantonment at Mirzapore. After a week he would send Blake's report and my few belongings on to Calcutta. After three weeks he would leave. I retraced my steps. I spied the dust kicked up by the troops' horses in the late afternoon. I remained at a discreet distance until I was certain they would have made camp for the evening. They were putting up their tents in a mango grove when I rode up and began to unload my packs. Blake looked up. He pressed his lips together in disapproval.

'You're going back in the morning with the Rao's men,' Blake said.

I laid out my bed, then took myself off under a tree with Mountstuart's *The Courage of the Bruce* and my bayoneted musket on my lap and lost myself in the verse until it became dark. Blake sat with his back to me, but eventually Mir Aziz picked up his huqqa and came and sat by me. He puffed for a few minutes and then said, 'Chote Sahib, it is better if you return. Please.'

'You are staying,' I said.

'I have many reasons, and I am many years older.'

'It is not just my being young and rash. I cannot leave now, it would be – dishonourable, an abandonment of a sacred charge.'

He gazed at me in the dark. 'We will speak tomorrow.'

The next morning the Rao's escort turned back for Doora, but I would not go with them. Blake did not address a word to me. I took a perverse pleasure in the knowledge that he was angry.

Mir Aziz said simply, 'Chote Sahib, I ask you humbly. Return to Mirzapore.'

I shook my head.

We climbed slightly uphill under an umbrella of sal trees, with the sun continually breaking through the leaves, and the undergrowth thick on either side, tracing small paths until I had lost all sense of our direction. The trees became sparser, and large rocks and boulders began to strew the way. Somewhere I could hear the sound of water.

By a small tank and a broken old tomb where the trees had fallen away entirely, a native stood, watching our approach. As we came closer, I confess a feeling of dread began to take hold of me. Blake turned and looked at me once, then dismounted. As we came closer I saw that the man's face was hard. He was thin-lipped and had small, black, bird-like shiny eyes, but I could see he smiled. There were heavy lines etched from eye to chin, and a mass of finer ones around his eyes and mouth. He was short, held a long wooden staff, and he was quite well dressed, wrapped in a great shawl of fine cotton that covered his head, his spindly legs ending in a pair of soft Bundelkand slippers. He hailed us and waved. Blake went up to him and they exchanged greetings. Blake began to speak and the watcher listened, his gaze shifting urgently between Blake and me, but he did not stop smiling.

How persuasive Blake was, I do not know, but after some minutes the man agreed to join us, walking beside Blake. Behind them came Mir Aziz, and lastly myself, leading our horses. Perhaps a mile on along the path we came upon four more men, taller than the first, more poorly dressed, but powerful-looking. One man led an ass whose harness was laced with small bells which tinkled as it walked. It seemed that no explanations were needed. The men bowed and uttered a greeting, *'Namaste!'*

Blake said, *'Aule khan salaam.'*

We set off again. Blake was at the centre of the group, and it was not clear who was leading and who following. There was sporadic talk, led by Blake and our original guide, and I thought I heard Mountstuart's name, but I was not sure. Mir Aziz spoke occasionally in answer to a question. No one spoke to me, but now and then one or other of our new escorts would look back at me doubtfully, concerned, it was clear, by my evident Europeanness. In the late afternoon we came upon a larger gang of ten or twelve natives who appeared to be in the act of setting up camp for the evening. I could not tell if they affected not to know our guides, but they surged towards us, greeting us all enthusiastically, and insisted we set up our tents near them.

'Are these the men we seek?' I asked Blake quietly.

'I think so. The leader, the little bird-like one, calls himself Gulab. He likes to talk of "his people", who are further on into the forest.'

'What do your omens say, Mir Aziz?'

He looked at me sadly. 'I heard the cry of the *ullu* – the owl – in the day, sahib.'

'That is a bad omen, is it not?'

The dark came, and the evening seemed to take on an almost delirious quality. They called us over to eat with them. There were a number of fires, but we were brought, with some ceremony, to sit round the largest. They welcomed us and showed us friendly faces. They separated us from each other by planting themselves between us.

The food was like dust in my mouth. Blake and Mir Aziz said little. Our hosts chattered and joshed with each other, for all the world as if it were a night like any other.

Our first escorts brought out a drum and two very crude stringed instruments, one plucked, one played with a rude bow. The gathering listened as they performed. There was a gentle breeze and the night felt velvety. At some point I looked down and saw that my musket had gone. The native next to me grinned in a friendly manner. When the musicians finished playing, the leader, Gulab, began to tell a story. The audience laughed and clapped. I became aware that we were each surrounded. I knew what was coming. It was just as Sleeman had described, just as I had read in his book: men behind us, pressing in, apparently enjoying the music; one man on each side to hold us down when the time came. I could not bring myself to look behind me to see if the man I could sense at my back had a scarf – a *rumal* – in his hand. We would sit and wait for it, like lambs. I tried to brace myself.

Blake leant across the circle and said to me quietly, though somehow the words came clearly across the music, 'The advantage of living is not measured by length, but by use; some men have lived long, and lived little. You've done well, and honourably.'

The storyteller stopped speaking and called for refreshment. Mir Aziz looked over at me. He smiled and stretched his hand out to me in a strange, almost brotherly, gesture. *It will be now*, I thought.

As the storyteller drank, there came the screech of an owl from high in the trees above us. Even as I lifted my head to look up, I knew what was coming.

I felt a hard blow on the head, the light fluttered, my hands were grabbed, then there was another blow, and then darkness, then nothing.

PART FOUR

Chapter Thirteen

I could not see, but I could feel twigs and stones digging into me. I could not move my hands nor feel my legs. My head throbbed. I was pulled upward, but my legs would not work. Something fell hard across my shoulders, stinging and heavy. That roused me. My legs held after that. I shouted out to Blake and Mir Aziz, and was rewarded with another blow. Something – a stick, a knife – prodded me in the back, and obediently I staggered forward. My face was tied tightly in a cloth; my mouth was very dry.

The stick, constantly needling me in the back, prodded me onward. We walked for what seemed a long time. There were no voices, just the constant snap underfoot of grasses and leaves. At last someone seized my shoulders and half pushed and half hoisted me into a room of some sort. I could tell I was no longer outside because the sounds had changed. I was thrust on to a dirt floor. There I rolled over and passed thankfully into unconsciousness.

When I awoke I choked. My mouth was so dry and full of dust that my tongue stuck to its roof. I still could not see. I endeavoured to spread the little moisture under my tongue about my mouth. My face and chest were pressed into the earth. The cloth about my face smelled rank, of old sweat and other unpleasant things. My hands, still tied, were awkwardly twisted into my stomach. All was silence. I struggled to sit up and braced myself for another blow, but none came. I put up my hands to dislodge the cloth from my face, pulling it down past my chin. It was pitch black and I wondered for a moment if I was blind, but abandoned myself to the relief brought by the cold air pouring into my mouth and lungs. I longed to lay my head down and lapse into oblivion. Instead I examined myself for injury. There was grit on my lips and in my nostrils. I was sore, but nothing felt broken or bleeding. The floor beneath me was dry and dusty, the wall behind me rough, and the air still and cool. I was as cold as I had been since coming to India. I thought I must be in a cave. I began to make out shapes in the gloom. I felt cautiously around myself, and to my right laid hold of a prone body. I felt for the head and made out the ragged top of an ear.

'Blake? Blake!' I whispered, as loudly as I could.

He barely breathed. I shook him gently, and then more urgently, pulling his head free of his blindfold. Hindered by my bonds, I tried to rub his hands, then to slap him on the cheek. He began to cough, eventually turning to one side to hawk upon the ground. I swear, I was never so glad to hear an expectoration in all my life.

I got on to my knees and tried to haul him up by looping my arms about him from behind and then propping him against the rock wall. 'Are you injured?' I whispered.

For a moment there was no answer, just shallow coughing and wheezing. 'Nothing that hasn't been knocked about a good deal before,' he said, his voice little more than a croak. We sat for a while. He whispered, 'Damn me, what I'd do for some water.' Then he said, 'There's someone here with us.'

There was a rustling, a tiny shift, a light breath some way to my left.

'Mir Aziz?' I said urgently.

'Alas, no.' The voice had a languorous, drawling quality to it. 'I told you to go back to England, Jeremiah Blake. See what happens when you disregard my advice?'

Blake said, 'Company sent me to look for you. Couldn't leave you to the "deaf tyranny of fate" and all that, could I?'

'That is one of Byron's, Jem, not one of mine.'

The voice reminded me of a rakish uncle of mine who had resided – when he could afford it – in Bath and of whom my father had greatly disapproved.

'Damn me,' Blake croaked, 'must have misremembered.'

'My line – if you recall – speaks of "slipping the rusty bonds of circumstance". The metaphor is quite different.'

I recalled it very well.

'Magnificent as it is, Xavier, I'm more in need of a cup of water than some stirring lines.'

I felt I had been struck ten times across the head. In the course of our travel, I had moved from a sneaking suspicion that we should never find Xavier Mountstuart, to a conviction that someone in Jubbulpore had done him to death, to a belief that we would probably never find out what had become of him. The sudden confounding of these presumptions, encountering the man in a cave in the midst of the Mofussil, was almost too much to comprehend.

'You are the very apex of mundanity, Jem,' Mountstuart said. 'And you are speaking like a plebeian again. After all those years of practice.'

'I am a plebeian, Xavier.'

'Well, there's a water crock somewhere about.' There was a shuffling and the sounds of gentle tapping. 'They have deposited us among their stores. There is a wick and a tinderbox. Like the deity on the first day, I shall make light.'

There was the sound of flint clicking and a small flame appeared. It lit a small wick floating in a bowl of ghee, which did little to chase back the darkness, illuminating only a limited space about it. There was a clack of pot on pot and the sound of water pouring.

'My dear young man, will you oblige me?'

It took me a moment to understand he meant me. I sprang forward to take the bowl in both hands and brought it to Blake's mouth. He drank greedily, then stopped and pushed it at me. I gulped and swallowed and choked, and gulped again, then used my sleeve to try to clear the worst of the grit from my face and mouth. When I was done, I turned to look surreptitiously at my hero.

The light, as I say, was dim, so it was hard to make him out clearly. He was older than I had envisioned him, and bore the marks of captivity. He was very thin, his once blond hair longer, darker and wildly unkempt; he had a stringy beard. His long fingers were grimy, his face dark, whether from dirt or sun I could not tell. But the famous dark brows furrowed over the famous eyes – I fancied even in the gloom I could just see their blueness. He was dressed in a thin shirt and pyjamas and native sandals, and had about him a blanket.

Around him there were jars and sacks and small crates. To his left, the cave narrowed to a dark hole; to my and Blake's right was another larger exit.

'Well,' Mountstuart said conversationally, 'I am most flattered you have come. It has been some time, hasn't it, Jem?'

'Five years. Before they told me, I didn't even know you'd returned from England.'

'You were still rotting away in Blacktown when I came back, an ill-tempered recluse barring the door to visitors.'

Blake exhaled slowly.

'Wallowing in grief,' Mountstuart went on, 'having cast aside every privilege you had won. That *I* had made possible for you. Having wasted all the advantages that had come your way. Because of a native woman. For God's sake, Jem, I trained you to speak like a native, not to become one.'

'She was my *wife*, Xavier. I was proud to call her such, and I loved her. You of all people should have understood that,' said Blake quietly.

'You knew how things worked,' Mountstuart went on. 'You might have lived with her quite respectably in the traditional manner, as your *bibi*, but you had to marry her and thrust your choices in everyone's faces. And then all the rest followed. The contrariness, the insubordination.'

'Contrariness and insubordination. That's good, coming from you.'

'I am an aristocrat, and that allows me a certain leeway. Besides, I understood the boundaries.'

Blake's voice was uncomfortably calm. 'Well, I chose my path, it was not forced upon me. Do you really wish to argue?'

'No, by all means let us not.' There was silence. 'So, you are still with the Company.'

'It was the price of staying on.'

'You recovered your captaincy then?'

'I didn't want it.'

'What do they have you doing?'

'Cleaning up their mistakes, small and tawdry things mostly.'

'*Plus ça change*,' said Mountstuart languidly.

'The mistakes were on a grander scale then.' There was suddenly the sound of breathy chuckling. Then at last, Blake said, 'Xavier, why'd you come back?'

'Oh heavens, Jem! For the money of course! The estate is mortgaged to the hilt. I must have something to live on.'

'Hence *Leda and Rama*,' said Blake, drily.

'It's good enough.'

'It is a masterpiece!' I said.

'My dear young man, it is hardly that. But it should make me some money and do some mischief in Calcutta.' Mountstuart let out a long and elegant sigh. 'I came back because I missed it. I could not abide the endless grey, and those long damp winters.'

'Xavier,' Blake said, 'we were three. Have you seen or heard about another captive? A native. His name is Mir Aziz.'

'Not one whisper. I have seen only you. I imagine they would have killed him at once. I am alive because I am European – and famous, of course – and they do not know what to do with me.'

Neither of us spoke.

'They have, by the way, treated me really quite well. They now let me more or less live among them. I generally sleep in a house on the edge of a nearby hamlet. I have learnt a particularly recondite and little-known dialect from a fellow from north of Etawah, and a plethora of fascinating details about their sexual practices. Tell me, have you been in Doora? How is Vishwanath?'

'Well enough,' said Blake, with the smallest hint of impatience. 'Surviving assassination attempts. Is there something to eat?'

'There is roti and a little dahl left from my breakfast. You are welcome to them. There may be something in the sacks. Poor Vishwanath. His court has always been a veritable pit of snakes.'

He reached about for the food. 'Perhaps you will introduce your young companion?'

'May I present Lieutenant William Avery, not quite of the 7th Bengal irregular cavalry. A great admirer of yours. Avery, Xavier Mountstuart, esquire.'

'Truly, I am deeply honoured, sir,' I said, suddenly breathless. 'I know all your verse, I came to India because of your writings. I cannot tell you how—'

'An admirer, you say?' he said, 'how refreshing. Jem has always been curiously resistant to my work.'

'I've told you, Xavier, no man is a hero to his valet.'

'Oh God, is he still quoting Montaigne?' Mountstuart drawled. 'I wish I had never given you that book. Can you tell me, young man, how my new book is faring? Does it sell?'

'It is the talk of Calcutta, sir. I had to bribe the bookseller for my copy.'

'And the reviews?'

'Scandalized, sir.'

'How gratifying.'

'This is the way out?' said Blake, pointing to the right where the cave narrowed.

Mountstuart nodded. 'We are quite deep in, deep enough to keep their supplies from spoiling. From the outside one can hear little.'

Blake stood up unsteadily, took the light from Mountstuart and hobbled towards it.

'It turns to the right. It is some way before one reaches the open air.'

'How many?'

'Between fifteen and twenty. It varies.'

'Do you have any idea of the hour?' said Blake.

'Mid-afternoon. I think we have some time. Here, eat this, we can talk of escape later.'

We tore at the rotis, smearing the last of the dahl on them, and stuffed them into our mouths. He contemplated us, settling the blanket around himself.

'So, you came to rescue me. And may I say what a fine job you have done of it so far.'

'Buchanan sent me to find you. Brought all his pressure to bear – threats, promises. Told me you had disappeared into the Mofussil for the sake of a poem about a Thuggee chieftain. I didn't believe it.'

'Buchanan, eh? Not Theo Collinson? No word from him?'

'He's out. Returning to England, I heard. Buchanan's Chief Military Secretary and very senior in the Political Department.'

'So he clawed his way to the top. And Collinson gone. I would not have predicted that.' He shrugged. 'But to return to me. It is an excellent story, no? The great poet seeks out the Thugs to enshrine them for ever in verse! I have actually been composing a ballad in my head while I have been here. I already have several thousand lines. Not that anyone will buy it. It is all novels now; ballads are sadly out of fashion.'

'What were you really doing, Xavier? Sleeman hates you.'

'Perhaps you might tell me.'

'I think someone in the Company asked you to look into the Thuggee Department. I wonder why?'

'Again, I am sure you have divined the answer.'

Blake said nothing.

'The Board of Control in London invited me to investigate Thuggee,' said Mountstuart, 'but in secret. There have been certain disagreements between London and Calcutta regarding the growth of the Thuggee Department. Calcutta loves it. The Board, however, is terrified of rumours of misdemeanours. It worries they fuel those in Parliament who would transfer India to direct rule. It knows it cannot afford a scandal that demonstrates misgovernment. I was commissioned to look into the Thuggee Department but Sleeman was not to know the reason why. I am to give my report to the Governor General.'

'So there had been rumours.'

'There were always some sceptics, like Lushington in Bharatpore, but Calcutta has always dismissed their concerns. An officer from Jubbulpore has lately been in correspondence with the Board in London about his concerns. He disappeared last year. There was some confusion about how he met his end: some say it was fever, others that he was shot.'

'And what were your conclusions?' asked Blake.

'Much the same as yours, I imagine,' said Mountstuart.

'There is no such thing as Thuggee.'

'What?' I said.

'Thuggee exists only in the mind and writings of Major William Sleeman,' said Blake. 'There is no secret fellowship of Thugs that acts across Hind. There is no Thug language. There is no common method of killing. There is no Thuggee cult of Kali.'

'Just so. And Calcutta cannot see it, for the Thuggee Department is too great a success,' said Mountstuart. 'But I am curious, what set you off?'

'You, go all the way to Jubbulpore for a poem? You were always happy enough to make it all up before. And Sleeman's book, *Ramaseeana*. A secret language of Thugs? What language? Words you would find in any rookery in any bazaar anywhere in Hind. A few phrases of thieves cant, the language of the poorest and meanest castes. As for his "Thug omens" and rituals – a list of superstitions and old customs common to ryots and petty thieves, anywhere between here and Lahore. And the so-called family trees – when you examine Sleeman's lists, hardly any of them had been born into "Thuggee". Some had been adopted. Plenty had no children or family at all. Many had been driven to banditry for a season or two because the harvests have been bad and land rents have gone up. As for the Approvers, many are bandit chiefs escaping the fate they deserve by delivering their subordinates up to the authorities and saying what Sleeman wishes to hear.'

I put my head in my hands. 'How is it then that no one else has been granted this great revelation other than yourself?' I said, wearily.

'My dear young man, how many Europeans who read Sanskrit and speak Persian spent so much time in the filthier parts of the Calcutta bazaar?' said Mountstuart. 'How many know the native gutter as well as Jem? Not one, I should hazard. Besides, so many in the Company long for it to be true.'

'As for Kali worship,' Blake said scornfully, 'every bilker, every knuckler and a thousand others will call upon Kali. She is the patroness of thieves and vagabonds, of wives and farmers and many others. Everything he writes of Kali shows no understanding of the Hindoos – but that of course is hardly surprising, as almost no Company man does. And as for that so-called Thuggee temple at

Bindachal, it bears no relation to Sleeman's descriptions. I'd be surprised if he had ever been there. And the word itself means trickster or deceiver, not strangler.'

'This is madness. We are in the clutches of a band of Thugs, and you are saying that day is night and night is day. I do not believe it.'

'Let me give you some history, young man,' said Mountstuart. 'One can glean from Sleeman's records that there were some years ago a number of bandit gangs from the Etawah district, north of here, that called themselves Thugs, but they were known as much as swindlers, cheats and mountebanks as murderers.'

'In the bazaar in Jubbulpore,' Blake broke in, 'they tell comic stories about Thugs cheating men out of horses, or talking them out of their savings.'

'But it is certainly the case,' Mountstuart went on, 'that the Thugs often preyed on travellers, like many dacoits. The truth is there are dacoits and bandits all over Hind that will kill their victims before robbing them so as to leave no witnesses. Sometimes they befriend them, sometimes they simply attack. Sometimes they throw them down a well, sometimes they strangle them first.

'Now, in '28 and '29, the Company resolved to act against the Thugs, not because natives were being murdered on the roads – that had been happening for years – but because Dhunraj Seth, the richest banker in Hyderabad, had lost three huge caches of rupees and gold on the road between Hyderabad and Indore to a number of gangs who called themselves Thugs. He demanded reparation. The Company happens to be vastly in debt to Dhunraj Seth. But once the bandits were caught they were hard to keep in prison, because they would not confess, or they would change their pleas. So Major Sleeman did a thorough job of catching them; he executed Feringhea's quite innocent nephew, you know, in order to persuade him to be captured. Then he prevailed upon them to confess, using many methods including his rack. Then he made certain that no one would go free.'

Blake nodded. 'In Saugor and Nerbudda territory,' he said, 'two testimonies from an Approver or an informer are enough to condemn a man. Trials are conducted in English so the accused understand nothing. If a native is arrested by the Thuggee Department, he will be found guilty.'

Mountstuart laughed. 'Sleeman may be a hypocrite and a bore,' he said carelessly, 'but he has a formidable talent for organization and administration – not qualities I myself have ever aspired to, but the records and the maps have a certain genius, for all they have been put to ill-intended purposes. From Sleeman's papers I judged there were no more than a few hundred men among the Thug gangs and their occasional hangers-on, and by 1832 they had all been caught. Some were hung, some transported to penal camps in Sumatra and Penang. The rest were sentenced to years of hard labour at the gaols in Jubbulpore and Saugor.'

'Where almost all of them – the poor hangers-on, the lookouts, the grooms, the cooks – have died,' Blake said. 'Meanwhile, the chiefs who turned Approver – or who give Sleeman the folk tales he loves – live out their days in the School of Industry.'

'But as the Thugs declined,' Mountstuart continued, 'the Thuggee Department grew ever greater, and Sleeman's officers are now everywhere from Hyderabad to Rajputana. I believe that since '32 some 3,000 more natives have been arrested and found guilty.'

'Do not tell me they are all innocent men,' I said, faintly.

'No,' said Blake. 'Plenty are dacoits and brigands and common criminals from all over Hind. Many are the poorest and lowest castes; some take to crime in desperation, for some it's a way of life. There has been great hardship in the countryside in the last ten years. Plenty are wandering people, vagabonds who might filch and steal a little, nomad tribes like the Gonds and Bhils who have fought the Company's orders to settle in one place, unfortunates whose crime is little more than that they continue to travel around and they are poor. There are others who have been arrested on the basis of denunciations of informers, who make money from it. They are rounded up by Sleeman's officers, who are now to be found in almost every part of Hind, all trained to see Thugs where there are none, and they are sent to Saugor and Nerbudda because it is quicker and easier to find a man guilty in the Territory than anywhere else in Hind. But they are not Thugs, and their children are not bound to be Thugs, and it is a lie.'

'Sleeman fell so under the spell of his own invention that he cannot see its fallibility,' said Mountstuart. 'He is in thrall to his system, and it has corrupted him. It began with the Approvers, who after a few beatings would tell him what he wished to hear, and then elaborated beyond his dreams. Did you see Feringhea? A fascinating succubus. A man who will fit himself to every situation. He'd sup with the devil and lick the spoon. Such a talent for survival and destruction. A mesmeric gift too, I fancy. A Thug in the old sense of the word, a trickster and deceiver. He saved his own skin by making himself indispensable to Sleeman's vision of Thuggee, offering up blood-curdling tales and dark magical rituals that Sleeman longed for. The Thuggee we know is a mixture of Feringhea's stories and Sleeman's fancies. The final seal of Sleeman's corruption was the rack, the breaking machine, whose existence he is so at pains to deny.'

'And the Company loves it,' Blake said. 'The Thugs create fear and demonstrate the degeneracy of Hindooism, and the Thuggee Department shows that the Company is fitter to rule than any native prince, and it conveniently despatches those the Company wishes to rid itself of.'

'But we saw Thugs hang,' I persisted. 'They invoked Kali.'

'Those men were Gonds,' said Blake. 'If they had not worn kurtas and been covered with flower garlands you would have seen the scars which show their tribe and caste. They were told their families would be paid a subvention if they would call upon the goddess. If you remember, only one did.'

'How do you know?'

'I broke into the gaol and spoke to them, just as I broke into the Thuggee bureau to see the papers Sleeman guards so carefully, and other places.'

'Mr Hogwood's home?'

'Yes.'

'And his servant?'

'Had a large bruise on his head, no more, I swear it.'

'Jem is an extraordinarily talented lock-picker and house-breaker,' Mountstuart said. 'And if I may continue, I have written a report for the Board of Control in London, which our hosts have curiously shown no desire to divest me of.'

'What are the charges?' said Blake.

'The first: that Thuggee as described by Major Sleeman does not, as you say, exist.

'The second: that a system of justice has been allowed to develop in Saugor and Nerbudda whereby a native may be found guilty on the flimsiest of evidence; a state of affairs initially set up to sentence known criminals, but which has now been extended in a manner which is quite beyond control.

'The third, and connected to the above: that in the interests of maintaining and extending the authority of the Thuggee Department, hundreds, if not thousands, of natives quite innocent of Thuggee or indeed any brigandage have been condemned in Saugor and Nerbudda.'

'I am also of the opinion,' said Blake, 'that Thuggee is being deliberately used as a means of justifying intervention in independent states the Company regards as not sufficiently biddable. Those accusations that the Rao protects Thugs sit very conveniently by the attempts to assassinate him. I would not be at all surprised if there are imminent plans to depose him. And there will be plenty more of it.'

'Oh, Blake! Surely now you go too far.'

'Verily,' said Mountstuart wryly, 'Thuggee has a thousand uses. I must say I had not thought of that. I told Vishwanath a little about Jubbulpore, but I did not tell him as much as I might have. The old sense of loyalty to the Company, I suppose. I felt I should wait until I had presented my findings to the Governor General before I said more.'

No one spoke for a while. For myself, the first burst of excitement at finding Mountstuart was overtaken by a great wave of fatigue. I tried to doze, but I could not: their revelations raced about my head, seeming at one moment quite preposterous and at others horribly credible.

At last I said, 'Might I please make two observations, gentlemen? You say Thuggee does not exist. But we watched that grave being dug up and saw a native party that had been killed not two months ago in the Thug manner. And why then are we imprisoned in a cave by a band of dacoits who behaved just as Thugs do?'

'It is confusing, I know, my dear young man,' said Mountstuart. 'But let me tell you something most intriguing. My captors told me they have been brigands, Thugs, what have you, for many years. They used to despatch their victims in whatever way was most easy or appropriate – with a knife, with a blow, sometimes with the *rumal*. As for burial, sometimes they buried their victims, sometimes they simply left them, or threw them in a stream or a well. But now they always kill with the *rumal* and dig the round "Thug" grave. It is as if by describing Thug rituals, Sleeman has brought them into being.'

'It seems,' I said wearily, 'a little far-fetched.' My head was spinning.

'How is it then do you think that Mauwle happened so easily on the Thug grave when the Approvers could not find it?' asked Blake.

'Hogwood said he had a nose for it.'

'Nose, my arse,' said Blake. 'There were marks on the trunks, three identical marks cut into the trunks of the three mango trees nearest to the grave. A circle with two lines through it on each trunk. I noticed them as I watched Mauwle oversee the diggers. He must have known what he was looking for. I knew they must have some significance, but I could not see then what it was.'

'I have begun to wonder,' said Mountstuart, 'whether this band, which was described to me as the last Thug gang, has been permitted to survive and to perform its gruesome murders just as Sleeman described, in order to keep the fear of Thuggee primed. An occasional Thug murder keeps the Company anxious.'

'A mark on a tree!' I said, now quite exasperated. 'That could be anything – part of the Thug ritual! Listen to yourselves! You are suggesting that the man who launched the whole campaign against Thuggee, who has pursued the Thugs tirelessly for the last ten years, is deliberately allowing – encouraging even – this gang to do its evil work, and that it then tells his men where it has left the bodies?'

'I do not believe it is in direct communication with Jubbulpore, for if it were I do not think I should still be alive, but as Jem has said there are ways by which it may send messages.'

'How did they realize what you were about in Jubbulpore, Xavier?' Blake asked. 'What did you do? Could you not have held your fire?'

'I was not brimming with tact, Jem, it is true,' Mountstuart said, a little tetchily, 'but I could not resist baiting Sleeman. All his fine aspirations to raise up the natives, and that insistent lying about the rack. I found it sickening.'

'Do you not think he is shamed by the machine and that is why he hides it? And was that all you did, Xavier?'

'Don't scold me, Jem. I am entirely well, you need have no fears on that account. Though it is likely,' he conceded, 'that my rashness drew their attention.

'Sleeman cannot bear contradiction, I could not hide my disgust, and we argued. He decided I was poisoning his creation: his work, his town. His men, let us not deny, would do anything he asked. That prize monster Mauwle took to stalking my lodgings. Every night for that last week, he would walk in grinning, brandishing his sabre, and ask me how I still liked Jubbulpore. On the last night Sleeman quite lost control of himself. He told me my inability to understand his work and my misrepresentation of it threatened everything he strove for. I had never seen him so furious. Rashly, I told him he had no idea what I could do, and I laughed at him. He said I was mad and he would have me arrested. I left. I meant to return at once to my lodgings, but instead I decided to walk round the native environs of the cantonment, which I found less unbearably respectable. By the time I returned to my lodgings, it was very late. There were men in the compound, but I had the great good fortune to see them before they saw me.

'They were armed with knives, and I knew they had been despatched to kill me. My monkey, Auckland, had returned earlier. I watched them wring his neck. I managed to hide in the shadows in the lea of the outside walls of the compound. I was certain they would find me, and two of them came very close, but at the moment when I was sure they would come upon me – the moment I was sure I was as good as dead – they were called back to the compound. The others had found some money, which I was sorry to lose, and some papers – nothing important, scribbles, though they didn't know that. They waited until just before dawn, then departed: their presence would have been quickly remarked upon by daylight. I slipped back into the compound to retrieve what I could as quickly as possible. The place had been torn apart, my possessions were strewn everywhere and every scrap of paper had been taken. I had, however, buried the important ones in the dirt. I left then and there, sleeping by day, travelling mostly by night. When I got to Doora I asked Vishwanath to keep my presence secret. It is hard to exaggerate the extent to which Sleeman is the great power in the central states.'

'There were rumours in the bazaar that someone had tried to kill you,' said Blake, 'and others that you'd slipped out of Jubbulpore in secret. The matchmaker Maa Amala said she had arranged a guide for you. She also said that you enraged the Major by trying to seduce Mrs Sleeman.'

'Good God, never!' Mountstuart said. 'She was far too virtuous for me.'

'You called your monkey Auckland?' I said, dazedly. I puzzled for a moment, then light dawned. 'After the Governor General?'

'I saw some similarities.'

'I cannot accept that Major Sleeman would countenance murder,' I said.

'That attack outside Doora. Do you think that was an accident too?' said Blake.

I shook my head. 'It is too much,' I said.

But then I thought of what I had said to Sleeman about Blake that day we had left Jubbulpore. *If it is true*, I thought, *then I brought Sleeman upon us.*

'Why after all this you actually chose to go looking for Thugs,' Blake said, 'I cannot think. It didn't seem – rash?'

'Why should it? These gangs did not have the reputation of murdering Europeans. I have encountered plenty of brigands before – we both have. And I am, after all, the king of the poets. I believed them to be the last true Thug gang, the Kitree band. You may have heard of them at Jubbulpore.'

'We heard of them.'

'At first I assumed they had escaped capture by keeping to themselves, and I wanted an untutored native account of Sleeman's campaign. I was sure they would confirm my conclusions. I planned to meet with them, return to Doora, and make my way down to Calcutta to present my report to the Governor General. Unfortunately, they have proved all too susceptible to my charms and will not let me go.'

'Did it occur to you that that book of yours might have used up a little of your credit with the Governor General?'

'Jeremiah, how very trite of you to say so.'

'And I suppose the Board didn't know about it?'

I sighed with frustration. 'Perhaps we might talk about what we are to do, how we might escape?' I said.

A murmur of echoing voices, one overlaying the other, began to come from the caves to our right. We listened, each tense, as the exchanges grew closer and closer.

The man I knew as Gulab came into the cave. He carried a lamp in a bowl of ghee like our own, and an unsheathed sword.

'Gentlemen,' said Mountstuart, 'I think you may have met our host. He goes by many names: Gulab, Chotee the singer, Salman, but he is most often known as Rada Kishin.'

He was followed by a native I did not know, who was also armed. Two more men followed, carrying bowls which they placed on the ground. There was a plate of bread and a bowl of curry and small blocks of something crystalline and hard.

Gulab, or Rada Kishin, spoke. His black eyes shone. He gestured at the food. Blake answered. Rada Kishin laughed. Blake said something about Mir Aziz. Rada Kishin shook his head. For a moment he looked solemn. He lifted the scabbard he had fastened to his belt. It was black and intricately decorated with silver wire. Mir Aziz's scabbard.

'Sar,' he said, breaking into English, 'he is dead. It is our way. We can do no other.'

'Why not us?'

Rada Kishin smiled and spoke softly in Hindoostanee. Then he inclined his head to Mountstuart, and then to Blake and then finally to me. We listened to their footsteps echo through the caves and out into the open air. I thought of the last moment I had seen Mir Aziz and how he had tried to calm and prepare me, though he must have known our likely fate.

'"The wounded snake can kill as long as life remains,"' said Mountstuart. 'Gentlemen, we do not have long.'

'I beg your pardon?'

'It is what Rada Kishin said to me,' said Blake. 'He means they cannot allow us to live and will kill us in the morning. For one Englishman they were willing to postpone sentence; three are too dangerous to them. They will decide how best to dispose of our bodies and then they will kill us.'

Chapter Fourteen

'We cannot rush them,' said Mountstuart, 'we have not a hope.'

Blake began to search among the sacks.

'I do, however,' Mountstuart went on, nonchalently, 'have the whisper – the suspicion – the seed – of an escape. That said, I have not been able to prepare as much I would have liked, as I have not spent much time in here recently.'

'Xavier!' Blake said impatiently.

'If you must have the prosaic version. I had a good deal of time here alone at first, and I explored the caves behind us. They seemed all to come to dead ends. One, however, does not. It is stoppered with earth and grit. I managed to excavate a hole large enough to crawl through. On the other side there is another sequence of caves. One leads to a rockfall. There is a hill of shale and stones, and at the top there is a small hole through which one can see daylight. I had been slowly enlarging it towards the day when I had presumed I must eventually escape, but I had not expected my departure would be so imminent.'

'Where does it comes out?'

'I have no idea.'

'We'll burn through these ropes.' Blake raised his hands. 'We'll eat, then we will inspect your hole. If we work through the night, will it be enough?'

With a large and theatrical gesture Mountstuart turned his arms outward as if he himself were posing a grand question to which he did not have the answer. Blake ripped off a piece of a hemp sack and twisted it into a spill, which he lit with the lighted wick. He applied it to the rope about my wrists, encouraging me to work at the fibres until they parted. I did the same for him. He told me to eat, and I readily acquiesced. Mountstuart hardly touched a mouthful, but

Blake, like some clucking mother hen, pressed it upon him. There was bread and *goor* – the sugar that Sleeman said the Thugs ate when they entered the cult. It was sinfully delicious: sweet, hard, with a taste that reminded me of burnt toffee. Blake scavenged the cave for useful things: Mountstuart's tinderbox, two blankets, a water skin that leaked a little, a sealed pot of ghee, the remnants of our meal. Everything he did with a sense of intense purpose, never hinting in any way that he might consider our plight hopeless, and his conviction propelled us on.

We set off, Mountstuart – who, it transpired, was rather shorter than I had expected – holding our fragile light in its bowl of ghee, and, in a leather pocket that he hung about his neck, the report he had written for the Governor General. Blake had the tinderbox, the spare pot of ghee, wicks and blankets, and I the water skin. We limped through one shadowy cave to another, until at length we arrived at Mountstuart's earth bank. The way through was like nothing so much as a rabbit hole. Mountstuart took off his blanket, thrust the light and his hands into the hole, following with his head, and forced his way through. Blake came next, pushing the blankets and ghee ahead of him, and I last. The hole was tight, and the process of stuffing in one's shoulders and feeling them lodge tight, extremely unpleasant. But we got through at last, and Mountstuart led us another few hundred yards to a high cavern where a steep hill of stone, shale and rubble stretched from floor to roof. 'At the top, I have made a small hole. I do not know where it emerges,' Mountstuart explained. 'And there is space only for one to work at a time.'

It was Blake who edged up the hill of stones first. His ascent was slow. He had very little light, having declined to carry the lamp for fear he might drop it and cast us all into darkness, and every too-robust footfall caused the surface to slide. But eventually he gained the summit. I could just make him out kneeling at the top.

I closed my eyes. I longed only for oblivion. But what I saw was the afternoon that I had gone to tell Major Sleeman about Blake.

*

At the Thuggee bureau I had asked for Hogwood or the Major, wondering if I should at last be permitted to enter its portals. It was the former who had arrived. Without a word, he had ushered me in. In the first room, half a dozen inscrutable native clerks sat at desks poring over piles of paper, and a vast *punkah* moved back and forth overhead. It was quiet, cool and exceedingly orderly. Two walls were fitted with deep glass cabinets which were packed to overflowing with despatch boxes and papers tied with different coloured ribbons. A third was covered with large maps and pencil sketches of natives' faces and heads drawn from different angles, some even from the back of the head. We walked through a door that swung energetically on its hinges afterwards. No one looked up.

With each step I was more and more discomfited. Hogwood gave me an encouraging pat and walked me to the Major's study. The Major was sitting at his desk, and had just set aside his morning huqqa. I hesitated in the doorway. The room was crammed with papers, books, stones, artefacts and sketches, much of it locked in glass cabinets or stuffed on to shelves.

Hogwood said, 'I took the liberty of bringing the Lieutenant in to see you.'

The Major looked up and frowned. 'Lieutenant Avery, is there something I can do for you?'

'I am so sorry, sir, if it is an awkward moment. I will return at your convenience.' I suddenly felt I had made a mistake. 'It is a most awkward matter, one I would much rather not raise . . .'

'I see,' said the Major.

'I shall remove myself,' said Hogwood. I had hoped he would stay, but he edged out of the room, walking down the corridor to his study, where I heard him issuing directions to an unseen clerk. Then the door shut.

'Well, Lieutenant, say what it is that troubles you so.' He had not invited me to sit, and so I remained standing.

'Major Sleeman, when I was in Calcutta, when I received my orders to accompany Mr Blake, Colonel Patrick Buchanan—'

'Patrick Buchanan, the Chief Military Secretary?'

'That is him, sir.'

The Major looked mildly surprised but shrugged. 'Continue.'

'Colonel Buchanan told me that one of my tasks was to . . . to . . . well, sir, it is a very delicate matter and an unpleasant one.'

The Major folded his arms.

'He told me that though Mr Blake was extremely good at his job, he was not always the most . . . the most reliable of men.'

The room, the entire bureau for that matter, seemed extraordinarily silent.

I lowered my voice. 'By that I do not think he meant that he was cracked in the head or anything of that sort, but that he could be' – with every word I felt increasingly uneasy – 'erratic, and held some unusual opinions. He said that I should observe Mr Blake, and that if I noticed anything that might be described as "untoward behaviour", that seemed to suggest that he might be straying from his duty in searching for Mr Mountstuart, that I should consider taking the matter – that is, reporting his behaviour – to a senior officer. He mentioned you, Major Sleeman, as someone I might approach, if I had to.'

'Go on.'

'This is not something I wish to do, sir. Mr Blake has many impressive qualities.'

There was a flicker of impatience. 'I can see that this is causing you some discomfort, Mr Avery, but it is time to come to the point,' he said.

'Of course, sir.' My voice was a little shaky. 'Major Sleeman, you should know that I am most concerned that Mr Blake may have lost his way with this investigation. You will have noticed that he seems quite obsessed by Thuggee. Believe me, it is just the same if not worse when I am alone with him. He seems to have almost forgotten that his task is to find Mountstuart. I know that he makes repeated visits to the native parts of town, I am not sure what for – he refuses to apprise me of his suspicions. He also disappears at night. I know that he has made a number of clandestine visits to the prison, indeed that he has actually broken into it. I do not believe he has any hare-brained notion to free the prisoners or anything of the sort, but that he goes to speak to them, and I suspect he is preoccupied by some thought that there is something here – something he judges not right – that he must discover or expose.'

Major Sleeman looked quite bewildered. He leant his elbow on his desk and rested his chin in the arch of his finger and thumb.

'Well, Mr Avery. You have done the right thing, even if you have left it exceedingly late. I understand how distasteful this must have been for you. But I am glad that you have come to me. I may do little more than write to Calcutta to let them know what a potentially dangerous individual they have on their hands. I shall certainly let the Governor General's office know that you did not spare yourself in the pursuit of your duty, that your loyalty has been tested and not found wanting.'

'Thank you, sir.'

'I could, I suppose, detain Mr Blake.'

I paled. 'I thought perhaps it would be enough simply to tell you.'

'Actions like these have consequences, Mr Avery. To be honest, though he is plainly a most unusual individual, it is evident Mr Blake is also an erratic and angry man and possessed of some dangerous opinions. The Thuggee Department, on the other hand, has nothing of which to be ashamed. We have consistently seen off our detractors, of which he is evidently one.'

He thought for a moment. 'May I count on your discretion? I would rather that you said nothing about our talk for now; I imagine you, too, would rather it remain confidential.'

'Yes, Major Sleeman.'

Pebbles and rocks were skittering down the sides of the mound. Blake had come down. His hands were bleeding. He announced he had cleared a space large enough for two to sit. He insisted Mountstuart and I bind our hands in strips of blanket. We took our positions at the top of the great stone mound, our backs bent, our arms stretched ahead of us. My fingertips could feel the edge of the top of an opening blocked by the stone pile itself, and from it there issued a whisper of warm air and a darkness that seemed not quite so deep.

We set to, scooping away rocks and pebbles, attempting to move the shale as fast as we could without dislodging the stones beneath us and precipitating our own fall. Within minutes my fingers were torn. From time to time, the strangeness of my situation presented itself to me afresh: sitting next to my hero in a dark cave in darkest India, too tired and preoccupied to speak of my admiration.

The hours passed and we laboured in turns. The dust made Mountstuart wheeze and his whole frame shook. Watching him ascend the mound was almost painful. For myself, I became light-headed with the effort, my bruises sang with pain and my back ached. Our fingers bled. Only Blake seemed indefatigable, tirelessly taking his turn when we slid exhausted down the shale slope. The hole, meanwhile, became larger, but still we could not see what was on the other side, and when Blake dropped a stone through it we could not hear it hit the ground.

The light on the other side began to turn from deep black to slightly lighter purple. Dawn was approaching. The hole was almost deep and wide enough for one to slide through. Blake tore one of the blankets into strips and then Mountstuart tied them together for a makeshift rope. It was so much like some escape from Sir Walter Scott, I almost laughed. Mountstuart elected to go through first, as the lightest, with the makeshift rope about his chest in a knot that he said could be easily loosened, and some of our meagre baggage. I volunteered to take his weight as the tallest and heaviest. He wedged himself through until his head, arms and upper body filled the hole and all I could see was the dim outline of his hair and beard.

'Dear young man, could you impel me through the aperture? It is rather snug, but I will manage with a little more force behind me.'

I took hold of his shoulders and gave as great a thrust as I could. He uttered a sudden 'Oh!' and his upper half slid through. Just in time, my hands closed on the cotton rope which I had wound about my leg and sat upon. I struggled to keep my balance and not let go. We had agreed to communicate in signs as far as possible for fear of being heard. For some minutes I simply paid out the rope. Then I jerked upon it as hard as I could.

'Let the rope down,' he rasped. I paid out the cloth as far as I dared, gritting my teeth: my hands – already raw from the rocks – cried out when the cloth dragged.

'Can you see the bottom? Can you find footholds?' I whispered as loudly as I could. Just as the weight became insupportable, it was abruptly relieved of its burden and I pulled it up. There was a whisper from the ground.

'I am down.' I heard no more.

The light was brighter now. Blake was climbing up the mound behind me with our few stores. 'I will hold the rope for you,' I said. There was nothing to attach the rope to; whoever was last would have to navigate their way out and down without help.

'You do not need to.'

'I am younger than you and have a better chance of climbing down. You must go with Mountstuart to confirm his report.' I had words prepared. 'I am not necessary. I—'

'Get through that hole. Don't worry on my account, I can climb almost anything. You can catch me if need be.'

'Blake, listen to me. In Calcutta Buchanan told me that my task was to watch you. He said that you might not be altogether reliable and might go astray and that if you did I should report you to a senior officer. That day before we left Jubbulpore, your questions were so erratic and you had made Major Sleeman so angry, and I could not see how it had anything to do with Mountstuart, and I was so worried about the gaol. I went to see him about you. I told him about your night visits. He asked me to keep silent about what I had said. I betrayed you.'

For a moment I thought Blake looked quite shocked. He collected himself almost immediately. 'Don't torment yourself, Avery. You obeyed your orders. Besides, we are here not because of anything you did in Jubbulpore, but because I insisted on following Xavier.'

I did not move.

'Now, Avery,' he said. 'You've read too many of Xavier's books. If you don't go through, you'll delay us.' He forced the rope under my arms. 'This end releases the knot,' he said.

I put both feet into the hole and he pushed me through. The air on the other side was noticeably warmer. I kicked my legs against the rock on the other side and wrenched my arms through, and as I swung back to the rock my head struck an outcrop of rock. Half-stunned, I could just make out Mountstuart some forty feet below me on a dirt floor. There was light behind me. The rock wall was puckered and dented, and I felt for handholds to see if one might indeed climb down it. But my fingers could attach to nothing substantial and so I allowed the rope to lower me down, coming to a halt with my heels some ten feet above the ground. I pulled at the knot, felt the rope slip from me and fell to the ground. I grimaced.

'Ah, the joys of firm ground,' said Mountstuart. The grey early-morning light was creeping in through an opening a hundred yards away, half hidden by what appeared to be thick foliage.

Above us, I could just about make out the shape of Blake working his way through the hole with little difficulty, though I had fancied myself somewhat thinner than him. Then he was splayed against the rock wall like nothing so much as a spider on its web, and he began to descend. His feet found holds where I had seen none, and his fingers stuck to the stone as if glued there. Mountstuart applauded soundlessly as he reached the ground.

'My dear Jem, any circus would still find a niche for you.'

Blake frowned, raised his fingers to his lips and pointed to the opening. He pointed at himself and began to slide soundlessly towards it.

At the cave entrance he paused, moved out into the greenery and was gone. We waited for some minutes. He reappeared and beckoned to us. Looking out, I could see we were high up and the landscape was mostly scrub. Twenty yards below us there was a copse of trees. Blake pointed. I bolted for it. In the grass to my left I saw a prone figure – a dead man, a scout or watchman, I suppose. I remember little of that run. We continued for as long as we could: headlong through tearing undergrowth, past screaming birds and monkeys, as far as we were able. On and on we went, through our strength and beyond, as if we were being chased by all the hounds of hell. At length, I heard Mountstuart stumble and fall on to the damp red ground. I stopped. He was gasping and looked at the end of his strength. My chest felt near rupture. Blake threw himself against a tree and gulped for air. The stone dust had left us looking like pale, bedraggled ghosts.

'We must press on,' he said. He took the water skin and drank. Then from under his arm he removed a bundle of cloth and a knife. I realized he had taken them from the fallen native. A knife, some cloth, blankets, water and a little food: all our possessions. I thought fleetingly of my books and the lengths I had gone to preserve them. Now I truly had nothing in all the world. From round his neck Blake fished out a small damp leather purse. In his hands were the remains of the opium ball. He pulled three small pieces from it, each the size of a pea. Mountstuart picked himself up and saw my doubtful look. In daylight I could see for the first time the famous brooding dark eyes, rather sunken in his face but still as powerful as I had seen described.

'Eat it, young man. It relieves pain, it soothes coughs, it calms an unruly gut, makes weariness disappear, and conjures renewal from nowhere,' he said, and put his in his mouth and began to chew on it.

I obeyed. I had forgotten the strangeness of the opium: the bitter taste, the texture of beeswax.

'But where are we? Where can we go?'

'It is all one. We must remove ourselves as far as possible, as swiftly as possible,' Mountstuart said.

'East lies that way,' Blake said. I wondered how he knew; the sky was grey and I could not gauge the compass points, but I wanted him to be right.

'Look, Avery, we're at a high altitude. We must be somewhere in the Vindhya mountains. If we walk parallel to them, keeping them to our left, we'll eventually get to the Ganges and Mirzapore.'

Remarkably quickly, the opium began to take effect, a knot of warmth beginning in my chest and working outwards, soothing my pains, and my legs were able to work again. Even Mountstuart slowly regained a little colour and began to breathe more easily.

For hour after hour we stumbled on, fear and opium lending

power to our limbs. Past sal tree after sal tree, past strangler vines, past shrilling birds and inscrutable monkeys, over twisting roots, broken creepers, through clouds of quiet yellow butterflies, on small paths worn by the feet of animals that led nowhere. Blake would fall back occasionally to obscure our tracks with a leafy branch, but he could not hide the broken grasses that advertised our presence so thoroughly. Several times he took us across small streams and pools, and each time we filled the water skin and drank. After a while the trees seemed to swell into one curtain of punishing green, and the strangler vines seemed like nooses, and the noise of the jangal became one long screech. The glow of the opium began to recede, and an anxious fretfulness took its place. The thought of our pursuers weighed upon me. I expected to hear their cries at any moment. With the fear came the crushing thoughts. They could not afford to let us escape; they would pursue us for ever. We had no idea where we were; we might wander in this wilderness until we starved. Calcutta was 600 miles away. The thoughts sucked at me, and beneath them was a more yawningly awful thought: that such evil could exist where I had been so persuaded there was good, and that I had played a shameful part in our discovery. My strength failed, even as my companions, so much older than I, persisted. I was so ashamed – especially before Mountstuart – but I found I could not place one foot ahead of the other.

Blake came to stand beside me. 'Come, Avery, we must go on.'

'I am sorry, but I cannot. You must leave me here.'

'Come on, William.' He put my arm across his shoulder and took my weight. 'We can go a little further. You have to get back to Calcutta, if only for that girl. The fair one at the levee. She liked you. Well, better than she liked the others, for all the good it may do you.'

'She did?' I said doubtfully.

'She did. Now, I have come up with a foolproof plan to return us to Calcutta, but it relies upon you playing the role of a mute native woman.'

Despite myself, I managed a choking laugh.

'There. Another step, and another. I don't joke, William. Xavier and I have returned from worse spots than this, have we not?'

'Most assuredly,' Mountstuart said, panting. Blake had found him a stick, and it was clear he needed it.

'We . . . once . . . escaped . . . from . . . Karachi,' Blake said, breathing heavily, 'disguised as a nautch and her ugly girl servant. The Company wanted – still wants – a route into Central Asia. We made a survey of the port and the city. But the Talpurs do not like European spies. Mountstuart made a lovely nautch, but he was younger and prettier then. I had to pluck his eyebrows. The cries of pain were something to hear. I was a most credible sullen servant, fluent in Pashto. We ran across Sindh with nothing to eat save what I could steal for a week.'

I laughed a little again.

'That's the ticket, William. Just a little further. You should know that your hero's books are compendiums of fabrication and falsity.'

There came a breathless 'Huh!' of outrage from Mountstuart.

'A mountain of falsity. This man is not the elevated being you think him, Avery – but then, to be fair, no one is. To paraphrase Montaigne,' he glanced back at Mountstuart, who gave a cross grunt, 'even when you're sitting on the highest throne in the world, you're still sitting on your arse. I've found that a very useful maxim. As I was saying, all those daring escapes: one man and his noble steed pursued by thirty angry hill-tribesmen. Nonsense. He escaped from every one dressed as a woman. I was there, arranging his skirts. I was always on foot; he rode the donkey. For three years I had blisters and he had no eyebrows. Just a little further, and I will tell you the truth. You will never see Xavier in the same light again.'

We went on. Blake told a story about Mountstuart attempting to break into a nawab's harem, and being saved by himself and an elephant. Mountstuart said it was a damned lie, though it was true that the Mahommedan ladies were very voluptuous, even if the opium they ate left them full of lassitude. I found that I had walked another five miles quite absorbed with their bantering.

The light began to go, and we looked for somewhere to bed down, eventually hiding ourselves in the deepest undergrowth we could find. 'They will not be able to follow our tracks in the dark,' Blake said. I was not sure I believed him. Mountstuart, who was almost too fatigued to eat, uttered a sceptical 'Ha!'

Blake brought out the last of our food and shared it between us. He opened the small pot of ghee and we rubbed it over our blistered hands and feet. Thus fortified, we lay down to sleep.

I expected to slide immediately into unconsciousness, but though I was as utterly exhausted as I had ever been, dark thoughts surged upon me: Macpherson dead, Nungoo dead, Mir Aziz dead, the Company full of ugly secrets.

When I woke, my head was groggy and throbbing, my feet and hands were raw, my stomach painfully empty, and my ears ringing with the sounds of daybreak. Overlaying all was a lurking sense that our pursuers might not be far. Blake was bending over Mountstuart, his hand inside the neck of the other's shirt. I watched, Mountstuart fast asleep, while Blake pulled out a purse much like his own and from it produced another small brown ball of opium, which he then slipped into his own.

He broke off a thin twig from a neem tree and handed it to me. 'Go and wash yourself, you'll feel better,' he said. 'There's a stream over there, you can hear it. We must be off soon.'

When I returned, Mountstuart was awake and dusting himself off. He looked exhausted, inclined his head regally at my morning greeting without a word, and stalked off to the stream. He was no better humoured when he came back. Blake gave us both a piece of the opium.

'It'll get us through another few days if we cannot find food,' he said. Mountstuart stared at him hard, but said nothing.

It seemed as if there was a drill pressing upon my forehead. 'Where will we go?

'We can't go back to Doora. They may have someone watching the roads.'

'But Calcutta is 600 miles away.'

'We need simply to get far enough so that our captors' – I noted he did not say 'Thugs' – 'will give up their pursuit. We'll make for

Mirzapore,' he said firmly. 'It is not quite ten days since Mrs Parkes said she was meeting the Governor General's party in Mirzapore. She will only just have arrived. We will catch the Governor General at Mirzapore before he goes north. Put Mountstuart's findings before him. Add mine. I judge the distance to be around eighty miles. We can certainly do it.'

'A mere eighty miles,' I said. 'And in which direction?'

'This way.' He set off briskly. Mountstuart picked up his stick, gave a sigh and followed.

The opium did its work. We ran through jangal, sometimes thicker, sometimes sparser, with never more than an animal track to guide us. There were streams everywhere and we drank often to fill our bellies. Gradually, the fear of capture subsided. What remained racing round my head was the thought that we might roam this featureless jangal for ever and never strike humanity. But when my pace slowed, Blake would fall back to walk beside me. Sometimes he told me stories – how they delivered horses to some grandee in the Punjab, while fulfilling some secret spying mission – or he described the views from the hills near Thibet. Sometimes he asked me to describe scenes from home, what I admired about my sister, what I remembered of my mother. I even spoke of my father – though all my recollections seemed to me very dull by comparison. His words distracted me, and my trying thoughts slipped away, until all that was left was the need to place one foot in front of the other. The pace, however, was clearly telling on Mountstuart. He looked pale and ill, and he said not a word. Towards late afternoon, as we came once more to the end of our strength, Blake began to talk about his exploits with Mountstuart.

'The things we did for the Company,' he said. Mountstuart had slowed down, and his face was pale and streaked with perspiration. He did not answer. 'Do you recall Burmah?' Blake went on.

'Burmah?' said Mountstuart, visibly drawing himself together. 'How could I forget Burmah?'

A few minutes passed. 'Absurd, risible episode. Preposterous,' said Mountstuart. Blake began to walk a little faster, and we tried our best to keep up.

'It was '24, young man. The Company had its eye on Burmah. Disastrous campaign, though the Company did end up with Assam and Manipore and what have you. They sent us ahead of the army into the jangal. Someone at the Political Department had heard the Burmese set great store by a white elephant whose coming would foretell the return of the Buddha. If we had the elephant, they reasoned, the people would welcome our army. And so we were sent to find it.'

'A mythical white elephant?' I said.

'That is correct, young man. Strangely, though we looked high and low, we could not find it anywhere, could we, Jem? In the meantime, we learnt the dialects of some of the forest tribes, the Kayin and the Mon, who did not overly love their overlords. They hid us from the Burmese, who would have happily disembowelled us. We advised the Company that the tribes would rise for us if we could offer them the chance of a small independent state under Company rule. But naturally it did not listen. The familiar story. The tribes rose on their own, and the Burmese slaughtered them in great numbers.

'That was in those first years, when Jem was a shrimp of a thing. The first time I saw him I knew immediately that I could use his unique talents. He could pass himself off as anything, Bengal street child, Pathan goat herd. He was usefully small and could climb up and through everything. I trained him, and when he was ready I took him off with me to Punjab and Kashmir. Such a shame he grew.'

Mountstuart stopped, and took several deep unsteady breaths.

'Now, Jem,' he said, and it seemed to cost him something to speak. 'Have I sung sufficiently for my supper? I need my piece. I cannot walk on without it.'

Blake stopped. Slowly he brought out the purse around his neck. He pulled off a small piece and held it out.

'Is that all?' said Mountstuart.

'It will have to last until we reach Mirzapore,' Blake said. 'You know that.'

'Let us hope we find it,' said Mountstuart, but he took it. We tramped a few more hours in silence until the light failed, and then stopped. I slept almost where I fell.

In the morning, Mountstuart had stomach pains, but Blake coaxed him up and handed us both a small piece of the opium. I hesitated.

'Take it,' said Mountstuart with a thin smile. 'It takes years to become as I am.' I pretended not to have heard, but put the morsel in my mouth, noting with mild alarm that it seemed less unpleasant than before.

We began to walk, Blake and I shouldering the last of our baggage, but still Mountstuart struggled. He muttered that his limbs hurt. At first he insisted he would not accept our offers of help, but eventually he let us take it in turns to support him, and so we made progress, but more slowly than we had done. All the while, I could see that Blake was marking our way, observing the sun, and looking out for signs of occupation as we went. In the early afternoon the forest thinned, and he stopped by a stream and smiled.

'There is a village up ahead,' he said. The rush of relief I felt was so great I almost stumbled, bringing Mountstuart with me.

'How can you tell?'

'By the way the undergrowth has been worn and eaten by goats, and the bark has been harvested. The trees thin ahead. There'll be fields. I shall go in, you stay here. Take shelter in the trees if you can.'

I would have protested, but Mountstuart folded his legs up and crumpled on to the ground and I could see he could go no further, nor safely be left. I too, truth be told, was at the end of my strength. So I watched Blake prepare himself. First he made himself a turban. Then he wound strips of blanket from our escape rope around his legs and arms. He stepped into the stream and covered his feet in mud until they were dirty and grey enough to belong to an elephant, or a much-travelled native, and then took Mountstuart's sandals. He tore strips off his kurta. In one he cut holes for eyes and mouth, and wrapped it around his face. The others I helped him tie round his hands. He finished by donning one of the blankets. Almost nothing of him could be seen but his feet. He took the branch Mountstuart had used as a stick, and shaped it with the knife into a stake. Then he bent over, and in one movement seemed to shrink and age several decades.

Mountstuart sat up, better humoured. '*Et voilà*,' he said. 'The leper.'

The jangal floor was thick with dead leaves and twigs, but there was little undergrowth to provide cover. 'It would be best if you could get him up into a tree,' Blake said, doubtfully. 'You'll be safer.'

I looked at Mountstuart. 'I cannot see how that can be done,' I said.

We ventured beyond the trees, through the tall grass, and eventually came to what appeared to be an abandoned irrigation ditch on the side of what had once been a cultivated field. Mountstuart and I sat down in the shadow of a tree. Blake did his best to disguise our tracks – though he was dissatisfied at the results – and I watched him walk back to the stream, cross it, and continue east into the trees on the other side. Mountstuart fell asleep almost immediately. I was relieved. I lay back and watched the light dapple the leaves, and tried to set aside the worries that crowded in: that I might not set eyes on Blake again, that Mountstuart was in no state to go any further. I dozed.

At length, Mountstuart hauled himself up.

'If I do not have some form of verbal exchange I shall die of boredom,' he said. He seemed much brighter than he had been for two days. 'Young man, you say you came to India because of me. You may tell me which of my works you particularly admire, but first, how did you come to be attached to Blake?'

'It still seems quite unlikely to me, sir,' I said. 'I was sent to Black-town to summon him to Government House.'

'So, you dislodged him from that miserable hole in Blacktown?'

'Only just, sir,' I said. 'I think I aggravated him out.' He smiled, a lazy, amused, charming, tired smile. 'Then I was sent along with him for lack of anyone else.'

'How flattering.'

'Oh no, sir, they did not know how much of an admirer of yours

I was. I was given a copy of *The Courage of the Bruce* when I was fourteen. I have carried that copy, and all the others, all the way from Calcutta to Doora. It's gone now, of course.'

'I am honoured.'

I quoted my favourite verses, and he seemed pleased and talked a little about where he had been when such and such had been composed. He spoke of Runjeet Singh, the Lion of the Punjab, about meeting Lord Byron, about his first years in India. He talked of the Rao, and of other native princes he knew; of his dislike of Sleeman and the new missionaries from England and how India had changed, of the report that had been taken by the Thugs, of his new poem. He was animated and amusing, and his words tumbled out at almost too great a speed, and his eyes seemed huge and their pupils tiny little drills. He asked me about my time in Calcutta, and laughed uproariously at my answers, and then about my family and my home, which he plainly found less scintillating. Eventually, he came to a stop and we drifted again into silence. The thought that Blake might never return, held at bay all this time, returned, and the familiar sense of dread took hold.

Towards dusk there came the sound of brushing grasses and light footfalls. I pushed Mountstuart into the grass and flattened myself as best I could. A bundled figure hove into view. He whistled – a sound I thought I had not heard since I was in England.

'Blake?'

'Hush!'

Though I had seen him don the disguise that morning, I was still surprised. It might have been another man, older, inches smaller, bent out of shape, hands like claws, and leading, of all things, a donkey, which was carrying several packs and a large pot. He pulled off his hood and mask and unbent himself. 'I have roti, rice, camel's milk, walnuts, cloth and sandals.'

'Walnuts?' I said.

'It's the end of the season, we are lucky,' he said. 'We'll eat the nuts and boil the shells to darken our skin.'

Mountstuart stood up.

'See the conqu'ring hero comes! Sound the trumpets, beat the drums!' he said.

Blake stared at him, then slowly tethered the donkey to a tree. The food was like manna. Like nectar. Even the odd salty taste of the camel's milk was good. In under the trees, Blake lit a small fire and filled his pot with water, and we cracked open the walnut shells, He said the village was called Seetabad. He had begged a few things and stolen others, including the donkey, and had established that the road that ran through it led north to Mirzapore. Our fortunes seemed suddenly transformed. I was more cheered than I had been since Doora, but he seemed distracted.

'However did you take the donkey?'

'I take no pride in it. It is some ryot's livelihood and it will soon be missed, so we will have to move.' He sighed. 'But I have other news. I thought we would have gone far enough, but they are still pursuing us, and are not far. Two bands of travellers passed through Seetabad this morning: one was a group of musicians. The second, I imagine, was the rest of them. One of them was carrying a fine black and silver-inlaid scabbard. Very distinctive.'

'Mir Aziz had a most distinctive scabbard just like that,' I said.

'Precisely. I calculated about fifteen men in all. I don't know which way they went. But they are more determined in their pursuit than I had expected them to be. They should long since have melted back into the Mofussil. I fear they must have decided that they cannot afford to let us go; they are more persistent than I expected. If they return here, they'll hear about my thefts. This place is too small for such happenings not to become widely known. We cannot stay. We must head for Mirzapore as fast as we can. We will travel tonight. It's possible we'll find a Company civilian in one of the next villages.'

'But you have not rested at all, and I do not know how far Mountstuart can go.'

'I'll keep up. The donkey is for Mountstuart.'

The water boiled and we tossed in the walnut shells. It turned a dark muddy brown. When it had cooled, Blake took a muslin rag and rubbed the mixture into his face, the backs of his hands and fingers, his neck, his arms, his feet and legs. The result was surprisingly effective. Mountstuart and I followed suit, and to finish we all dipped our hair in the mixture. I was pleased, but Blake shook his head.

'Your eyes are too pale, your features too European, you are not built like a native, your feet are too smooth, and every time you open your mouth you betray yourself. If you had a beard and a smattering of Pashtu you might pass for a Pathan. But you don't, and we must be inconspicuous. And so, Avery, a mute native woman it will be.'

'Though it must be said that a six-foot native woman is hardly a common sight,' said Mountstuart.

I was aghast. 'You joke.'

'I was never more serious in my life, William.'

I protested that my Hindoostanee had come on in great strides, that I should be hobbled and of little use in a fight. I pointed out that Mountstuart had far more practice in playing a woman. I pleaded that I might be a hooded, mute native man. Blake was immoveable.

'Don't be downcast, Avery. After so many years of reading Xavier's verses, you will be able to tell your own tale of how you escaped the Thugs disguised as a native matron. You'll be the toast of Calcutta. And it is really not so uncommon. Why, at any one time throughout the country hundreds of young men escape from prisons, and steal in and out of zenanas to visit their lovers, dressed as women.' He was only half-joking.

There was little to be done. Blake produced cloth from his packs, Mountstuart and he wrapped their heads in pugrees, tied their trousers into rough dhotis, and wrapped blankets over their shoulders and heads. I, meanwhile, was swathed head to foot in the remaining blankets, and gave up my boots in favour of sandals – it was all I could do to prevent Blake from burying them. Mountstuart insisted that he inspect my walk, which he told me was not nearly demure enough. He demonstrated his patented 'begum's carriage' – 'Young man, I have used this many times in tight scrapes,' he said – and insisted that I imitate him. Blake watched.

The moon was high and the night clear, and our strange little caravan was well lit: Mountstuart astride the donkey; Blake, his head hooded in his blanket and limping a little; and I, constrained from head to foot by my hateful robes. Blake's plan was to gain the road, then walk parallel to it through the trees as far as we could before dawn. At first my sandalled feet caught on every creeper and root, and though they permitted me to uncover my face, I was regularly admonished for lifting my skirts too high as I strode. But the night was cool, and I was protected from the worst of the biting insects, and with every step we drew closer to Mirzapore. It was almost pleasant. One could hear the chirp of humming creatures and occasional night calls – the *chuck chuck* of nightjars, the screech of an owl, the cackle of some sinister hunting animal. Once we tiptoed past an old broken temple, fearing to rouse any holy man who might make his home there. The hours passed.

Just before sunrise the trees thinned and we found ourselves in the fields on the outskirts of another village. Several had the small covered platforms on which labourers kept watch for animals coming to eat the crops. At this time of year we did not expect to encounter watchers, but we were careful. We had agreed that we would avoid such places until we found a settlement large enough for a bazaar of sufficient size that we would not be too conspicuous. We walked deeper into the trees, found a hollow beneath a spreading tree surrounded by high grasses, and slept.

When I woke, Blake had gone to survey the village. I waited, the emptiness in my stomach almost painful. Mountstuart woke and looked about, ill-humouredly. He did not acknowledge my morning greeting. Blake returned with some bread. It was hardly enough to feed all three of us, and he was solemn and once again seemed preoccupied.

'Really, Jem,' Mountstuart said testily, 'the bleeding heart is too much. It may be some poor native's supper, but it is our survival.'

'It is not that,' said Blake sombrely. 'We haven't shaken them. They're still after us. They asked about three Europeans. Or if anyone had seen any group of three travellers. We could wait until they pass on, but the village is too small to steal from without attracting attention. And we must get you to Mirzapore. I reckon it as twelve or thirteen kos. Not more than thirty miles. We must trust to our disguises and take to the road, it's busy enough.'

'But you have hardly slept,' I said.

'And there is no need to make speed on my account,' said Mount-stuart, almost haughtily.

'Xavier, you took the store. You took it all. There is none left.'

'I had to, Jem. Besides, it was mine. And I am sure you have a little left somewhere.'

'I don't.'

'Do not give me that accusing look, young man,' Mountstuart said, looking at me. 'You understand nothing!'

'I am not giving you any kind of a look!' I answered irritably. 'And why can you not for once use my name? I do have a name, you know.'

'Xavier can't remember anyone's names, never could. Too much trouble.'

'He knows your name,' I said accusingly.

Blake did not dignify this with a reply.

It was a wide dirt track, not unlike the Poona road we had taken south, but it was busier – most of the time. We met herds of goats, groups of singing pilgrims, a series of camel caravans, beggars and holy men. Then there were long periods when the road was empty. I could not decide which I liked less. When the road was busy I was stared at, no doubt because I was perceptibly taller than any woman on the road. I shrank from the scrutiny, pushing into the back of my hood and looking down so I could see even less. When it was empty I expected that small party of musicians with a mule at any moment. I should have felt better if I had not felt so confined and constrained by my skirts, or if I had had a weapon of some kind, but Blake had our one knife. And we made slow progress because of my woman's garb and because Mountstuart had trouble remain-ing on the donkey, and so I had to hold on to him. As the day continued, he became testy. He began to slouch and sway, and to mutter in English that his limbs were aching and that he needed to rest. In vain we frowned at him, and Blake rebuked him in some unfamiliar dialect, but he ignored us. Blake, meanwhile, acted as our scout, falling behind to see who was coming, or striding ahead to survey what would greet us.

It was early afternoon and the road was quite empty when he ran up behind us.

'They are coming up behind us. Maybe a quarter of a mile. We cannot outdistance them.'

Chapter Fifteen

Ahead of us was a small battered stone Hindoo temple with the usual steep carved steeple, and a little tank next to a large neem tree. Sitting rather glumly beneath it was an unkempt old man, one of those sadoos or holy men who attach themselves to old shrines or temples and live off what they can beg. He had a white beard with a knot tied into it, and his ribs and his forehead were painted chalk white. He wore nothing but an old yellow dhoti, and placed before him there was an old wooden bowl. There was no question but that he had seen us. In any case, the jangal had thinned and retreated to the hillsides some way away, and around us was an area of scrub in which it would not be easy to hide. With Mountstuart unable to walk, there was no hope of running to the shelter of the trees in time.

Blake approached the old man. At first the old native refused to look at him and shook his head. Then he spoke in a high querulous voice.

'He says if he lies about us and they find us, they will come back and kill him. He says if he helps us and they find out, they will kill us and then him,' Blake said. But he did not give up. He sat down and began to talk, pointing at Mountstuart and myself. The minutes passed and my impatience mounted – soon they would be able to see us and there would be no escape – but I feared to speak lest I spoil Blake's argument. Leaving Mountstuart sagging on the donkey, I approached Blake and tapped him on the shoulder. I could hear the pleading in his voice. He looked up and pulled my hood off, and went on speaking to the sadoo.

When he finished speaking, the sadoo contemplated us for some minutes. His face was a picture of worry. But Blake had softened his heart. He stood and gestured towards the little temple. I helped Mountstuart from the donkey and supported him in. The sadoo showed Blake a place to tether the beast where it was just hidden from the road, and then he too came in. There was barely room for all of us, and Blake and I stood to give Mountstuart room enough to sit. The sadoo propped what had once been the temple's wooden door, now rotted and splintered, against the lintel and took his place under his tree.

We did not wait long. We could hear them coming, the voices and the ass with its little tinkling bells. They stopped to speak to the sadoo. I held my breath and looked at Blake and prayed that Mountstuart would not forget himself. The sadoo answered calmly enough. There were a number of exchanges. Blake listened intently. Someone walked round the circumference of the building, and then the party seemed to stop. I realized after a few moments they were taking water from the tank. For several minutes nothing was said. Then someone mounted the little steps to the temple entrance. Blake closed his eyes. There was a hearty blow on the door. It rocked but did not shift. As one, we pressed ourselves back into the shadows, though had the door opened we would all have been instantly visible. Standing on that top step, but inches from us, one of our pursuers barked out something to the sadoo. Back came his voice, calm, reedy and insistent. The footsteps descended. There were the sounds of baggage hitched up, and the tinkling of the ass's bells, and they seemed to be off.

We remained in that little space for what seemed like an age. The ass's bells rang in my ears for long after it must have ambled out of earshot. The sadoo came and with some effort pushed the door away, and we spilled out into the air. Blake lifted Mountstuart on to the donkey as gently as he could, thanked the sadoo and explained that to our shame we had nothing to give him. He shook his head, looked at us shrewdly and raised his palms upward. I understood he was giving us his blessing.

'He says in case they turn back we can walk into the trees, and as long as we don't stray too far from the edge, we will never be far from the road. He reckons there is a town ten miles on with a good-sized bazaar. There is a dak bungalow there.'

We turned from the road and walked through the scrub into

the trees. We stopped to rest among the trees for a while, then pressed on as night fell. The land began to rise and off ahead, darker than the sky, we could see the sides of the Vindhya mountains. Mountstuart grumbled a little and began to shake. Blake took off his own blanket and wrapped it around him. For several hours we walked in near silence. Then Mountstuart began to talk in a taut whisper.

'You know, Jem, I cannot remember my own lines. They were all in my head, but now I cannot remember them.'

Some minutes later he said, 'I am sorry, Jem. I am truly sorry. I am the wreck of myself, Jem, I should never have come back. But you should have come to England with me. We would both have been better there.'

'There was nothing for me in England, Xavier.'

'You would have saved yourself this. You would not still be serving those damned bastards.'

'You came back.'

'The Board wanted me. They were so insistent. I was the only man for the task. How could I refuse? All was well until Jubbulpore. I simply need a little regularly, and then I am almost as I was. But of course Sleeman – dull puritan that he is – has banned the sale of opium in the bazaar at Jubbulpore. Finding it was harder, and it made me a little . . . erratic. Then in the cave, in the dark, alone, I could not think. The lines would not come. And they were so generous with it.' He laughed drily and it turned into a cough. 'And it relieved so much. The lines poured into me.'

A little while later he said, 'Let me tell you the story, young man, of my first encounter with Jem.'

His voice rallied a little and he pulled himself up. 'It was in the Bangbazaar in Calcutta. As I wandered through the stalls, I heard a screaming argument, a cacophany of adults shouting, and in their midst a little piping monkey voice, swearing fluently in English and Hindoostanee and something else I later discovered to be Irish. I turned a corner and found a crowd of furious shopkeepers closing in on a shrunken little urchin boy with the unmistakeable pinched features of the English lower orders. He was screaming back at them in perfectly colloquial – if profane – Hindoostanee. I thought he must be about eleven years of age, but later reckoned him to be fourteen.'

Mountstuart's voice trembled with anger and affection all at once. Blake was silent.

'He was no better than a thief. Indeed, he was a thief. His parents had been hanged or transported, I know not, and he had been sent out on the Company's shilling as a drummer boy, and now he had been caught stealing. The scene was most diverting, but I was curious about the creature, so I pushed my way into the crowd and offered to pay off the shopkeepers – it cost me a goodly sum – and caught him by the ear before he could run off. He had been in Calcutta for six months. In that time, he had taught himself the dialect of the bazaar and a deal of Irish from the common soldiers in his troop.

'He was a trial to one and all, one and all, disobedient and inso-lent, and he had a remarkable talent for filching and thievery and all manner of dishonesty. And he had a magpie mind, which had picked up all kinds of strange and glistening bits of fact and nonsense. I had a fancy to do something with his talents, and an idea of what he might be good for, and his regiment was not sorry to see him go. I found a Company moonshee and put him to work: his letters, Hin-doostanee, then Sanskrit and Persian. But he was a little animal, a proper little criminal.'

His voice dropped as if he had used it all up. 'He would collect his daily grog ration in a water skin inside his trousers, and sell it on at a profit to the soldiers more thirsty than himself. But we beat that kind of conduct out of him.'

A little later he said, 'I am getting old, Jem.'

He continued to shake. Blake stopped, carefully rearranged Mountstuart's blankets, opened the water bottle, poured a little into the cap and gave it to him.

When the dawn came we were at the foot of a fortress town that looked more than promising. There was no argument this time, we would all go in together. We were at the end of our strength and if we could not find food or help here, it would be hard indeed to go on. Blake said there should be a decent-sized bazaar, and if there was a working dak post we might exchange the donkey for food and shelter and send a missive by dak runner to Mirzapore. It should arrive within the day and we might get help by the morrow.

'But we should not come in together in case they are looking out for us. You must walk with Mountstuart; I will come alone and find you.'

The town walls were tall and the colour of the dark red earth: a good start, I thought. But through the gates there were clusters of mean little huts, and as we walked further on it was evident the town had seen more prosperous times. Once grand houses had been overtaken by palm frond and vine, and there was little sense of trade and bustle. We pushed on towards the bazaar, hopeful but anxious. It was a sore disappointment: an all-but-abandoned square, a few sorry stalls and a tank where natives were watering their live-stock. I brought the donkey to the tank to drink, and tried not to sink into despondency. I helped Mountstuart off the beast and set-tled him on the tank's steps, for there was nowhere else I could put him. He did his best to appear able, but he was plainly not well, and my rather too successful attempts to help him dismount drew looks – though his ill health had the effect of discouraging our audience from examining us too closely. Taking care that my face was covered and my eyes shadowed by my hood, I looked about. There was very little to see. Someone was selling food in a corner; dogs sniffed rubbish. No sign of our pursuers at least, but none of Blake either. And so we sat by the tank, and I helped Mountstuart to water, and we waited. I wondered if I could find anyone to buy the donkey, but abandoned the notion as I had not the energy to pursue it.

At length I spotted Blake. He walked purposefully across the empty market, limping slightly, his hood deliberately obscuring his features. He hailed us in some dialect of Hindoostanee that I could not understand. He came to Mountstuart's other side and mut-tered, 'We must get him back on the donkey, we must move quickly.'

I did not need chivvying. We hurried as fast as we could across the square. Then, just to one side of us, a party of riders came into the market making for the tank – a European officer, and with him eight cavalry sepoys in Company livery. I felt such relief I could hardly breathe.

'Thank God!' I cried – but it came out an indistinct croak. 'Thank God! Sir! You've saved us!'

The European turned round, looking for the provenance of the voice. I threw back my hood and pushed aside my veil, barely aware of the startled natives about me.

'Who is that?' The European turned, standing up in his saddle, obviously bemused, as were the ryots standing about. I was a most peculiar sight. He took off his helmet and looked over.

It was Hogwood.

'Good heavens, Lieutenant Avery?' Looking distinctly slight and small without his helmet, he pulled his horse around and rode up to us, squinting. 'Lieutenant Avery! The hero of the hour! What on *earth* are you wearing?'

Our desperate need suffocated my confusion at seeing him. Many thoughts crowded into my mind but I thrust them away. 'We have been walking for five days with almost no food. We are all out.'

'You must be,' he said, quite astonished. He took our party in. 'Is that . . . Is that Mr Mountstuart? Great heavens!' He dismounted.

Mountstuart raised his hand feebly, but did not speak.

'Mr Mountstuart is not at all well. We rescued him from a band of Thugs – dacoits,' I said.

'Great heavens!' Hogwood said again. 'How absolutely extraordinary!' He stared at the dirty creature on Mountstuart's other side. 'Mr Blake, is it you? I should never have known you.'

Blake nodded. 'I heard there was a Company officer in the town.'

'May I say again, Avery, that you look quite extraordinary.'

'The Thugs – dacoits – trailed us for days. We were forced to adopt disguises.'

'I see.' Hogwood looked us over again, sounding more incredulous and as if he was on the verge of laughter, then suppressed it.

'Dear me, I forget myself. What can I do for you – food and water to begin with, I imagine?'

'Food, water and rest,' said Blake.

'Mr Mountstuart is all out, and he may require other . . . ah . . . refreshment,' I added. 'We need to get to Mirzapore as fast as possible. If you can help us see to Mr Mountstuart, feed us and get us some horses, we can be on our way.'

'Of course,' said Hogwood, his eyes straying back to Mountstuart. 'What of your two servants?'

'Mir Aziz was killed; Sameer is in Mirzapore.'

'I am sorry for that. Well, it happens that I am on my way to Mirzapore myself. Perhaps we can travel together? I am told the place is still quite impossibly crammed with the Governor General's people and the army. Really, this is the most extraordinary coincidence. I am checking on a number of new dak post stops and am here only for today. The town, as you see, is run-down and it has only recently been decided that it should be built up again. It is likely to be months before another European comes again.' He shook his head in disbelief.

'Mr Hogwood,' said Blake. 'Mr Mountstuart needs medicine urgently. I must find a pan seller and something to pay him with. I can ensure the Company reimburses you, but we are without anything of value . . .'

'Of course, I should have some coins,' said Hogwood. Though I was starved and exhausted and knew there was no alternative, I could not help averting my eyes with embarrassment as Hogwood felt around in his various pockets before retrieving several blackened rupees. 'Please. My jemadar knows this place. He will help you.'

'I am grateful,' said Blake. He began to rattle away quietly in the jemadar's ear.

'We have pitched our tents just beyond the walls, Avery. If you and Mr Mountstuart come with me, we will make plans to get you to Mirzapore, and if you are able, you must tell me about these Thugs.'

He called out orders to the sowars. Two dismounted and offered us their mounts, but I worried that Mountstuart would not be able to sit on a horse without my help, and brushed the men away.

'Avery,' Hogwood said. 'My sowars can support him. Rest yourself.'

I was given a horse, and was glad to have it.

Hogwood's tent had been erected in the overgrown grounds of a once grand native mansion. It was a splendid affair (I wondered for a moment if it was the tent under which I had sat watching the bodies dug up outside Jubbulpore, but dismissed the thought), with fine carpets, and a curtained area where there was a charpai, a wooden bath, and a copper basin and tripod just like the one I had abandoned in Calcutta. Once we had sat Mountstuart in a deep reclining chair thick with cushions, Hogwood went to arrange matters and servants began to bring out food: rice, wheat cakes, boiled eggs and cooled water to begin with. By the time Blake arrived, there was fricasseed chicken, omelettes, custard, bananas and custard apples; and a bottle of cold claret. So much food, indeed, that simply looking at it made me feel a little sick.

'I have sent a sowar to Mirzapore to inform the authorities you are on your way,' said Hogwood, returning to the tent. 'In my humble opinion you should rest for a while – perhaps take a bath to prepare yourself for civilization – and leave your journey until the morning.'

Blake was encouraging Mountstuart to eat a modest plate of rice and egg. I thought I saw him slip a pellet of something into Mountstuart's hand. The sight was both touching and strangely upsetting.

'I am afraid, Mr Hogwood, we simply cannot wait,' said Blake, looking up. 'But we will take a short rest. It may seem perverse, but we have our reasons.'

'But Mr Mountstuart is clearly exceedingly weak. If you wait until tomorrow, we can bring him back on a bullock cart.'

It was Mountstuart who now answered. 'My dear young man, your hospitality and concern are most gratefully received, especially in view of our last meeting. But it is imperative I reach Mirzapore as soon as possible.' His voice was not much more than a rasping whisper, but even so he brought to his words a certain dramatic flourish, and a faint hauteur, which I wished he had spared us.

'Yes, of course.' Hogwood looked abashed. 'But may I say that if your inclination to leave swiftly is in any way related to the awkwardness occasioned by your stay – both your stays – in Jubbulpore, or indeed the suddenness of Mr Mountstuart's departure, I would beg you to lay that aside. We may take different sides in . . . in, er, certain arguments, but I truly wish to help in any way I can. I am particularly concerned about these dacoits or Thugs who held Mr Mountstuart. You say they pursued you. That is very worrying. If you can spare the time to tell me what passed, I would be most grateful.'

'I have a meeting with the Governor General I cannot afford to miss,' said Mountstuart. 'I have some documents I must lay before him.'

I thought Hogwood paled slightly at Mountstuart's words, but I was not sure.

'As to my story, having quit Jubbulpore rather abruptly, you will remember, I travelled the forests of Saugor and Nerbudda, and was taken prisoner by a brigand gang, who were, nevertheless, moved to keep me alive. They were, I must say, a fascinating group. I hope to write something about them. They call themselves the last true Thugs, and go by the name of the Kitree band, and their leader is a man named Rada Kishin.'

Hogwood gasped. 'I do not know what to say. Lieutenant Avery, do you not recall, this is the gang who we believe murdered that poor family we exhumed while you were in Jubbulpore? It seems they have suddenly become exceedingly and dangerously bold.'

'It so happened that Mr Blake and this young man stumbled upon my captors,' Mountstuart went on, as if Hogwood had not spoken – it seemed the opium was having its effect, 'and were taken prisoner too. At which point our hosts concluded they had too many European guests and prepared to despatch us. We realized we must escape. We did so, and then walked through the jangal to evade our pursuers, until we found the road a few days ago. They, however, continued to pursue us. Indeed, we feared they might have followed us into this very town. The pursuit has weakened me, but I am determined to reach Mirzapore as soon as I can. That, I think, is a fairly succinct summary of events.' He let his head fall back among the cushions.

I thought of everything Mountstuart had left out, including all that Blake had done. I frowned very slightly at him. He tightened his lips almost imperceptibly in such a way that left me in no doubt that I should say no more.

Hogwood leapt up. I had never seen him so animated. 'You think they may be near here? This is an opportunity we cannot afford to miss! I shall send two of my men to make inquiries back the way you came. If I accompany you to Mirzapore today, I can have a whole fresh cavalry unit from Mirzapore out here by tomorrow.'

'A whole unit?' Blake said.

'Major Sleeman's writ runs all the way along the road, Mr Blake,' said Hogwood, smiling slightly. 'Ah yes, I must send a message to Jubbulpore. Can you tell me anything about where you found them? I think we might finally be able to apprehend the whole band!' He paused for a moment.

'You must all eat and then rest for a few hours. I will make arrangements and have fresh horses ready for when you rise. If you can hold out for a few hours more' – he looked at Mountstuart doubtfully – 'you will have all the comforts of civilization by the end of the day.'

I looked at Blake. It was evident Mountstuart could not move at once. There seemed to be no alternative. Blake nodded.

'That is a relief,' said Hogwood. 'If you will excuse me, I will set our plans in motion.'

Then he tapped his head and laughed.

'Heavens, Avery! Your story has quite distracted me. I must congratulate you on your *other* exploits! Everyone from Poona to Benares must have heard of how you shot the tiger and saved the Rao of Doora's life. You are quite the hero!'

I had not meant to sleep but I could not help myself. I woke stiff, apprehensive and wishing I felt stronger. Hogwood said that with fresh horses we ought to reach Mirzapore in three hours, even making allowances for Mountstuart. He had arranged for two sowars to go ahead to announce our coming and scout the road. Two would accompany us. Two would stay with the baggage carts and servants and make the slow journey the next day. It was perfectly usual and acceptable practice.

It was just after midday. The sun was high but the temperature was pleasant. We made good speed. Blake appeared his usual silent self, but I did not believe he was entirely easy in himself. Mountstuart was managing better than I would have imagined – whatever Blake had given him seemed to have restored him for the moment. I glanced at Mountstuart: whatever became of us, I could not see how he might be mended.

We had ridden for about half an hour when Hogwood, out ahead, pulled up. He undid the water bottle at his side and took a draught. We all took a moment to do likewise. The road was wide, four or five horses might have ridden abreast, but dense jangal had taken over from scrub and the leaves leant slightly in the breeze.

Silently, out from the trees to our left stepped a native. And then another. And another. Dark faces, well shod, draped in blankets, all with staves and knives. And then another, a familiar figure this time: Rada Kishin. In each hand he carried a pistol. One was a Collier repeater. I was sure it was mine.

The two sepoys drew their swords and prepared to fight. Kishin shot one, who toppled off his horse; the dacoits seized the other's horse and pulled him off, one stabbing him as he fell.

'Mr Mountstuart,' called Hogwood, 'to me.' He drew his pistol.

From the trees stepped the ghost of a familiar figure. But he was no ghost. He strode through the others and stood at their head next to Rada Kishin, who carefully reloaded his pistol.

'Mir Aziz!' I cried.

'Chote Sahib, Blake Sahib, Hogwood Sahib.' He bowed. His dark silver scabbard sat on his hip. He was entirely composed. He bowed to Mountstuart. 'The *malik-al-shuara*,' he said. 'I am honoured, sar.'

'Mir Aziz,' I whispered, 'what is this?'

'Chote Sahib, you should have heeded me. Why did you not go to Mirzapore?'

I looked over at Blake. He stared at Mir Aziz. I thought, *There are many of them and we have no weapons except Hogwood's rifle.* And a worse thought: *Do we have Hogwood?*

Blake shook his head. 'I should have seen it,' he said. 'Buchanan didn't send us to find Xavier and bring him back, Avery. He intended us to bring Mir Aziz to Xavier. Mir Aziz is to make sure Xavier disappears for good, and that we do too. Isn't that right, Mir Aziz?'

'We take these three,' said Mir Aziz to Hogwood. I could not read his face. He kept his pistol cocked. Mir Aziz walked up to my horse and took hold of the bridle and handed it to one of the men. He smiled reassuringly.

'You are making good fight, Chote Sahib, I am proud of you,' he said. 'But there is nowhere to go.'

I had no answer. The sheer degree of the betrayal was almost too much to comprehend. Mir Aziz walked over to Mountstuart, inclined his head again and took his reins. Mountstuart uttered a fatigued sigh.

No doubt we all looked exhausted and defeated. Perhaps that was why Rada Kishin was so casual as he reached to take Blake's reins. It was a mistake. As he stretched across, Blake – moving faster than I had imagined possible – slipped from his saddle and landed behind him. With one arm he grabbed Rada Kishin round the neck and with the other he put a knife to his throat. The Thug, or dacoit, leader – whatever he was – struggled, then let his weapons drop.

'Avery, here!' Blake shouted. For a moment the dacoits hesitated. I kicked the man holding my reins in the back and he fell forward, then I jumped from my horse and ran to Blake, picking up Rada Kishin's pistols.

'Mr Hogwood?' I said.

One of the other dacoits stepped towards us, brandishing his sword. Blake said nothing, but he jerked Rada Kishin's head back and nicked his neck. A thread of blood trickled from it. The dacoit chief shouted and the man stepped back hastily.

'They are eight and we are four,' I said to Hogwood. 'You and I both have guns. We can win this fight.'

'I am sorry, Avery,' said Hogwood, and he rubbed his forehead in a familiarly weary gesture, 'but these are my orders. Mr Blake, you cannot be allowed to reach Mirzapore. I must thank you, by the way: I never thought to come face to face with Rada Kishin himself.'

'I did not want to believe it of you, but I see it is true,' I said. 'You know what they will do to us. And for what – something that brings shame on the Company. I thought you were a good man.'

'There are greater things at stake, Avery. I am sorry, I bear you no personal ill will, but I must do what I am told.'

'By Colonel Buchanan?' said Blake, placing the tip of his knife once again at Rada Kishin's throat. Hogwood stared at him, broodingly. 'Come, Mr Hogwood, tell me. As a last request and all that.'

'By Buchanan, yes,' Hogwood said, breaking into a half-smile. 'Order must be maintained. You cannot be found. Mr Blake, you really must put down your knife.'

'And Buchanan holds the gears of promotion,' said Blake.

'He does. I am an able man and I am not about to spend another ten years killing myself in the provinces.'

'That attack outside Doora. That was you.'

'I assumed, wrongly as it turned out, when I realized what you were about, Mr Blake – thank you by the way, Lieutenant Avery – that you must be stopped.'

'And the men at the bungalow who came for Mountstuart, that was you too?'

'Mr Mountstuart made a lamentable agent: it became all too clear what he was doing in Jubbulpore. He was, moreover, quite out of control. And if he had died then, Mr Blake, you and Lieutenant Avery might have been spared this.'

'And in Doora. You're sending money and guns to the Rao's rivals.'

'The Rao is an unstable feature. In the long term he has no place in the Company's India, for all Lieutenant Avery's admirable deeds.' He sounded impatient.

'And Sleeman?' said Blake.

Hogwood said, with the merest trace of a sneer, 'Major Sleeman is a very effective policeman. He catches those he is told to catch.'

'And now, acting on Buchanan's orders, you are going to have these men – these Thugs – murder us.'

'Enough. You will come with us,' said Mir Aziz. He jerked Mountstuart's reins; the horse took a jerky step and Mountstuart clutched the saddle, swaying. He looked very pale. Blake brought his knife closer to Kishin's throat, and I trained my pistol upon Mir Aziz.

'If you harm him I will shoot you dead where you stand, Mir Aziz,' I said. 'So. You take Buchanan's orders too?'

Mir Aziz quietened Mountstuart's horse. 'Does it matter, Chote Sahib?'

'It does to me.'

'I do the work of the Department. In times past, Blake Sahib is doing same. What? Did you think a mere native should behave better than your own countrymen?

Blake said, 'Yes. I thought you would. Or at least fight for yourself, not some dirty Company plot.'

'Men do what they must, Jeremiah Blake,' said Mir Aziz. 'Now, talking is finished.'

'Indeed,' said Hogwood. And he raised his pistol and shot Mountstuart.

Mountstuart gasped, flung out his arms and fell sideways from his saddle. Indeed he did not so much fall as throw himself on to Mir Aziz. His legs tangled in his stirrups and his horse was dragged along with him. Mir Aziz was knocked off his feet.

Blake uttered a great roar and cut Rada Kishin's throat. I saw a jet of blood spurt forth as I slipped behind his horse to gain time before the other dacoits gathered themselves to attack. Two of them came at us from the front, using the riderless horses to shield themselves from my pistols. Another had circled us, drew his tulwar and advanced on Blake. Hogwood remained on his horse a few yards from the furore – I suspected he had intended not to dirty his hands at all in the matter of our disappearance. Now he jerkily began to reload his gun, while Mir Aziz was still trying to disentangle himself from Mountstuart's horse.

I was so intent on the scene, I did not see the dacoit come in close by the side of my horse. He dived at my left side and stabbed at me with a knife in his right hand. Somehow he misjudged his thrust; it bounced off my shoulder and I spun around, shooting him in the face at close range. He fell. With that pistol discharged, I had only the Collier.

By now our horses were dancing with fear, but their excitement prevented our enemies from throwing themselves upon us. Two more came upon me, shifting and ducking so I had no clear shot. One came close enough to land me a blow with his stave that almost knocked me senseless. I learnt then that men fighting for their lives have an advantage over men who fight for any other motive. I staggered and the other tried to skewer me with his knife, but I pulled away and the blade merely cut my upper arm. I shot him, and then the other. Neither was a clean kill, but both went down in a pool of their own blood, gasping and struggling as the life leaked out of them.

Behind me, Blake was surrounded. He cut about him, but one dacoit grabbed him from behind and as he struggled another prepared to run him through. The Collier felt hot, and its aim was imperfect even for a pistol, but I got a bullet into Blake's attacker and another into the man on his back. Those were my last bullets. I saw Blake stab his blade twice into each of the wounded men. That left one dacoit, Mir Aziz and Hogwood. More than enough. The dacoit came after Blake, who was panting and gasping and covered in blood, much of it his own.

Hogwood wheeled about on his horse, still unwilling to involve himself in the skirmish. I picked up a sword. Mir Aziz walked towards me. His sword was out of its fine black scabbard, his pistol was in his other hand, and he smiled. He was clean and unbloodied; he too had planned to keep himself unsullied. As he approached, Hogwood lifted his reloaded rifle, uncertain whether to shoot Blake or me. He decided upon me. We were not far and it was an easy shot, but before he could pull the trigger Blake lifted his short dagger – the one with which he had killed Rada Kishin – and threw it fast and hard into Hogwood's eye. Hogwood screamed and fell heavily from his horse on to the ground. But the dacoit with whom Blake had been struggling lunged forward and made a deep thrust. Blake deflected it with his left hand. He toppled with a gasp and, as he fell, he jammed his sword upward into the dacoit's thigh. The noise was like a pig being stuck.

Now it was Mir Aziz and me.

I raised my sword and stepped towards the right, away from his sword hand. He stuffed his pistol loosely into his belt. I knew how good he was, far better than I, and stronger too. He came closer and we exchanged parries. I struggled even to match those first two blows. I realized I was at the end of my strength.

He took a step back and said, 'You cannot win, Avery Sahib. But I will make it quick and clean.'

I shook my head and stumbled back. Mir Aziz came on, and I kept backing as he slashed down. I half stumbled on a stone, and then he was above me, at first striking down with the sword, and then, when I blocked him, pressing down with his weight so that I slipped on to my back. I tried to scrabble backward, but he kept advancing, breathing hard but calm, determined to finish me. My retreat was halted by a tree root. I could not withdraw any further, and I was at his mercy. He stood over me and prepared his downward thrust. I did not try to parry, but in my desperation there came a last burst of strength born of the pure desire to survive, and I threw myself forward like a pocketknife, grabbed the pistol in his belt, twisted it round and discharged it straight into his stomach. He gave a grunt and sat down.

I stood up and tottered away. 'No,' he gasped. I turned. He was leaning on his elbow, and beckoned me with some difficulty. The blood was already blooming all across his stomach. He looked up at me steadily, his breathing ragged. We both knew it would be a slow death. I picked up his sword. He nodded and shut his eyes. Mine, I found, were wet, but I pushed the blade between his ribs and into his heart.

Blake was a mass of wounds: a cut in his thigh, another in his side, and blood was pouring from his hand, but he was alive. Mount-stuart lay crumpled in the dust where Mir Aziz had thrown him aside. The red stains on his side reminded me of the tiger's hide – a memory that seemed joined to some other man's life. I was glad his face was not marred. I managed to retrieve three horses. When I returned, Blake had crawled over to Mountstuart's body. He began to mutter.

'I was wrong. I was so wrong. I was so wrong. It wasn't Sleeman. It was never Sleeman. You were right, Avery. You said he was misguided. He believes all of it. It is Buchanan who knows what Thuggee is, and will not have it exposed. It was Buchanan all the time. He had me find Xavier so Mir Aziz could kill him.'

'But Colonel Buchanan is the Chief Military Secretary,' I said. I was becoming alarmed, I had never seen Blake in such a state, and I was most concerned about the blood.

'He also works,' said Blake, 'as Xavier and I did, for the Secret and Political Department. Always had his own stratagems. A bastard always.'

He was very pale. Very gently I took his arm. One of his fingers was dangling from his hand.

'Do you have any more opium, Jeremiah?'

It was an effort for him to look at me, and then his gaze was dull. 'I never had any. There was none to be found. I gave Xavier some beeswax. He knew what it was, but he gathered himself anyway.'

Then he set his jaw. 'Buchanan played me so well. He knew that I could find Xavier, and that if I disappeared no one would be much surprised or alarmed. He gave me a clever native, knowing that I of all people would be more than likely to take him into my confidence, and an innocent, knowing I'd weaken and take him under my wing. And I did both.'

After that, he barely spoke. I cut strips from Mountstuart's blanket and bound all his wounds, especially his hand, as tight as I could. I managed to drag Mountstuart on to a horse though it cost me more than I admitted. I had a melancholy recollection of Nungee in his shroud, balanced across a saddle, just as Mountstuart now was. I had to tie him on. Blake was hardly able to stand, but he made me retrieve Mountstuart's report from the slim wallet he had carried around his neck. I did not think that he would be able to ride on his own. I almost had to lift him into the saddle. He sagged terribly, but he would not let me ride behind him.

Thus we came to the barracks at Mirzapore: two riders, one near unconscious, and the body of the most famous man in India. Blake could not, by then, walk. I carried him in.

Chapter Sixteen

I t seems to me that the stories – the myths – began the very moment that we arrived at Mirzapore. By that time, Blake was not conscious and I was covered in blood and filth, and very weak. There was a sepoy waiting for us on the edge of Mirzapore near the barracks – I learnt later that Hogwood's sepoys had already delivered the news of Mountstuart's discovery, rescue and imminent arrival. I suppose Hogwood and Mir Aziz had planned to present themselves as the sole survivors of the Thug ambush that was to cost our lives.

When the sepoy saw us he turned and ran back into the barracks. I remember dismounting, stumbling over to Blake and drawing him from his saddle so I could carry him. He was a dead weight and I almost fell over. I tied the reins of Mountstuart's horse to my arm and walked through a stone arch into a parade ground. On the other side of it a cluster of officers were walking, then running, towards me. There were many sepoys.

'I am Lieutenant William Avery,' I said as they reached me. I was by now breathing very rapidly and had to catch my breath. 'I have the body of Xavier Mountstuart. We were attacked some twenty miles outside Mirzapore. My colleague Jeremiah Blake is sorely wounded and requires medical assistance.'

There was uproar. People kept arriving and everyone seemed to be talking at once. Again I tried to explain. Mountstuart had been murdered, we had fought for our lives, that much was understood. As for the rest – Hogwood, Thugs, dacoits – no one quite seemed to listen, or perhaps I did not describe it correctly. I could hear the different versions taking wing about me, though I endeavoured to correct them, but I was having some difficulty in breathing. I remember thinking the snatches of words were like small birds hopping further and further beyond my grasp as I tried to round them back up. But by then, I was more concerned about Blake than the babble about us.

'I must have a doctor!' I cried. Someone tried to take Blake from me but I shook him off.

'Confound it, man, can't you see you are badly cut?' someone said. And I saw it was true: there was a deep slash in my upper arm that was bleeding. I remembered the time before, on the road near Jubbulpore, when I had not noticed, and it all seemed very puzzling, and then it began to hurt.

'Lieutenant!' someone said to me sharply, and I came to myself. Two native orderlies had arrived with a stretcher, and I was persuaded to lay Blake upon it. I followed them into a quiet room off the parade ground where there were two clean white beds. I longed to lie down on one. I later learnt the regimental hospital was being rebuilt and so we were saved the depredations of a crowded flyblown dormitory. A gruff medical man and a number of native orderlies set about cleaning me up and attending to Blake. I remember asking the medic if he would clean our wounds as Blake had mine, with ghee and herbs. He looked at me as if I were mad and said Blake was so far gone that like as not he'd die and the hand would certainly have to come off. At that I stood up and shouted that I'd die first. The orderlies crowded round and with gentle hands forced me to sit again, and the medic, seeing my agitation, reluctantly allowed that he would do his best and that he had seen the ghee cure. A major came. It transpired they had been expecting us – without any great optimism – for some time, for Sameer had presented himself a week before at the barracks with Blake's despatches and a tale that we had gone to rescue Mountstuart from the Thugs. The Major said he must hear what had taken place. The medic said my wound must be attended to, but the Major was insistent. The medic raised his voice, and the Major reluctantly withdrew with promises that he would return.

All in all, they said, I was lucky, the muscle was torn but the bone was not splintered. They wanted to remove my clothing, but I would not take it off as Mountstuart's report was tucked inside my shirt and so they had to cut my sleeve off. They bandaged me and put me to bed. I endeavoured to stay awake to watch Blake – who lay quite motionless – but I succumbed to sleep in the end.

When I woke, Sameer was seated cross-legged on the floor by Blake's bed. He stood up and took my hand and began to utter a stream of his usual nonsense. I realized he was saying, 'I sent your books.' After that, he went back to his post by Blake's bed, whence he would not be dislodged. Blake had not woken. The Major returned with a younger officer who took notes. He said that I must have a talent for getting into dramatic scrapes, and that all Mirzapore had heard about the Rao's tiger hunt. He said Mountstuart's body was to be buried with all due honours, and he asked me to tell him how Mountstuart had met his end. It was hard to be clear, to put everything in the right order. I began with our capture by Rada Kishin and how Blake had saved us, confining myself to a sketchy description of Mountstuart's fragile state. On the subject of their conclusions about Thuggee and Jubbulpore, I could not even begin. When I came to the point when Hogwood found us, I began to sweat.

'Mr Hogwood was a fine Company man,' said the Major. 'He was due for promotion. His is a sad loss. Major Sleeman will be most upset.'

I steeled myself. 'It was Hogwood that shot Mountstuart,' I said.

The Major and his secretary looked at me as if I had gone mad. 'You are not yourself, Lieutenant Avery,' said the Major.

I looked him in the eye.

'I swear on my life, sir. I saw Hogwood shoot Mountstuart in cold blood, deliberately.' I went on to describe the ambush, Mir Aziz's arrival and the subsequent fight. I ignored the amazement, nay disbelief, on the faces of my listeners. When I concluded my account, the Major seemed aghast.

'Furthermore, I have in my possession a document written in Mountstuart's own hand concerning the work he was doing before he died. Most important work commissioned by the Board of Control in London. He entrusted it to Mr Blake, who in turn has entrusted it to me.'

We both looked at Blake's prone form. *The Major does not expect him to survive*, I thought. I hurried on.

'Mr Mountstuart intended to deliver it directly to the Governor General. I suppose that task now falls to me. Oh God, is he still here?' I started up and immediately felt exceedingly dizzy.

I reached into my shirt with my good arm and drew out Mountstuart's envelope. The Major stared at it – as well he might, the dark blots across its surface could not have been anything but blood – and his eyes grew almost round with astonishment. He put his hand out for it, but I drew back and thrust it again into my shirt.

'I am sorry, sir, but I can surrender it to no one but the Governor General himself,' I said.

'I do not think that the Governor General is in the habit of granting audiences to lieutenants,' he said, a little stung. 'I must say, moreover, that I do not understand how it was that you and your companion came to be tramping the jangals of Doora in search of Mountstuart in the first place.'

'Mr Blake and I were charged with finding Mountstuart by Colonel Patrick Buchanan, at Government House in Calcutta in late September.' Buchanan's name stirred some response in the Major; I did not dare begin on the subject of him. 'Mountstuart paid with his own blood to get this to Mirzapore,' I said. 'I do not mean any disrespect at all, but I cannot give it up to you.'

The Major considered for a moment. 'The Governor General has decided to remain in Mirzapore for Mountstuart's interment,' he said. 'You were with him when he died, and of course there is the whole Doora issue. I suppose something may be done.'

I felt very tired after the interview and drifted off to sleep.

When I woke there were four men about my bed, peering at me: two civilians and two senior officers. I was too bleary to make out their faces, save for one short, plump, bespectacled man with small black eyes, who stood closest to the bed.

'Ah, Lieutenant Avery,' he said, 'you are awake. I am the Governor General's Political Secretary, Sir William Macnaghten. I believe you have something for him. If you will give it to me, I will ensure he receives it.' He had an odd little black brush of a moustache that inched its way across his upper lip.

'But it needs Mr Blake, sir,' I said. 'The Governor General must see him. He knows it all, sir, and more. You must have the complete picture.'

Sir William Macnaghten pulled his brows together and contemplated the recumbent Blake.

'The Governor General gives the oration at Mountstuart's funeral in a few days and then afterwards goes on to Allahabad. I am sure he will wish to meet the men who were with Mountstuart when he died. We will do our best to arrange an audience. In the meantime, I am the Governor General's closest aide, Mr Avery. I must be firm. The document, please.'

I was relieved to be shot of it.

I woke the next morning feeling considerably better. Blake was still in a bad way, very weak. We had by then been moved to separate rooms and Sameer firmly ejected. The doctor said the officers were deciding what to do with him, as he belonged to no regiment, though he claimed to have worked for the Company for some several years. I said that I would vouch for him, and that he deserved only praise and reward for his conduct. But he was not allowed back, and when I proposed to get up and take a turn outside, an officer came and said that I must keep to my room and rest until we saw the Governor General.

'And may I be the first,' he said, suddenly very warm and taking my hand – then releasing it for fear that his impulsive gesture might cause me pain, as I was much bruised and bandaged – 'to shake your hand, Lieutenant Avery! Everyone talks of you. The tiger hunt in Doora. And now Mountstuart's last stand! Well, it is quite something. I should say no more, but the camp is abuzz. We all hope to drink your good health – both your healths – in due course!'

For several hours I lay in my bed feeling strangely unsettled. Then I went to sit with Blake, though the orderlies were reluctant. He had woken but barely spoke. His arm and hand were bandaged. I knew they had taken off two of his fingers, and there was considerable doubt as to whether he would win through at all. For many hours he had lain in a stupor, but by early evening he had recovered enough to take some water and a little nourishment. As he ate, I told him about my interview with the Major and the Governor General. He sat for a while then called for paper and pen and lay back, cradling his arm in his lap.

'I need to explain it to you,' he said, and his voice was not much above a hoarse whisper. 'In case I am not well enough to see the Governor General. You must listen to me and you must take notes.'

'I am sure you will be well enough,' I said.

'Nevertheless,' he said. He took another breath, swallowed, and drew himself up again and winced. 'I was wrong about Sleeman,' he went on. 'He may hate all contradiction, but he is not knowingly corrupted. He wants too much to be seen as a good man. He longed for a dark secret foe to fight for the soul of Hind, and he convinced himself he found one. It's there in his book. His endless questions about Kali, alongside the Thugs' answers, all different, all contradictory.'

'What about your innocent victims? The hanged tribesmen.'

'Oh, that is true enough. At Jubbulpore, they long since ceased to listen to what their captives say. Thuggee and banditry is the story and everything is made to fit within it. It is a crime, but a different kind of crime.'

'Hogwood then.'

'You know most of it already. He was Buchanan's creature, the Political Department's man in Jubbulpore. He had two private dak runners to send correspondence. That's how I used to work. One for the normal channels, one for secrets. In my certainty about Sleeman I forgot that. It was he who wrote to Buchanan about the true reason for Xavier's visit and then that he'd disappeared. In the bazaar there was a rumour that the 'small magistrate' had sent men to kill Mountstuart. I thought they meant Sleeman, because of his short stature, but since I was sure that Xavier had left Jubbulpore, I dismissed it. What they meant was the lower, junior magistrate: Hogwood. And at the exhumation, remember, he was over by the tree when they found the grave; he saw the marker and pushed

Mauwle to the right place. I'm sure Mauwle was quite suggestible: he loves to be right.'

I could see it, the two of them by a tree, Hogwood tracing his fingers across the bark, and then Mauwle starting to pace the ground beneath it; I remembered him handing over his letters to the two dak runners the day I came to see him.

'Hogwood knew about Rada Kishin's band and how they were allowed to continue their business to keep alive the fear of Thuggee, and the accusations that Vishwanath Singh was protecting Thugs. But he never had any direct contact with them. It would have been too dangerous. So Buchanan did not know where Mountstuart was, but he probably had an inkling that he had been taken. Perhaps Hogwood had heard something from Doora.'

'From Doora?'

'He admitted he had been sending money to the Rao's enemies. In his bungalow, I found a ledger I didn't understand. I could not see what it was for. I think it was a record of money and correspondence sent to Doora to the Rao's rivals. It is just the kind of ploy Buchanan likes. Weaken a state through bribery and promises to one faction you'll never keep.'

'So he and Buchanan encouraged the attempts on the Rao's life?'

'At second hand. It is not surprising. It is the kind of thing Mountstuart and I did, though not so overtly. And I would never have put the records on paper.'

He was finding it hard to keep his eyes open.

'One more thing. Your friend Macpherson. I don't believe his death was an accident. Then his reputation ruined.'

'Macpherson never gambled and barely drank. I do not believe he would have stolen papers,' I said. 'And the last thing he said to me was that he had forced me into something I'd never asked for. I have thought a deal about that in the last two days.'

'Killed and discredited. Similar things were done in my time, but to influential natives in the independent states. Early on, I was convinced they deserved it. Then I came to believe that things were more complicated.' He yawned and winced again.

'I think Macpherson became concerned about the oddness and

secrecy around our party. I bet he found something – most likely about Mir Aziz. Buchanan wanted it kept quiet. If I live I'll find your moneylender and we'll get the truth of it.'

'It is all so dirty,' I said bitterly, 'so rotten. I keep asking myself, should I resign my commission? I do not know what to do.'

'The Company is a vast creature of many heads and many arms. It is not all rotten, at least I am not sure it is.'

'But you don't believe in it.'

'I am a dangerous radical.' He gave a thin smile. 'I believe it is a mechanism for the domination of one people by another for the latter's enrichment. And I have no answer as to what should take its place.'

'I cannot see it so baldly as that.' I did not want to argue. There was one more subject I had resisted raising.

'And what about Mir Aziz? Was he a Thug? How could he be if he was a Mahommedan?'

Blake was silent for a while. 'There has always been more mixing between Mahommedans and Hindoos than the Company likes to admit. Especially among dacoits. Lots of Mahommedan Thugs in Sleeman's books. Another inconsistency in his Hindoo romance.' He coughed a little. 'The Company employed Thugs before. Feringhea ran Ochterlony's secret department. Course, the Company didn't know who he was. Perhaps Buchanan needed a Thug. Remember what Feringhea said? "Let the government pay me and I will do its work"?' Then he shook his head. 'But I don't think Mir Aziz was a Thug. He was a very effective agent and sometime assassin.'

His eyes closed.

'I must sleep now.'

The Governor General's tent was not one tent but four, each one lined up against the next to make a square, each connected to the others by passageways. Around them, like a rippling scarlet fence, was a curtain of red cloth some nine feet high. Beyond the red curtain there was tethered a great menagerie of animals: an honour guard of camels and their riders, two elephants, cages of chickens, sheep and so forth. Then there were the palanquins, the horses, the servants, the Governor General's advisers and secretaries and their households. Further on there was a whole field of baggage camels, an endless train of bullock carts, and more elephants. And that was but one small part of the cavalcade and its dependents and supporters. I had been told there were 12,000 people in the procession, and as many animals, if not more. My head hurt even to think of it.

As we made our way from our rooms to the enclosure – I on my two feet, Blake in a sedan chair carried by four bearers, for he was not strong enough to walk – those we passed stared at us and mumbled to each other. It was a relief to pass through the red curtain and then into one of the four tents, which was itself divided by a long white muslin curtain. In this anteroom we were kept waiting for some time. From the other side of the curtain one could hear the muffled sounds of voices engaged in discussion. Blake was very quiet. I hoped he was gathering his thoughts, but I worried that he might simply be struggling to remain upright. He had refused to take the opium I had had Sameer find for him, and I knew better than to ask how he was. At last there appeared a bland-faced civilian who looked so completely as one expected a respectable Company civilian to, he might have been pressed from a mould. He spoke in a low, confidential voice as if he were generously imparting a very great secret.

'Lord Auckland will see you now.'

I elbowed my way through the curtains, and Blake was borne aloft by the bearers. We came into a large enclosed space in which the light had taken on the yellowed tone of the tent's canvas. There were several high-backed, wooden, upholstered chairs, a number of small occasional tables, and a beautifully carved, polished-wood desk on which there was a metal box and a silver tray. The many servants and bearers began to leave the tent through the opposite curtain.

Behind the desk stood Lord Auckland, the Governor General. I had never been introduced to anyone of such elevated status before, and I was tongue-tied. At first sight he seemed very long and thin and elegant and easily confident in the way of his class. His expression was quite benevolent. Standing behind him was the small, plump, moustachioed man to whom I had delivered Mountstuart's report, and at a little distance in a large cane chair was another large, generously stomached and well-chinned man, who remained seated. I found his face familiar, but I could not place it. I looked to Blake. He took in the other man's presence but said nothing, and something in that nothing convinced me he knew him.

'Welcome, gentlemen,' said the Governor General. 'The last companions and rescuers of the great Poet Laureate of the subcontinent! What a great loss both for poetry and for India herself!' His voice was unexpectedly high and husky.

'Mr Blake,' he went on, 'I hope your wound is not troubling you too much?'

Blake first inclined his head, then shook it, and said nothing. His silence entirely confounded the Governor General, who looked quite nonplussed for a moment. The former's inscrutability was so in character I had to suppress a smile.

'And you must be young Lieutenant Avery, who saved the Rao of Doora from a tiger! With one shot you transformed our relations with Doora. Well done! Remarkable story, young man. Quite marvellous! We are exceedingly pleased. I am certain garlands and accolades await. I know my sisters are very keen to make your acquaintance. Gentlemen, you are about to be the toast of India.'

'A lucky shot, Your Excellency,' I stuttered.

Lord Auckland looked down at the small man with the spectacles as if in need of prompting.

'The Governor General is delighted to make your acquaintance, but is rather short of time,' said the small man.

'My Political Secretary, Sir William Macnaghten,' said the Governor General.

In his chair, Blake sat up and took a breath. There was no disguising that he was far from strong, but he managed to speak with more force than I had expected.

'Then I'll be as brief as I can, Your Excellency,' he said. 'You may have heard by now something of our story, but so as to scotch any myths or fabrications: Xavier Mountstuart was murdered ten miles from Mirzapore, not by a band of dacoits – or even as I've already heard it said, by Thugs – but by a Company magistrate, Mr Edward Hogwood, on the direct orders of the Chief Military Secretary and head of the secret section of the Secret and Political Department, Colonel—'

Sir William Macnaghten noisily cleared his throat; the Governor General twitched slightly and stared at his hands.

'Buchanan.' Blake spoke fast and urgently. 'The Colonel sent Lieutenant Avery and me to find Xavier Mountstuart in the full expectation that we too should not return—'

'Mr Blake, these are very, very serious accusations,' said Sir William Macnaghten.

'I know that only too well, sir. I do not make them lightly. The object of the exercise was to prevent Mountstuart from delivering to you and to the Board of Control in London this report, which proves that Thuggee is not what Major William Sleeman claims it to be, that the Thuggee Department has dangerously overreached itself, that hundreds of natives have been wrongfully sentenced and others have died in vast numbers in Territory gaols of disease and starvation.'

The Governor General had now turned his face to one side, as if he was trying to put himself as far from Blake as possible.

'I think, Mr Blake, the Governor General has heard as much—'

'It was also to prevent the discovery of two further crimes,' Blake went on, ignoring Macnaghten and speaking almost feverishly fast. 'Firstly, that at least one other murder has been committed in order to maintain the fiction and avoid exposure, and secondly, that Buchanan has sought to exploit the supposed threat of Thuggee in order to justify the deposition of at least one independent native ruler, the Rao of Doora, and has in addition fed funds to the Rao's rivals in order to—'

'Mr Blake, enough!' said Sir William, quite angry. 'May we pause for a moment?'

'Let me add that I have come to believe that Major Sleeman was not a witting part of this, but Buchanan and his agent Hogwood were. I also accuse Buchanan of conspiring to murder Lieutenant Avery's friend Frank Macpherson, who I suspect found out the true purpose of our journey.'

The Governor General pursed his lips. Sir William looked furious.

'This is very shocking. I can hardly believe it,' said the Governor General in his high, husky voice. His neck, I saw, was especially long and swaddled in a white cravat which gave him a slight air of being an invalid. At the same time there was something boyish and undefined about his face – disconcerting in a man of fifty-odd. He had large, soft eyes, soft, flat schoolboy hair, and his skin was pale and lined as if he had not been enough outside. It was lent a particularly unhealthy hue by the strange colour of the room.

'Sir William may recall that some years ago he had reason to read my reports. He knows that I am not given to exaggeration,' said Blake.

'Very serious, very unpleasant accusations,' the Governor General went on. 'They will take some time to digest.' He clasped one pale hand over another and looked up at his Political Secretary.

'They are more than accusations, Your Excellency,' said Blake. 'The evidence is in Mountstuart's report, collected at the behest of your colleagues on the Board of Control in London, and must surely now be acted upon.'

Both men looked up sharply. 'I hope you are not presuming to tell the Governor General his business?' said Sir William.

'No. Not at all,' said Blake, looking back and forth between the two. His mouth tightened.

'Your Excellency, Sir William,' I said nervously, 'I can personally attest that everything Mr Blake says is true. More than that, you should know that Mr Blake's own investigations confirmed all that Mr Mountstuart writes, that he it was who discovered Mr Mountstuart's whereabouts, masterminded our escape, ensured our survival in the wilderness, kept our spirits aloft when all about seemed lost. I owe him my life several times over.'

Sir William gave me a look in which it was clear that he did not think I had helped. 'I think the Governor General has heard everything he should,' he said. Lord Auckland stood up. The exercise seemed to require considerable exertion.

'Mr Blake, Mr Avery,' he said absently, as if his mind was only half upon us, 'you have performed great exploits, you have made great efforts. You have done remarkable work. Britain will be proud. The Company wishes to reward you. I have, I am afraid, a great number of other things to deal with. We are many days behind our planned advance into the north. I have full confidence in Sir William, he will pursue any further matters pertaining to these, er, these, er . . . I wish you both well. Brave deeds, brave deeds, indeed. By the way, gentlemen, did you know we have a new monarch? King William passed away in June. Young Victoria is Queen.'

Sir William fixed his eye upon us, and I bowed low – as custom demanded – as if to some native potentate. Blake coughed and sank into his chest, to avoid, I suspected, having to make an obeisance. The Political Secretary clapped his hands, and a small procession of bearers and servants appeared from behind the curtain to conduct the Governor General to his next assignation.

When the Governor General was safely out of the tent Sir William said, 'Mr Avery, pray be seated. You must understand that the Governor General cannot be expected to hear the details of such things.'

'I am sorry,' Blake said, falling back into the chair, 'I do not understand.' His face was very pale, and damp with perspiration.

'I think you understand very well. This is a most sensitive subject. If the Governor General were in any way associated with it . . .'

Blake summoned himself again. 'But he has been here barely a year. None of the opprobrium need attach to him. Sir William, the Thuggee Department is a mechanism that has gone criminally wrong. It must be closed down – this is why the Board in London sent for Mountstuart. He was led to believe the Governor General would be primed for his report. Colonel Buchanan must be—'

'Must? Must? Are you suggesting we shirk our responsibilities, Mr Blake? Are you questioning my rectitude? You are right on the threshold of insubordination. As I recall you have been there before and with disastrous consequences. The matter will be dealt with. Your efforts will be rewarded. But you must be discreet. Let me be as clear about this as I can be.'

From inside the pocket of his black frock-coat, Sir William drew out a sheaf of papers: a bent and creased envelope spattered with brown spots, and a cleaner leaf with notes upon it. Mountstuart's report and my notes on Blake's explanation. He placed them on the silver tray. From the metal box he took a phosphorous match and a small vial. He poured the contents of the latter over the papers and struck the former against the side of the box. An alarming burst of orange fire shot from it. He picked up the papers by one edge and placed the other side in the flame. They took immediately.

'No!' I was up before I realized. Sir William gave me a nasty, fish-eyed look and dropped the papers on to the tray, where they proceeded to burn in a lively manner. I felt cold and sick. Blake sat entirely still. He looked at the envelope burning, then up at Sir William, and fixed him that slow, hard look of his. Macnaghten looked away.

'All right. I shall be plain,' he said stiffly. 'Lieutenant Avery, may I suggest you sit down? Gentlemen, the Company requires this.'

He waited, as if expecting some response. Neither of us spoke.

'Have you any idea how many Europeans there are in India?'

I shook my head. Blake stared straight ahead.

'A few thousand. And how many of them? Countless, swarming, teeming millions. A few thousand Company men govern millions, bringing order, peace and prosperity where there was chaos, war and unrest. It is a feat of great and precarious balance; it requires unity, and sometimes an occasional necessary myth.'

'You are saying that the Thugs are a necessary myth?' I said.

'Even if not everyone he arrested was strictly a Thug, Major Slee-man has made the roads of India safe. The campaign against Thuggee shows the natives we have the determination, and, yes, the ruthlessness, to destroy a murderous caste thousands of years old, an immutable evil woven into the very fabric of this country. It shows that the Company cares for their welfare. It shows that we are fitter to rule than the selfish native princeling fawning over his favourites and counting his jewels. Sleeman has given the Company an extraordinary triumph. Would you take this away from us? India must have order; without it there is chaos and we are all – European and native – at risk.'

'But the roads aren't safe,' said Blake. 'Hundreds of innocent men have been killed to prove that Hind is degenerate and we should rule it. Sleeman has propagated a lie. It's an imaginary enemy, a false panic, and such things have consequences. It has reinforced every prejudice Europeans hold against the Hindoos. It makes it ever easier for Europeans to view them with disgust and misunderstanding, to deride and dismiss their customs and habits and to trumpet the superiority of their own. And it provides the Company with an easy and dishonest justification for marching into any independent state you wish.'

'Your passion for the natives,' said Macnaghten, 'is both touching and misplaced. Do not be a fool, Mr Blake. Consider the outcome you desire. Thuggee exposed as fiction? There would be uprisings, rebellion, mutiny. There is already unrest about the famine.'

'Hardly improved by the 12,000 men the Governor General plans to lead through the heart of it.'

'Think of it, millions turning on thousands, Mr Blake, women and children murdered. And do not imagine the natives would triumph. There would be such an outcry that even if the Company failed to subdue it, regiments from England would. Imagine the retribution. Thousands more dead. Think on it. The scandal in London, the careers destroyed and, perhaps, the destruction and disbanding of the Company itself. Is that what you seek?'

'Don't try to frighten me with your talk. The Company's rotten. Maintaining this lie won't save it,' said Blake. 'It doesn't need me to bring about its destruction. The rebellion will come, the Company will fail.'

Macnaghten sighed and looked at Blake through his glasses as an exasperated schoolteacher looks at a recalcitrant pupil.

'Dear me, Mr Blake, radical talk! You cannot truly believe India

would be better without the Company? We give it order and discipline, culture, reason, opportunity, faith, peace, stability. This
country cannot rule itself. It needs us, and we are but a few. If we
left the natives to themselves they would be at each other's throats
in minutes, to say nothing of ours. There is never a moment when
there is not a raja terrorizing or oppressing his people, or being
murdered by his family. The choice is simple: your silence ensures
peace and order, and nothing is more important than that.'

'I give it twenty years.'

'Mr Blake!'

'I understand,' said Blake. 'You want to be discreet. You can be
discreet as you disband the Thuggee Department. Buchanan can be
quietly dismissed and then prosecuted for murder.'

'Mr Blake, you force me to be direct. There is no report on the
Thuggee Department, there never was. We require – nay, we
demand – silence on this from both of you. But we also recognize
your considerable efforts and your abilities. India will recognize
them. They will be rewarded. Lieutenant Avery, you were hoping
for a cavalry regiment? That can be arranged. We will confirm your
lieutenancy in a regular company. There will be, I guarantee, good
prospects for promotion, though you should perhaps have some
actual experience. We are likely to see action before long near the
Afghan border. That may interest you. You could also, if you wished,
transfer to the Political Department. You will have entrees into the
Company's highest circles; you have already as good as received an
invitation from the Governor General's sisters. Your career is made.
And as for your debts, we can make arrangements. Is there anything
else?'

'Colonel Buchanan offered me passage back to England should
we succeed,' I mumbled. 'And, sir, something else. My friend
Macpherson met an untimely end. I cannot be sure what happened,
but I believe his reputation has been unfairly traduced. I think the
accusations against him are unfounded. My silence is dependent
upon his reputation being restored.'

'I see,' said Sir William, disconcerted. 'Well, I suppose we can look into that. It seems you have some thinking to do about your future, Mr Avery.

'Now, Mr Blake, what do you want? Name it. You are about to become a hero. There is a place for you here. You are a capable man. What about an Assistant Resident? Anywhere you like, where you can practise your languages and indulge the natives to your heart's content.'

Blake said nothing. I wondered how much strength he had left.

'Time was,' Macnaghten continued, pushing his spectacles up his nose, 'I seem to remember, all sorts of fine futures were predicted for you. Now is your chance to revive your fortunes. Do you want your captaincy? Naturally in return we expect no talk beyond this place of murders and plots and conspiracies within the Company. No doing down of Sleeman or the Thuggee Department.'

I could not see Blake accepting any of Macnaghten's offers, but I also could not see how we could refuse.

'How will you report Xavier's death?' said Blake.

'A great Englishman cut down in his prime by marauding Thugs,' said Macnaghten promptly. 'A hero of the Empire. The two of you, his trusty supporters, fighting for your lives. There will be a great monument erected in Mirzapore. There will be poems, paintings, I am sure. His memory will not be disgraced.'

'With Hogwood dying in a brave attempt to mount a rescue.'

'Of course.'

Blake stared at Sir William. His eyes glittered. 'I don't like your methods. I find I can't stomach your vision of this place any more either. I'll take nothing from you.'

'Take care, Mr Blake. Do not dig your own grave twice. You are still a member of the Company. We can give, and we can take away.'

In a wheezing flat whisper, 'Don't threaten me, you piece of filth.'

'Jeremiah!' I sighed.

Macnaghten uttered a kind of angry yelp. If he had been a fighting sort of a man, I think he would have launched himself upon Blake.

'I told you!' he said excitedly, for the first time looking back at the large man in the armchair who had sat so quietly that I had quite forgotten him. 'I told you! He is quite beyond redemption. There is no point trying to reason with him. He has the manners of the gutter! Mr Blake! Let me tell you, you have single-handedly once again destroyed your future in the East India Company, and this time for good! I will have you court-martialled. I will have your household dispersed—'

'Sir William, does it not seem to you that such threats might be just a tad excessive?' said the large man, pushing himself up off his chair and strolling towards us. 'Just at the moment Jeremiah Blake does not look as if he will live beyond next week. In which case, you will have nothing to fear. He is, however, a determined man, and quite likely to survive simply out of pure pig-headedness. And though I am certain he will dislike it inordinately, he is shortly to become quite famous, whether you like it or not. A court martial? I do not think you would want to have him make his accusations under questioning. Most inconvenient.'

'I do not have the time for this,' Sir William said.

'My advice to you, Mr Blake,' said the large man, 'is to give up on it. It is a bad job. The Company will have your silence, one way or another.' I studied his features, and was sure they were familiar: a long, soft, curving nose; a little, round, padded receding chin; little arched eyebrows and small brown eyes.

'I don't want your advice, Collinson,' said Blake.

'You should take it, however, Jem, and you may call me Sir Theo,' he continued smoothly. 'Macnaghten, you are quite right, you do not have time for this. Allow me to take the reins. I know Mr Blake of old, and I feel sure that I can find a way of overcoming his reservations.' He gave Sir William a smile that would have seemed quite innocuous, save for the introduction of several pointed teeth. It gave him the look of a well-fed fox.

Sir William wanted to leave, but was uncertain whether he should.

'You had better arrive at an agreement, for if you do not, the Company will have to take measures,' he said pompously. 'Good

297

day to you, Mr Avery. If I were you I should seriously review my association with this man.' He nodded curtly, hurried to the tent's curtained entrance and pushed his way through.

The large man settled into the chair behind the Governor General's desk.

'Lieutenant Avery, I am Sir Theophilus Collinson. Once upon a time Mr Blake worked for me.'

'He was the Company's finest fixer,' said Blake. He grunted slightly as he shifted his weight in the chair. 'A finger in every curry in Hind, we used to say. But I heard the Company had washed its hands of you, and you were bound for London.'

'Oh, Blake, be pragmatic for once! You may find it hard to stomach, but Macnaghten is not wrong about the need to keep order. And your young friend agrees, I can see it.'

I looked away.

'Moreover, Sir William and the Governor General have ambitions in the north, and no whisper of trouble will be permitted to get out, let alone reach London. Buchanan is on his way up country to negotiate with Runjeet Singh on Sir William's behalf. They will not rid themselves of him, not just now, he is too useful, even if he does overreach himself. And just as you said, Thuggee is too powerful a myth. But I can tell you that next year Sleeman is to be moved from Jubbulpore to the north, to begin a new campaign against the Badhak dacoits.'

'So they're after Afghanistan, eh? So much for Macnaghten's desire for peace. And the poor old Badhaks, they aren't dacoits, just a tribe of gipsy wanderers, no better or worse than the rest.'

'Really, Blake, your sympathy for the vagabond poor is quite exhausting. Now listen to me. If you try to bring this out, you will be treated as mad or dangerous. You might well find yourself court-martialled. Nor will they stint on your young friend here. You know how it works. Let it pass, let them reward you. Let yourself be valued as the man who found Mountstuart and kept their secrets. There are plenty who will admire you the more for it. I speak as someone who knows your worth, and someone who liked and admired Xavier, even as I saw his frailties.'

Blake would not acknowledge him. He seemed very pale to me. There was a long pause.

'And as someone who regarded Xavier Mountstuart as a friend, I undertake to ensure, no I swear to you, that Patrick Buchanan will not live to see Ireland again. That he will pay for what he has done. You know I am good for it.'

Blake looked at him.

'But I must have your word – and yours too, Mr Avery.'

'Sir Theophilus,' I said, 'I would give you my word, but I have already told at least two people that Hogwood killed Mountstuart.'

'The Company can have its way in most things, but a few unfortunate rumours – well, it must live with them. It deserves them. But you are not to speak of it again, or that promising career will be over.'

'No, sir. And my friend Macpherson's reputation?'

Collinson did not blink. 'That can be arranged.'

'You can have my silence, Collinson,' said Blake. Sweat was streaming down his face, 'in return for Buchanan, if I live. If I die in the next week, I've made arrangements, letters already sent to Calcutta.'

'Then we shall have to make sure you live,' said Sir Theophilus, displeased.

'I don't want anything from the Company,' Blake said. 'I've had my fill of it. I don't know why you defend it. It was quick enough to spit you out when it no longer liked the taste of you.'

'Ah well, Jeremiah, I am the realist, you are the idealist. I always liked you for it, that and your relentless curiosity. What I have never liked is your arrogant conviction of your own righteousness, your belief that your cleverness and your much-vaunted honesty make you a better man than the rest. In this world they merely make you a more dissatisfied one.'

Blake seemed to drift off for a moment, then he said, 'You're right. If I had not been so sure of myself I might have saved my friend's life. Have my silence. And my commission. I resign everything. I won't watch the Company choke the life out of all it touches. I'll go back to England.'

'I see now what this was,' Sir Theophilus said musingly. 'This was a test. One last chance for the Company to prove itself to you. Sir William calls you naive, and he is right. Times have changed, and they will not return to how they were. You may not like it – I will be frank, I do not like it much either – but there is nothing to be done. This latest escapade planned by Macnaghten in the north, let me tell you, will be a costly disaster. But no one wishes to hear my opinion on the matter. So I smile, note my objections and remove myself.

'We are not so far apart in our opinions, Jeremiah Blake. Let us not pretend that the Company was ever a model of disinterestedness. Profit and advantage were always its motive. But you are right: it has changed and is changing. When I first came here, we recognized the qualities of this place. We admired its literature, its architecture, its music, the ingenuity of its peoples. I counted among my friends the finest native families of Calcutta, and I was glad to visit their homes. I fell in love with a lady from a noble family, and she bore me four sons. Now time has passed, the Company has grown in power and reach – and let us admit it, you and I played our parts in helping it to do so. At the same time it has become squeamish about those who were once its hosts and are now its subjects. It demands they speak English and it scorns to learn Hindoostanee. It always had a taste for land and territory, but now rapacity is dressed up as righteousness. A niggardliness and cruelty has crept into its dealings with natives. I do not believe this has been in the best interests of India, its people or us. But it has served the Company well. I find myself at odds with the men who rule at Government House; my sons are less and less welcome in European company unless they are willing to present themselves as subordinates. This, however, is what passes for Progress and there will be plenty more of it, both here and in England. I do not believe it can be stopped or prevented.

'Now, should you live beyond the next few days, and there is a good likelihood you will not, it just so happens that I am returning to England in the new year. Some interesting offers have been made to me. Should you also decide to return, well, you have very particular talents, Blake, you should exploit them.'

'I don't want your help,' Blake said.

'Do not be a child, Blake,' Sir Theophilus said. 'There is no point in returning to England in order to be destitute. You will need to make a living; you will need a patron.'

Blake slumped in his chair. He looked extremely unwell. Sir Theophilus called for the bearers, and I prepared to follow.

'Not you, Lieutenant Avery,' he said. 'No. I want you to tell me everything, from the beginning.'

Chapter Seventeen

February 1838

I t was one of those warm, dry February days that neverthe-less hinted at the burning heat to come. The sky was the blue of a washed-out cloth, and the river dark and shiny. On its far side one could see the grand mansions of Garden Reach. The ghats were chaotic, crowded and dirty as always, but the smell of fish was less pungent today and there was a good breeze up the Hooghly. The tender had arrived to take the passengers from the wharf down the Hooghly to the deeper water off Sagar Island, where *The Marchioness of Blandford*, a 900-ton East Indiaman, waited for them. The helmsman fussed about with the ropes, impatient to be off, but some travellers were still awaited, and so we stood on the ghat, eking out the last moments on land. The trunks had gone off earlier that morning, so there was little to carry. There were several grizzled elderly gentlemen, presum-ably taking retirement; and a couple of younger men going home on leave. Some four or five ladies in flounced dresses and puffed sleeves waited in their carriages until the last moment. Their small children ran about, pursued by breathless ayahs and bearers.

The day after our audience with the Governor General, I attended Mountstuart's funeral. There were hundreds of mourners. I should not imagine that above three or four had ever met him. The Gover-nor General spoke the oration, describing a man I did not recognize, and a death which bore no relation to what I had seen. But I had reluctantly come to the conclusion that Macnaghten and Collinson were right: much though I disliked it, the secret would have to be kept, order must be maintained.

It did not prevent the surge of anger as I listened to the Governor General's words and knew he knew that he lied. And so I had decided that, whatever happened, I would resign my commission and return to England, as Blake planned to. It was arranged that we would travel down the Ganges by boat to Calcutta as it would be a great deal less exhausting than the land journey. Thence we would take an Indiaman for England.

I did not share Blake's radical opinions, but I felt a loyalty to him which I could not easily explain, and whenever I thought about Mountstuart, I felt an anger that made me wish to break all the familiar bonds of conduct and obedience. It was particularly difficult whenever I was asked about our time with Mountstuart. This happened a great deal, for I was constantly approached by officers and civilians wanting to shake my hand, drink my health or invite me to dinner. Pretty young women appeared from nowhere to congratulate me. They wanted to hear about the tiger hunt and Mountstuart's last stand. I must admit that even as I replied uneasily to their questions, it was pleasant to be so feted. Yet all was increasingly cast into shadow by my worry about Blake, who was still very weak.

In the days after the meeting Blake rallied, his wounds knit and he became stronger, but he was very silent. I was sure he blamed himself for Mountstuart's death and, I surmised, a great many other things too, and I wished to tell him he was wrong. By the end of the week, however, he had sickened with a fever. I hoped it was one of the familiar sweats to which old hands were prone, but the surgeon said the source was Blake's hand, and it must come off. Blake refused to countenance the notion, though I begged him to relent, and I feared perhaps he wanted to die. I watched him grow weaker and weaker, though we bathed the wound thrice daily with ghee and Sameer found dried wormwood in the bazaar which we gave him for the fever. The surgeons were not impressed, but I was a hero now, and so my demands were met, with ill-disguised scepticism, it must be said. Eventually Blake passed into unconsciousness.

For a day he could not be roused at all. Then he woke, very weak. I was summoned to his bed and he said that whatever happened to him, I should stay in India.

I protested, but he said, 'Don't take me as your example, Avery. The world is the way it is, and if you can it's better to live comfortably with it than bump along against it. Don't throw away your chances before you've had them. I think you would not regret some more years here. I know there's little for you in England.'

I told him I would not think of it.

He was very frail for several days afterwards, but then began to improve. We took the boat to Calcutta a few weeks later, taking our leave of Sameer, who, following certain interventions on our parts, had been granted a prolonged leave to return to his village, and a place in his old regiment where other members of his family still served.

In Calcutta, Blake began to prepare for his departure and fought off all attempts to make a hero of him. He did his best to disappear from our story altogether, though he never showed any disapproval of my enjoyment of our celebrity. When asked about how we saved the Rao, or his discovery of Mountstuart, or the days of pursuit, or our final encounter with a notorious Thug leader, he would smile gnomically and fall silent. Not that our reluctance to speak of the subject made any difference. Just as Theophilus Collinson had said, Mountstuart's end seemed to collect rumour and myth, no matter what the official accounts described.

Some days after we arrived in Calcutta I went to a dinner where an elderly man came up to me, took my hand, fixed me with a steady look and said quietly, 'I know the truth about Mountstuart's end, sir. I know what you have struggled against.' Seeing my anxious look, he drew me close, put his mouth to my ear and whispered, 'Freemasons!'

I haunted Blake's house in Blacktown, telling myself I was ensuring he convalesced properly, but really because there was no one in Calcutta with whom I felt as at ease. He was arranging pensions for his retainers and tying up old business. I would witness the tail-end or the beginning of some unlikely farewell: a well-to-do half-caste widow with a brood of orphans; a tearful Irish rope-maker; a feverish red-faced captain shaking his hand with an intensity that seemed a little excessive; a native moneylender who was keen to let me know he shared with Blake a love of Persian poetry.

All the time, however, I pondered what Blake had said about staying on. Truth be told, despite all that had taken place, part of me wished to stay in India, to see more and do more. My homesickness, meanwhile, had almost gone. I still thought often of Louisa and of the places I loved, but more often I remembered how difficult it had been between my father and myself. I thought of how unimpressed the wider family would be if I returned now. What I would do to put food in my mouth, I had no idea. In my wilder moments I imagined being in London with Blake, but I had only to envision what an impossible pair we should make, to see it for the fantasy it was. Besides, I knew that it would be hard enough for Blake to find his feet in London, and I had not been made for cities.

Something else had taken place too. Among the notes and letters I had received on returning to Calcutta was one from Helen Larkbridge.

'*My dearest William,*' she wrote,

> *Will you allow one who holds the warmest and liveliest memories of you to let you know with how much excitement and pleasure we have learnt of your extraordinary adventures, and to congratulate you on your even more extraordinary bravery? It seems an age since you left Calcutta, so determined, so grim-faced, so ill-used in the loss of your dearest friend. How I wish I had overcome my own maidenly weakness, had braved your stern and steely manner, had thrown off the dead hand of convention, and had offered you the comfort and the tender words that were in my heart. I cannot tell you how much I regret that I did not.*
>
> *If you can find a moment, a tiny space, among the many far greater and more important demands now made upon your society, perhaps you might consider calling upon me? It would be so very good to see you again.*
>
> *I sign myself, your affectionate friend,*
> *Helen Larkbridge*

I had been been told that Helen had 'come to an understanding' with Lieutenant Keay. That is to say, she was all but engaged to him, though he had returned for the time being to Benares. I could not, however, resist calling on her.

She had been lodging with a rather grand merchant family who spent a good deal of time on their estates near the Governor General's mansion at Barrackpore, giving her the run of their Calcutta mansion. When I arrived one cool, bright afternoon, I found her alone but for the servants.

'William!' She smiled, but cautiously, and held out a gloved hand. I kissed it and looked up. She was transfixingly pretty. She wore a dress of soft sprigged muslin, and about her the air seemed scented with jasmine. 'I can hardly believe it is you!'

'I too.'

After that we sat awkwardly for a while, I asking dull questions about Calcutta acquaintances, she answering as animatedly as she could. After a while, there seemed little left to say.

'Perhaps I should go,' I said.

'No!' she said. She drew her hands together. 'William, I feel as if I do not know how to speak to you. You seem so . . . so battle-hardened, so far away from Calcutta foolishness. Please, I have a confession to make. I fear it makes me seem very forward. I should say at once that Lieutenant Keay and I have an understanding, but I felt that if I did not conspire in some degree I should never manage to speak to you properly.' She looked over at me, quite serious. 'I gave out that I was not receiving today, and I sent my chaperone across town to pick up some pills for a headache. And now I feel quite a fool.'

I laughed. I was bemused. I thought for a moment. 'Perhaps we might start again,' I said.

'We shall have some tea,' she said, and clapped her hands. She ordered me to tell her the story of my adventures, and I told the version I had become accustomed to telling, and she listened and laughed and gasped, and I thought how enormously pleasant it was to have my story listened to by a lovely girl who knew me, at least a little. She seemed to understand when I wished to stop talking of it, asking about Blake instead. And when I had finished, she said, 'And so you are torn between staying and going.'

'Yes, I feel my duty pulls me in two directions. I do not know what to do.'

'For my part, William,' and she looked down blushing, 'though I have no right to say it, I should rather you stayed.'

I left, once more hopelessly smitten.

Two weeks after we returned to Calcutta, Collinson made good on the first part of his promise, regarding Frank Macpherson's reputation. It was suddenly widely known in Calcutta that he had been dreadfully misrepresented, and his affairs had been confused with a recently deceased former Company officer called Francis McFierson, a man of shady reputation who, quite apart from being vastly in debt, had been drummed out of his regiment for theft and embezzlement and was thought to have died somewhere north of Delhi. The papers he was supposed to have taken turned out to have been accidentally mislaid within his department. It seemed remarkably unconvincing and thin to me – and still did not explain his murder – but everyone about me seemed to find it perfectly plausible. Blake, meanwhile, found the moneylender to whom Frank had apparently owed so much. At first the man had claimed to know nothing about the matter. Then, after a certain pressure was brought to bear, he had admitted that a gentlemen at the Secret and Political Department had offered to overlook certain irregularities in his affairs if he would claim, and substantiate with documents, that Frank Macpherson – a man he had never met – had been considerably in debt to him. Such fraudulent claims carried the threat of a prison sentence and ruin, and the moneylender was extremely anxious to keep secret his part in it. So there seemed little doubt that Buchanan had had a hand in Frank's death. Blake believed he must have stumbled upon the real reason for our journey, and Buchanan had feared he might tell me. Of Buchanan himself, we had heard nothing.

Meanwhile, opportunities dropped into my lap. My lieutenancy was confirmed, and I had been offered two posts: one in a cavalry regiment going north with the Governor General, or another keeping an eye on the independent state of Gwalior, both of which I initially refused. I had also discovered on arriving in Calcutta that Lieutenant O'Keefe, to whom I was so disastrously in debt, had succumbed to the cholera only weeks after Macpherson had died. He had left no dependents, a pile of IOUs – which were judged void – and a cache of valuables won from idiots like me. He had not been much liked, and our messmates had gone about religiously returning his winnings to their former owners. I thus recovered my father's pocket watch and ring.

Some days later the Rao's tigerskin arrived for me, along with two tightly wrapped packs that Sameer had sent from Mirzapore. I had not expected to see them again. Inside were my books, much battered and in some places reduced almost to pulp, and the Rao's bag of gems, which I had all but forgotten. I knew I should hand them in to the Company treasury, but something stopped me. Call it dishonesty, greed if you like, but I baulked at giving the Company all it would have of me. I asked Blake what to do.

'Keep them,' he said. 'As restitution. For Macpherson's sake, for Xavier's, for the Rao's. Or what you will. But don't give them to the Company. It's had plenty from you.'

Discreetly, Blake turned a couple of my stones into cash. I paid the last of my debts, bought three fine shawls of the best quality and a pearl necklace, and sent them, and a long letter, home to my sister. I ordered a complete set of Mountstuart's works from England, all the back issues of Mr Boz's *Pickwick*s, and decided to consider myself a man of means.

When I told Blake I was thinking of staying, he nodded. He said it was a good decision. Afterwards, however, I could not shake the feeling that I was betraying him, nor the perception that when he left there would be only one other person – Helen Larkbridge – on the whole continent of Asia whom I trusted or cared about.

A week later Helen and I were engaged, and I decided to join the regiment going north, so we agreed we would marry quickly so she could travel with me. The courtship had been swift, but we had seen a great deal of each other over the weeks. She had told me that though I had been far from the most eligible of her suitors, I had always been the one she wanted, but having few advantages save her looks and some good family connections, she had told herself she must marry well. And before I had left for Jubbulpore I had seemed so distracted and serious she had been convinced I was lost to her.

'I cried for several days,' she said. 'And then I picked myself up and accepted Keay.'

I was impressed by her honesty. We both wrote to Keay, who had, after some initial and justified complaint, graciously agreed to stand aside.

Helen was the one subject I had found myself reluctant to discuss with Blake. The loss of his own wife seemed to make the subject awkward, and I had the feeling he would disapprove of the speed of our engagement.

The day before he left, I found Blake walking by the water south of the Hooghly ghats. We stood contemplating the river for some time.

'You came to tell me something,' he said.

'Yes. I am going to marry Helen Larkbridge.'

There was the merest moment of hesitation, but I felt it. 'Congratulations,' he said, and as if to make up for that moment of uncertainty, again, 'Congratulations.'

'You think it a mistake.'

'No.' He paused. 'But it's very soon. You could take your time. You do not know each other very well, and she knows very little about India.' I could tell he was choosing his words with care. 'And you've seen things that have changed you. It may be hard for her to understand.'

'I do not think I can do without her.'

He sighed. We looked out on to the water.

'I came here to say goodbye to my wife. Her name was Anwesha. She was Hindoo. She made me promise when she was dying that I would burn them both and scatter their ashes here.'

'Them?'

'She died giving birth to our son. He was stillborn. She died a day later. My first thought on waking is of her, and my last before sleeping.'

*

So now Blake and I stood on the quay, and the tender bobbed in the water. In a carriage at the end of the wharf, Helen waited for me.

Blake was in full European civilian dress, with his frock-coat over his hand, hiding his missing fingers. I wondered whether he would ever wear native clothes again. Several ladies took curious peeks at him. He had got very thin, and his shoulders hunched a little against the warm breeze. I reminded myself how hardy he was.

'Do you have sufficient funds?' I said. Along with everything else, Blake had refused to accept the pension the Company had offered him. I did not know how he had paid his passage.

'The griffin debtor asks me that?'

'I am, as you know, remarkably liquid these days.' From my pocket I brought the small black bag which the Rao had presented me, intending to put it in his hand.

'I am not doing too badly myself, William,' Blake said, pushing it away. He rummaged about in a pocket and brought out an identical black bag. It clicked satisfyingly.

'Two big sapphires and a diamond. Enough to pay for my passage, and something for when I get to London. You should know that I wrote to the Rao – I can still get a confidential message from one end of the country to the other – to tell him about Sleeman and Hogwood. I thought he should know.'

I nodded. 'Collinson will deliver his promise?' I said.

'I trust him to.'

The ladies and their children and servants were clambering into the tender; the old gentlemen were following them.

'Goodbye, Jeremiah, I wish you well. More than well.'

'Goodbye, William. Take care of yourself. Send my good wishes to Miss Larkbridge.' He took a breath. 'Take your time. You don't need to rush into anything.' Uncharacteristically, he did not meet my eyes.

'I have this for you,' I said.

'What is it?'

'Letters from Collinson. Letters of introduction for London.'

'I don't want them.'

'Please, Jeremiah. Take them. He came to see you when you

were sick in Mirzapore and gave them to me. He said he would have work for you in London.' I held them out.

His face twisted with exasperation. 'What do I know of London?' But he took the packet reluctantly and slipped it into the pocket of his coat. I grasped his right hand and shook it vigorously, unwilling to let go.

'I will never forget you, Jeremiah, as long as I live.' I looked down, ashamed. 'Forgive me.'

'For what?'

'For staying.'

'What's to forgive?' he said. 'I spent half my life here. How can I reproach you for wanting to stay?'

'I hope we might meet again, one day.'

He smiled at me again, both reassuring and mildly irritated.

'I am quite able to look after myself, William. I did so for many years before I met you.'

He disengaged his hand from mine, then touched me very lightly on the shoulder. He looked out one last time over the familiar crush of human forms and debris of the wharf. Then he began to clamber into the boat, teetering alarmingly and clutching the side. I resisted the urge to dart forward and catch him.

When the tender pulled off, I stayed on the wharf, watching the sailors strain against the oars. I stayed until I could no longer see his features and his head was a tan blob and his body a clean white dab. All about me the natives pressed, rolling barrels, lifting sacks. The smell of dried fish floated up from the ghats, pricking my nostrils. Just before I turned away I thought I saw a spray of white confetti hang in the air for a moment, before it floated down to the water.

Jeremiah Blake and William Avery will return in The Infidel Stain *(see page 325 for an early glimpse of the first chapter).*

Historical Afterword

In 1857, twenty years after the fictional events recounted in this book, the Indian mutiny, or Great Rebellion as it's known in India, broke out. One of its direct causes was the East India Company's annexation of the large independent state of Oudh the year before. The mutiny's suppression would be the Company's last act: the British government decided it was no longer competent to run India, dissolved it, and took over government itself. There are, incidentally, a number of well-attested stories of Britsh officers evading capture during the mutiny by disguising themselves as women.

William Sleeman (1788–1856) was an energetic Victorian with an extraordinary capacity for work. He was the first person in India to find and identify dinosaur fossils; and the first to collect reports of 'wolf-children' – the stories that later inspired Rudyard Kipling to invent the character of Mowgli in *The Jungle Book*. He wrote enthusiastically and authoritatively about horticulture, and introduced new farming methods and new crop strains to bring higher yields. He was a brilliant linguist who loved the landscape of India, was deeply curious about its culture and had a genuine – if sentimental and paternalistic – desire to improve the lot of the Indian peasant.

Sleeman's main claim to fame, however, was the ruthless campaign he led in the late 1820s and 1830s to suppress the Thugs, the roadside bandits who befriended, then strangled, then robbed their victims and dedicated their corpses to the Hindu goddess of death, Kali. His systems – maps, lists of Thugs describing among other things their aliases and distinguishing marks, family trees, and so on – were the precursors of modern policing tools. Although he was already a very effective public administrator, it was Thuggee that made Sleeman's career: he became Superintendent of a new cross-India department pursuing Thugs and dacoits, and ended his career as the Resident – the senior Company official – in Oudh, whose takeover by the Company in 1856 he opposed.

Sleeman produced a series of articles and books about the Thugs, describing them as an organized India-wide guild of murderers bound by generations of intermarriage, and detailing their customs, rituals and language. His writings quickly captured the imagination of the British in India, and then the public at home. By the mid-1830s the Thugs had become notorious bywords for the evils of the dark, mysterious East, inspiring simultaneously horror and excitement. In 1839, *Confessions of a Thug*, a now unreadable Gothic novel by Philip Meadows-Taylor, a former soldier in India who claimed to have worked on the Thuggee campaign (in fact his material comes straight out of Sleeman's writings), became a huge British bestseller. Thugs, or sinister oriental figures like them, went on to appear in other novels, such as Wilkie Collins's *The Moonstone*. Some think that Charles Dickens intended to introduce them to his unfinished novel *The Mystery of Edwin Drood*. In the 1850s, a spate of muggings in London in which the victim was rushed from behind and his hat pushed down over his face spawned a city-wide (and completely unjustified) panic that Thugs had arrived from India.

Since the 1960s, however, Indian and British historians have begun to question the idea that the Thugs, and Sleeman himself, were all that they seemed. Some dispute that the Thugs – as described by Sleeman – ever existed at all. The subject is still hotly debated. It seems likely that 'Thuggee' emerged from an amalgam of stories, colonial fears, moral panic and Sleeman's own dark imaginings. Sleeman himself seems to have seized on the idea after reading reports by a Company magistrate called Thomas Perry from 1815, who had beaten a series of 'confessions' from a young bandit called Ghulam Hussein, which became increasingly detailed as the beatings and confessions progressed. Hussein described himself as a 'Thug', a word which meant deceiver, trickster or conman in Hindustani. Under pressure to explain an increase in local roadside murders, Perry gradually came up with a picture of a caste-like group of organized criminals called Thugs. But his Thugs never mentioned Kali, or strangling, or a special language, and were more likely to toss their victims down wells than bury them. What Slee-man does seem to have done – without quite realizing it – was for the first time to collect and write about some of the traditions of peasant, nomadic and criminal culture in India, rather as in Britain writers were for the first time taking an interest in working-class culture.

In traditional histories of the British Empire, Sleeman's success was put down to his brilliant system of maps, indexes and family trees. In Indian folk memory he comes over as a more brutal, un-subtle figure. Mike Dash's book about Sleeman's campaign, *Thug*, quotes bandits arrested by Sleeman speaking anxiously about 'a ma-chine for torturing Thugs'. Kevin Rusby's *Children of Kali*, a book about criminality in India, quotes townspeople from Jabalpur (the modern spelling of Jubbulpore) – 150 years after the event – describing how Sleeman strung up the Thugs from trees along the road from Jabalpur to Mirzapur (Mirzapore). My own mother-in-law, who spent many years in Chennai (then Madras) in southern India, spoke of 'Thuggee' Sleeman as famously ruthless and famous for using torture to extract confessions.

At the time the British were quick to accept Thuggee at face value. Sleeman's 'discovery' came at a moment when the character of the British occupation of India was undergoing a profound change. Traditionally, Company employees had – while mainly try-ing to make as much money as they could – been relatively tolerant and respectful of the Indian culture in which they lived. Many had relationships with, and children by, Indian women. Some were actively enthusiastic about India. They studied its languages and lit-erature, admired its traditions, adopted its fashions. British scholars resurrected the dead language of Sanskrit and traced its influence as the root of most European languages.

However, as the Company extended its territory and authority across India through the 1820s and 1830s, less sympathetic, more dis-missive attitudes began to take over. New arrivals were increasingly reluctant to mix with Indians and to learn local languages. They were more likely to see local customs and religions as degenerate and even evil, and were quick to emphasize their superiority over the Indians they governed. The reasons for this were many and complex. Among them was the arrival of more British women in the colony, one effect of which was to make Anglo-Indian relationships increasingly taboo. Another was the arrival of evangelical missionaries and government officials to whom Hinduism represented idolatry. Then there was the need to justify the Company's increasing authoritarian presence in India. The simplest, or at least most self-serving, explanation was that the Europeans were morally superior to the Indians, who required their civilizing influence. In the 1820s and 1830s, the Company began wars with Burma, took over states such as Coorg and Mysore and insinuated itself into Jaipur, where it was claimed the local rulers were either incapable, unruly or just plain bad. (This strategy would be formalized in the late 1840s by Governor General Dalhousie's 'doctrine of lapse', whereby the Company could take over an independent state if the ruler was 'manifestly incompetent or died without direct heir'.) The Thugs illustrated precisely why India needed the East India Company and its civilizing influence. Sleeman's campaign, meanwhile, demonstrated how effective and benevolent Company rule was.

Another powerful idea that Sleeman helped to plant – or certainly to establish – in the British colonial mind was that of hereditary criminality. Once the Thugs were thought to have been suppressed in the mid-1840s, Sleeman and his successors at the Thug and Dacoity Department went in search of other groups who fitted the template, and gradually the idea of 'criminal castes' evolved. The subject became a kind of pseudoscience in India, and was so prevalent that by the late nineteenth century English books on the Indian caste system routinely contained sections on hereditary criminal castes: the Pardaso – Muslim vagabonds and robbers; the Lambani – highwaymen who were said to kidnap children; the Rasmusi – 'hereditary robbers' who masqueraded as watchmen; and the 'Beels' or 'Bhils'. What these groups had in common was that they were in reality rarely distinct castes as the British liked to think, and – like European gipsies – they were poor and nomadic and therefore easy to scapegoat, and hard to govern and keep tabs on; many of them would now be described as tribal peoples.

Sleeman died in 1856 just before the mutiny, in the midst of a sea voyage back to England where he was going to recuperate from ill health.

Fanny Parkes (1794–1875) lived in India between 1822 and 1845, mostly in Allahabad, halfway between Calcutta and Delhi on the Grand Trunk Road, where her husband was an East India Company 'civilian', or civil servant, in charge of ice-making. During the cool season she travelled without her husband, whom it was said went mad in the winter. Unlike many Company wives Fanny embraced India and was enraptured by its beauty and variety. She learnt Hindustani and the sitar. Her diaries, published in 1850 and now available in a shortened edition as *Begums, Thugs and Englishmen* (Eland Books), describe Hindu rituals, the Indian landscape, Thug trials, sailing on the Ganges, and the lives of the high-born women in the zenanas (women's quarters), while bemoaning the status of married women in England and the colonists' lack of respect for Indian culture. To a twenty-first-century ear they are utterly beguiling.

Henry Derozio (1809–31) was a young radical mixed-race teacher, as described in this book, who after his death remained a profound influence on the movement known as the Bengal Renaissance, the great surge of creativity that took place in Calcutta in the mid-nineteenth century, of whom the best-known figure is the great Indian poet and writer Rabindrath Tagore.

Sir William Macnaghten (1793–1841) was an East India Company civil servant who served in the Secret and Political Department, then became secretary to Governor General Sir William Bentinck, and Chief Political Secretary to his successor, Lord Auckland (1784–1849). He is best known as one of the instigators of the disastrous First Afghan War (1839–41), one of the most shameful and disastrous moments of British rule in India. During 1837 and 1838, Lord Auckland and his entourage – including an army of almost 10,000 soldiers and camp followers – spent seven months travelling up the Great Trunk Road from Calcutta to the northern hill station of

Simla. They travelled through a terrible famine in the Agra region which claimed 800,000 lives, and which, though the Governor General provided some relief, was not helped by the vast procession of hungry mouths marching through it. Along the way, Macnaghten, a confirmed Russophobe, persuaded the Governor General that the ruler of Afghanistan, Dost Mohammad, was encouraging the Russians to invade northern India and should be deposed. In fact Macnaghten and his allies vastly exaggerated the danger of Russian interference and deliberately ignored Dost Mohammad's willingness to negotiate with the British. But though the justifications for the invasion were flimsy to say the least, Auckland sent Macnaghten and the 'Army of the Indus' into Afghanistan in late 1838. The campaign was a disaster, and Macnaghten was assassinated by Dost Mohammad's son in 1841. The Army of the Indus began a chaotic withdrawal from Kabul in early 1842, and only one survivor made it to the British outpost of Jalalabad a few weeks later. Dost Mohammad was reinstalled, ruling Afghanistan until his death in 1863. Auckland was ignominiously sacked and recalled to England in 1843.

Glossary

afeem opium poppy

akhbarat news sheet

attr (attar) essential oil extracted usually from rose petals

baboo (babu) rich Indian Calcutta grandees; originally a term of respect which, under British rule circa 1837, came to have slightly derogatory connotations

Bahadur Company colloquial name for the East India Company

Bangbazaar the bazaar in Calcutta

begum honorific given to India women of high rank

bele Thug burial site

bhisti water carrier

bhurtote strangler in Thug gang

bibi a native mistress

brandy pawnee brandy and water

Bundelkand (Bundelkhand) Indian region north of Vindhya mountains

chakla brothel

charpai low bed supported by webbing

Chote junior, as in 'Chote Sahib'

churidar pyjama bottoms, tight at the bottom

civilian East India Company civil servant (as opposed to soldier)

dacoit roadside bandit; **dacoity** is banditry

dak Indian postal delivery by relays of runners or horses

dak bungalow house built near dak stops along main routes across India, where Europeans would pass the night when travelling

darwan porter/doorkeeper

dastar Sikh headgear or turban

Deccan plateau of southern, central India, south of the Satpura mountain range

dhobi-wallah laundryman

dhoti a long loincloth

dirzi tailor

diwan first minister

gaddi short-legged Indian chair, very low to the ground

gaz Indian measure of length, approximately a yard

ghat broad steps down to water

ghazal love song, ballad

goor crystallized cane sugar

hakim healer

harkara runner or escort

hinna henna

huqqa water pipe for smoking tobacco

iqbal luck

jangal jungle

jemadar lowest Indian comissioned officer in East India Company, or chief or captain of a criminal gang

katar an Indian dagger

khansaman steward/butler

khitmatgur a male servant who waits at table

kos Indian unit of distance; about two and a quarter miles

kurta loose, long-sleeved shirt

Multanni mitti Fuller's earth

lakh a thousand

lobster insulting word for an English soldier, referring to his characteristic red coat

loll shrub chilled claret

machan high platform in tree used for hunting

maharaj/maharaja title or honorific meaning 'great king'

mahout elephant rider or keeper

Marathas warlords who ruled over areas of central India between Bombay and Calcutta, defeated by the East India Company in 1819; the Marathi language is still in widespread use in these areas and among the Maratha caste today

Maulvi respected Muslim religious man in India

mehtar sweeper

Mofussil outback, countryside

moonshee Indian language teacher or secretary; Persian honorific for someone who had learnt many languages

napi barber

nautch Indian dance performed by professional dancing girls, usually without many clothes

nawab Muslim ruler

nujeeb irregular Indian soldier

parda curtain between men and women, derivation of purdah

Pegu small, sturdy pony from Burma

pugree (puggaree) type of small turban

puja Hindu religious ritual

punkah-wallah servant who works a ceiling fan

rao title given to Indian prince or king, similar to 'raja'

rumal yellow scarf allegedly used by the Thugs to strangle their victims

ryot Indian peasant farmer

sadoo (sadhu) Indian holy man

sardar prince or nobleman

sarpech turban jewel

sepoy Indian soldier in the East India Company armies

shikar hunt

shikari huntsman

simkin Champagne

sircar steward, domestic servant

soor swine

sowar Indian cavalryman in the East India Company armies; a **camel sowar** is a camel driver who would travel fifty miles a day to deliver messages

suttee practice of burning a widow on her husband's funeral pyre

swoddy English slang for a soldier

syce groom

Talpurs rulers of Sindh (now in eastern Pakistan)

tank artificial lake or reservoir

tawaif courtesan

tulwar Mughal-style sword with a thin, curved blade

tuncaw salary

ullu owl

writer young Englishman employed as a clerk, manager and/or accountant by the East India Company

zamindar large-scale landowner and tax-collector, often an aristocrat, principally in Bengal

zenana another word for the harem or woman's quarters of a well-to-do Indian family

Acknowledgements

A neophyte when it comes to India and its history, I have relied on many good books. I can't name them all, but I would pick out in particular Mike Dash's *Thug*, Eland Books's reprint of Fanny Parkes's wonderful memoirs, *Begums, Thugs and White Mughals*, as well as their reprint of John Beames's *Memoirs of Bengal Civilian*, Richard Holmes's *Sahib*, Charles Allen's *Lives of the Indian Princes*, Christopher Bayly's *Empire and Information: Intelligence Gathering and Social Communication in India*, and Emily Eden's *Up the Country*. I want to thank my infallible agent, Bill Hamilton, and my editor, Juliet Annan, for sticking with me as I ventured into new territory, and for eternal good humour. Caroline Pretty, my copy-editor, was an absolute pleasure to work with. Most of all, I'd like to thank my husband John, without whom I would never have dared make a stab at fiction, for his support in everything.

The verse quoted on page 69, 'The love of power, and rapid gain of gold . . .', is adapted from Lord Byron's *Don Juan*, canto III, verse 14; the real thing can't be improved upon.

Read on for an extract from
book two in the Blake and
Avery series, *The Infidel Stain* . . .

The Infidel Stain

Prologue

The still, quiet shop was a blessed shelter from the biting cold. She had risen at four to walk the six miles to Hackney Road and back, and all the way she had hung on to that half-hour when she would creep in, fall gratefully into a dark corner, shut her eyes and cast aside her cares. Just for a short while, before he came down. Sometimes she thought it was the place she liked best in the world, not just for the physical refuge it provided, but because the old familiar smells and tools – the smell of ink, of lampblack and linseed oil, the musty dry scent of paper, the boxes of type and gravers and burins – were so comforting.

She did not like to come too often, for she did not want him to grow tired of her, and so she had waited and stored up this morning's visit. He had never seemed to mind finding her there though, not even when at the start she had taken things – not much, just a bit of paper, or a storage box, or a piece of type, a tiny perfect 'x' or 'm' that she would rub between her fingers. He had shown her how to get in so no one could see, and sometimes, when he was opening up, he would send her out to the coffee stall and have her buy one for herself.

The street was quite empty. Even the coffee seller wasn't out yet – he would still be serving the late-nighters and early-morning comers on the Strand. She made her way past the darkened shopfront, into the narrow alley around the side, behind the outside steps. Under them, and out of sight of prying eyes, she cleared away the old bricks from in front of the small square door that barely came up to her waist, took the small key tied to a bit of string from out of her skirts, placed it in the old rusted lock and turned it.

Squatting down on her haunches, she edged through. She avoided crawling as it messed her skirts and her basket and she was selling today. There was a small cavity between the little door and the print room where they stored boxes and type and, having inched through the gap, she came out into the room at last.

It was very dark. She stood, brushing herself down. Dawn would not come for a little while, the front was shuttered and the cracked window in the back had been blacked out; he had taken to doing this recently, claiming that it stopped the cold coming in at night, but she reckoned he was working on something he wished no one to see. She knew the room well so she was not concerned, and it was a relief to be out of the wind. She could hear it whistling outside, trying to find its way through the cracks. Arms outstretched, she began to walk across the room to the far wall, taking care not to disturb any boxes or piles of paper. To the right of her, she could just make out the silhouette of the press. In the darkness it seemed to loom even bigger than usual.

Then her boot slid from under her and for a moment she lost her balance and thought she would fall. She swore quietly as she righted herself and clung to her basket. The floor was wet. She lifted her skirt, took another big step and grimaced. It was slippery here too. Perhaps a cat or rat had knocked over some ink. No. He would not have been so careless. Maybe one of his old workers had broken in to sleep off the night's excesses and knocked over a bottle, or spewed up, or worse. He hadn't had anyone in recently, but it had happened before. The writers and illustrators were all soakers and topers, the lot of them.

'That you, Seymour?' she said. 'You drunk?' But there was no answer. 'Mr Wedderburn? Nat?'

Standing there in the dark she began to feel uneasy. She was, she realized, holding her breath. Some instinct told her to lay her hands on something solid and she took a quick step back, feeling for the wall. But she lost her balance again and went down, one hand going out to break her fall, the other grasping the basket. She cursed again. Her hand was wet, and the stuff was all over her skirt. She rubbed her fingers together. Sticky, slightly thick even. Not piss then, nor booze either. She sniffed and pulled herself up quickly, keeping clear of the great piece of machinery in the middle of the room. The sense of foreboding deepened, and the thought came upon her that there was someone else there, in the dark. She could hear nothing, but even so fear rose in her. As quickly and quietly as she could – though it was too late for that, she knew — she made herself feel her way around the walls to the back window. She found the tool bench next to it and put her basket upon it. She stretched up to pull the piece of old blanket away from the window frame. The sky was just beginning to lighten and the room was suddenly a good deal brighter. Her fingertips and palms were stained with something black like ink. But she knew it was not ink. She did not want to turn around, but she forced herself to do so.

The sight imprinted itself upon her eye, like a flash of light, though the light itself was poor.

Blood, terrible and black like ink, everywhere. As if a great, hideous bucket of it had been poured out. Blood soaking through his trousers and pooling on the floor, where her boots had spread it into the corners. Blood etched and painted over his face, across his arms and on to his chest. Blood spewing, along with his guts, from a deep and livid cut in his stomach, as broad and wet as a mouth. And his black-stained body, draped over the bed of the printing press, head propped against the platen, arms dangling off each side. Like Jesus, it suddenly came to her before she pushed the thought away, taken down from the cross.

PART ONE

Chapter One

I t was a cold, bleak day, and the sooty brick of the city made it
seem all the greyer. I had not long returned from India, and
years in hot climes had lost me the habit of English cold. I pulled
my coat more tightly around me and checked my pocket watch
for the tenth or twelfth time. I did not wish to be late.

It was only the second time I had ever been to London. The first
had been when I was a child. I recalled almost nothing of it save that
we had visited my rich, scowling great-uncle at his gloomy abode in
Golden Square – a place which greatly disappointed me as I had
expected it actually to be golden – and I had seen a hurdy-gurdy
man with a dancing dog in the street. This time, I had been in London less than a day and, while I marvelled at it, I also felt I was not
entirely fitted for the capital and its overwhelming deluge of sensations, nor for the whole brave new world that I had encountered
since my return from India.

I had left England a country traversed by horse and carriage; I
had returned to find it in thrall to steam and iron.

The day before, I had taken my first train journey, riding the
Exeter mail-coach to catch the Great Western Railway at Swindon,
bound for the Paddington terminus. I had sat on the wooden pews
of the second-class carriage and watched the air fill with steam, felt
the thrust of speed, heard the clank and chug of the wheels on the
rail, and watched the curious effect of the countryside melting into
a blur of green as it rushed past the window, or rather as we rushed
past it. We had reached a speed of thirty miles an hour. It was
remarkable and thrilling, and yet it left me ill at ease. I had grown up
in Devon and was accustomed to slower, country ways. We had
threshing machines of course, but the women and children still
gleaned the fields after harvest. Mills, mines and steam machinery
had all been a very distant prospect. Now the whole country seemed

to be hurtling towards an unpredictable future of engines, belching chimneys and noise – noise everywhere. It was a world I did not recognize and one in which I was not sure I had a place.

Of course, London stirred and excited me too. I was lodged in the most fashionable part of town, in handsome rooms equipped with every convenience, at the Oriental Club in Hanover Square. I had admired Trafalgar Square and the slowly rising girth of the column to Nelson. I had walked down Whitehall to observe the foundations of the new Houses of Parliament. Everywhere ambitious new constructions were rising up. But I was also unsettled by the chaos and scale of the city, its crowded raucous streets, and the sense of being alone in a vast multitude of unsmiling faces. Nor was I overfond of the city's particular kind of ubiquitous, black grime – an oily, sooty extrusion that seemed to bear little relation to country dirt.

I emerged from the Blackwall railway terminus – an elegant new brick building with a hotel and custom house attached, rather incongruous against the rough landscape behind – on to the East India dock road. I consulted the scrap of paper on which my directions were written and walked towards the great stone gateway of the East India dock itself, which loomed like the entrance to some stolid Hindoo palace. I had been brought here by my second train journey – from the Tower of London on the Blackwall railway. This had provided glimpses of a meaner London: a moving picture of shabby streets, half-finished terraces and dilapidated workshops; then, as we moved further from the city, scrubby marsh, broken fences and overgrown market gardens half shrouded by murky, low-lying wisps of fog; and vast stretches of open dock filled with masts and populated by beetling stevedores.

The walls of the East India docks were pasted thick with bills, most of them advertising the lower sort of popular papers such as the *Ironist, Bell's Life in London* and *Woundy's Illustrated Weekly*. In the lea of the walls, small sheds and shacks served drink and tobacco, and a crowd of poor-looking sailors and stevedores clustered around them. On my side of the highway there was a new church, an old timber-framed house and, next to it, a rickety, smoke-blackened edifice that announced itself in large faded letters as 'The Hindoo-stanee Coffee House and Seamen's Hostel': my destination.

The door was stiff and rattled. I found I was slightly breathless. I pushed past a thick canvas curtain and entered a dim-lit room of exposed brick. There were perhaps twenty or thirty men seated at tables, eating. It took me a moment to take in that all were Indian natives. Rushing between the tables, two or three more young Indian natives carried bowls and collected plates. The air was thick, warm and slightly fetid, a familiar marriage of perspiration and curry smells that I had not expected to encounter again. I removed my coat, hat and gloves. No one paid me any mind.

Most of the diners were dressed in the thin calicoes and canvases of the southern oceans that would have provided little comfort against the bitter cold outside. Some looked quite ragged, and in far from good health. There was a low buzz of talk, but mostly they simply ate, with a dedication that bespoke considerable hunger. I concluded they must be Lascar sailors come in from the docks. Puzzled, I looked about again, more carefully. In a fireplace at the far end of the room, a large grate overflowed with glowing embers. Above it hung a wooden crucifix with a painted sign attached to it which read 'Jesus saves'. To the left of the fireplace in a corner sat a lone European eating his dinner. He seemed as down-at-heel as the Lascars around him.

It was over three years since we had last met.

He was scooping up his stew with shreds of rotee, eating in a calm, methodical manner, and had about him the insistently soli-tary, aloof quality that until that moment I had quite forgotten. The surge of concern and pleasure I had felt was succeeded by a twinge of unease. I ignored it and pushed my way through the close-set tables towards him, and when I reached the table I said warmly, 'Jeremiah!'

'Captain Avery.' He looked up, his expression guarded.

'Mr Blake,' I mumbled. Involuntarily, I took a step backward.

'Sit down,' he said, gesturing with his piece of bread, and returned to his food.

I pulled out a chair and wedged myself in, looking for somewhere to place my coat and hat, electing at last for my own lap, and attempted to quell my feeling of bitter dismay. I realized that I had forgotten more about Jeremiah Blake than I had remembered, and cursed myself for a fool for having dropped everything and rushed to London.

A plate was set down before me along with a steaming bowl of curry and another of rice, from which Blake began to help himself. Reluctantly, I put a spoonful of curry upon my plate and took a furtive look at my companion. He seemed to me frail and more lined than I remembered, and his skin was slightly clammy. He kept his left hand, with its two missing fingers, under the table. His clothes looked hardly sufficient against the cold. His rusty, threadbare suit had clearly been through several owners; the waistcoat had lost all but one button, and the neckerchief – closer to yellow than white – was pinned on, probably to hide a tattered shirt beneath. I was suddenly reminded of Mr Dickens's painful descriptions of the London 'shabby-genteel'. On the table next to him was a small bundle that included a battered hat and a ragged muffler and what Mr Dickens might have described as 'the remains of an old pair of beaver gloves'.

My mind teemed with questions. What had become of him? How was he earning his living – was he, indeed, earning his living at all? How had he learned I had returned from India? For the moment I felt too awkward to ask any of them.

Blake looked up suddenly and fixed me with an appraising stare.

'What is this place?' I said.

'Hostel for Lascar seamen,' he said. Then he scooped another mouthful of curry on to his rotee and put it into his mouth.

'So,' I tried again. 'Three years. More.'

Blake nodded.

'How have you been?'

'Well enough. You were in Afghanistan,' he said, deflecting my question.

I remembered how much he disliked talking about himself, and I nodded.

'Decorated for bravery, promoted to Captain, I heard.'

'Yes.' I shifted uneasily.

'Papers say the war's going well.'

'Is it?' I said.

'Isn't it?'

'I do not keep up.'

'And you married Miss Larkbridge.'

I did not wonder how he knew these things, and I was not surprised that he did.

'We are expecting our first child. That is to say . . .' I stopped, not wanting to say more. 'It was one of the reasons we decided to return home.'

I half expected him to press me on the matter, but he said nothing. Silence. Long pauses, I recalled, did not discomfit Jeremiah Blake. He leaned back and wiped his hands on a handkerchief he drew from his pocket. I could not forebear to look for the two stumps on his left hand, but the movement was swift and then he wrapped his right hand over the left, so it was impossible to see the missing fingers. He tapped his right forefinger on his left knuckle and looked at me. His hands seemed somewhat red and chafed, but it was hard to be sure if this denoted he had fallen on hard times or was simply due to the ravages of the winter.

'Have you,' I said, casting around for a subject, 'visited Mr Haydon's painting at the Egyptian Hall?'

'*The Death of Mountstuart?*' He shook his head. 'You?'

'I went yesterday. There was an hour's queue to see it.'

'And?' said Blake. He took another bite of rotee.

'Let us say it is lively rather than accurate.'

Mr Benjamin Haydon, the history painter, was exhibiting a large canvas purporting to show the now notorious ambush and murder of the poet and adventurer Xavier Mountstuart by a gang of Hindoostanee bandits known as Thugs. Death had transformed Mountstuart into a saint and a martyr, famous and revered across Europe. In the painting, he lay in the foreground, reclining on the ground in a beautifully laundered white shirt, one arm raised in elegant defiance, as a mass of bloodthirsty Thugs attack him with knives. To the left, in the background, two other Europeans fought off a battalion of savages with pistols. Jeremiah Blake and I were those two Europeans, the only living witnesses to what had actually taken place.

'Mr Haydon wrote to me in India,' I said, 'asking for an account of what happened. He said he wanted *colore.*'

'Didn't listen to you then.'

'I said that I could not help him. I did not get the impression he would much have appreciated my version. Besides, I do not like to talk of it. I assumed he must have approached you.'

'Mmm,' said Blake noncommittally.

We met each other's gaze at last.

I said, 'Are you in trouble, Blake? Is that why you wrote to me? Forgive me, but I cannot but notice you seem, well, not exactly flushed with good fortune. I mean, finding you here, among these poor wretches, I . . .' I trailed off, not sure how to proceed. 'If you are in straitened circumstances, please, Jeremiah, let me be of assistance.'

For the first time he looked almost amused. 'No,' he said.

'No, you will not accept my help?' I said.

'No, I am perfectly well, William. I eat here because I like it. It reminds me of the street stalls in Calcutta. I talk to the sailors, keep up my Hindoostanee. And when he's minded, Mohammed cooks the best Bengali food in London.'

'Indeed?' I said. I glanced doubtfully down at the dark brown mess on the plate before me. It did not smell too bad. 'I have taken rooms at the Oriental Club. They say it has the best curry chef in England – you really should let me take you.'

'No,' said Blake.

'No?'

'I'll never set foot in that place.'

'No, of course not,' I said. 'Foolish of me to ask. But, Blake, I have to say, you do not look well. And your clothes are . . .'

'I've had a bout of fever,' he said irritably. 'That's all. It returns every so often. Especially in winter.'

'Well, you have managed to mystify me entirely, Blake. I have no idea why we are here, save that you have a taste for the cooking, nor why I have journeyed the seventeen hours from Devon to London. You should know that when I received your letter I dropped everything and came at once. I suppose I should not be surprised. But I think you might oblige me with some explanation.'

'I wrote to you because I have an appointment with someone who wishes to meet you too.'

'Me?' I said, bemused.

'You may decide you don't want to meet him, but since you're here . . .'

'Someone in London who wants to meet me?' I said stupidly.

'Viscount Allington.'

'The Evangelical?' I said, even more puzzled.

Blake nodded.

'He asked for me? For us?'

'He has some particular work – a case, a task – for you and me. But you're under no obligation to take part. You can leave if you want.'

'You and me? But how . . .'

'Theophilus Collinson knew you'd returned. Recommended you.' As he said the name, Blake's expression darkened. We had both had dealings with Collinson, the former head of the East India Company's secret department, before his return to London. In India, it had been said that he had a finger in every curry. Blake did not trust Collinson, but he had offered him his patronage in London. At the time Blake had declined it. I was flattered, and at the same time experienced a pang of disappointment. It was not Blake who had summoned me at all.

He just wanted a decent book to read ...

Not too much to ask, is it? It was in 1935 when Allen Lane, Managing Director of Bodley Head Publishers, stood on a platform at Exeter railway station looking for something good to read on his journey back to London. His choice was limited to popular magazines and poor-quality paperbacks – the same choice faced every day by the vast majority of readers, few of whom could afford hardbacks. Lane's disappointment and subsequent anger at the range of books generally available led him to found a company – and change the world.

'We believed in the existence in this country of a vast reading public for intelligent books at a low price, and staked everything on it'
Sir Allen Lane, 1902–1970, founder of Penguin Books

The quality paperback had arrived – and not just in bookshops. Lane was adamant that his Penguins should appear in chain stores and tobacconists, and should cost no more than a packet of cigarettes.

Reading habits (and cigarette prices) have changed since 1935, but Penguin still believes in publishing the best books for everybody to enjoy. We still believe that good design costs no more than bad design, and we still believe that quality books published passionately and responsibly make the world a better place.

So wherever you see the little bird – whether it's on a piece of prize-winning literary fiction or a celebrity autobiography, political tour de force or historical masterpiece, a serial-killer thriller, reference book, world classic or a piece of pure escapism – you can bet that it represents the very best that the genre has to offer.

Whatever you like to read – trust Penguin.